San Miguel

ALSO BY *T. Coraghessan Boyle*

San Miguel

T. Coraghessan Boyle

VIKING

VIKING
Published by the Penguin Group
Penguin Group (USA) Inc., 375 Hudson Street,
New York, New York 10014, U.S.A.
Penguin Group (Canada), 90 Eglinton Avenue East, Suite 700,
Toronto, Ontario, Canada M4P 2Y3
(a division of Pearson Penguin Canada Inc.)
Penguin Books Ltd, 80 Strand, London WC2R 0RL, England
Penguin Ireland, 25 St. Stephen's Green, Dublin 2, Ireland
(a division of Penguin Books Ltd)
Penguin Books Australia Ltd, 250 Camberwell Road, Camberwell,
Victoria 3124, Australia
(a division of Pearson Australia Group Pty Ltd)
Penguin Books India Pvt Ltd, 11 Community Centre, Panchsheel Park,
New Delhi – 110 017, India
Penguin Group (NZ), 67 Apollo Drive, Rosedale, Auckland 0632,
New Zealand (a division of Pearson New Zealand Ltd)
Penguin Books (South Africa) (Pty) Ltd, 24 Sturdee Avenue,
Rosebank, Johannesburg 2196, South Africa

Penguin Books Ltd, Registered Offices:
80 Strand, London WC2R 0RL, England

First published in 2012 by Viking Penguin,
a member of Penguin Group (USA) Inc.

10   9   8   7   6   5   4   3   2   1

Grateful acknowledgment is made for permission to reprint an excerpt from "Musee des Beaux Arts" from
Collected Poems of W. H. Auden. Copyright 1940 and renewed 1968 by W. H. Auden. Used by permission of
Random House, Inc. and Curtis Brown, Ltd.

Map illustration by Milo Boyle and Karen Kvashay Boyle

Publisher's Note
This is a work of fiction. Names, characters, places and incidents either are the product of the author's imagination
or are used fictitiously, and any resemblance to actual persons, living or dead, business establishments, events or
locales is entirely coincidental.

LIBRARY OF CONGRESS CATALOGING-IN-PUBLICATION DATA

Boyle, T. Coraghessan.
   San Miguel / T. Coraghessan Boyle.
      p. cm.
   ISBN 978-0-670-02624-1
   ISBN 978-0-670-02629-6 (Export Edition)
   1. Lester family—Fiction.   2. Waters family—Fiction.   3. Sheep ranches—Fiction.   4. San Miguel Island
(Calif.)—Fiction.   5. Domestic fiction.   I. Title.
   PS3552.O932S26 2012
   813'.54—dc23
   2012004731

Printed in the United States of America
Set in Minion Pro
Designed by Alissa Amell

For Milo,
who careened down the dunes and provided the electricity

About suffering they were never wrong,
The Old Masters; how well they understood
Its human position: how it takes place
While someone is eating or opening a window
or just walking dully along.

—W. H. AUDEN, "MUSÉE DES BEAUX ARTS"

Author's Note

In retelling the story of the Waters and Lester families during their time on San Miguel Island, I have tried to represent the historical record as accurately as possible, and yet this is a work of fiction, not history, and dialogue, characters and incidents have necessarily been invented. I would like to acknowledge my debt to three texts in particular—*The Legendary King of San Miguel*, by Elizabeth Sherman Lester; *San Miguel Island: My Childhood Memoir, 1930–1942*, by Betsy Lester Roberti; and *Mrs. Waters' Diary of Her Life on San Miguel Island*, edited by Marla Daily—and to express my gratitude to both Marla Daily and Peggy Dahl for their kind assistance with the research for this book.

San Miguel

N

Point
Bennett

Elephant
Seal Beach

1 mi.
1 km.

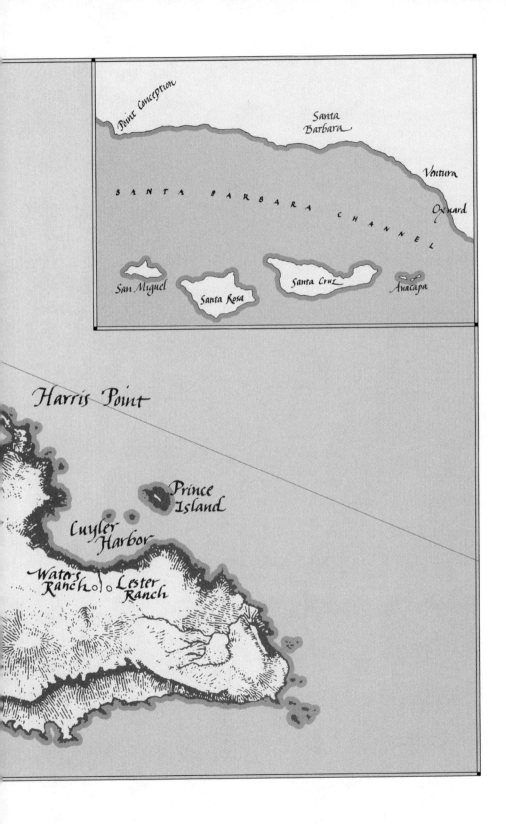

Point Conception

Santa
Barbara

Ventura

Oxnard

S A N T A   B A R B A R A   C H A N N E L

San Miguel

Santa Rosa

Santa Cruz

Anacapa

Harris Point

Prince
Island

Cuyler
Harbor

Waters
Ranch

Lester
Ranch

PART I

Marantha

Arrival

She was coughing, always coughing, and sometimes she coughed up blood. The blood came in a fine spray, plucked from the fibers of her lungs and pumped full of air as if it were perfume in an atomizer. Or it rose in her mouth like a hot metallic syrup, burning with the heat inside her till she spat it into the porcelain pot and saw the bright red clot of it there like something she'd given birth to, like afterbirth, but then what would she know about it since she'd never conceived, not with James, her first husband, and not with Will either. She was thirty-eight years old and she'd resigned herself to the fact that she would never bear a child, not in this lifetime. When she felt weak, when she hemorrhaged and the pain in her chest was like a medieval torture, like the *peine forte et dure* in which the torturer laid one stone atop the other till your ribs cracked and your heart stalled, she sometimes felt she wouldn't even live to see the year out.

But that was gloomy thinking and she wasn't going to have it, not today. Today she was hopeful. Today was New Year's Day, the first day of her new life, and she was on an adventure, sailing in a schooner out of Santa Barbara with her second husband and her adopted daughter, Edith, and half the things she owned in this world, bound for San Miguel Island and the virginal air Will insisted would make her well again. And she believed him. She did. Believed everything he said, no matter the look on Carrie Abbott's face when she first gave her the news. *Marantha, no—you're going where?* Carrie had blurted out before she could think, setting down her teacup on the low mahogany table in her parlor overlooking San Francisco Bay and the white-capped waves that jumped and ran in parallel streaks across the entire breadth of the window. *To an island? And where is it again?* And then she'd paused, her eyes retreating. *I hear the air is very good down there,* she said, *very salubrious,* and the little coal fire she had going in the grate flared up again. *And it'll be warmer, certainly. Warmer than here, anyhow.*

They'd been up before dawn, gathering their bags by lantern light on the porch of the rented house at Santa Barbara. If it had been warm the previous afternoon under a sun that shone sturdily out of a clear cerulean sky, it was raw and damp at that hour, the sky starless, the night draped like heavy cloth over the roof and the rail and the twin oleanders in the front yard. The calla lilies along the walk were dulled to invisibility. There wasn't a sound to be heard anywhere. Edith said she could see her breath, it was so cold, and Marantha had held a hand before her own mouth, feeling girlish, and saw that it was true. But then Will had said something sharp to her—he was fretting over what they'd need and what they were sure to forget, working himself up—and the spell was broken. When the carriage came down the street from the livery, you could hear the footfalls of the horses three blocks away.

And now they were in a boat at sea, an astonishing transformation, as if they'd crept into someone else's skin like the shape-shifters in the fairy stories she'd read aloud to Edith when she was little. A boat that pitched and rocked and shuddered down the length of it like a living thing. She was trying to hold herself very still, her eyes fixed straight ahead and her hands folded in her lap, thinking, of all things, about her stuffed chair in the front parlor of the apartment on Post Street they'd had to give up—picturing it as vividly as if she were sitting in it now. She could see the embroidery of the cushions and the lamp on the table, her cat curled asleep before the fire. Rain beyond the windows. Edith at the piano. The soft sheen of polished wood. That time seemed like years ago, though it had been what—a little over a month? The chair was in Santa Barbara now, the piano sold, the lamp in a crate—and the cat, Sampan, a Siamese she'd had since before they were married, given up for adoption because Will didn't think it would travel. And he was right, of course. They could always get another cat. Cats were as plentiful as the grains of rice in the big brown sacks you saw in the window of the grocer's in Chinatown.

She'd had a severe hemorrhage at the beginning of December, when they'd first come down to Santa Barbara, and she'd been too weak to do much of anything, but Will and Edith had set up the household for her, and that was a blessing. Except that now they were going to have to do it all over again, and in a place so remote and wild it might as well have been on the far side of the world. That was a worry. Of course it was. But it was an opportunity too—and she was going to seize it, no matter what Carrie Abbott might have thought, or anyone else either. She heard the thump of feet on the deck above. There was the sound of liquid—bilge, that was what they called it—sloshing beneath the floorboards. Everything stank of rot.

They'd been at sea four hours now and they had four more yet to go, and she knew that because Will had come down to inform her. "Bear up," he'd told her, "we're halfway there." Easier said than done. The fact was that she felt sick in her stomach, though it was an explicable sickness, temporary only, and if she was ashamed of herself for vomiting in a tin pail and of the smell it made—curdled, rancid, an odor that hung round her like old wash—at least there would be an end to it. Will had admonished her and Edith not to put anything on their stomachs, but she'd been unable to sleep the night before and couldn't help slipping into the kitchen in her nightgown when the whole house was asleep and feasting on the dainties left over from their abbreviated New Year's Eve celebration—oyster soup, sliced ham, lady fingers—which would have gone to waste in any case. Now, as the boat rocked and the reek of the sea came to her in the cramped saloon, she regretted it all over again.

She was trying to focus on the far wall or hull or whatever they called it, sunk deep into the nest of herself, when Ida backed her way down the ladder from the deck above, grinning as if she'd just heard the best joke in the world. "Oh, it's glorious out there, ma'am, blowing every which way." The girl's cheeks were flushed. Her hair had come loose under the bonnet, tangled black strands snaking out over the collar of her coat in a windblown snarl. "You should see it, you should."

The idea lifted her for just an instant—why shouldn't she go out on deck and take in the sights? She wasn't dead yet, was she?—but when she got to her feet, the ship lurched and she sat heavily again.

Ida's face went dark. She seemed to notice the bucket then and the way Marantha was holding herself. "Are you all right, ma'am? Can I get you a blanket?"

"No," she heard herself say, "I'm fine."

"What about the bucket—could I empty the bucket for you? So it—so you don't have to—?"

"Yes, that would be nice." She felt her insides clench at the thought of it, of what was in the bucket and what Ida would have to do with it out there in the

5

wind with the waves careening away from the hull and the bow pitching and pitching again. "But how's Edith managing?"

"If you can believe it, she's at the wheel right this minute, with your husband—Captain Waters, I mean—and the man who runs the ship, Captain Curner. He's letting us take turns, anybody who wants. Me too. That was me at the helm not five minutes ago." She let out a little laugh. "Could you tell the difference?"

And now suddenly Marantha felt her mood lift—Ida could always do that for her, every minute of her twenty-two years on this earth a rare adventure—and she found herself smiling. "I could. I knew it was a woman's touch—it was so much smoother." They both looked at the bucket then. "And that," she said, pointing, "that came up when the men were at the wheel, no question about it."

"But you know, it's not half as rough as it can be out here, or as it normally is this time of year, or so Captain Waters says."

"So it could be worse."

"It could."

"You're not affected?"

"No," Ida said, spinning herself round in a mock pirouette, "not at all. Captain Waters says I've got my sea legs. And Edith, Edith too—she has them. Sea legs. That means you—"

"Yes, I know." She paused, looking round her at the scatter of bags and provisions, the few sticks of furniture Will had allowed her because it just wasn't practical to ship all that furniture across until they had a chance to gauge how she was acclimating. "But can you believe it's the new year already?"

"I can."

The boat fell into a trough, then climbed back again. She folded her arms across her chest, trying to put pressure there, to hold everything in, because she could feel the next cough coming, and the next cough would bring on another spasm, she was sure of it. "It all seems to go by so quickly," she said, and she wasn't really talking to Ida anymore.

She was out on deck when the island hove into view (*hove*: that was the term, wasn't it? From *heave*, because everything on a ship was constantly heaving,

6

including your stomach), and she saw it as a tan lump marbled with bands of the purest white, as if it were a well-aged cut of beef laid out on the broad blue plate of the ocean for her and nobody else. But it wasn't beef they would be eating in the days and weeks and months to come, it was mutton—and turkey from the flock the previous tenant had introduced. And fish, she supposed, because wasn't the ocean here abounding in all species and varieties of fish? But then she'd never developed much of a taste for fish—aside from lobster, that is, which wasn't really a fish, was it?—and she couldn't think of a single way to serve it but baked in a dish till it was dry and tasteless.

There was a wind in her face, a cold wind freighted with pellets of cold salt spray, canvas flapping, ropes singing, wind, but it felt good, felt pure, and the tightness in her chest began to give way. By the time the boat came to anchor in the bay below the sole house on the island, the house that was theirs now, along with everything else within her purview—the rocks and gulls, the sand dunes careening down the slopes, the sheep that were like scraps of cloud scattered randomly across the distant green hillsides—she was so excited she was like a child herself, like Edith, who hadn't spent more than twenty minutes belowdecks the whole way out. Will had warned her that the house was nothing special, a wood-frame sheepman's place, built seventeen years earlier by their new partner in the Pacific Wool Growing Company, Mr. Mills, but that didn't stop her from picturing it in her mind's eye through every day of the past two months. What would it be like? The rooms—how were the rooms arranged? And the views? Would Edith have a room of her own—or would she have to share with Ida? And what of the hired man, Adolph Bierson, whose face she hadn't liked from the minute she laid eyes on him at first light that morning? And Jimmie, the boy who'd been out here looking after things these past months—where did he sleep?

The boat swung round on its anchor so that the island was behind her and she was gazing back the way they'd come, beyond the mouth of the harbor and across the iron-clad waves to the mainland that was visible now only as a distant smudge on the horizon. Then they were lowering the skiff, Will scampering round the deck like a man half-fifty who hadn't taken a minié ball in the soft flesh just above his left hip at Chancellorsville, and yes, she, Edith and Ida were to go first, along with a jumble of sacks and boxes, with Adolph at the oars and Jimmie to meet them on the beach with one of the mules and the sled to bring them up the long hill to the house. And she shouldn't worry, Will insisted, his big sinewy hands steadying hers as he helped her down the rope ladder to the boat with his eyes on fire and the smell of his breath sharp with the aftertaste of his own excitement, because today was a holiday and they were going to have the remainder of the afternoon to themselves. "I'm not worried, Will," she said in the instant before she started down the ladder, "not when I'm in your hands," but with the way the wind was blowing she couldn't be sure he'd heard her.

The House

Getting the boat to shore without overturning it in the surf was no small thing, but Adolph, grim as a soldier under fire and with the long muscles of his arms straining beneath the fabric of his jacket, managed it. For a long while they'd simply sat there, just outside the line of breakers, and she'd begun to grow impatient—and the girls had too—because here was the beach laid out before them and there the path up to the house, and what was he doing, this clod, this Adolph, when they were all so eager to set foot on terra firma and see what the house had to offer? Finally, though, she realized what it was—he was timing the surf, looking for an opening, the interval between a set of waves that would allow them to shoot in atop the previous one before the next came to smash them against the shore. She counted wave after wave, the seabirds screeching and the boat lurching beneath her, and then suddenly Adolph was at it, rowing furiously, the oarlocks protesting and the spray flying in their faces, and in the next moment they were ashore and leaping from the boat to tug at the painter and pull it high up the beach, and never mind their shoes or skirts or the way the wind beat the brims of their hats round their faces.

To the girls, it was a lark, both of them wet to the knees and laughing in great wild hoots even as she herself managed to save her boots, skipping on ahead of the sheet of white foam that shot up behind her and fanned out over the beach as far as she could see, though the hem of her dress was dark with wet and sprinkled with the pale flecks of sand already clinging there. She was breathing hard from the exertion, but deeply, and without restraint. If she hadn't known better, if she hadn't hemorrhaged just last month, she might have thought there was nothing wrong at all.

The sand gave beneath her feet. Tiny creatures, translucent hopping things, sprang all around her. The smell was wonderful—sea wrack, salt spray, the newborn air—and it brought her back to her own girlhood in Massachusetts and the sultry summer days when her father would take the whole family to the shore. But it wasn't sultry here. Far from it. The temperature must have been in the low fifties and the wind made it seem colder even than that. "Edith!" she cried out. "You'll catch your death in those wet clothes," and she couldn't help herself, though she should have let it go.

Edith wasn't listening. Edith was fourteen years old, tall and handsome, as physically mature as a girl two or three years older, and she had a mind of her own. She deliberately went back into the surf under the pretext of unloading the bags from the rear of the boat when she could just as easily have started at the front, and she and Ida—who should have known better—were making a game of it, snatching up this parcel or that and darting up the beach to tumble everything in a random pile even as Adolph trudged through the sand, a bag under each arm and dragging two of the oak chairs behind him without a thought to the finish or the cushions she'd sewn for the seats. In the meantime, the steamer trunk she'd so carefully packed with her personal things—letters, stationery and envelopes, writing implements, her jewelry, the clothes she'd folded and tamped into place—was still in the boat, its leather surface shining with wet. She wanted to shout for him to fetch it before it was ruined, but she didn't know how to command him, barely knew him, and the sour look he gave her didn't help matters.

Flustered—and cold, shivering—she glanced round her in irritation, wondering where the boy was with the mule and the sled to take them up to the house. And that was another thing: she couldn't for the life of her imagine what sort of sled they were talking about. The sleds she knew were for coasting down snowy hillsides or they were horse-drawn sleighs, with runners, for snowbound roads, but this, as Will had tried to explain, was a sort of travois—the path was too narrow and rough for a cart and so things had to be dragged up and down from the house. The house that was invisible from here, though she craned her neck till the muscles there began to throb. All she could see were pocked volcanic cliffs fringed with a poor sort of desert vegetation.

"I'll race you!" Edith shouted, waving a pair of hatboxes high over her head, as Ida, her face lit with the purest pleasure, sprinted up the beach with her suitcase.

"Girls!" she cried. "Stop it now. Show some dignity."

Ida, dutiful, slowed to a walk, but Edith kept on, her skirts dark with wet and her heels kicking up sand, and she didn't stop till she mounted the ridge that marked the high-tide line. She might have gone on running all the tortuous way up the path to the plateau beyond and right on into the house, if the boy hadn't appeared at that moment, mule and sled in tow. For an instant, Edith just stood there, staring, and then she dropped the hatboxes, turned on her heels and came running back, giggling, while the boy—Jimmie—stood there gaping as if he'd never seen a girl before in his life, and maybe he hadn't. Marantha gave a wave of her hand and made her way up the crest of the dune to him while he bent to the boxes Edith had dropped.

As she got closer she could see that the sled was a crude affair, constructed of the salvaged railway ties that composed one of the chief sources of building material here on this treeless island, two lengths forming the struts across which sawed portions had been nailed into place to create a slanted bed. In the center of it, lashed firmly down, was a rocking chair, and that must have been for her, so that she could ride behind the mule, an innovation of Will's, no doubt. And that was touching, it was, the way he cared for her, the way he thought matters through so as to make things easier on her. She caught her breath and then climbed up over the lip of the dune that traced the margin of the beach, the wind snatching at her hat so that she could feel the pins giving way and had to use her free hand to hold it in place, all the while clutching her overstuffed handbag in the other, the fingers of which had already begun to go numb under the pressure. To make matters worse, she caught her shoe on something, a loop of kelp or a scrap of driftwood, and stumbled so that she had to go down on one knee in the sand.

The boy just stood there as if he'd grown roots, staring from her to the retreating form of Edith and back again. He looked—this was her first impression and she wanted to be charitable—not stupid, really, but amazed or maybe hypnotized, a short, slight, dark-haired boy with sunburned skin, a retreating chin and eyes as black as the mud at the bottom of a pond. When he saw her stumble a second time, it startled him into action, and he came running to her, his arms flung out awkwardly for balance. Without a word, he reached a hand to help her as if she were an invalid already, and she wondered how much Will had told him.

"You must be Jimmie," she said, trying to mold her face into a smile of greeting.

11

He ducked his head. Colored. "Yes, ma'am," he said.

"I'm Mrs. Waters."

"Yes, ma'am," he said. "I reckoned that."

She turned her head to direct his gaze toward the beach. "And that's my daughter, Edith, in the azure hat, and the serving girl, Ida. And the man—"

"That's Adolph, ma'am. I know him. We—he—well, he come out already once to help me work the sheep and suchlike . . ."

"Yes," she said, rubbing her hands together against the cold. "Well, I hope you'll all get on nicely." And then, looking to the sled and the mule with its skittish eyes and ears standing up as straight as two bookends and the path that wound its way through the chaparral and up the hill to where the mysterious house awaited her, she added, "The chair—I presume that's for me?"

He nodded, stabbing at the sand with the toe of one boot. His hair was too long, she could see that, greasy strands of it hanging in his eyes beneath one of those caps the Irish workmen favored. His fingernails were filthy. And his teeth—she'd have to introduce him to a toothbrush or he'd be gumming his food by the time he turned twenty.

But here came the wind again, gusting now, and the sand driven before it like grapeshot. "Very well, then," she said, and again he just stared. A long moment unfolded. "What I mean to say is, what, exactly, are we waiting for?"

There was no room for Edith on the sled once they'd loaded it with everything it could carry, and so she stayed behind on the beach to help Ida and the men unload the skiff on its successive trips to the schooner and back. Edith had pestered her—she wanted to go now, wanted to see the house and her room and the sheep, and why couldn't she just walk up on her own?—but Marantha was firm with her. She was needed below, on the beach, and she'd see the house in good time. Jimmie stared at his feet throughout this colloquy, which, given Edith and her temperament, lasted longer than it should have, and when Edith finally turned and stalked off he gave the mule a swat and they started on up the path.

The boy led the mule by the reins, walking in a loose-jointed way, sauntering as if he were out for a stroll, but the grade was steep and the mule was laboring. Within minutes its flanks were steaming. A cascade of mud and stones flew out from beneath its hooves and she was twice spattered, three times, four. She could smell the animal's breath, rank and ragged, careening down the length of it on the wind that grew stronger as they rose in elevation. Her neck ached. Her mouth was dry. Steeling herself, she gripped the arms of the rocker as it jerked from side to side and the heavy struts of the sled scraped along the path, gouging two deep furrows behind them.

As they climbed, she saw that the path wove its way through a natural canyon, which fell away to the thin muddy margin of a creek some thirty or forty feet below. The sky was a uniform gray. Birds started up from the scrub and shot at a diagonal across the gap of the canyon to vanish out of sight. The mule wheezed and sighed. She felt a cough coming on and fought it, breathing fiercely through her nostrils and holding herself as rigidly as she was able. The rocker groaned, the sled chafed. And then, just when she thought they were going to go on forever, up and up till they circumvented the clouds and reached a whole new continent in the sky, they emerged on a plateau in a blast of wind-driven sand and the house was there.

It took her a moment to get her bearings, the mule kicking up clods, the boy swinging the sled in a wide arc across the yard so that it was facing back down the canyon even as he reached up for the hame of the animal's collar and jerked it to a stop. She didn't know what she'd been expecting, some sort of quaint ivy-covered cottage out of Constable or Turner, hedges, flowerbeds, a picket fence—*a sheepman's place*—but this was something else altogether. This couldn't be it, could it? She looked to the boy, expecting that he'd let her in on the joke any second now—this was the barn or the servants' quarters or bunkhouse or whatever they called it and in the next moment he'd be chucking the mule and leading her on to the house itself, of course he would . . . but then it occurred to her that there were no other structures in sight, no other structures possible even in all that empty expanse. Jimmie was watching her. A gust caught her like a slap in the face. The mule shuddered, lifted its tail and deposited its droppings on the barren ground. She pushed herself up from the chair, stepped down from the sled and strode across the yard.

Her first impression was of nakedness, naked walls struck with penurious little windows, a yard of windblown sand giving onto an infinite vista of sheep-ravaged scrub that radiated out from it in every direction and not a tree or shrub or scrap of ivy in sight. There was nothing even remotely quaint or cozy about it. It might as well have been lifted up in a tornado and set down in the middle of the Arabian Desert. And where were the camels? The women in burnooses? She was so disappointed—stunned, shocked—that she was scarcely aware of the boy as he pushed open the rude gate for her. "You want I should put the things in the parlor?" he asked.

She was in the inner yard now, moving as if in a trance toward the door, which even from this distance she could see had been sloppily cut and hung so that there was a wide gap running across the doorstep like a black horizontal scar. The windowsills were blistered, the panes gone milky with abrasion. A jagged line of dark nailheads ran the length of the clapboards, climbing crazily to the eaves and back down again as if they'd been blown there on the wind, the boards themselves so indifferently whitewashed they gave up the raised grain of the cheap sea-run pine in clotted skeins and whorls that looked like miniature faces staring out at her—or no, leering at her. She recognized this as a delusion and delusions only came when the fever settled on her, but she didn't feel feverish at the moment, just weak, that was all. Weak and disordered. As if that weren't enough, just as she was about to lift her foot to the front steps, in the very instant, a quick darting shadow—snake, lizard, rodent?—whipped out in front of her and she had to stifle a scream, but the boy was right there, doing a quick two-step, bringing the heel of his boot down on the thing, which was only gristle and blood in the sequel.

"Ma'am?" The boy was fumbling to pull open the front door for her, wearing a puzzled look—she was the invalid, acting strange, an animated wraith like Miss Havisham, a harpy, a witch, and she knew she had to snap out of it, embrace the positive, be strong and assertive. She willed herself to pass through the door and into the front room, thinking at least there were two stories, at least there was that, and then she was staggered all over again.

Will couldn't expect her to live here—no one could. The room was uninhabitable, as crude and ugly a place as she'd ever seen in her life. The floorboards were innocent of varnish or even oil and they were deeply scuffed and scoured by the sand, which seemed nearly as comfortable here as in the yard. There were no curtains on the windows. The furniture, such as it was, consisted of half a dozen wooden chairs, a long bare table etched with the marks of heavy usage and a bleached-out sideboard that looked as if it had been salvaged off a ship—which, she would learn, was in fact the case. No rug. No paintings, no china, no decoration of any kind. Worst of all, no one had bothered to cover the walls, which had been crudely whitewashed, apparently from the same bucket that had been put to use on the exterior. This wasn't a room—it was just an oversized box, a pen, and at the rear of it were two bedrooms the size of anchorites' cells and an even cruder door that gave onto a lean-to addition that served as the kitchen. Everything smelled of—of what? *Sheep.* That's what the place smelled of, as if the whole flock had been using it as a barn.

"Ma'am?"

She came back to herself suddenly—the boy was there still, wanting something. He gave her a pleading look—he was only trying to help, she could see that, only trying to be efficient, to unload the sled and bring it back down for Will and the girls and Adolph to load up again and again so that all they'd brought with them could be arranged here in this sterile comfortless rat-hole of a house that no amount of hope or optimism or good cheer could begin to make right, and she realized, for the second time in as many minutes, that she was making him uneasy. Worse: she was frightening him.

"Yes?"

"Should I—? I mean, do you want that I should—because Captain Waters is going to be wondering where I got myself to and he can be awful sharp sometimes . . ."

"Yes," she said, and her voice sounded strange, as if her air passages had been choked off, and she had to struggle to command it. "Go ahead. Do what you must. Shoo, go on!"

The coughing didn't start till he'd ducked out the door and into the wind-whipped gloom of the day and it carried her to the unfinished stairs that were like the steps in a child's tree house and on up them to the carpetless bedroom she would share with Will and the sad four-poster bed with its greasy curtains and the counterpane that smelled not of her husband but of sheep—only, and inescapably, of sheep.

The Bedroom

It was anger—and despair, that too—that gave her the strength to strip the bedding and tear the bed curtains from their hooks, to ball them up and fling them on the floor for Ida, because what was he thinking, how could he ever imagine she'd regain her strength in a freezing hovel like this as if she were some sort of milkmaid in a bucolic romance? They could have gone to Italy and baked in the sun till her chest was clear, the lesions dried like figs on a tin sheet and the flesh come back to her limbs, her breasts, her hips and abdomen—or even Mexico. A tropical place. A desert. Anyplace but this. His own selfishness was at work here, she knew that in her heart. Even as she sat there on the stained mattress trying to fight down her feelings, coughing and coughing again till her throat was raw, she couldn't help accusing him. But then she'd been guilty too. She was the one who'd given him the last of her savings, the last of the money left from James' estate, to buy in here as equal partner with Mills because she knew if she didn't she would lose him. He was an enthusiast, he wanted to better himself, saw his chance and took it, but he was her husband too and he'd loved her once, loved her still, though she knew she wasn't much use to him anymore—not beyond what her money could bring, anyway. The thought—and it wasn't the first time it had come to her—shrank her down till she was nothing, a husk like one of those papery things you saw clinging to the bark after the imago unfurls its wings to beat away on the air.

She could hear them below, the heavy tramp of feet, boxes set down with a dull reverberant thump, a soft curse, the door slamming. She wouldn't go down there. Wouldn't move. Wouldn't do anything at all but just sit here until Will came up the stairs with his doleful eyes and penitential face and gave her an explanation, courted her, saw to *her* needs instead of his own—or just held her, just for a moment. There was the slam of the door

16

again, sharper footsteps, thinner, like the beating of a hammer against a sheet of tin, and then the girls' voices rising to her in a pitched-high gabble that gave her no comfort at all. Edith said something. Ida responded. Edith went off again. She strained to hear, but the walls and floors distorted the sense of it till she couldn't tell whether they were as heartsick and disoriented as she herself was or caught up in the novelty of the place and the day and the task ahead of them. There went Edith. There Ida. And then one of them was in the kitchen, a banging there, metal on metal, and it was Ida, it had to be, settling in.

It was only then that she lifted her eyes to the room, to see again where she was, to study the peeling whitewashed boards that ran up the walls and across the ceiling without differentiation, the window cut there like a dark demonic eye, the plain porcelain chamber pot set in one corner in advertisement of its function, the water-stained armoire in the other, its mirrored door dull as a sheet of lead. The next cough caught in her throat and she took a shallow wheezing breath and held it, then pushed herself up and went to the washstand. There was a pitcher of water there beside the basin and a chipped ceramic cup that seemed to have some sort of residue at the bottom of it. She breathed out, then in again, then once more, deeper now, expanding her lungs, and the cough didn't come. How long the water in the pitcher had sat there she couldn't say—was it from Will's last visit? Or had the boy freshened it that morning? No matter. She lifted the pitcher to her lips and drank till droplets spilled down the front of her jacket.

The moment passed and she felt marginally better. She was going to have to get control of herself, will herself to get better and be the sort of wife she knew she could be if she could just get past this sinking feeling that had brought on the spasm as much as anything else because hadn't she been breathing freely down there at the beach? Less than an hour ago? And wasn't the air pure, just as Will had promised? That was when she turned and caught a glimpse of herself in the mirror. There was a figure trapped there beneath the dull sheen, a figure that mimicked her every motion though it didn't look like her at all, and that was because the mirror was cheaply made, a pure lens of distortion like one of the mirrors in the fun house at the arcade. The woman staring back at her had a wasted filmy look, the flesh tightened at the jawline and raked back around the orbits of the eyes, and when she stood up straight in her traveling clothes and arched her back and threw out her chest, she saw nothing there, just a pinched descending line from the pale blotch of her face to the fixed hem of her brown twill dress.

She moved closer, ignoring the sounds from below—a clangor, a thump, Will's voice raised in command—and took a good hard look. And then, without even knowing what she was doing, she was loosening the jacket and unbuttoning the shirtwaist to reveal her camisole and the white tatting that edged it. Her clavicle—was that what it was called?—shone in the weak light as a hard raised slash of bone over flesh so bloodless it might have been the flesh of a veal calf. Fascinated, she peeled the camisole down to the upper edge of her corset—never mind the cold—and there were her breasts revealed. What had been her breasts. Nothing there now but the nipples, as if she were a child all over again. She'd lost weight, of course she had, she'd known that all along. The first doctor had put her on a milk diet and then the second— Dr. Erringer, the one who'd auscultated her and listened and thumped and pronounced the inescapable diagnosis in his soft priestly tones—on red meat, and she tried to eat, she did, but what the mirror gave back was undeniable, unthinkable, fraught and ugly and pointing to one end only because this wasn't the fun house but the real and actual.

I'll tell Will, she was thinking, frightened all over again, terrified. Tell him it's not going to work, tell him I need sun, not gloom, comfort, pampering, civilization, that this is all wrong, wrong, wrong. Tell him I can't be his wife, can't sleep in the same bed with him, can't do what's expected of a wife because my bones won't stand it, my lungs, my breasts, my heart, my heart . . .

When was the last time they'd been husband and wife? Before her hemorrhage. Before December, anyway. And before that, after she'd begun to lose weight and Dr. Erringer had informed her that consumption was not hereditary as people had believed all these years but a disease caused by infectious agents, by microbes that were so small as to be invisible, she'd been afraid for Will, afraid of infecting him, and yet he was needful and she was too and their marital relations went on. With one proviso: she wouldn't kiss him. Wouldn't kiss anyone, not even Edith—not on the lips. That was her true terror—not that she herself would succumb, which on her bad days she saw as increasingly inevitable no matter how much Will tried to talk it away, but that she would infect the ones she loved the most.

She turned away from the mirror, buttoned herself up and crossed back to the bed. The chill of the place—of a room in a wind-besieged house that had been allowed to go cold because there was no one there to feel it, because it had been derelict, run-down, cheerless—set her to shivering, and she wouldn't wrap herself in the filthy bedding no matter if she shivered to death, but she laid herself down on the mattress, using one arm for a pillow, pulled up her legs and curled into herself. Sleep, that was what she needed. If she could just rest a bit, she'd feel better, she knew she would. She closed her eyes. Her breathing slowed. And the room, with its wheeling drift of dirt and the stained armoire in one corner and the chamber pot in the other, vanished into nothingness.

The Kitchen

She awoke to a distant thumping, as if to the beating of an outsized heart, a heart as big as the house itself. Thump, thump, thump. For the first moment, staring at the unfamiliar walls, she didn't know where she was, and then it all came back to her in a rush: she was on an island raked with wind, an island fourteen miles square set down in the heaving froth of the Pacific Ocean, and there was nothing on it but the creatures of nature and an immense rolling flock of sheep that were money on the hoof, income, increase, bleating woolly sacks of greenback dollars—or at least that was the way Will saw it. Will, whose footsteps, heavy tread, were coming up the stairs to her, thumping, thumping. She held herself very still, counting off the intervals between her breaths, fighting back the urge to cough because one cough, the first one, would lead to another and then another, till the whole unraveling skein played itself out all over again.

The footsteps stopped outside the door. Then there was a knock and Will's voice, soft and inquisitive: "Marantha, are you there? Are you asleep?"

She was gathering herself—it was New Year's Day, they were in their new home, here now and no place else, and they were going to put things in order, celebrate the day, live and breathe and take in the air, the virginal air—but she wasn't ready yet. She needed a minute. One more minute. She didn't answer.

The door pushed slowly open and there he was, Will, standing in the doorframe peering in at her, his look poised between the elation she knew must have been surging through him and the duty he felt toward her. The duty to frown and commiserate and fold his big busy hands up in front of him as if he didn't know what to do with them. "Is it bad?" he said, and he took a step forward, as if to come to her, but she didn't want him, not yet.

She spoke without lifting her head. "We're going to have to do the washing," she said, her voice toneless and rasping, the voice of a woman shrinking into the grip of her own skin as if it were no more than a sack, a coat. "I hope you understand that. Right off. First thing."

"Yes," he said, snatching a look at her face before his eyes went to the wall, the window, anyplace but the space she occupied, "yes, of course. You're right." He was a big man, six feet tall and well over two hundred pounds, solid, powerful, her man, her strength, and she felt sorry for him in that moment, sorry she couldn't share in his enthusiasm, but one thought only was going through her head: They'd spent ten thousand dollars for *this*? The last ten thousand dollars she had to her name? What if things didn't work out, what if the boat didn't come, or what if it did and then went aground and wrecked under the load of the shorn wool that was the profit of the place? Then what would they do? Kill sheep and wear their skins and go around hooting like the Indians who'd given up on this lump of rock all those eons ago, who'd died of misery and want for all she knew?

"It's all right," he said, more softly now, and his eyes came back to settle on her. "We'll have it all washed and dried out before bedtime, you'll see."

She didn't respond for a long moment. "Send Ida up," she said finally. "And Edith. Where's Edith?"

And then everything shifted as if she'd turned the page of a book. Will eased the door shut. She heard his tread on the stairs, heard Ida's voice, Edith's. She sat up, setting both feet squarely on the floor and the floor didn't move because it wasn't the deck of a boat, everything fixed and solid now, this mineral world, this place where she lived. She took a tentative breath and held it, and in the next moment the weight was gone from her chest and she was breathing freely, thinking of all the things that needed doing, the wash, the clothes, the furniture, unpacking. She felt ashamed of herself. So what if the place was dirty? That was a temporary condition. It could be cleaned. Made presentable. Comfortable, even. Anyplace could.

She stood. Brushed at her skirt to smooth it down. And then she was out the door and in the upper hall, heat rising to her from the iron stove below and the damp lingering reek of sheep driven down by the scent of the coffee Ida was brewing on the kitchen stove, God bless her. She went to the kitchen first. Ida, a smear of something darkening one cheek—ash, grease?—gave her a frantic look. "I was just making up a tray for you—coffee, with two lumps, the way you like it, and buttered toast."

"Don't trouble yourself," she said, "you've got enough to do, I can see that. I'll take it here."

"Here?"

There was a hutch in the far corner, the glass in the upper portion cracked, its paint (olive and cream, with dabs of yellow to represent the blooms of the flower pattern on the cupboard doors) stripped to the bare wood in random patches as if it had been gouged with a sharp implement or maybe even gnawed. An oilcloth-covered table with two chairs stood beside the back door, just beneath the window. On the wall behind it, running from the door to the stove, there were two lines of hooks, and from the hooks, blackened pans hung suspended. Along with a cleaver. A boning knife. What looked to be some sort of flail—or no, it was a flour mill. And beside that, in the corner where the stovepipe ran up into the unfinished eaves, a homemade calendar fastened to the wall with a single nail, its leaves curling at the edges. She moved closer, squinted her eyes. The calendar showed the month of March, 1886, almost two years ago, and she saw that one of the dates had been circled in black, the tenth.

"Ma'am?" Ida had lifted the tray from the counter and was holding it out before her in offering.

"Set it on the table, would you?"

She went up to the calendar, ran a finger over the neat circle of ink. Mrs. Mills. It must have been Mrs. Mills who'd marked the date as special, and what was it, an anniversary? A birthday? She'd met the woman only once, in the house at Santa Barbara, and she remembered her as graceless and plain, her clothes out of fashion and her hair gone gray, a woman not much older than herself who'd spent the better part of seventeen years on this island, in this house. Who'd sat at this table and laid out the days and months in a neat grid, who'd selected Wednesday the tenth and marked it in anticipation of an event that was long past now. History. Everything was history.

"Do you miss it?" Marantha had asked her. "The island? After so much time spent there, I mean?" It had taken the woman a moment, as if the thought had never occurred to her. Then she leaned back in the chair—the men were out of earshot, on the front porch, perched on the railing and jawing away like long-lost brothers, the afternoon grand, sun striping the carpet and carriages sailing by on the street as if they were boats on a stream—and let out a long sighing breath. "It does get lonesome out there, I'll say that. But the quiet does you good. You don't have all the dirt and noise of the city. The criminal population. Cheats, lawyers. Of course, my boys—Jack and William—was eager to get out. No females out there, you see?"

Seventeen years. Mrs. Mills. *Call me Irene.*

She didn't sit—she felt full of energy suddenly, as if she were somehow in competition with the absent woman, a housewife herself, a farmwife, at least for the time being. Instead, she ate standing up, leaning over the table to sip from the cup and pick the toast up off a cracked plate she'd never laid eyes on before. One of Mrs. Mills', no doubt. One of the sheepmen's. She studied the unfamiliar cup in her hand, paused to chew, swallow. A quick image of Charlie Curner flitted through her head, his boat riding the waves and the mainland looming up on him. "Ida," she said after a moment, "have you seen the crate with the dishes?"

"They must be in the yard yet. Or the front room." Ida had already been out back, at the cistern, and the big laundry pot had been set to boil atop the stove. The sheets would go there, if anyone could find the soap they'd brought, and the bed curtains and the rest, and Will would have to string up a length of rope for a clothesline, or did they already have one here? They must have. Even sheepmen, even Jimmie, had to have washed their clothes, if only to keep them from rotting away to rags.

"Well, wouldn't it be a good idea to have them brought back here so they can be sorted and put on the shelves? We can't be expected to eat off a bare table, or, or"—she held up the cracked plate—"this rubbish."

"I don't know, ma'am, but there's an awful load of boxes out there, just a jumble of things the men have gone and dropped down without bothering even to see what they are. I can't make hide nor hair of them."

"But I clearly labeled them—you saw me."

Ida just shrugged. This was hard on her, she could see that. Everything was in chaos and there were a thousand things to do, not the least of which was to prepare the meal, the holiday meal, and here was the bird itself—how could she have missed it?—laid out on the counter beside the iron sink, neatly gutted and plucked, just as if it had come from the butcher.

"The turkey," she said. "Was that from—?"

"The boy killed it this morning, while we were on the boat, is what I gather, because Captain Waters give him word when he was here before Christmas to make things ready for us. There's a whole flock of them running about the yard, you know. Chickens too. You should go and have a look, you should. The sun's just broke through and it's a glorious day out there. It'll lift your spirits, I'm sure." She turned back to the stove, to the potatoes boiling there in an unfamiliar pot, a sheepmen's pot, blackened and battered. "And Captain Waters says we're to stop what we're doing, all of us, by three o'clock, because it's a holiday and he's going to take us out and show us over the island."

She couldn't see much out the window, which was as clouded with abrasion as the ones in the front room. But she saw the outline of the pens there in the yard, the wooden slats of the fences, and beyond them the long gradually sloping rise that culminated in the high point of the island, Green Mountain, 831 feet above sea level, a measurement Will had taken himself with his transit. Eight hundred thirty-one feet. He was proud of that figure, inordinately proud, as if he'd captured one of the Alps and reduced it to fit here to scale on his own private domain.

"We're all in a high state of excitement, so," Ida said, turning to the chopping block now and the turkey that wanted stuffing. She chopped onions and celery, fragmented a heel of bread, her movements neat and circumscribed, her shoulders dipping and rising as she worked through her tasks, her feet sweeping through a graceful arc on the bleached-out floorboards till she might have been dancing in place. She was a pretty girl, pretty enough, though no match for Edith, and a good worker, solicitous, kind, dutiful above all else. Her parents were Mullinses, out of County Cork via Boston and the Gold Rush that had washed them up penniless in San Francisco. She was a poor girl, that was all, poor Irish, but after three years of having her in the house now Marantha considered her as much a daughter as Edith herself, or very nearly. "To see over the island, I mean," Ida went on, glancing over her shoulder. "The flock. And the seals too. Can you hear them? That's them barking in the distance."

She caught her breath a moment. There was the creak and rustle of the stove, the hiss of water coming to a boil. Men's voices, muffled, giving and taking orders. And something else too, an undercurrent of concerted vocalization that might have been the basso ostinato of a distant choir. Seals. Barking. Or no, singing, singing their own immemorial songs to the sea and

the island, and to what else? Fish. They sang to fish, the god of fish, the pro-
vider and nurturer of all the flashing silver schools of the sea. She tried to
picture them—she'd seen them in San Francisco, lying inert on the rocks at
the edge of the Bay—dun things, black, tan, bleached white. Those seals
belonged to no one. But these, strange to think it, the ones singing even now,
belonged to her.

The Flock

From the kitchen she went down the hall to the main room (the parlor, she'd have to call it, the parlor cum dining room) and started sorting through the boxes, looking for her plates, the cutlery—and sheets, where were the sheets? The men had left everything in a jumble, just as Ida said, and things had gotten wet, unfortunately, so that the ink had bled and smeared on the boxes she'd so meticulously packed and labeled back in Santa Barbara, working through long punishing afternoons when she'd barely felt equal to getting out of bed. They were outside now, the men—she could see them through the window, their hats and shoulders glazed with sun, Will, Adolph and Jimmie—and they seemed to be fussing with the mule and the sled. But there were two mules now and a horse too and Will was bending suddenly to jerk a supple darkly shining object up off the fence post and clap it over the horse's back—a saddle, the stirrups dangling and the horse flinching with the surprise of it. And then, speaking of surprises, she saw that there was a dog there with them, a sheepdog with a piebald coat and two mismatched eyes, its tail sweeping back and forth in the dirt.

A dog. A horse. Turkeys. Seals. She couldn't begin to imagine what else would turn up in this embarrassment of riches—and what about the sun overhead, did she own that too? Or the effect of it, the power it radiated to the grass so the grass could sprout and the sheep could batten on it and frolic and grow out their coats? The dirt, the dirt was hers. Or half hers. Or no, a quarter, when you factored in Hiram Mills. And Mrs. Mills. She had a quarter interest too. They were like four gods, their own pantheon.

She went to the front door—never mind how poorly hung it was—and pushed it open on the pale streaming sunlight. The wind had died. It was almost warm. All the scents of nature came to her at once like a dose of smelling salts—the barnyard and its ordure, the wildflowers blanketing the hills, sage, lupine, the sea—and it was as if she'd never been alive till this moment, because this wasn't the exhausted sterile atmosphere of the parlor, the restaurant, the public library or the doctor's office or any confined space, but something else entirely. It was primitive. Untainted. Fresh. Fresh air, the air that would cure her. It was true, everything Will had told her was true. How could she have doubted him?

"Will!" she cried out and watched him turn away from the horse, a neutral look on his face because he didn't know what to expect, complaints, demands, trouble, and before she could think she was coming across the yard to him, pinching her skirts to keep them out of the mud. The hired man and the boy stood there frozen. The dog lifted its eyes. "Will," she said, "it's glorious. Everything is. I'm just—didn't you say you were going to take us for a ride?"

There were three chairs lashed to the sled this time—two rockers, for her and Ida, and a straight-backed chair for Jimmie, who was to drive the mule. "I've swapped out the mules," Will said when they'd gathered there in the yard, all of them still in their traveling clothes because there hadn't seemed much sense in changing into anything fresh, not till dinner, anyway. "General Meade here, I've hitched him to the sled because he's stronger but less predictable than Plum"—and here he looked to Edith—"who as you can see I've saddled up for someone to ride. I'll be on Mike"—he nodded toward the horse, which was poking its muzzle into the dirt around a poor sprout of yellowed weed—"and since Adolph's going to stay behind to look after things, the turkey, in particular, isn't that right, Ida?, I guess that elects you, Edith."

Edith gave him a look of surprise and then she flushed with pleasure.

"Here," he said, "let me help you up," and Edith went to him and Will dropped one hand down so that he could take her foot, put an arm round her shoulder and ease her up and into the saddle. "Now, you'll go sidesaddle today, till you get used to him, but we'll have you riding astride in no time. You wait and see."

Then he mounted the horse, wonderfully agile for a man his age, commanding, erect, the hat raked down over one eye as if he were one of the cowboys in a dime novel, and Marantha realized she'd never seen him on a horse before, never even dreamed he had the skill of it. Maybe it was

27

something he'd learned in the Army, before she knew him. Maybe that was it. It had to be. Because in the seven years they'd been married he'd never ventured beyond the hansom or cable car, not as far as she knew. "Are you comfortable there, Minnie?" he asked, using his pet name for her even as he leaned down and steadied the reins so that the horse's hooves did a quick little dance and the mud exploded beneath them.

"Yes, I'm fine," she said, though she dreaded the yawing and jolting that was to come. She gripped the arms of the rocker, braced her feet, made sure of her hat.

"All right," he said, nosing his horse around, "you go nice and easy now, Jimmie. This isn't a race."

The boy didn't respond. He merely flicked the switch at the stolid black rump of the mule—General Meade—and they were off, the dog darting on ahead with a high tremulous yelp while Ida swung anxiously round to shout over her shoulder to Adolph, who stood there in the yard like a post, his arms dangling and his face expressionless. "Don't you let that turkey dry out," she called. She was trying to add something else, some further admonition, something about basting, but the sled dropped into a hole and her voice got away from her.

They hadn't gone two hundred yards before the sheep began to appear, wedge-faced aggregations of them staring stupidly from either side or lurching out of the way of the mule at the last second. Yellow eyes, the black slits of their pupils. Wool caked with filth. Sheep. If they'd looked vaguely romantic at a distance, like souls set adrift, up close they were anything but. The smell was stronger here, a working odor of massed bodies, of sweat, urine, excrement. All she could hear was the sound of their ragged mindless bleating like a perpetual complaint, and underneath it the pulsing indistinct chorus of the seals.

Will led on, heading toward a bluff beyond, where apparently there was another canyon that gave onto the beach, another beach. The plan was to picnic by the shore, walk the strand and collect seashells while Jimmie went off to pry abalone from the rocks for a New Year's chowder to complement the turkey and potatoes. That was fine, but this business of the sled was something else altogether. She held tight as it swayed side to side, lurched over stones and hissed through the long troughs of sand, Ida shouting with glee and the boy rising up out of his seat to coax the mule on. At first she was nervous about Edith, afraid her mule would bolt or throw her or step in a hole and go down atop her, but as they went on she saw how confident Edith was—and alert too—and how the mule really was gentle, ambling along like one of the ponies Edith used to ride at the park when she was little. She was thinking about that, about the time when there were just the two of them, before Will had come into her life, and how dense and rich those days had seemed, James dead and buried and Edith there to take his place, to be stroked, loved, supported, when Will, riding high above them, swung his horse round to come up beside the sled and lean down to her.

"You see that, Minnie," he crowed, waving his arm in a grand gesture to take in the whole scene, from the dwindling furrow the sled had cut behind them to the crown of Green Mountain and the far-flung clusters of sheep that seemed to be everywhere, palely glowing under the benediction of the sun. "That's just a fraction of the flock, which Mills puts at four thousand, and that's before the increase of this year's lambs."

He was grinning down at her, looking more alive than she'd seen him in years, his excitement running on ahead of him. "I can see them," she called back, the sled jolting so that she had to hang on with both hands. "Just look at the lambs trying out their legs. The way they kick."

Edith was on the opposite side of the sled, not twenty feet away, her shoulders swaying gracefully beneath the crown of her hat as the mule worked its haunches up and down, picking its slow deliberate way through the scrub that was alive with pale green shoots of new grass and wildflowers as far as you could see. She was about to call to her, to point out the lambs, when Edith pulled up short, tugging at the reins so that the mule jerked back its head and planted its feet, all motion gone out of it in an instant but for the slow metronomic swishing of its tail. Edith arched her back, raised a hand to shield her eyes. "Oh, look," she said, pointing now, "look at that one all alone. Is that one alone? Over there?"

The dog had already spotted it, scrambling his paws to bolt through the grass and circle it twice, his bark fluent and pitched high. The lamb, its umbilical still trailing away beneath it, merely blinked at him, as helpless as a fallen leaf. The ewe was nowhere to be seen.

"You better shut that dog up or he'll drive all the ewes off their lambs,"

Will said, addressing Jimmie, who stopped the mule with a single guttural command, sprang down from the sled and began wading off through the vegetation, the dog dancing on ahead of him.

"Nipper!" the boy called. "Nipper, heel!"

It was too much for Edith. She slid from the saddle as naturally as if she'd been doing it all her life and hurried after him, and in the next moment they were all on foot, the whole party, she and Ida and Will too, pushing through the scrub to where the lamb stood apart from the flock that spun out in all directions, each ewe with one or two lambs and sometimes three, lambs in the hundreds sprung up like mushrooms after a rain. There was that odor, that intense odor, as of things fermenting. Suddenly it was cold. She put a hand to her throat, pinching the collar of her coat to keep out the breeze that seemed to have come up out of nowhere. When she got to where the lamb was, the dog was sitting on its heels and Jimmie and Will were standing there gazing down at it as if it were some rare specimen. Edith, looking flushed, bent to it with a sprig of fresh grass. "Here," she was saying. "Here, little thing, take this."

"It don't want grass," Jimmie said flatly. "Milk's what it wants. Mother's milk."

"Poor thing," Marantha heard herself say, and at that moment the animal let out a bleat so hopeless and weak you'd have thought it was dying right there before their eyes.

"They each of them has his own call and his own smell—that's how the dam finds them," Jimmie said. "But every once in a while, nobody knows why, the ewe'll reject her own lamb."

"Can we keep it?" Edith pleaded. "Nurse it, I mean. Because if its mother—"

Will was standing beside her, gazing down on the bony narrow skull, the ears slick with afterbirth, the slit yellow eyes, the lips opening and closing on nothing. He had his hands on his hips the way he did when he'd made up his mind about something and that irked her because she could see what was coming. "You can't just blunder on an animal and assume it's abandoned," he said, and his voice was wrong, all wrong, too hard by half. "Because sometimes the ewe comes back—isn't that right, Jimmie?—and that gives it a far better chance of survival than having to rely on somebody who, for all the

30

height and heft of her, is still a child, feeding it six times a day from a warmed-over pan of milk."

Edith never even glanced at him. She just straightened up and turned to her, to her mother, and repeated herself: "Can we?"

And what did she say? She said, "Of course, of course we can," and she was looking at Will when she said it. "We can't just leave the poor animal out here to starve, can we?"

The Lamb

Dinner that first evening was a homely affair, hardly festive, but it was better than it had a right to be considering where they were and the transformation that had taken place in the interval of just over twelve hours, from the time they pulled themselves out of bed on the mainland till now, with night freshly descended over the island. The table had been moved to the center of the room and covered with a cloth, there was a fire going in the potbellied stove to take the chill off the place and Will had lit a pair of lanterns that threw rollicking shadows across the walls every time somebody moved. She took a glass of wine when it was offered her and raised it to Will's in a toast to her new life and her new family, all of them, even Adolph and Jimmie, who were seated at the foot of the table, looking abashed. For them, there was beer, and for Edith a bottle of sarsaparilla. Whatever had afflicted her earlier, whatever her fears, the day and the sun and the novelty of the moment had pushed it all away and she felt calm now, calm and steady and even grateful.

The abalone chowder was a pleasant surprise, unexpectedly rich and flavorful, heavily peppered and simmered down in the cream from the milk of the cow Jimmie had led in from the pasture a week earlier after its calf had died—that and the butter they'd brought with them from the mainland. If she hadn't known better, she would have thought she was spooning up an oyster bisque at a candlelit table at Fior d'Italia in San Francisco. And Ida did a splendid job with the turkey, which, while it wasn't as moist as it might have been, nonetheless hadn't been scorched or dried to jerky either, which was quite a feat under the circumstances.

On the other hand, they were eating off of a mismatched assortment of chipped plates she herself had found in a dirty cupboard in the kitchen after discovering they'd somehow forgotten the box of Wedgwood china that had once belonged to her first husband's mother. Or that the cutlery had been left behind too, so that they had to alternate between an odd farrago of forks and spoons and pass round the two bone-handled knives that had been standing on the kitchen windowsill for God knew how long.

That was crude. So crude it had almost brought tears to her eyes, but she'd held back—just as she'd held back that morning when the coughing started up again—because she didn't want to spoil things for Will. This was his idea, his venture, his dream, and he'd talked it up so many times over the past months it had become a litany of success and increase and health abounding, and now the abstraction had been made concrete. He was beside himself, his eyes shining above the thick regimental mustache as he laid out his plans for the road, the outbuildings, the sheep and hogs and all the rest, even a boat— if they couldn't build one out of scrap they'd save up and buy one of the working boats in the harbor at Santa Barbara, once the wool came in. She'd never seen him happier. He hummed to himself as he carved the turkey, then danced round the table as he served it out in great steaming slabs and all the while the talk never stopped. Increase, that was his theme. Increase and improvement and profit.

Edith seemed in good spirits too, chattering away with Ida, giggling, shooting glances down the table at Jimmie, who blushed and turned his face away, and at Adolph, immovable Adolph, who sat there as if he'd been carved of stone. It was a relief. Especially after the way she'd fought against the move, throwing one tantrum after another, as if to leave her piano and dance lessons and the new friends she'd begun to make in town were the end of her life. *There's no choice in the matter*, Marantha had told her. *The deed's signed, the money paid out. Think of someone other than yourself for a change.* And Edith had thrown it right back at her: *I am. I'm thinking of you.*

But now, in the flush of arrival and settling in, everything seemed to have changed. The mule ride had clearly thrilled her. The novelty of the place. The turkeys roosting in the grass, the lovely mother-of-pearl seashells she was already planning to work into beads for a necklace, the wildness and isolation of the hills and valleys that bled away in the mist as if they'd never been there at all.

"It's like *Wuthering Heights*," she'd said as they were setting the table for dinner, "like the wild moors with their lowing herds and wandering flocks. Exactly like." And then she'd looked beyond the window and into the yard where Jimmie and Adolph were cutting and stacking lengths of root and driftwood for the stove. "Only where's my Heathcliff?" And then they'd both laughed, and that felt good, because it was the first time in weeks, at least since they'd begun the ordeal of organizing and packing and ordering supplies and foodstuffs from one shop and another, that Marantha felt the burden lift from her.

And then there was the lamb. They could hear it bleating from the yard throughout the meal and it kept on bleating even after Edith had given it a bowl of stove-warmed milk, letting it suck the liquid from her fingers as if it were at the teat, and it bleated when they cleared the table for cards and the Ouija board and it kept on bleating when she and Will climbed the stairs to their bed with its fresh-washed sheets and dubious counterpane and the bed curtains that were still damp to the touch.

For a long while she lay awake, listening to it, though she was exhausted and couldn't have moved a finger even if the bed had caught fire. There were furtive scurryings in the dark—mice, as she was to discover, legions of them that overran the place and made it their own, as if she and Will were only leasing it from them—and an intermittent scraping she couldn't place. It might have been the sheepdog scratching at the door or some other animal nosing round the house looking for a way in, seals lumbering up at night, seabirds, owls, what did she know? Or maybe it was her imagination, maybe she was hearing things, her nerves at a pitch and the silence so uncompromising, so different from the way it had been on Post Street, where there were always voices, hoof beats, the creak and clatter of wagon wheels, distant music, life.

Toward dawn—she must have dozed, because she started awake with the pain in her chest that felt as if some thing were living inside her and struggling to get out—there came a series of soft distant barks that weren't like the barking of a dog at all, or the seals with their raucous eruptive cries she'd heard as clearly as if they were right out there in the yard. She listened for a long while, puzzled, until she realized that the sound must have been coming from the foxes Will had told her about, Lilliputian things the size of a house cat that stole through the night and made off with the turkeys and chickens and the eggs they laid in neat cups of grass and couldn't defend in the dark. It was a dull sound, spaced at intervals, and after a while it dragged her back down into sleep.

If she dreamed, it was of sunshine cascading off a vine-covered wall and the grapes hanging there plump with dew, but before it was full light she was awakened by a knock at the door that pulled Will up out of his sleep with a grunt of alarm. "Hush," she murmured, reaching out a hand to him, "hush, Will." And then she thought of Edith. "Is that you, Edith?" she called.

A muffled voice. "Yes, Mother. May I come in?"

Edith had taken the smaller upstairs room, just behind theirs, and Ida had been installed in one of the anchorites' cells below. Jimmie and Adolph, thankfully, had their own bunks in a long squat one-room outbuilding where the hired shearers stayed when they came out twice a year to collect the wool for shipment back to the mainland.

Will was already sitting up in bed, heavy-chested and pale in a nightshirt that could have been cleaner, his feet placed firmly on the floor and one hand scratching vigorously at the thinning hair of his scalp. "Just a minute," she said. "I'll come to you." And then, though she still felt weak from yesterday, felt as if all the blood had been drained from her, she got up, wrapped a robe round her and went across the bare floorboards to the strange door that opened on a house she barely knew.

Edith was just outside the door, already dressed, though the first thing she noticed was that she'd been slipshod with her corsets, always slipshod, as if proper attire didn't matter. It looked as if her dress were sagging off her in the rear, which was inexcusable. She might not have been conscious of it, though she'd been told a thousand times, but it made her look no better than a charwoman or one of these immigrant wives with their greasy hair and the faint line of a mustache darkening their upper lips. She was irritated, and before she could catch herself, she began to cough, not in a spasm, it wasn't as bad as that, but her throat closed up on her again and Will, pulling on his trousers, roared, "Get her a glass of water—can't you see she's having a spasm!"

"No," she heard herself say, her eyes tearing now, "no, I'll be all right," but it was as if some clawed creature had hold of her throat and wouldn't let go. It took a long moment, Edith rushing into the room to snatch up the water glass despite the fact that Will was half-dressed, and then she had it to her lips and she felt the claws ease their grip. She took a deep wheezing breath. And then, standing there in the doorway, feeling light-headed and weak, endured another long spiraling moment before she could ask her daughter what the matter was.

"It's Ariel," Edith said, and suddenly her eyes were brimming.

"Ariel? Who's Ariel?"

Will's voice came down like a hammer, hard and disapproving: "The lamb."

She didn't understand. "Lamb?" she repeated stupidly.

"Mother, he's cold. He's been bleating all night. He's shivering."

She became aware then of the sounds of the morning, of birdcall from beyond the window, of Ida, below, slamming the door of the stove, of a low murmur of voices from the yard—Jimmie and Adolph—and beneath it all, faint as the creak of a door's hinge, the weak trailing bleat of a motherless lamb left out in the cold of the night. Then she was following Edith down the stairs and out the door into the wind that tirelessly skimmed the frigid air off the surface of the ocean and drove it over the island. The lamb was there, tethered in the yard, its eyes dull and unfocused. It had been curled into itself on the ground, but when they came out in the yard it stood shakily and made as if to bleat, yet no sound came out.

Jimmie and Adolph, sipping coffee out of dented tin cups, looked on in-differently.

"Do you see, Mother?"

It was Edith's idea to carry the animal into the house and set it down beside the stove, where it could be warmed, though that didn't seem sensible, not at all. You didn't bring barnyard animals into the house, not unless you were an animal yourself. The creature was going to die, she could see that in an instant, anyone could, but the look on Edith's face, the way she took charge and insisted, melted her. "All right," she said, following her daughter through the front door and into the parlor cum dining room of the house that was like a barn itself, "but you'll have to tether it to the stove, because I will not have that thing running through the rooms and, and, *relieving* itself, do you understand?"

Edith was already bending to the stove, the animal held fast in her arms, and she was rocking it like a baby, like her own child. "Yes, Mother," Edith said mechanically, not bothering to glance up at her.

"And any mess it makes"—she held it a beat—"you are responsible for. Solely responsible. Do you hear me?"

The Wind

Why she was always expecting the worst, she couldn't say, except that her illness had colored her view of the world, dragged her down, made her see for the first time in her life what lay beneath the surface of things. People made plans, invested their money, educated themselves, raised children—and for what? For the promise of an afterlife? For the glory of God? To forge another link in the chain of being? She didn't want to be a cynic, not with Edith to worry over, not with Will and the household and all the rest of the responsibilities that bore down on her day and night. She truly wanted to believe that her life had purpose, that they would make money out of this venture instead of losing the last capital she had, wanted to believe that living out here on this island would repair the damage to her lungs and that Edith's pet would recover and grow stronger by the day—and she would have prayed for it if she hadn't lost the habit.

The day flew at her, full of complications. Every time she came into the parlor, there was the lamb, tethered to the stove, and Edith nursing it. It smelled of urine and the pellets it scattered across the horse blanket Edith had spread beneath it. Frail, withered, its skin sack-like and loose, it stood shakily and then fell back into the bundle of its limbs. Still, by dinnertime that night she had to admit that the animal seemed to have taken a turn for the better, gazing up alertly out of its resinous eyes as Edith patiently fed it, one sopping finger at a time. "Do you see, Mother?" she said, running a hand down the length of it while it strained forward, pressing itself to her.

"It's certainly an improvement," she said, "don't you think so, Will?"

Will had just come in from the yard, where he was building a toolshed with the help of Adolph, a kind of make-work in advance of plowing and sowing the fields and widening the road when the seed and sticks of dynamite arrived on Charlie Curner's boat, promised for the second week of the

37

month. His face was sunburned. There was dirt under his nails. "Yes," he said absently, but then he glanced down at Edith and the lamb and his eyes came into focus. "Damned foolishness, if you ask me."

Edith's shoulders tensed. The lamb let out a soft bleat, as if in protest.

Marantha didn't tolerate profane language in the house, because it was cheap and it lowered them all, not just the profaner but the household itself, and Will knew it. She drilled him with a look. "That was a harsh thing to say, Will. If you'd like to know, Edith sat up with that animal half the night and she's been entirely diligent about feeding it and cleaning up after it too. Give credit where credit is due."

He didn't bother to respond. He just stalked through the room and down the hall to the kitchen, where the washbasin was. She could hear him saying something to Ida and then Ida's voice, fluttering back at him.

Edith glanced down the hall, tucked her skirts under her and sat lightly on the floor beside the lamb, pulling it to her. She stroked its ears, whispering to it, her chin trembling with her emotion. "I don't understand why anything I do, no matter what, is always wrong," she said finally. "Am I wrong? Am I always wrong?"

What she wanted to say was something along the lines of *Mind your skirts, now,* or *You'll get filthy down there,* but instead she just shook her head and said, "No, not at all."

The following morning the house awoke to sunshine. It was warm enough for the lamb to go out into the yard and Edith went with it, though as the day wore on Edith was in and out of the house a dozen times, helping Ida roll out the one decent carpet they'd managed to bring with them, hanging pictures and rearranging the furniture in an effort to make the room more homely. Twice, driven to distraction by the animal's incessant bleating, Marantha had to remind her to go out and feed it, and by late afternoon Edith, her feet up on a stool and a novel propped open in her lap, seemed to have forgotten about it entirely. Night fell. They were in the kitchen, helping Ida prepare the meal. Ida was talking about the mainland, about what people would be doing back there right at that moment and how strange it was to think of it. "They'd be going out," Edith said. "To the concert hall. To hear music. To see a play."

"And to the restaurant after," she put in. She could picture it, the tablecloths, linen napkins, fruit piled high on the sideboard, cheeses, a steak buried in onions and mushrooms and the waiter there at your elbow. A glass of sherry. The murmur of voices. *May I bring you anything else, madame?*

Ida paused a moment—she was dredging chicken parts in flour while the oil snapped in the pan before her—and gazed over her shoulder at the darkened window as if she could see all the way across the channel to the coast beyond. "Or the sweetshop," she said. "Wouldn't that be the thing?"

And then the meal was served, chicken fricassee, fried potatoes, beans in tomato sauce and cornbread. Will said grace and the platter of cornbread was making its way round the table when the background palaver of the wind fell away for an instant and a thin plaintive cry inserted itself into the silence. At first she didn't know what to make of it—was it a bird brought down in the wind? The mice? A fox? Or was it the dog, whining at the door of the bunkhouse? Will didn't seem to have heard. He was going on about the schedule for the coming weeks, how once they'd plowed the fields and got the seed in they would turn their efforts to converting the path into a legitimate road so as to facilitate bringing supplies up from the harbor, the same theme he'd been stuck on through the course of every meal thus far. She was about to ask if anyone had heard anything, when Jimmie spoke up.

"That'll be your lamb," he said, flicking his eyes round the table.

Will looked up in irritation. "That is," he went on, and he was addressing Adolph now, Adolph alone, "if Curner ever gets back here with the things we need. And that's another thing—he might be a good man at sea, Curner, but he can't begin to make the grade when it comes to giving attention to what people order in plain English or even reading a simple itemized list, if you want to know the truth."

The lamb. It was out there in the dark and if Edith had forgotten about it so had she. She pictured it huddled against the fence under the vault of bleak glittering stars, the wind probing, hunger settling in like a disease.

"The thing of it is"—Jimmie snatched a quick glance at Edith—"a newborn lamb has no more protection against the cold than a naked baby."

Edith set down her fork and looked wildly round her. "We can't leave him out there—he'll die, he will."

No one said a word. The windows were black, the stove hissed and creaked with the fire in its belly, Ida glided in from the kitchen with the coffee pot in one hand and a second platter of bread in the other. "Mother?" Edith was appealing to her, her eyes stricken and her inflection rising. Their first crisis, she was thinking, the first sour note to spoil Will's idyll. And Edith would have her way. Edith always had her way.

But not yet. Let her learn to wait. Let her learn that her mother wouldn't always give in, or at least not without a struggle. She took a sip of water—mineral-heavy and sulfurous—patted her lips with her napkin, took up her fork. Though the chicken was excellent, really first-rate, she found she didn't have much appetite. She'd meant to force herself to eat—the sight of herself in the mirror had frightened her more than anything any doctor could have told her—but tonight she just didn't feel equal to it.

"Mother?" Edith repeated.

She didn't want to play peacemaker, didn't want to quarrel, but she could see Will was spoiling for a fight and she had no choice. "Couldn't we put it in the barn—to get it out of the wind?" she offered. "And—oh, I don't know, find it some old blankets or straw or something? How difficult would that be?" She looked past Will to where Jimmie sat beside Adolph at the end of the table, forking up beans as if he hadn't eaten in a week.

The boy just shook his head. He was the authority here—he knew the flock like no one else. "No, ma'am," he said, his eyes on his plate, "there's no amount of blankets that'll keep that animal alive through a night like this." He gave her a tentative smile, clearly pleased with the attention. "You hear that wind?" he said. And she did, they all did, the noise of it overwhelming the ticking of the stove, their collective breathing, the rattle of utensils against porcelain. "There's a gale coming," Jimmie said, dropping his eyes to the plate again and shoveling up a quick mouthful of beans. "And this," he said, chewing, "is just the announcement of it."

That was enough for Edith. Without asking permission to get up from the table, she rose from her chair, darted across the room, out the door and into the night. A moment later the door was flung back again, the salt tang of the ocean rushing in on the wind, and here was Edith, her mouth set, leading the lamb into the room. Will let out a low curse, a crude epithet he must have picked up in the Army, and this wasn't the first time Marantha had heard it, but it humiliated her now, here in company, angered her, and she called out his name sharply, even as Edith knotted the animal's tether round the legs of the stove and slid back into her seat at the table without a word. The hired men never lifted their heads. Will fumed, but held his tongue. And the lamb, as if wiser than she would have credited, didn't make a peep. Or bleat, that is.

There was a long moment of silence, in which the wind once again became the dominant feature, and then she looked to Edith and said one thing only: "Do you mean to tell me, young lady, that you're not even going to wash your hands?"

The wind kept up all night, just as the boy had said it would. It was furious, unrelenting. She'd never experienced anything like it, not even the hurricane that had come raging up the eastern seaboard to uproot the big weeping willow in the front yard of the house she'd grown up in. Every time she thought the wind was dying, it seemed to come back all the more furiously, rattling the windowpanes and rushing under the eaves in a sudden violent blast. Will had warned her about the weather here—San Miguel was the northernmost link in the chain that made up the Channel Islands, the first landfall for the storms sweeping down the coast—but the warning had been buried so deeply beneath layers of praise for the pastures and the views and the romance of the place (and the air, never forget the air) she'd barely heeded it.

Until now. Now, as she lay there in the dark, the thing in her chest quiet for once, she was afraid. The wind kept beating, keening, unholy, implacable, and it was as if it were aimed at her and her alone. As if it had come for her. Come to blow her away across the waters and force her down beneath the waves, down and down and down to the other place, darkness eternal. The roof heaved, the house rocked and groaned beneath the joists. Everything seemed to compress, as if waiting to blow like the cork from a bottle. She wanted to waken Will, wanted to cling to him and feed off the low consoling murmur of his voice, but she didn't because she knew he needed his rest— now more than ever—and there was nothing he could have done in any case, nothing anyone could do except God, and God had deserted her. Will was right there beside her, but she'd never felt more alone. She couldn't sleep. She'd never sleep again. And though she needed to get up and relieve herself she was afraid to move, as if even the slightest perturbation would upset the balance and bring the whole ramshackle structure crashing down around her.

Finally, the pressure on her bladder became too much to bear and she pushed back the blankets and got out of bed, the floorboards cold beneath her feet and the air a shock. The darkness was absolute and she had to feel her way, expecting at any moment to trip over the chair or the steamer trunk or pitch headlong into a yawning black pit. She wasn't one to complain—all she wanted was what was best for Will and Edith—but wasn't it supposed to be warm here, wasn't that how it had been advertised? Or *warmer,* at any rate? That was what she was thinking, muttering to herself, and then her outstretched fingers came in contact with the wall and the wall led to the corner, but she couldn't find the pot because it was the wrong corner, and by the time she got done fumbling blindly around and understood her mistake the pain in her abdomen was so insistent she was afraid she was going to wet herself, wet right through her nightgown like an incontinent child, and how would she explain the stains on the floor or the reek of the soiled garment? Frantic now, she moved to her right, and here was the door and its cold iron handle and beside it a new wall altogether. She worked her way along this wall, step by step, her feet frozen, the wind screaming and screaming again, and then her shin struck something solid and the pot clattered in protest.

She tried to be quick about it, lifting the lid and positioning herself as best she could in the darkness, but then, perversely, her flow wouldn't come. She was thinking of the W.C. and how astonished she'd been to learn that it was a full three miles and more from the house (to keep the sewage downhill from the spring, Will had claimed, though he'd clearly been ashamed of himself for having overlooked the matter now that there were women in the house, and he'd promised to move it closer, much closer, as soon as he was able) and how utterly barbaric that was, when finally it came in a sudden hot rush and she cleaned herself quickly and climbed back into bed.

In the morning, it was still blowing. Outside—and she wouldn't realize this till later—the sand was mounding its drifts against anything that stood erect in the yard, the walls of the house and outbuildings, the fences, even the flagpole, so that the men would have to spend the whole morning shoveling it away. Will was asleep still, breathing deeply. There was no other sound but for the wind. After a while she eased herself out of bed, put on her slippers and wrapper and went downstairs to make herself a cup of tea to soothe her nerves. She wasn't thinking of Ida sleeping behind the flimsy door of the windowless room at the bottom of the stairs or of the kitchen stove that had gone cold in the night or the wood to stoke it—and she wasn't thinking of the other stove, the one in the main room behind her or of the lamb tethered to its legs. No, she was thinking of the wind and how it was a wonder it hadn't shattered the panes of the windows and crushed the walls like paper, thinking how cold the house was, how alien, and wondering for the hundredth time in the past three days just what she'd gotten herself into.

It wasn't till she'd lit the kitchen stove, filled the kettle with water and set it there on the stovetop to boil that she turned and came up the hall to the main room with the notion of stoking the fire there too. Only then did she think of the lamb. And she thought of it only because it was lying there stiff on the floor, the cord twisted round its throat where it had fought against it in the dark—twisted, and twisted again.

Jimmie

By the end of the first week she'd begun to feel stronger, so that she was able, at least for a few hours each day, to oversee the household and even take on some of the cooking herself—by way of a change and to free Ida for other tasks, not the least of which was to scour some of the sheepmen's dirt out of the place. The floors were the most objectionable, pocked as they were with the impress of a generation of shearers' boot heels and stained with grease and lanolin and worse. It went without saying that the kitchen was filthy, but she put Ida and Edith to work on it and before long it was almost tolerable, though it would never be what anyone, even a blind man, would call clean, not unless the walls and floor and fly-spotted rafters were torn out and set afire and the carpenters came in and started all over again. For the most part, she left dinner to Ida—she was to avoid all exertion if she had any hope of recovery, or so the doctors claimed, and by evening she was always at her lowest ebb—but when Jimmie and Adolph came up to the house one morning with a dozen lobsters from the pots they'd put out, she took it on herself, as a daughter of New England, to show them how they should be prepared.

Will had finished the shed and repaired some of the fences, and now he had the men working on the preliminaries of converting the path down to the harbor into a serviceable road. The day was overcast and cold, though the air, for once, was still. After examining each of the lobsters carefully to be sure they were sound, she went out the front door and across the yard to where the men were working. Will was in his shirtsleeves, slinging a pick. Adolph was filling the wheelbarrow with dirt and Jimmie was standing there with his hands in his pockets, waiting to dump it over the side and down into the canyon. "Jimmie," she called, "would you come here a minute? I have something I'd like for you to do."

She watched him exchange a look with her husband.

"I'll just need him for a bit," she said, though it wasn't the truth.

Will set down the pick and took a minute to wipe his face with his handkerchief. She could see that he wasn't happy about it, but he nodded to Jimmie and Jimmie crossed the yard to her.

"I want you to go down to the shore and bring me back some seaweed."

He tugged at his cap, brushed the hair out of his eyes and shot a single look over his shoulder in Will's direction, but Will had already turned back to his work. "Seaweed?" he echoed.

"You'll need the mule."

It took him the better part of an hour and when he returned he had enough kelp with him to bury the sled twice over. She was at the window with her sewing when he came up the road and she saw that Will and Adolph said something to him as he led the mule on past them, and then she was out in the yard and waving him around back of the house where she'd selected the spot for the pit in a stretch of sandy soil. "I want you to dig here," she said.

"Dig, ma'am?"

"A firepit," she said, and he gave her a blank look. "For the lobsters?"

He repeated her words, very slowly, and she could see that he thought she'd gone mad—or no, he was just confirming the conclusion he'd reached on that first day when he'd hauled her up the hill behind the mule.

She couldn't help but smile. "Don't you worry," she said, "I know what I'm doing. Now, I'm going to want it roughly here"—she bent to project an imaginary line with the tip of her forefinger—"and it should be, oh, maybe three feet deep and at least that many long. Once it's done, I'm going to want you to fill it with wood and build the biggest fire you can, understood?"

He simply nodded and slouched off to get the shovel, and if Will was going to complain—and she knew he would, taking the boy off the job like that—well, she had no doubt the result would be worth it.

She had Ida serve the lobsters with the last of the butter they'd brought over from the mainland and there were roasted potatoes to go with them. Edith lit a candle. Ida brought out a pot of beans and a plate of fried dough. Will said grace, a few murmured words, and then the two knives went round as everyone pried at the shells of the lobsters to get at the sweet white meat that had cost them nothing but effort, meat as free as the air and the salt seawater that surrounded them. "Good, isn't it?" she said, trying a bite of it herself, though these weren't the lobsters she knew because they lacked claws and the claws held some of the most succulent morsels, but then none of them would have known that but Will, and Will just said, "Yes, delicious."

There was a silence, the only sounds the cracking of the shells and the play of their utensils. Edith was struggling to crack hers with a fork only, as Adolph had one of the knives and Will the other, and she wasn't speaking to either of them because of the way they'd reacted to the death of her lamb. Will had been especially harsh. "You see what comes of your willfulness," he said, as if Edith hadn't been distraught already, blaming herself over and over. He'd looked down at it, at the staring eyes and the ragged red line at its throat where the cord had dug in, its legs splayed and tongue like some black wedge of meat it had tried to swallow. "Take that thing out in the yard where it belongs," he said, or no, he was practically snarling, and then he turned his back on her and stamped down the hall to the kitchen. And Adolph, as if it were any of his business, had not only criticized her at breakfast that morning so that she left the table in tears, he'd insisted on dressing the carcass for its meat and then tacking the hide out on the wall of the shed to dry in the wind. "And why?" Marantha had demanded. "Why would you want to do that?" He'd looked up at her insolently, chewing around the heel of bread he'd just shoved into his mouth, a hired hand who should have been taking his meals out of doors—and would have, but for Will's democratic feelings. "For gloves," he said. "Kid gloves. The softest thing in this world." He'd hesitated, looking her dead in the eye across the expanse of the table. "But for one other thing I can think of."

Will had been in the kitchen, out of earshot, and lucky for Adolph, but she hadn't forgotten the incident—and neither had Edith. And since that morning, at her pointed request, the hands had been taking breakfast and luncheon in the kitchen or out in the bunkhouse, but Will—she'd never told him what the man had said, not in so many words, for fear of Will's temper and what he might have done—still insisted on all of them taking dinner together.

And so here they were, cracking lobster and passing round the plate of potatoes like one big family, and when Ida came into the room with her own plate and took a seat beside Jimmie, it was Marantha who broke the silence. "Ida," she said, and this had been prearranged between them, "aren't you forgetting something?"

"Lord yes, ma'am," Ida said, tapping her forehead in pantomime and jumping up as if the chair were a bed of hot coals. "How ever could I have forgotten?" They all watched her cross the room and head down the hall for the kitchen.

"What's all this?" Will asked, looking up at her.

"Oh, nothing much," Marantha said, trying to keep her expression even. "Just a treat, a little something extra—for Jimmie." The boy's eyes jumped to hers. "Because he was the one who did all the work and it's only right—"

And here was Ida, hoisting the big platter over one shoulder like a waiter in the finest restaurant, only to set it down before Jimmie, still steaming and redolent of the sea.

"Go ahead," Marantha said, and now it all came out, now she was laughing, now she was a girl again, as the boy, with a look of bewilderment, plucked one of the long pale wet strands of kelp up off the platter and held it out before him on the tines of his fork. "Go ahead—it's the best part."

When Charlie Curner did finally arrive from Santa Barbara—two days late—she was the first to spot the sail in the harbor. She'd been sitting at the window in the bedroom, working at her scrapbook, feeling faintly nauseated after the few bites of luncheon she'd forced herself to swallow (the last of Edith's lamb, which Ida had stewed with carrots and potatoes till it had lost its consistency and melted away into the gravy, though Edith still wouldn't touch it, subsisting exclusively these past days on eggs and porridge), and she'd glanced up from the nameless pink flower she was pressing flat between two sheets of paper, and there it was. She had to look twice to be sure her eyes weren't deceiving her, and then she lifted Will's binoculars down from the hook beside the window and focused in on the boat till it came clear and she could see that it was Charlie Curner standing at the helm and not some Chinese abalone fisherman or a poacher come to rob them of the odd sheep when their guard was down.

Her blood was racing. She stood abruptly from the chair, spilling the scrapbook to the floor, and then she was out the door and down the stairs crying out the news. They all dropped what they were doing—Ida emerging from the kitchen with her hands white with flour, Edith closing her novel on one finger and darting out the front door to call to the men, who were already laying down their tools—and it was as if they'd been marooned a year instead of just a week and a half. Edith ran on ahead, the afternoon glowing around her in the sun that climbed up out of the mist like a hot-air balloon, her arms pumping and the heels of her shoes shining with a thin skin of mud. Marantha was hurrying too, thinking of the letters everyone had promised—her mother back home in Boston, Carrie and the others in San Francisco—and of her plates and cutlery and whatever else Charlie Curner had managed to bring to brighten the dull round of their days. Not two weeks yet and it seemed as if there were nothing else, no other world, no place but this. Even then, even in her excitement, she knew she would never last here, no matter what she'd promised or how hard she tried.

She ran out of breath before she was halfway down, and so she stopped herself and found a rock to sit on while below her, in the bay that stretched away to the flat gray nullity of the ocean, Charlie Curner pulled at the oars of his skiff and Edith stood at the scalloped edge of the breakers, waving her handkerchief high over her head. She watched the rest of them emerge from the canyon in miniature, their heads bobbing and shoulders weaving, Will and Adolph bringing up the rear while Ida and Jimmie sprinted past them to splash into the surf with Edith and haul the bow of the skiff up out of the surge as if it weighed nothing at all. It was a moment of high excitement: What had he brought them? What news? Had he remembered the flour, the sugar, the pickles she'd asked for specifically on Edith's account? The calico? The gingham?

She watched them unload the packages, wishing she'd thought to bring the binoculars with her—though she squinted her eyes, she really couldn't make out much detail at this distance. Was that the crate she'd packed her dishes in? She couldn't be sure. All she wanted—she'd give anything—was to be down there with them, to race Edith all the way, but her legs wouldn't carry her and her breath wouldn't come. She'd been a strong runner once, the fleetest girl in her school, but that was a long time ago. Before James, before Will. Before the first annunciatory cough.

Below her, she saw them gathered now around the gesticulating figure of Charlie Curner, the news of the world come to them in a pantomime she couldn't decipher and words she couldn't hear. She hoped he'd remembered to bring the newspapers. And magazines. She'd expressly told him . . . but then she caught herself. If he brought her china, that would be enough. And the letters. The letters above all else. She told herself not to expect too much, because Charlie Curner wasn't their personal agent but only another hired hand, after all, and the process of getting and ordering—of itemizing, of *caring*—was far from perfect. After a while, long before Jimmie came dashing up the trail for the mule and sled and the others began carrying the crates and sacks and brown-paper parcels up from the beach, she turned and started back up the hill, head down, moving deliberately, counting each of her breaths as if they were the only form of news that mattered.

She was up all that night, feeling feverish but refusing to admit it, her cough shallow but steady, the pain beneath her breastbone a dull intermittent thing she drove down with the patent medicine that was forty percent alcohol and no fooling herself about that and cup after cup of hot tea leavened with milk. The parlor was hers alone, no sound but for the ticking of the cast-iron stove and the patter of the mice on their nightly foray into the cupboard—and how she wished she had Sampan with her now, not only to put the fear of retribution in them but to feel him warm in her lap and listen to the soft grateful catch and release of his purring as she stroked his ears and the downy chocolate fur of his face and tail and delicate curled-up paws. She'd read through all her letters twice—two from her mother, whose news of home seemed almost exclusively of weather reports and funerals (*How I envy you, dear, out there in sunny California, because it's been the bitterest winter here anybody can remember since your grandmother's time*), one from her cousin Martha in Brookline and one each from Carrie Abbott and Susannah Kent in San Francisco—and now she was busy answering them. Charlie Curner—and she didn't at all like the kind of looks he'd kept giving Edith at dinner, a married man of forty, forty at least—was asleep in his berth on the schooner he'd named for his wife and would be setting sail after breakfast, and so she had no choice but to get the letters finished and addressed before he left. Either that or wait God knew how long.

She was still in the wooden chair by the stove when the sky began to lighten outside the window. She'd written twenty-two pages to her mother and every one of them, every line, was as sunny as her mother supposed the weather to be. Her health was fine, the air bracing, Will working like ten men to improve on their investment and Edith growing into a fine young lady who could not only play the piano and sing and dance like an angel, but also ride as well as any woman in the country—and here was her joke—Annie

Oakley excepted. With Carrie she was more forthcoming, if not entirely honest, and if she complained of the weather and the difficulty of setting up a household in such a wild place, she put a brave face on it too, as if everything— the dirt, the cold, the bare planks of the floor and the crippling pain in her chest—were as easy to put right as snapping your fingers. When she heard Ida stirring, she sealed the letters, left them on the table where they'd be sure to be noticed and tiptoed up the stairs to slip into bed beside Will.

She awoke to an empty bed and a sudden brutal squalling that cut through her like a jolt of electricity. One moment she'd been floating in her dream (the grapes again, the wall of the villa, the sun), and in the next she was lurching awake to this shriek, these shrieks, one mounting atop the next, as if a whole tribe of the Indians that had once lived here were having their throats cut, one by one. For a minute she didn't know where she was, the bed curtains like the walls of a tomb, the light crepuscular, the air damp, refrigerated, foul with her own breath, and then she was coughing and at the same time trying to fight the thing inside her and flinging back the curtains on the world she lived in now, the world circumscribed by the bare walls, the washstand, the chipped ceramic pot and the water-stained armoire. And all the while the shrieking went on, spiraling up and up until it broke in a squeal of pure immitigable outrage.

Coughing, clutching her nightdress at her throat, she went to the window and there he was, Jimmie, in the yard below, in the pen where the pigs were kept. He was doing something to them, torturing them—torturing *her*—and before she could think she thrust open the window and shouted out his name. He looked up in bewilderment. It was two o'clock in the afternoon. The schooner had left the harbor. There was the banging of Will's pick from somewhere down the path that would become a road. And the wind, the wind of course. "What are you doing?" she demanded, but her voice had lost its timbre and it wasn't a human voice at all but the squawk of some reiterant bird.

"Ma'am?"

"That noise. You get away from those animals. Shame on you."

He was a hundred feet away. The pigs—they were six, the boar, two sows and three shoats left from the last litter—had backed away from him, pressed in a moil against the fence. "The Captain's orders, ma'am. He says they got to have rings struck through their noses to stop them digging."

50

She was outraged, weak, pale, stripped down to nothing, coughing and coughing again. A shade drew across her eyes. It was the contagion and it took hold of her tongue and lodged a wad of phlegm in her throat so that she thought she was going to gag. The boy didn't know. He didn't care. She watched him turn back to his work. Finally it came up, a hard ball of sputum that was like the gristle cut from a piece of meat, and she clenched it there in her handkerchief until her voice returned to her. "I don't care what Captain Waters says, you stop that now, do you hear me?" Whether he heard or not, she couldn't say, but the next pig was already screaming.

She slammed the window shut and went to the door, calling down the stairwell to Edith, Edith who would go out there and give that boy a piece of her mind and get him to stop this, this insolence, this cruelty, but her voice failed her again. "Edith," she called, croaking now, croaking because the disease was consuming her from the inside out, strangling her, taking her voice away, syllable by syllable, "Edith!"

A moment. Then Edith was there at the bottom of the stairs, her face pale and insubstantial in the shadows that infested the place. "Yes, Mother?"

She couldn't catch her breath.

"Are you—? Can I get you anything?"

"Tell that boy"—and now the shrieking rose again, uncontainable—"to stop that this instant . . . I'm not—I need rest. Today. Just today. Tell him—"

She watched Edith turn abruptly, heard her footsteps on the scuffed wooden planks of the lower hallway and then the parlor, heard the door creak open and slam shut again. Then she moved to the window and threw up the sash and Edith appeared in the yard below.

"Mother says to stop that. You, Jimmie. Mother says—"

The boy had dropped his tool—and what was it, some sort of clamp to drive the hard metal ring through the animal's flesh?—and he was staring at her out of his black expressionless eyes. "The Captain said to."

Edith crossed the yard to him. Even from here Marantha could see that her corsets were unfastened again. She was wearing an apron over her skirts. Her hair flowed down her back in a tangle because she hadn't bothered to put it up. She was hatless. "I don't care what he said, Mother's not feeling well and you're to stop that now."

"You can't boss me."

"I can. And I will." Edith put her hands on her hips, cocked herself on one leg as if she were posing for a movement in one of her dances. Then she slowly unfolded one hand and gestured to him with her index finger. "Come here," she said.

The boy looked around him to see if anyone was watching, then he swung the gate aside, pulled it shut behind him and came to where she stood in the yard. "What do you want with me?" he asked, looking her in the face for the first time.

Her voice was soft, so soft Marantha could barely hear it. "Anything I feel like," she said.

He took a step back, dropped his eyes. "You can't boss me," he repeated. "You're only fourteen."

"Fifteen. In a week and a half. Which is older than you."

"I'm nineteen."

"Liar."

There was a silence. Marantha could hear the pick ringing still in the distance, tempered steel essaying rock. "Eighteen, anyway."

"Liar. When's your birthday?"

"Don't know."

"How can you not know your own birthday? Are you that stupid?"

"I'm not stupid. I'm as smart as anybody. Smart as you."

"Then how is it you don't even know when you were born?"

"Because my mother's dead. And she never—" He was working the toe of his boot in the dirt, his characteristic gesture. "I mean, I never . . . I'm eighteen years old."

"Liar."

The pigs were watchful. The sun was wrapped in gauze. The pick rang. And then Edith pulled the boy to her, their heads so close they might have been kissing, and Marantha felt a shock go through her. "Edith!" she called, though she didn't hear what Edith said next, but she heard Jimmie, his voice pitched low yet clearly audible as he recoiled from Edith's grip and took an awkward step back. "All right," he said, "I'm fifteen. But that's still older than you."

The Rain

It came in the night without preliminary, a sudden crashing fall against the shingles of the roof that woke her, gasping, from a dreamless sleep. At first she thought it was the wind, another sandstorm churning across the island to bury them like Ozymandias, but then she heard the gutters rattle and the swift plunge of the cisterns and knew that the real rain, the rain they'd been waiting for, had arrived. All she could think was that Will would be pleased— and she should have been pleased too, rain like money in the bank, but she hated the dampness it brought because dampness was the ally of the thing inside her. And of the mold. The mold that crept over every stationary object in the house like a biblical plague, the furniture spotted with it, clothes greasy to the touch a day after they'd been washed, the pages of her books marked and sullied, eaten away from the inside out, rotted, decayed. But she had to stop herself. The rain was the important thing and the rain was a blessing. She repeated the thought aloud, as if to convince herself, her voice a dying whisper in the dark, lost in the susurrus of the rain. For a long while she lay there listening to the trill of the gutters, everything adrift, until finally her thoughts floated free and she fell asleep again.

She woke to a persistent drip. It took her a moment, a wand of feeble gray light caught in the crack of the bed curtains, the world coming back to her in all its preordained dimension, before she realized that the blankets were wet—not damp, but wet, soaking. She looked up and saw that the canopy above her was bellied with water, and here came the drip, exploding on the pillow beside her. And then another and another. She called Will's name— twice—but he didn't move, his breathing slow and heavy. Then she was shoving him, heaving against the dead weight of him until he came up sputtering as if the waters had already closed over them.

"What is it? What?"

"The roof's leaking."

"What do you mean?"

She tore back the bed curtains, angry suddenly, furious, and thrust the wet blankets at him. "The bedclothes are wet, that's what I mean—can't you feel it? The whole bed—" That was when the breath went out of her and the first hacking cough of the morning snatched the words from her mouth.

And what did he do? Did he put his arm around her, fetch her a glass of water or the bottle of medicine and her teaspoon? No. Cursing—predictably, as if Jesus Christ had anything to do with it—he heaved himself out of bed and slammed round the room, pulling on his clothes in a frenzy of hate. "Jesus Christ, can't I have a minute's peace? Can't I even get a goddamned night's sleep when I'm so worn I can barely— Edith! Where's Edith?"

"Let her be," she said, fighting down the cough. She was out of bed now, crossing the room in her nightgown to the stand that held the water pitcher and her medicine, and the roof was leaking here too, a steady drool of dun-colored water trickling down to splash the floor at her feet. The medicine was useless, she knew that, but it deadened the sting of her throat and fought down the pain in her chest, at least temporarily. She measured out a teaspoon and took it, wincing at the taste—bitter herbs in a tincture of alcohol that turned the inside of her mouth black—and then she took a teaspoon of cod-liver oil and washed it down with a glass of water, and all the while her feet were getting wet.

Ignoring her, Will tore open the door on the corridor and shouted for Edith. He was in shirtsleeves, his braces dangling, his pale calloused heels naked to the thin seep of light coming in through the window. "Goddamn it, where is she? Edith!" In the next moment he snatched the chamber pot out of the corner, threw up the sash and flung the contents out into the yard, not even bothering to rinse the thing out before heaving himself across the room to position it under the leak. Where it immediately began to splash over. On the floor. Filthy. Everything filthy. And then Edith was at the door, barefoot, in her nightgown, rubbing at her eyes.

"Don't just stand there," he snapped. "Can't you see what's happening here? Help me move this bed—your mother's wet, the bed's wet. Here, take this corner—no, no, here, this way, *push*."

She wanted to say something—Edith wasn't decent, he was too harsh with her, too bullying, there was filth on the floor—but she didn't. Instead she pulled her wrap tight around her, eased on her slippers and went out into the hall and down the stairs to the kitchen, where she knew it would be warm at least and the coffee she could already smell was brewing in the pot.

It rained without relent throughout the morning and into the afternoon and showed no sign of slacking. The windows steamed over. Water came in under the front door, a great lapping tongue of it, so that she had to lay a towel there—and then get up and wring it out every twenty minutes. Anything that could hold liquid—pots, pitchers, dirt-rimmed buckets dragged in from the barn, the dishpan—lay scattered across the floors, upstairs and down, ringing maddeningly with a persistent tympanic drip. And of course they had to be emptied too. It was a new job, a full-time occupation, and it took her out of herself: she didn't have pause to feel weak or sick and if she coughed she hardly noticed.

Luncheon was a subdued affair, Edith half-asleep, Will brooding over the leaky roof and the damage to the road—he'd been out there in his mackintosh three times already, plying his shovel uselessly in the muck—and it was a struggle to keep up a conversation. Ida was no help. She was having her own trial in the kitchen, where the jointure of the slant roof and the back wall of the main house gave up a flood like Niagara, the floorboards soaked through, mud everywhere, and so she took her meal at the kitchen table with the hands. There was a stew of mutton—the eternal dish—three-days-old bread, the last of the wheel of cheese Charlie Curner had brought them. Marantha talked just to hear herself, but nobody was listening.

Afterward she tried to interest Edith in sewing or a game of cards or reading aloud from Dickens or Eliot, but Edith just gave her a look and went upstairs to shut herself in her room. And Will—Will was up on the roof with a bucket of tar he'd heated over the stove and nothing she could say about the danger could dissuade him. "You'll break a leg," she shouted at him as he went out the door. "Or your neck. Then where will we be?" She kept glancing out the window, expecting to see him splayed in the mud under the eaves, thinking of the time he'd broken his foot stepping off the curb in front of the apartment and how savage he was with her through every waking hour of his convalescence, as if she'd somehow been to blame. He was impossible. Demanding. Insulting. She'd very nearly left him then. She'd actually gone

55

down to the station, Edith in tow, and inquired about the price of two tickets to Boston before she came to her senses.

She sat and rose again, sat and rose. The pans filled, she emptied them. At one point, she settled in by the stove with a book but she couldn't concentrate. The rain hissed at her, mocked her, erected a solid gray wall beyond the windows, one more barrier between her and where she longed to be.

It was past four when Will finally gave it up. There were two abrupt thumps from the direction of the front porch—one for each boot—and then he came through the door in his stocking feet, the wet mackintosh hanging from him like sloughed skin. His head was bowed, his shoulders slumped in exhaustion. He looked defeated, looked old—older than her father was when he died. The thought complicated the moment—her father had been nearly seventy, sick for years with a malady no one was able to diagnose, all his vitality reduced to the effort of staying alive—and she had to fight it down before rising from the chair and hurrying across the room to him. "Here," she said, taking hold of his wet sleeve, "let me help you off with that."

He didn't offer any resistance. He merely stood there, dripping, so depleted he could barely raise his arms. He smelled of the outdoors, of the workings of his body, wet hair, sweat gone stale—and of tar, the odor faintly sweet and strong as any perfume. His hands were blackened with it, as if he'd pulled on a pair of mourner's gloves on his way to a funeral. "I did the best I could," he said.

"Don't worry about that now, we'll manage." She folded the mackintosh over one arm and led him to the chair by the stove, where he sat heavily, and then she was fussing over him. "I'll get you some dry clothes—and tea, I'll have Ida brew you some tea. Or would you like something stronger?"

"I'll have a drop of that whiskey—if you'll join me. Will you?"

Her first impulse was to say no, because what had she become but a crabbed miserable thing who said no to everything, to every pleasure and delight no matter how small or meaningless? Whiskey. She hadn't tasted whiskey in so long she couldn't remember what it was like—and then, suddenly, she could. In the old days, the early days of the apartment when Edith was little and the evening sun striped the walls and lingered over her potted geraniums as if each leaf and flower were lit from within, Will would come home from work and she'd fetch the bottle and the siphon and they would sit at the window sipping whiskey sodas and watching the life of the street below. She smiled, laid a hand on his shoulder. "Yes," she murmured, "I'd like that."

For the next hour she sat there with him, just the two of them, and she felt a great peace settle over the house. The rain kept up, but the dripping was intermittent now, the tar having done its job—or mostly so—and she left the door of the stove open so they could watch the play of the flames. Ida was in the kitchen, busy with the meal, Edith shut in her room still, the hands out in the bunkhouse—she could see the soft glow of their lantern in the window there and it was as if they were miles away, as if they were on a ship and the ship was a beacon at sea. When the dark came down, she didn't bother to get up and light the lantern on the table.

"It's pleasant, isn't it?" she said. "To sit here like this. Everything's been such a mad rush."

"I know," he said, "I know. But things are settling down now. I feel like we're actually making some progress—on the road especially. Or at least we were until this damned rain came along."

The whiskey eased the rawness of her throat. She'd expected it to be harsh, but it was just the opposite—it was silken and cool and had the placatory effect of her medicine, only it tasted so much better. And it wouldn't turn her tongue black. At least she hoped not. "Damned?" She tossed the epithet back at him, but lightly, because she was feeling good and she didn't want to nag at him, but really, how could something soulless, an element at that, be damned?

"I'm not saying we shouldn't be thankful for the rain—it's just what we want if we expect the animals to thrive, and it'll replenish the spring and fill the cisterns, and that's all to the good. It's just that I expected something more gradual, a good soft soaking rain—"

"Not a deluge."

"No," he said, shaking his head and reaching for the bottle. She watched him pour himself a measure, then lean forward to pour for her too. "The devil of it is to think of the work we put into that road, and all for nothing—it's washing out right this minute, the banks caving in, rocks strewn everywhere, worse than it was when we started on it. Much worse. I tell you, I'm half-mad just thinking about it." He took a long sip of the whiskey. "At least Curner brought the dynamite. At least there's that."

"But not the dishes."

"It's just like the war," he said, waving a hand in disgust. "The Engineering Corps was bloated with men like Curner, half-wits and incompetents who couldn't follow a requisition form if their lives depended on it—matériel would be wanted for an assault and it was sitting useless on one loading platform or another somewhere up the line and no one could say where or why. And none to take responsibility, you could wager on that. It was always the fault of Sergeant Such-and-Such or maybe his brother. Or some officer sitting behind a desk somewhere. But don't worry—we'll spell it out for him, make a list, item by item. And what do you think we'll put right at the top?" He gave her a grin. "Minnie's dishes."

"And cutlery. And my linens—where are my linens, I'd like to know?"

"Yes," he said, tilting his head back to drain the glass, "all that." In the light of the fire he looked solid, looked young again. Or younger than he had when he came through the door. "But the dynamite's the thing. Because without it we're never going to be able to make a road of that footpath before the shearers come, there's just too much rock. And Mills lectured me on the subject, you know that—those wool sacks can weigh three hundred pounds apiece and they're apt to catch on any of the turnings and take the whole lot over the side of the ravine, mule, sled, driver and all. I wouldn't want an accident," he said, shifting in the chair so that his wet socks left two broad dark stripes on the floorboards. "Especially not out here, with the nearest doctor eight hours away."

The nearest doctor. She meditated on that a moment, seeing herself prostrate in the saloon of Charlie Curner's schooner, all sensation gone from her fingers and toes, the blood trailing away from the corner of her mouth and the black waves beating like fists at the hull. Did Will even know what he was saying?

There was a smell of cooking from the kitchen. Everything was still. She could feel the liquor inside her, a new kind of medicine, medicine that lifted you up instead of driving you down. "I don't like that man," she said.

"Who? Mills?"

"No," she said, and the mood was soured now, "*Curner.* Did you see the way he looked at Edith? He was leering, Will, that's what he was doing: leering. A man his age. It was obscene. I don't want him in this house, ever again, and I don't care what he does with my plates."

He said her name, whispered it, pleadingly: "Marantha."

"And Jimmie," she went on because she couldn't stop herself, all the worries she'd bottled up spewing out of her now, "he's no companion for Edith. Have you seen them together? Have you seen the way they, the way he—?" It was all too much, too mean and petty and low. "She doesn't belong here, Will, that's the truth of it. And neither do I."

A long moment passed between them. The bucket in the far corner began to drip again, the gutters rattled, the rain tore at the roof like a flail. Then he pushed himself up from the chair without a word, took the bottle by the neck and moved heavily up the hall toward the kitchen.

The Road

In the sequel, she stayed on in the dark, bringing the glass to her lips every so often, the rising chemical scent of the liquor in her nostrils, the taste of it on her tongue and in her mouth and the back of her throat. She meant to get up, light the lantern, help Ida set the table for dinner—rouse Edith; where was Edith?—but Will's whiskey, which had pushed her so high, weighed her down. She shouldn't have gone off on him the way she had and she regretted it now, already thinking of ways to make it up to him, to help rather than hinder. He was under a strain too. All the troubles of the place devolved on him, one worry chasing after the next—a week ago he was stalking through the corridors muttering darkly about the disaster they faced if the rains didn't come and now here he was with his hands tar-stained and his back aching and the road washed out. He was fifty years old, soon to be fifty-one. This was no kind of life for him. He was an educated man, skilled in his trade, one of the few men in the country who could reliably run a big printing operation the way he had on his brother's paper in Boston and the *Morning Call* up in San Francisco. He was a gentleman, not a common laborer. If he didn't watch himself he was going to end up sick or injured or just plain out of luck, like the palsied ragtag troop he so proudly marched with on Decoration Day each year, banners waving, bands playing, and every other man with his sleeve hanging loose or his leg gone at the knee. *You survived the war, Will,* she told him, *you don't have to fight another one.*

She emerged from her reverie to the sound of voices leaching out of the steady background thrum of the rain: Will's voice, Ida's, call and response. It was some trick of the atmosphere—or her own ears—because suddenly she could hear them as clearly as if they were right there in the room with her.

"Everything's all over mud," Ida said, complaining, but her tone wasn't the tone of complaint—it was airy and light, as if she were with Edith and the two of them had their heads together, half a breath from dissolving in giggles. "Just look at this floor. How can anybody expect me to cook in conditions like this?"

There was the sound of a chair shifting, the metallic groan of the hinges on the cabinet door, and then Will's voice, companionable, intimate: "Oh, I don't know, you seem to be doing a pretty fair job of it, even if you do have to wear a pair of gum boots under those skirts of yours. But you're always . . . what I mean to say is you, you're a very good"—he faltered, his words dense with whiskey—"really excellent. First-rate. But what's that, what are you adding to that pot?"

"Never you mind. You stay out of that now."

"Ida, Ida, Ida,"—denser yet, drawing out the vowels as if he were singing—"I know this is hard on you, but I swear I'll be back up there on the roof to tar over this gap here as soon as, well, as soon as the rain stops. The very minute."

"Stops? You really think it means to stop?"

"It's got to. Law of averages."

"Well, I don't. Not a bit of it. If anybody ever witnessed an example of God's retribution on the sinners of the world, this is it—muck and rain, rain and muck, that's all there is." There was the sharp unmistakable click of glass on glass, and was he pouring for her, was that it? "And I'm just the sort of sinner to throw myself in the flood and be done with it, truly now, because I don't think I can stand for another thirty-nine days and thirty-nine nights of this, can you?"

"So maybe I ought to see about putting a hull under the house, then—is that what you're saying?"

Ida, laughing: "Yes, that's exactly it. And maybe you'd better start in pairing up the animals."

"Good advice, capital, the best in the world. I'll do that just as soon as I've had my dinner. But beyond that, tell me, what sins could a girl of your age possibly have to atone for?"

A sigh. The rattle of a spoon run round the circumference of a cooking pot. Ida's voice, dropping low: "Oh, you'd be surprised."

And then there was a whole hurricane of noise, the back door flung open on the storm and slammed shut again, the floorboards groaning, feet stamping, and a new voice entering the conversation, Jimmie's, thin and adenoidal: "Jesus, it's cats and dogs out there."

She got up from the chair then and started down the hall. She could see them through the open kitchen door, framed there in the light of the lantern, the three of them, Will propped up on the table with his legs crossed, Ida at the stove, a glass of whiskey in one hand, stirring spoon in the other, and Jimmie, wet to the eyes and dashing the drenched cap against his thigh, moving into the circle of warmth. "What's for dinner?" he asked, and if he glanced up when she entered the room—if any of them did—it was only vaguely, without recognition, as if she'd already ceased to exist.

It was still raining when Will brought out the cards after dinner—they were four at whist, she and Edith partnered against Will and Ida, Jimmie watching their every move from a chair in the corner as if he were going to be examined on it afterward and Adolph gone out to the bunkhouse to do whatever he did there, stare at the ceiling, fling shoes at the mice, stew in his odious thoughts—and when nine o'clock came round and they damped the lanterns and went off to bed, it was coming down every bit as steadily as it had all day. She'd sat through the cards in as good a humor as she could muster, the room warm, Will sluggish though he'd put the bottle away and taken nothing with dinner but coffee and a cigar after, and she wasn't affected one way or the other when she and Edith wound up losing consistently, hand after hand, game after game, or at least that was what she told herself. Will was a master at cards and she wanted to be gracious about that, enjoying the game for what it was—an opportunity to escape the rain and the four walls and the endless yawning boredom of the place.

After saying goodnight to Edith on the landing, she went into her room to light the lamp there and prepare for bed. It was cold—bitter, damp, like plunging into the ocean—and she hurried over her toilette, bending quickly to wash her face in the basin and trying not to think about the apartment on Post Street, with its running water, hot and cold both, and the claw feet of the bathtub propped on the black-and-white tiles of the floor. By the time Will came up the stairs she was already in bed, shivering, listening to the rain on the roof and in the gutters and counting off the intermittent dripping of the three buckets set round the room. Nothing had changed. There was the washstand, there the pot. The only novelty was the angle of view, since the bed had been moved three feet to the left to defeat the most persistent leak, the one that had soaked through the canopy. Everything smelled of mildew.

She heard Will on the landing, in the hallway, each footfall descending like a blow, and then he was at the door, the door pushing partway open and his face hanging there in the gloom of the hallway—he was making an assessment of the prevailing conditions, of the leaks and the half-full buckets and the mood of his wife, and she couldn't blame him for that. "Minnie?" he called softly. "Are you awake still?"

She had a sudden urge to lash out at him—drinking whiskey with the help, with Ida, inflicting Adolph on her, ignoring her all evening except as an opponent to drub at cards while he built up Ida and tore down his own daughter as if to let her win a single game would annihilate him—but she checked herself. She was the one at fault. Everything had been so tranquil in the afternoon, the rain at the window, the fire giving up its heat, the neck of the bottle poised over her glass and then his and the two of them sitting down to a quiet chat for the first time in as long as she could remember, but then she'd had to spoil it. Had to nag at him. Truth told, she'd all but driven him from the room. Driven him to the kitchen. And she was on the verge of taking the thought one step further—*driven him to Ida*—but the thought was inadmissible, a fantasy, a delusion, Will her husband, Ida the servant, a second daughter, family. A child. All but a child. "Yes," she said, "I'm awake."

He edged into the room and shut the door gently behind him. He'd patted down his hair, though it had dried unevenly, and she could see that he'd scrubbed his hands to remove the tar, or most of it, anyway. "I see the leaks have stopped—or slowed at least."

"It's an improvement, yes," she said.

"As soon as it stops, I'll get back up there and fix it permanently."

She watched him move round the room, shrugging out of his jacket, unbuttoning his shirt, pulling the chair to him to sit and remove his trousers, a man getting ready for bed, the most pedestrian thing in the world, and intimate, deeply intimate, her man, her husband, and what had she been thinking? They were married. Man and wife. She loved him. He loved her. "If you like," he said, stripped to his underwear now, the hard muscles of his legs flexed against the grip of the cotton cloth, his arms hanging loose at his sides and the heavy spill of his abdomen suspended before him, "I can empty these buckets. It won't take but a minute."

"No," she said, "no need to bother." She sat up, pushed back the covers so he could see her there in her nightgown. Her throat was bare. Her hair ran loose over her shoulders. She was breathing steadily, easily, the cold and damp nothing to her, nothing at all—she was in Italy, that was where she was, and the sirocco had swept out of Africa to dry the ditches and scorch the fields. "Come to bed, Will," she said.

Next morning, he was up before her, up and out the door, thundering down the stairs to the kitchen and breakfast and then to his gum boots and mackintosh and the shovel that roughened his hands and tore at the muscles of his back and shoulders till he was so stiff some evenings he could barely straighten up. She wanted to massage him, rub his shoulders, ease his burden, but more often than not she was asleep by the time he came to bed. Last night was different. She was awake and present and after he'd turned out the light and come to her, his weight straining the mattress and she slipping helplessly toward him as if down a gentle sloping hill, she'd tried to be a wife to him, tried to open up, feel him, but she couldn't seem to let herself go. He groped at her, his fingers seeking her out, rucking up her nightdress, fastening on her breasts, the bulk of him rising up, pressing at her till she wasn't so much aroused as embarrassed—her shrunken breasts, her ribs that were like the stony reefs the tide exposed, the poor wasted shanks of her legs—and all she could think was that he was embracing a corpse. *You're so thin,* he murmured, working at her, working, kissing her throat, her ears, the parting of her hair, and in his moment of passion he actually took hold of her chin and pressed his mouth to hers until she spoke his name aloud, firmly, harshly, and turned her face away.

She felt ashamed of herself. Felt weak and inadequate. And as she lay there now listening to the rain that still hadn't let up, the rain that had become a burden, a weight that lay over everything, squeezing and compressing the air till it might have been raining inside her, raining in her lungs and her heart and her brain too, she thought of him out there on the road in the thick of it, his back aching, his shoulders on fire, plunging the shovel into the wet yielding earth as if it mattered, as if anything mattered. She forced herself out of bed, the first long spasm catching her by surprise. She coughed, heaved for breath, coughed. The pitcher, the glass, the little brown bottle, the spoon with its residue. And then her clothes. She took a long while dressing—no matter how low she might have been she had to think of Edith, of setting an example, because if she didn't do it, who would?—and then she drew up a chair to the mirror, combed out her hair and pinned it up.

The light was poor, but even so, even at a glance, she could see how reduced she looked. Her skin was porous, gray, stretched as tight as the lamb's hide Adolph had tacked up on the side of the barn, while her eyes seemed larger, disproportionately so, as if her features had sunk into them. She pinched her cheeks to bring up the color, but nothing came, and she resorted to her rouge, twin dabs of it worked into the hollows of her cheeks, but the effect seemed worse somehow. No matter. She had a duty to perform and that duty involved Will, her husband, who was out there in the rain, working for increase and profit, working for her.

It was ten-thirty in the morning by her pocket watch when she came downstairs, and it was past eleven by the time she'd brewed a full pot of coffee and wrapped up half a dozen sandwiches of lamb and onion in a towel she positioned beside the coffee in the depths of a straw basket. Then she put on her coat and hat, took up her parasol and went out the front door, down the steps and into the rain.

The footing was bad, but she'd expected that—what she hadn't expected was the feeling of release that swept over her as soon as the door pulled shut behind her. She was out of doors, only that, and it came to her that it was the first time she'd been out in days. The house loomed at her back, but she never turned her head. She was watching her feet, concentrating on keeping her balance in the roiling sepia mud that clung to the toes of her boots and sucked at her heels. The rain drummed at the parasol. Everything smelled of fresh-turned earth.

She found Will just beyond the second outcrop, wielding his shovel in a torrent, Adolph and Jimmie pitching in beside him, and it was like the day of the lobsters, only the wheelbarrow was filled with a yellow soup of diluted mud and all three of them looked hopeless. "I brought hot coffee," she said. "And sandwiches."

"You shouldn't have come out here in this," Will said even as he jammed the shovel into the ground and moved toward her, Adolph and Jimmie setting down their tools and moving too now, as if they'd been awakened from a dream.

"I know how hard you've been working," she said, her feet sliding in the muck, her shoes ruined and stockings soaked through, "and I just felt you could do with a boost, something to warm you, all of you." She couldn't set the basket down—it would have been washed away, sluiced over the side of the path and flung down into the ravine that was roaring now with its burden of crashing rock and churning yellow water—and she was having difficulty in trying to hold it out to Will and at the same time keep the parasol upright. In that moment she saw how absurd it was to have brought the basket to them—where would they drink their coffee or eat the sandwiches that would turn to paste the minute they took them up? There was no cover, no place to sit, the rain beating down without remit, everything in motion, gray above, dun below.

But they came to her, crowding in under the poor protection of the parasol, and they held out the cups she provided so that she could pour for each of them in turn and they took the sandwiches and lifted them to their mouths, their eyes gone distant as they chewed.

She wanted to say something about the conditions, how they really ought to think about giving it up for the day before someone got washed into the ravine or buried beneath a mudslide, but instead she turned to Will—Will, with his mustaches dripping and the crown of his hat collapsed round his ears—and clucked her tongue. "You poor man," she said.

He was chewing. He brought the coffee to his lips. "If you think this is bad, you should have seen it in the war."

Adolph's eyes were dead, Jimmie looked as if he were asleep on his feet. "This isn't the war," she said.

He gulped down the coffee, turned the cup over to drain the dregs and handed it to her. Then he rocked back on his heels, the rain driving at his face, and grinned. "I admit it," he said, "conditions could be better." And he looked to Adolph and Jimmie and then back to her again. "But at least nobody's shooting at us."

The Cake

Ida was first (her birthday was the eighth of February and Edith's the twelfth) and everyone felt they should make the day special for her, so even though it was raining again—*still*, forever, it seemed—and she'd barely slept and felt as if she'd been run through with a sword, Marantha was up early and shuffling round the kitchen, seeing to the flour, sugar, butter and eggs for the cake. Ida had already served breakfast, the men eating at the table in the parlor though she'd forbidden it, or thought she had, and now Ida was taking a mop to the floor there, everything smeared with mud and the very walls reeking of mold and rot and the sort of deep penetrating dampness no stove could ever hope to dry out. She'd given Ida a good dressing-down for serving the men in the house—and for the carpet too, because the carpet was hopeless after they'd got done with it. Ruined. Fit for the trash and nothing else.

"Don't be such a scold," Will had said, hateful, lecturing her, taking Ida's side, his eyes like pinpricks and his nose stabbing at her out of the tanned hide of his face. "You can't expect the hands to take their plates all the way out across the yard in this kind of weather. That's just unreasonable. Worse: it's inhumane." She'd felt mean and pinched and so she threw it right back at him: "Inhumane? What do you call serving up that poor child's pet for dinner? What about forcing your own wife to live like some gypsy in a caravan? You tell me that."

For herself, she'd breakfasted in her room on tea and toast with a bit of jam while writing in her diary, as if there were anything to report but rain and tedium and more of the same, and when the men had gone out to their digging, she'd come down to the kitchen. The stove was hot still, at least there was that. The kettle boiled right away and she had herself a second cup of tea, with two full teaspoons of sugar stirred in (why not—it wasn't as if she had to worry over her weight) and that gave her a lift. Of course, whatever she needed, whether it was a proper mixing bowl, a measuring cup or a whisk to beat the eggs, was either back in Santa Barbara or buried amongst the mouse pellets in some dismal back corner, but still she managed to find a suitable pan, grease it with the butter Ida had churned the day before yesterday and get things under way, using a teacup for measuring and one of the clay crocks in lieu of a bowl.

She'd creamed a cup of butter and was using a soupspoon to fold in a cup and two-thirds of sugar, as best she could measure, when Ida, mop and bucket in hand, pushed her way through the door. "Good morning, ma'am," the girl sang out, eyeing the pan as she crossed to the far corner to lean the mop against the wall there. The rain slackened momentarily and then started in again with a heavy thump, as if a tree had fallen against the roof, but that was impossible, the Spaniards having taken the last tree down for lumber a hundred years ago and the sheep making sure in the interval that anything taller than six inches was chewed right on down to the dirt. Or mud. In the next moment, Ida had the back door open on the roar of it and on the stomach-wrenching reek of the flooded W.C., which now stood just two hundred yards from the house, and here was the dog, soaked to the skin and trying to dodge past her even as she flung the bucket of dirty water out into the yard and slammed the door shut on it.

Marantha was at the counter—a whitewashed plank projecting from the wall and propped up on two sticks of wood indifferently nailed to the floor— and she barely turned her head. The eggs were next—eggs she'd collected herself at first light, bent over in Will's shroud-like mackintosh while the rain drummed at her back and the hens peered miserably at her from beneath the shed and the steps of the bunkhouse. She cracked three of them and carefully worked each into the mixture before adding the first cup of flour, feeling good, feeling competent and well, feeling useful, and she was so caught up in the process she entirely forgot about Ida, or that this was supposed to be a surprise.

"What are you doing, making an omelet?" Ida's voice seemed to come at her out of the ether, and when she jerked her head round in surprise, Ida was right there, not a foot away, peering over her shoulder. "Or is it bread?"

"No," she breathed, trying to mask what she was doing, "no, it's not bread. I—everything's fine. Just fine." She gave it a moment, and then, as casually as she could, she cracked the final two eggs and beat them into the mixture while adding the second cup of flour, a trickle at a time.

"I wouldn't want to speak where I'm not wanted, but isn't that too many eggs?"

She didn't know what to say. The kitchen felt very close suddenly. She could hear the dog whining at the door, and that was vaguely irritating because the animal was not allowed in the house and should have known better—let him go sprawl in the bunkhouse with Adolph and Jimmie. A moment drifted past. Ida hadn't moved.

"You know, ma'am, I'd be more than willing to help if you like," Ida said, and she was right there still, right behind her. "Wouldn't you be more comfortable in the parlor where you can rest by the stove while I finish up here?"

She could feel the strength radiating down from her shoulder to her forearm and wrist, the batter folding and folding again till she'd worked it smooth. Pound cake, the simplest thing in the world. She was working from memory, from her mother's recipe, and her mother's cakes had always been flawless, better than the baker's, better than anything her aunts or grandmother or anybody in the neighborhood could ever hope to compete with. She had a vivid image of a morning long ago, snow cresting on the woodshed, a tray of gingerbread cookies cooling on the counter while the sweet wafting aroma of the cake her mother had just taken from the oven filled the house and they sat at the window over cups of chocolate and watched the snowstorm transfigure the world. "What ever became of the vanilla extract?" she asked, as if it were an idle question, and she wasn't going to turn round, wasn't going to give up the pretense. "I hope we remembered it. With the kitchen things, I mean."

"You're baking a cake." Ida's voice had gone soft.

"That's right, yes." She let the affirmation hang in the air between them a moment, her shoulders busy, the spoon clacking in the depths of the bowl, and then she couldn't help but turn. Her smile—it was automatic, composed in equal parts of sympathy and embarrassment—wavered when she saw the look on the girl's face. "We were hoping to surprise you."

"You don't have to go out of your way for me, ma'am," Ida murmured, dropping her arms and folding her hands in her apron as if she meant to hide them. Marantha took her in at a glance: the men's gum boots, the neat mauve dress with its white lace collar, the hair so woolly it defied the brush. Her eyes were wet. Her teeth worked at her lower lip. "Because I don't usually—that is, we don't . . . not in my family—"

"Nonsense," she said, thinking of the Irish back at home in Boston, the eternal laundry, the ragged filthy children, the drunks and beggars. She set down the spoon and reached out her hand to take hold of Ida's. "Happy birthday," she said, running a thumb gently over the girl's palm. And the valedictory words were on her lips—*May you have many more*—when the cough surprised her and she had to turn away, had to hurry across the room, bent double, a handkerchief pressed to her face, to find the stool in the corner and sit there till she could breathe again.

It was a long morning. Ida kept fussing round her—"Can I get you something? A cup of broth? Would you like to lay down a minute?"—but once the spasm passed she insisted on finishing the cake herself. Of course she was going to finish it—what kind of birthday would it be if Ida had to bake her own cake? She felt light-headed, maybe a bit flushed even, but she poured the batter into the pan and shooed the girl away. "But, ma'am," Ida kept saying, "you don't know this stove—it's a neat trick to damp it just so—"

"I'm not helpless. I've been baking cakes since before you were born— believe me, I know what I'm doing." She glanced up at Ida where she was stalled at the door to the hallway, looking tragic. "Go, go on! You must have something better to do than stand here worrying over me—what about the mending I gave you? What about Edith's dress?" She turned away to pull open the door of the oven and felt the blast of heat in her face. And then the pan was in and the door shut and she straightened up and turned round to see that Ida hadn't moved. "Where is Edith, anyway?"

"Out walking."

"Walking? In this?"

"Yes, ma'am. She took her mackintosh and went out after she had her breakfast."

"But where?"

A shrug. "Just for a walk, that's all she said. Said she felt confined—you can hardly blame her."

She fought down an impulse to damp the stove—it was too hot, she was sure of it—but she didn't want to fiddle with it while Ida was watching. She said, "No, you're right. It's just that I worry."

"Of course you do, ma'am."

And that was that. Ida went off to her chores, and Marantha, though she felt overheated, though she felt the sluggishness invade her limbs and her lungs twist and tighten as if they were being wrung out like a pair of wet rags, sat by the stove and adjusted the damper and opened the door repeatedly to peer in at her cake though she knew she shouldn't have. Perhaps she nodded off for just a moment, she couldn't say. But the next thing she knew Will was there, the back door thrown open on the smoke issuing from the stove—and the cake, the cake that was blackened around the edges and as squat and hard and dry as a cracker—and her first thought wasn't for the cake or the smoke but for him, for how common he looked, how like a vagrant in his filthy wet clothes and crumpled hat. "Jesus," he said, his voice climbing the register, "what in Christ's name do you think you're doing?"

There was the smoke, the rawness of the outdoors, the look of him. "Baking," she said.

"Baking?" He threw it back at her, incredulous. "More like burning the place to the ground. Have you no sense at all? What do you think we took on Ida for?"

"Ida," she spat. "Always Ida."

"Well, isn't she the cook?"

"It's her birthday."

He was towering, huge, the mustache clinging wet to his face like some sort of bleached-out fungus, and he was trying to balance on one leg and jerk the muddy boot from the other. "I don't give a goddamn," he started and then caught himself. In the yard, in the rain, the faces of Adolph and Jimmie appeared and now they were crowding in at the open doorway.

She didn't care. She was angry, frightened, outraged. He couldn't imagine what she felt, none of them could. They were healthy, they were going to live, and she wasn't. Everything they saw before them was infused with the color of life, bright and shining even in the rain, but for her it was all dross. "You look common," she said—or no, she threw it at him. "And these men, these, these *hands,* will not take their midday meal in this house. *Will not,* do you hear me?"

She paused for breath then and no one moved, no one said a word, though

71

the smoke dodged and swirled and the cake blackened and her lungs rattled with the effort of drawing in the breath she so violently needed because she wasn't finished yet. "And I wish the place *had* caught fire," she said, but she was rasping now, all the resonance scoured from her voice by this thing with the claws, by the disease that plucked you up at random, that got inside of you and slowly strangled the life from you. "At least then we could leave this rat's hole and go back to, to"—she was coughing suddenly, coughing till she felt the sputum dissolve in a hot rush of blood she tried to choke back even as it filled her mouth and broke free to redden her lips and douse the front of her dress in a spatter of bright red droplets—"to civilization. Civilization, Will."

She held them with a look of fury until Adolph—and Jimmie, Jimmie following his lead—backed out the door and into the rain.

Will said her name once, softly.

"Don't speak to me," she said. "Don't ever speak to me again."

Edith's Turn

Four days later, it was Edith's turn. This time she let Ida do the baking, but she insisted on mixing the batter herself and sitting there in the kitchen till the cake came out of the oven plump and moist and perfectly browned across the top—she was Edith's mother still, no matter her condition. And every year since Edith had come to her from the orphanage, helpless, impossibly small and vulnerable, this perfect shining infant whose natural mother had tossed her aside like so much refuse, she'd baked a cake on her birthday—and on Christmas too. A cake. The smallest thing. And on this day, the day of Edith's fifteenth birthday—the twelfth of February, a day she'd marked with a star on the calendar the day they'd arrived—with the rain finally stopped and the sun burning bright in a cored-out sky, she'd risen from her bed with a fierceness of purpose. She didn't need coffee or tea or any other stimulant, just the cake pan, just the batter, just Edith.

It was a wonder, really, considering how low she'd been these past days. Confined to her bed, weak, bored, feeling useless, she'd lain there staring at the stained canopy and the curtains that hemmed her in, imagining she was already in her grave, a damp place, wet, reeking, the raw earth pressing down on her without mercy or appeal. She was feverish. Her dreams were dense, clotted with images of grasping hands and spectral faces that loomed up out of nothingness and vanished again just as quickly. She'd lost blood, too much blood, and though the hemorrhage hadn't been nearly as bad as the one she'd suffered in December, for which fact she was grateful, it had left her weak and disoriented all the same.

She'd forced herself to come downstairs that first night—for Ida's sake, to help her commemorate the occasion and lift the pall that lay over the house—and everyone had been in good spirits, all things considered. The cake was a humiliation, of course, Ida having had to produce another while she herself lay supine on the bed with the smell of it drifting down the hallway and up the stairs to mock her in her weakness and debility, and she hadn't been able to join in when Edith led a chorus of "Oh! Susanna," substituting "Ida" for "Anna," and yet still she felt fortunate to be there—moved, deeply moved— and couldn't keep from thinking about the following year and the one after that and who would be sitting there in her place. She looked up at Edith, at her face luminous with the pleasure of watching Ida unwrap the gift she'd given her—ribbons, blue satin ribbons Edith had brought with her from the mainland and kept hidden all this time—and she began, very softly, to cry. Will had looked away—she was angry with him still, though at that moment she felt so soft and fragile she would have accepted anything from him—and when she woke in the night, he wasn't there beside her in the bed.

It had taken her a moment, fumbling with the match and lantern, to understand why. "I don't want you here," she'd told him when he came to her at bedtime. He was hateful to her then, clumsy, shabby, the root and cause of all her troubles made flesh, his face hanging like a swollen pale fruit in the doorway. "Go sleep in the storage room," she'd said, "go sleep in the bunkhouse. I don't care. I don't want you here. I'm weak. I'm in pain. I—" But he was already gone, the door pulling shut softly behind him.

That was over now, gone, done, past. She didn't want to think of it or what it meant that he'd made his bed in the monk's cell across from Ida's room ever since and that she didn't care a whit whether he came back to her bed or not, not today. Today the sun was shining, the floorboards were drying out, the lambs growing into their limbs and all the birds in the world singing in unison while the cake, Edith's cake, sat cooling on the table. That was what mattered, that was all that mattered: the cake. And Edith. Edith's birthday. She got up and busied herself around the kitchen, thinking of all the things that needed doing—sending Jimmie for abalone, cutting wildflowers for the bouquet, finishing up the trim on the new dress she meant to surprise Edith with—and she was just sitting down at the little table against the window there, stirring a bit of milk into the porridge Ida had made for breakfast, forcing herself to eat, when she happened to glance up and see Edith making her way across the yard.

And who was that with her? Jimmie. Jimmie trailing along behind her like a moonstruck calf, the big straw laundry basket clutched in both arms as if it were filled with rocks, and why wasn't he at work? Why wasn't he clearing the road or plowing or sowing the grain—hadn't Will said they needed to get it in as soon as they had a break in the weather? Edith's face was perfectly composed, though her hair was disordered beneath her hat and her skirts were muddy, as if she'd been tramping the hills again, and she was saying something over her shoulder to the boy. In the next moment they both pulled up short, right in the middle of the yard, no more than fifty feet from the house, and Jimmie set down the basket, which did seem to be filled with stones—or no, seashells. They'd been at the shore, that was what it was, and she was just trying to sort that out—the two of them, alone and unsupervised, Edith's walks, her moods, the way the boy watched her at dinner as if her every word and gesture held some secret meaning, and what if it did, what if she'd been blind to what anyone could have seen as plain as day?—when Edith held out her hand and he went down on one knee in the mud to take hold of it. And then, without prompting, without taking his eyes from Edith's, he brought her hand to his lips.

All her pleasure in the day dissolved in that instant and she couldn't stop herself from rushing to the door and out into the festering wallow of the yard, her shoes muddied in an instant, her skirts blackened, all the blood left in her wasted body rising to her face and a strange yammering chorus of voices howling in her ears. Shock, that was what it was, ungovernable, unconscionable. She'd never . . . She couldn't . . .

Jimmie sprang to his feet. Edith lifted her eyes, distant eyes, defiant, as if she hadn't been caught out, as if she weren't ashamed in the slightest. There were so many things wrong with that tableau Marantha couldn't begin to list them. She tried to speak, tried to demand an explanation, but the words died in her throat.

The boy's trousers, filthy as they were, showed a spreading wet stain in the left knee, where he'd gone down in the mud. He put on a look of innocence. "Good morning, ma'am," he said, but he wouldn't meet her eye.

Edith said nothing.

She wasn't going to cough. She wasn't going to have a spasm. She was going to control her breathing, control herself. A cloud drifted across the sun so that a running sheet of darkness fell over the yard and raced up the far hill. The turkeys set up a gabble from their pen. She heard the sound of the dog barking at something somewhere. Finally—she wasn't going to cough, she wasn't—her voice came back to her. "Edith, you get out of that now," she said, and knew it was wrong, knew it was inadequate to what she was feeling and the tone she should have taken. *Don't make a scene,* she told herself. *Not in front of the help.*

"We're only playing."

"Playing? He—I saw him."

"He's my slave." Edith turned to the boy, who wouldn't raise his eyes. "Isn't that right, Caliban? Isn't it?"

Miserably, his voice hoarse with hopelessness, resignation, lust, he said, "Yes."

"I've had him fetching seashells."

Marantha tried to lift her feet from the mire, tried to edge closer, furious now, but it was as if she were frozen in place. "You're not to go unsupervised, unchaperoned, that is—"

"It's only a game, Mother." Edith looked to the boy now, to where he stood beside her in the mud, shrunken, slope-shouldered, his features pinched in concentration. "He'll do anything I say. Isn't that right, Caliban?"

"Yes."

"Speak up. I can scarcely hear you."

Louder now: "Yes."

"And what's my name?"

"Edith."

Edith snaked her hand out and slapped him so quickly he didn't have time to flinch. "What's my name?"

"Miranda."

"That's better. Now pick up that basket, take it around the house and arrange the shells on the porch there—and make sure you put the prettiest ones in front."

The boy bent to the basket without a word, lifted it—it was heavy, she could see that—and braced it on one hip. Then, the mud sucking at his boots, he struggled round the corner of the house and out of sight.

"You see, Mother?" A faint imperious smile, a cruel smile, a smile of superiority and willfulness. "He'll do anything I say."

That night, for the birthday dinner, Ida served an abalone chowder that was even better than the one she'd made on New Year's, followed by a pair of stuffed and roasted chickens (a special treat, since the flock had been decimated by the foxes and, Will claimed, an eagle that had made off with one of their best layers right before his eyes) with a side dish of rice and beans and a puree made from the last of the turnips Charlie Curner had carried over the previous month. She herself lit the candles and brought out the cake. Edith, in the new green dress that just exactly caught the color of her eyes, leaned over the table to make her wish and blow out the candles and everyone applauded.

"A toast!" Will proposed. He was at the head of the table, dressed in his best shirt and jacket, his hair newly washed and combed and his mustache neatly trimmed for once, and he reached down under his chair and came up with a magnum of the Santa Cruz Island wine he was always singing the virtues of, as if they too could establish a winery just by snapping their fingers, as if it were just one more money-making venture the island would give up to them in good time, though to her mind, the wind—and here it was again, picking up, rattling the panes and keening under the eaves like a chorus of the drowned dead—would blow the whole business, vines, trellises and grapes, right on out to sea. Everyone watched him draw the cork in silence as if it were a rare operation and he a magician in cape and top hat and she couldn't help notice Jimmie's eyes wandering to Edith, but then how could he resist—how could any boy, deprived or not, unless he was blind? Edith had never looked more beautiful. Maybe, she was thinking—and here the cork eased from the bottle with an audible sigh—maybe there was something healthful about the outdoor life after all.

Will made his way around the table, filling each of the glasses in succession, starting with her own, then Ida's, Adolph's and even Jimmie's—*Jimmie's*—and finally stopping at Edith's place. She wanted to say something, wanted to interfere—it wasn't right that a girl of Edith's age should take intoxicating beverages—but Will was already pouring. Edith had been animated all night, in high spirits, but she went silent now. Will poured the glass full, then poured for himself and lifted his glass high. "To the prettiest girl on this or any other island in the world! Or no," he said, correcting himself, "to the prettiest young lady!"

Marantha watched her daughter bring the glass to her lips, watched her sip and make a face before trying it again, emboldened, and taking a long greedy swallow. "You're not to go off with that boy alone," she'd lectured her the moment Jimmie had vanished round the corner of the house that morning. "It's not proper." Her heart had been beating wildly. The sun, so welcome a moment ago, hit her like a hammer. "Do you really imagine I have any interest in him?" Edith said, looking her straight in the eye. "He's a boy, a child, a weakling. And he's ignorant, as stupid as the stupidest sheep in the flock. Stupider." And what had she felt? Relief, certainly. But she had to stop herself from making a lesson out of this too, from reminding her daughter that there was no need to be cruel, that every person, no matter his station, deserved to be treated with dignity and respect, that—but what was the use? Edith was growing away from her, growing up, and here she was drinking the wine, drinking it greedily, and already holding out her glass for more. Which Will poured. And still her mother said nothing.

Edith led off the singing with "Blue-Tail Fly" and then Will sang his favorite, "The Battle Hymn of the Republic," in his strong cascading baritone, and everyone joined in. Ida got up to sing "The Rose of Tralee" and when they all applauded—was she tipsy?—she sang it through again. Jimmie was next. He rose to sing "Men of Harlech" in a voice so reduced you had to strain to make out the lyrics ("Men of Harlech, stop your dreaming/Can't you see their spear points gleaming?"), after which Edith excused herself and came back a moment later in a new costume altogether, in a loose flowing skirt without her corsets, and before Marantha could object, Edith announced that she was going to perform one of the dances she'd learned at school that went to the tune of Beethoven's "Für Elise."

"Since we don't seem to have a piano"—Edith was pushing back the chairs now and arranging the lamps for dramatic effect on the shelf behind her—"or anyone to play accompaniment even if we did have, I'm going to hum the melody myself." She paused to glance round the room. "Unless we can borrow a piano from one of the neighbors. And a pianist."

They were all watching her intently—Adolph, unfathomable Adolph, with his heavy brow and hooded eyes; Jimmie, with a faint fading smile pressed to his lips; Will, grinning proudly; Ida, sloppy suddenly, slouching, her mouth hanging open. Edith made as if to look out the window, the hem of the skirt rising daintily round her ankles as she bent forward and put a hand up to shade her eyes. "Do you think there are any wandering pianists out there?" She held the moment, bathing in the attention, and then looked directly at her. "Could you find one for me, Mother?"

Will let out a laugh and said to no one in particular, "Charming girl, isn't she?"

And then the dance began, shakily at first, Edith clearly having trouble coordinating her movements to the tune she had to produce herself, but she got stronger as she went on, so that even after Ida rose discreetly and vanished into the kitchen and the men passed round the bottle till there was nothing left, even after her voice faded away and the only sounds in the room were the rhythmic tapping of her feet and the wind in the eaves, she kept moving across the floor in a slow graceful arc, her limbs swaying to the music only she could hear.

The Eagle

All the talk was of the shearers—the shearers were coming, the shearers—until she began to think they were some messianic tribe bent on redeeming them all. She pictured men in silken beards and turbans, an oriental squint to their eyes and their shoes turned up at the toes, bearing gifts of spices and speaking in a strange tongue, but Will was having none of it. Will was in a state. He couldn't sit still, couldn't rest, working furiously at the road, scanning the horizon every morning for the telltale sail in the harbor, jumping up from the card table in the evening to pace back and forth until she thought the floorboards would wear through under his weight, and all the while lecturing Edith and Ida—and her too—about the state of the house. It had to be homelier, cleaner, more orderly—and why? Because it wasn't only the shearers who were coming, but Mills too. And not simply Mills, who was getting out, but the new man who was to buy in as half-partner, and it was their duty to show the place at its best. What would Mills think if he saw the state of the house as it was right this minute? Or the new man. Think of him. The real shame of it—and Will wouldn't leave it alone—was that they didn't have the wherewithal to buy out Mills themselves and set up as sole owners and proprietors and let the rest of the world go to hell.

"Imagine it, Minnie," he said. "Just imagine it. Our own island—our own country—and nobody to answer to. We could pull up the drawbridges and man the battlements. I could be king. And you—you, Minnie—you could be queen."

What could she say? She tried to be accommodating, tried to soothe him, tried even to scrub the place into submission, but the idea was a living death to her—the world was in San Francisco, in Boston, in Santa Barbara, not here. Queen? Queen of what? The sheep?

He put an arm round her waist, drew her to him and kissed her lightly on the cheek. "It's what I've always dreamed of," he murmured.

Then one night, after dinner, as she was going down the hall to the kitchen with the notion of brewing a pot of tea, she found him in his room—the former storeroom—changing into his work clothes. "You're not going back out there, are you?" she'd asked, incredulous.

The room was cramped and cheerless, but neat enough, she supposed, in a military sort of way. It was like an encampment on a battlefield, the bed no more than a cot with a single thin blanket drawn tight, his gear—a canteen, various tools and implements, his tripod and transit—arranged on various hooks projecting from the walls. He was sitting on the cot, pulling on a pair of stained and worn trousers she'd already mended more times than she could count. His socks were dirty, his shirt, even his braces. He didn't say anything.

"It's the dark of night. It's raining."

He shrugged. He was lacing up his boots now, though she'd asked him time and again to put them on and remove them on the porch so as to minimize the dirt in the house he was suddenly so very interested in keeping clean. "Seems like it's always raining."

She was silent a moment. "I'm sorry we haven't got the money, Will," she said. "I know how much this venture means to you, this place, I mean. You know if I had the money I'd give it to you"—she'd meant to keep any note of resentment out of her voice because he was her husband and she loved him and here he was sleeping separately from her because she was too weak to bear him—"but I've already given everything I have."

The room was close, windowless, lit only by a candle on a dish he'd set on an overturned crate by the side of the bed. "You're a martyr, a regular Christian martyr."

"Don't, Will."

He was busy with the other boot now, but he took time to glance up and hold her gaze. "Do you want to lose everything, is that it? Somebody's got to do the work around here, somebody's got to persevere. Yes, I want this place. Is that a crime? You can't know what I went through in the war—or after either, working the printing presses for my brother and then those idiots at the *Morning Call*. Dirty, demeaning work. Always somebody crabbing at you. Up in the morning, to bed at night, and for what? I want something of my own and if I have to work myself to death I'm going to get it."

She was standing in the doorway still, one hand on the frame as if she were a visitor in her own house. But then this wasn't her house and never would be—it was foreign to her, harsh and unacceptable, and so was this windblown island that might as well have been in the middle of the Amazon for all the diversion it offered. "You promised me we wouldn't stay past the first of June if I . . . if I don't improve. And I'm not improving, Will. It's too cold. Too damp." She felt a sadness so intense it was as if some machine had hold of her, some infernal engine, crushing the spirit out of her. "Too hopeless, Will, hopeless, do you hear me? If I'm going to die I want my things around me, I want society, comfort—not this." She lifted her hand to take in the room, the house in which it stood, the island and the sea and the distant cliffs of the coast beyond.

"You're not going to die."

It was a lie and they both knew it.

He was on his feet suddenly, brisk, towering, on his way past her and out into the night to work his precious road. "Goddamn it, Marantha," he said, his face so close to hers she could smell the stewed lamb they'd had for dinner on his breath—or his mustache, which he never even bothered to wipe properly—"it's not my fault. I didn't give you the disease."

"No," she said very quietly, "no, you didn't."

He was edging past her, nervous on his feet, guilty, ashamed of himself— and he should have been. He should have gone down on his knees the way he had when he proposed marriage to her in the front parlor on Post Street, Sampan a kitten in her lap and Edith curled up asleep with her china doll. Should have taken her in his arms and comforted her. Tried to imagine, for just an instant, what it was like to see the whole world fading to nothing all around you and none but the mute dead to understand or sympathize.

"Goddamn it," he said, cursing again, though he knew she hated it, "we have to go on, don't you see that?" His eyes were huge, apoplectic, his face flushed. "Life goes on, and what does life mean? Life means work, Marantha, *work*. And work is what I intend to do."

The rain stopped sometime overnight. She was awake, unable to sleep, racked with night sweats and thoughts of the beyond, when the thrumming on the roof abruptly ceased and in rushed the silence, shaping itself to fit the void—silence that was somehow worse than the rain, which was at least alive, or in motion at any rate. She stared into the darkness, too exhausted to light the lantern and take up her book, thinking of Will sleeping in his narrow bed in the room below her and sharing in the darkness that was general over the island and the sea and the continent beyond and would even now, on the eastern coast, where her mother would be getting breakfast in the kitchen of the house she'd been a girl in, be giving way to the light. Did she sleep? She supposed so. Eventually there was a period of blankness, but if rest was the purpose of sleep, then she didn't get much.

In the morning she felt so weak she could barely lift her head from the pillow. Outside the window the sky seemed a second roof, flat and gray and uninterrupted. Why she was alive, why she was breathing, why she'd been born on this earth only to suffer the way she had, she couldn't say. She lay there a long while before propping herself up with a pillow so that she could see out to the bay, to see if there was a sail there, but there wasn't. The shearers hadn't come. They were still on the next island over, plying their mobile trade, eating, drinking, taking their time. *The shearers are coming, the shearers are coming.* But not yet.

Ida brought a tray with breakfast: tea, toast, fried meat, but no eggs—eggs were suddenly precious, what with the exigencies of the cakes and the mortality amongst the flock. By the time she finished and washed, dressed and put up her hair, it was nearly noon by the clock on the shelf Will had erected for her on the wall beside the bed. That was an advantage of a house constructed willy-nilly of railway ties and whatever else washed ashore from the wrecks that ringed the island, she supposed—if you needed a shelf, you just nailed a board to the wall, aesthetic considerations notwithstanding. She took a moment to gather up her needlework, then went down to sit by the stove in the parlor. Ida was in the kitchen, baking bread and adding whatever came to hand—potatoes, flour, canned tomatoes, salt pork left over from breakfast—to invigorate last night's lamb stew. Will and Adolph were at work on the road, so far down now you couldn't see them unless you went to the second turning and peered over the edge there, tracing the line of the canyon to where the road switched back again and the raw earth gave up the fractured shells of its dynamited rocks. Jimmie was in the fenced-in field behind the house, sowing grain in the furrows he'd plowed the past three days. And Edith? Edith was out walking.

In the next hour, she got up twice to feed wood into the stove, and she was just easing back into her chair, thinking only of the pattern of the tea cloth she was working on—the figure of a scintillant red cardinal, seen in full flight, on a field of pale blue, just that, nothing more—when a movement across the yard caught her eye. What was it? Men, two men, first their faces, then their shoulders and torsos emerging from beneath the slope of the hill in gradual accretion, legs now, full figures, moving toward the house. One of them was Will, unmistakable in his patched clothes and seesawing gait even at a distance, and the other—this came as a shock—a stranger altogether. Had the shearers come? Was this a shearer, this lean, tall, fresh-faced man with a rifle in one hand and the clenched feet of what looked to be an enormous trailing bird locked in the grip of the other? She saw feathers, the reanimated flap of dead wings writhing in the dirt.

She set aside her embroidery, a single pulse of excitement shooting through her—*Someone new!*—and went to the door. The air was brisk, smelling more of the sea than of the flock. The pigs grunted from their pen. She could hear the chorus of the seals on the distant snapping cable of the wind.

"Minnie!" Will was calling, and here he was, coming round the corner of the house, the stranger at his side. "Come look at this."

She was wearing her carpet slippers, and despite herself, despite her excitement over seeing a new face, she didn't want to come down off the porch into the muddy yard, and so she held back.

The stranger—he was in his twenties, early twenties, she guessed, Ida's age—stopped in his tracks to gaze up at her with a look of wonderment on his face. He was unshaven, his beard the same nearly translucent color as the hair that trailed away from the brim of his hat and coming in irregularly, as if he weren't quite sure yet how to grow it.

"Are you—?" she began, then turned to Will. "Is this one of the shearers?"

The man let out a laugh. "Hardly, ma'am," he said, and came forward to tip his hat in a show of greeting. "My name's Robert Ord, ma'am, and I've done come out to these islands after the seals."

Will was grinning. "And guano. Don't forget the guano."

"Guano?" she echoed.

The stranger seemed to color, though she couldn't be sure because of the beard and his sunburn. "The leavings of the seabirds," he said, ducking his head and exchanging a glance with Will. "The white stuff. Very valuable to the farmers back on shore."

"White gold, they call it. Isn't that right, Robert?"

"Yes, sir, they do."

But where were her manners? He was a sealer, a collector of—of excrement—but he was a guest for all that and a new soul, a new face and voice and figure to drive down the tedium and bring news of the outside world. "Mr. Ord," she said, ignoring the fact that he still clutched the rifle in one hand and had just dropped the bird's blood-wet feet to employ the other in tipping his hat, "would you like to come in and sit by the stove? We were just going to brew a fresh pot of coffee and Ida'll have luncheon ready any minute now—"

"Yes," Will said, his voice drawn-down and dismissive, as if her invitation counted for nothing at all, "we'll be in directly. But look at what Robert's brought us." He gestured to the deflated bundle of feathers and claws at his feet, and she saw now what it was: an eagle. One of the fierce predatory birds that seemed to sail overhead as if they'd been propelled, their wings motionless as they caught the currents of the air and rose or plunged as they saw fit, fish eaters, opportunists, killers of lamb, turkey, chicken and shoat alike. She was stunned at the size of it—and the color, from the deep iridescent umber of its wings and torso to the perfect unalloyed white of its crown and tail feathers. Its talons were reptilian, the feet scaled like a chicken's and big as a man's hand. She hated it. It stole from Will, stole from her, but it was a complex kind of hate, hate that had awe mixed in with it, and a kind of love too.

"Nearly eight feet from wing tip to wing tip," Ord said, looking down at the massive spill of the bird. He nudged it with the toe of his boot, its head splayed awkwardly against the compacted mud, the talons clenched on nothing. "One of the biggest I've ever went and shot. And I tell you, I've shot plenty."

She studied the leathery slits of the eyes, locked shut now, and wondered what they'd seen from their vantage, so high up. What had the house looked like? The hogs? The turkeys? They themselves, with their explosives and guns and their figures that dwindled from the pyramidal crowns of their hats to the twin dots of their shoes.

Will's voice intruded on her reverie: "This one won't trouble us anymore."

It took her a moment. They were both watching her, smiling, proud, another obstacle out of the way and the evidence of it spread across the barren dirt at their feet. "But whatever will we do with it?" she asked.

"Do with it?" Will let out a laugh, and the stranger—Ord—joined in. "Bury it. Or maybe string it up over the barn as a warning to the others."

She felt cold. The smell of the sea seemed to concentrate itself suddenly, the fermenting odor of all the uncountable things washed up out of the waves coming to her as powerfully as if she were standing down there amongst them. And then a gust rose up out of the canyon, knifing through her, and in the instant she turned to retreat into the house she saw it fan the dead bird's wings till they rasped and fluttered and strove to take flight one last time.

The Shearers

If the shearers were late, if they were unpredictable, appearing when it suited them as they worked their way successively from one island to the other, it was beyond anyone's control, least of all hers. According to Will, Ord had heard from one of the fishermen that they were on the next island over, but nobody could be sure, since they could hardly send a cable, could they, and then Ord was gone with the seals he'd shot for their skins and a hold full of the guano he'd shoveled off the island in the mouth of the harbor, which looked to be no lighter for the lack of it. Twenty times a day she gazed out the window to the sea and there it was, its slopes so blindingly white with the leavings of the seabirds they might have been glaciated, Prince Island, and why they called it that she couldn't say. San Miguel had been discovered by a Portuguese named Cabrillo, she knew that much, and that he'd been sailing for the king of Spain, hence the Spanish name, but then everything was Spanish here, San Francisco, Santa Barbara, Santa Cruz, Los Angeles, California itself. Maybe the king had a son, but if so then why the English name? There must have been a word for "prince" in Spanish, though she didn't have an inkling as to what it might be. Of course, all that was more than three hundred years ago and there must have been a whole succession of kings and princes in the interval. If it were up to her—if she *were* the queen—she'd name the place for its chief attribute: Guano Island. Or better yet, *Heap.* Guano Heap.

In any case, the shearers were late. Mornings came and went, afternoons wrapped themselves in a swirl of mist, the nights dropped like a curtain—breakfast, luncheon, dinner, the washing, the dishes, cards, seashells, walks to the beach and back—and still no sail appeared in the harbor. "Where are they?" Will kept wondering aloud, his voice strained and pleading, but he wasn't addressing her or anybody else because no one had the answer except

God above or maybe Ord's mysterious fisherman, but his sail never showed itself either. "What's keeping them? How can we ever hope to make a profit if there's no one to clip the wool and take it to market?" Too anxious to sit in a chair for more than ten seconds at a time, he paced from one end of the room to the other, flinging out his hands in dumb show, and she would have offered him a whiskey just to calm him, but the whiskey was gone. He'd finished it. With Ida.

"They'll come," she said, trying to make the best of it, trying to assuage him, because his fears were hers and she could picture the sheep growing shaggier, dirtier, their wool so tangled and stringy it dropped off of its own accord, the shrubs decorated with it, the stripped stinking tracked-over mud bandaged in white, not a penny made and everything lost. Still, in a way, the delay was a blessing. Each day the shearers held off was a day Will could place his dynamite, blast his rocks, work the mule and the shovel and Jimmie and Adolph till the road began to take shape. He'd been driving himself furiously, the fences repaired, the barley and alfalfa in the ground and already sprouting, the shed erected and the roof of the house patched against the next deluge, and yet the road was little better than when they'd first started in on it—and the road was central to the whole operation. Will knew that. She knew it. And Mills—Mills especially knew it. And he would be here soon, on the boat that brought the shearers, with the new man, Nichols, in tow, and the onus was on Will to show them what he was made of.

Early one afternoon, just before lunch—it was the twentieth or twenty-first of the month, another day of exile, fog in the morning, sun breaking through at noon—she heard Will's voice in the yard and set aside her sewing to go to the door and greet him. He'd been blasting all morning, the soft muted concussions rolling up the canyon to set the windows atremble and resonate in the floorboards till she could feel them as a dull tingle through the soles of her shoes. Edith, who'd been helping her cut and sew curtains for the front window in the hope of adding a little color to the place, had turned to her at one point to complain about it. "It's so annoying, isn't it? It's like we're at war. Really, it's a wonder one of them doesn't lose an arm or a leg."

"Don't think such thoughts," she'd said automatically.

Now, rising from her chair, she said, "That'll be your father. You'll have to clear the curtains away so Ida can set the table." And then she was pulling the door open on a pale laminate sunshine, Will just mounting the steps of the porch with his hat and face and shoulders covered in an ochre residue of rock dust, everything ordinary, tedious, the round of the days as fixed as the stars in their slots, when she looked past him to where the two dun pincers of land cupped the bay and saw the sail there like a white knife plunged into the breast of the sea. "A sail!" she cried, the sudden intensity of her own voice startling her. "There's a sail in the harbor!"

Will stopped in mid-stride, one foot lifted to the step, dust sifting from his sleeves and hat and the folds of his trousers, his eyes snatching at hers as if he didn't believe her before he jerked violently round to stare out on the bay and see for himself. In the next instant Edith appeared at the door, her face wild with excitement. "Where?" she cried. "I don't see it." Will pointed— "There! Right there! Are you blind?"—and she shot down the steps, hatless, her best shoes ruined before she was halfway across the yard, even as Ida erupted from the kitchen and Jimmie, who'd been skulking round the corner of the house to take his lunch at the back door, reversed himself and started after Edith at a dead run. It took Will a minute, the heavy lines of his face lifting to take account of these new phenomena—a sail, Mills, the shearers— and then he was squaring his shoulders like the captain he was and shouting Jimmie's name with fierce insistence. "Where do you think you're going? You come here now."

The boy pulled up short, skidding in the mud as if his legs meant to go on without him. He threw a quick despairing glance at Edith, who was already approaching the first turning, and then came reluctantly across the yard, his shoulders slumped and feet dragging. Ida kept on. She'd crossed the yard and was at the mouth of the road now, not running exactly, but moving briskly, the apron flaring round her skirts, while Adolph, who'd apparently gone out to the bunkhouse to wash up, flung open the door there and stepped out onto the porch, a dirty towel in his hands.

"Ida!" Will cried, his voice breaking round a thin wire of tension and excitement. "You're wanted in the kitchen. You get in there now, and, I don't know, *prepare* something, anything. And coffee. Coffee in quantity. And, Adolph," he called across the yard, "you'll join me just as soon as I can get this rock dust washed off of me and change my shirt, and then we'll go down and help them unload. I won't be five minutes."

Marantha looked out to the bay again, to the sails and the ship enlarging beneath them, as if afraid it would have vanished in the mist like an optical illusion. But it was there, all right. The shearers had come. She should have felt relief but all she could think of was what they were going to do about dinner, where she would seat everyone, how they'd manage with the cracked plates and the mess of the place and the curtains that were laid out flat on the table instead of hanging airily at the windows. What would Mills think? What would Nichols?

But here was Jimmie, ragged and dirty and with his hair trailing down his neck like some aborigine because he refused to let her cut it, planted in the mud below her and looking up disconsolately at Will. "Captain?" he asked. "You want I should fetch General Meade and the sled?"

"That's right," Will said, smiling now, at ease, everything going according to plan. "Good boy, smart boy. He knows his business." And then he reached in his pocket, extracted a nickel and held it up to the light. "You see this? This is yours if you can hitch up the mule and get the sled down there to the beach in twenty minutes flat."

The boy just stared blankly. "What is it?"

"What is it? It's a nickel. It's money. You know what money is, don't you?"

Very slowly, as the schooner swayed in a web of diminishing waves and the distant hands furled the sails and the sun shone weakly in the gouges and puddles that hopscotched across the yard and on down the ravaged road, he shook his head. "Not much use for it, really," he said, looking out to sea and then gazing back up at Will, his eyes squinted against the sun. "Not out here, anyways."

The main thing the shearers did, aside from the shearing itself, that is, was eat. They weren't discriminating and they didn't want dainty foods or any of the dishes out of the recipe book she'd got from her mother who'd got it in turn from her own mother. Quantity was what they required: lamb, mutton, turkey and salt pork, with fried abalone if it was available, beans, bread, potatoes and the corn tortillas Ida quickly learned to press on the griddle and serve in great towering stacks, all of it drenched in a sauce concocted from rendered lamb fat, chopped onions, canned tomatoes, crushed chili peppers and a good fistful of every kind of spice in the pantry.

That first night, they were fourteen for dinner, including Mr. Mills and Mr. Nichols, the table extended by means of the desk from Edith's room and every chair in the house pressed into service, which still left them short so that two of the shearers had to make do with overturned buckets. She attempted to seat Mills at the head of the table—he was the one who'd built the house, after all, and the minute he walked in the door she felt out of place, an interloper, a squatter—but he wouldn't hear of it. "No, no, Mrs. Waters," he said, spreading his arms wide to take in the expanse of the room, the dim hallway and dimmer kitchen beyond, "this is your place now." He was shorter than she remembered, heavier, with a paunch and a pair of muttonchop whiskers that seemed to tug his face in two directions at once. His skin was mottled—patches of normal coloration alternating with parchment white, as if he'd been spattered with paint. Or guano. *This is your place now.* Cold comfort.

She sat at Will's right and she put Nichols—stiff, formal, a thirty-six-year-old bachelor who was dressed as if he were about to board the cable car for Nob Hill and who just happened to have ten thousand dollars to invest, or so Will claimed and she fervently hoped, hoped as much as she'd ever hoped for anything in her life—beside him. Edith, aglow in her new dress and barely able to contain her excitement—new faces amongst them, Nichols a gentleman and from San Francisco no less—was next to her, and Ida, in the intervals between serving the dishes, sat beside Edith. Jimmie was next to Ida, with Adolph across the table and the six shearers, dark silent men with leaping eyes who must have been Indians or Mexicans or some combination of the two, were at the far end. Will was in his Sunday best and she was wearing her blue dress, the one he liked so much, and she'd done her hair up in a chignon. There was a bouquet of wildflowers. She lit the candles herself.

The cuisine—a pair of turkeys stuffed with cornbread, a pot of beans, mashed potatoes and a puree of the butternut squash Mills had brought along as a gift, as well as coffee, bread pudding for dessert and red wine in quantity—might not have been the sort of thing the shearers were used to, but between the six of them, and Jimmie, of course, they reduced what was left of the turkeys to small reliquaries of chewed-over bones and scraped the serving bowls so meticulously Ida would have had to look twice to find anything to wash in them. To a man, they never said a word through the entire meal. From their end of the table came only the soft moist smack of mastication and the click of utensils, and if she'd spent a frantic half hour fretting over her table settings, it came to nothing. The minute they sat down, each of them produced his own knife, outsized things, sharp enough for surgery, and they used them variously as cutting implements, forks and serving spoons.

The irony wasn't lost on her. Four months ago she'd been entertaining the Kents and Abbotts in the apartment on Post Street, and now she was here in this drafty sheep-stinking ranch house, breaking bread with men who looked as if they'd never been introduced to a bar of soap. She sipped her wine and looked morosely round the table. Will was talking. Mills was talking. Jimmie murmured something to Adolph, who grunted, and Edith tried to draw Nichols out on the subject of the theater, but he said he'd been traveling and couldn't remember when he'd last been to a show.

She asked about Mrs. Mills—Irene—picturing her back in Santa Barbara in her comfortable house, the wind and the waves and the travails of the sheep nothing to her now, wondering if she dared ask about the date circled on the calendar, but Mills—*Call me Hiram*—just said she was fine. "Does she miss the place, miss it here, I mean?" she asked, and she couldn't help herself though she already knew the answer. "Oh, yes, of course she does," he said, his eyes locked on hers in the throes of his sincerity, though he was lying, anyone could see that. "We both do. It was a true . . . *privilege* to live out here."

The meal went on. There was small talk—news of the world, details relating to the running of the ranch—but it was Mills carrying the conversation and Mills was dull. The candles flickered and the stove hissed, emitting a faint scorched odor of the ironwood roots they'd dug up to burn, the trees themselves long gone, but the dense hot-burning roots remaining in the earth like buried treasure. Nichols didn't say much, responding when he was spoken to, offering up the odd comment on the tenderness of the turkey or the decor of the house ("Very nicely done, really—much more comfortable than I'd expected. For a ranch house"). He held himself with a rigidity that seemed to betoken a military background, either that or some sort of spinal complaint, and he wore a mustache identical to Will's, except that it was pure dead-of-night black, whereas Will's had gone to gray—or white, in fact.

In the expansive moment when Ida brought out the dessert, the pudding thick with raisins and drowning in vanilla sauce, Will, as if he couldn't bear it any longer, turned to Nichols and asked if by any chance he was a military man. "Or formerly, I mean. Like myself."

Nichols looked startled—or perhaps bemused. "Me?" he said, and here the mustache lifted at both corners of his mouth and a stained tooth edged in gold revealed itself. "Hardly. I worked for my father out of school, then went east for an education, which, unfortunately, I never succeeded in completing. For a degree, that is."

She was going to ask about that—*Was it one of the Boston schools?*—by way of finding common ground, putting him at his ease, but her voice stuck in her throat and she had to turn away and press a hand to her mouth, fighting the urge to cough with everything she had. They knew she was ill. They'd heard the rumors, she was sure of it, but she wasn't going to let it show, not if it killed her.

"And then," Nichols went on, tapping delicately at his lips with one of the mismatched napkins she'd managed to come up with, "my father passed on and left me a little something which Hiram here"—a glance for Mills—"has just about convinced me to put to work for my own benefit. For the benefit of us all, that is. You really do have an impressive operation," he said, his eyes drifting from her to Will. "A very unique opportunity, isn't it?"

Will assured him that it was—and so did Mills. It was a once-in-a-lifetime opportunity, Mills told him, and then repeated himself, "Once-in-a-lifetime. And as I think I've explained to you, the only reason I'm willing to sell is that I'm just too old anymore to be fussing around with boats and tracking sheep up in the hills."

She'd managed to catch herself, her eyes watering from the effort, a thin wheeze of regurgitated air rattling in her throat. Mills kept talking. He was a salesman, that was what he was. But his logic was faulty: he was no older than Will. And what did that have to say about this little transaction, not to mention their lives here? She wanted to step in, change the subject—couldn't they see they were pressing too hard, scaring him off?—but it was all she could do just to breathe at the moment. She held the wineglass to her lips, sipping, breathing, sipping, breathing, the first withering cough lurking just below the surface.

"No," Mills sighed, taking up his glass and setting it down again, "this is a young man's game, I'm afraid, though either partner could certainly run the place. Lord knows I did it, all on my own—till Will came in, that is—and for seventeen of the best years of my life. This place," he said, revolving one hand as if it contained a miniature crystal globe of the island and everything on it, "is a kind of paradise. Paradise right here on earth."

A silence descended over the table. Nichols dropped his eyes, no doubt calculating just how far that once-in-a-lifetime opportunity would take him. The pudding went round. Ida produced the coffee cups. The shearers looked sated, drowsy, ready to find their way out to the bunkhouse amidst the explosion of stars overhead and the yeasty warm wind-borne odor of the flock.

It was Edith who finally spoke up. "Yes," she said, her eyes fixed on Nichols, "it's all that, just as my father and Mr. Mills say, but I don't know if you realize how dreadful the weather can be. You've had sunshine today, and very little wind—"

"A little harsh weather can't put me off," he said, that faint smile lifting the corners of his mustache.

"But you can't begin to imagine," Edith went on, using her hands to elaborate. "It seems like we're living in the eye of a hurricane here—or not the eye, what do you call it? The edge, the outer edge." She shot Will a glance and Marantha recognized her look, a combination of the coquettish and satiric, as if this were all a grand joke. Was she trying to undercut him, was that it? Defy him? Squash the deal? It was her father who'd taken her out of school, disrupted her life, and now she was getting her own back, pushing the limits, needling him when he was most vulnerable. It was spite, pure meanness. "Edith," she heard herself say. "Edith, wouldn't you like another helping of the pudding? It's your favorite—"

Edith ignored her. "Mother's come here for the air, you know, and I can't think we've had three days of sunshine in all the time we've been here. It's damp, Mr. Nichols, damp and cold and unhealthy."

"Edith."

"And the wind." Edith had her dramatic face on, conscious that everyone was looking at her, even the shearers. "It's so fierce, so loud and hateful"—a pause, another look for Will, for her father, only him—"it just makes you feel so lonely you want to die."

And then there were the sleeping arrangements. Mills volunteered to take a place in the bunkhouse with Adolph, Jimmie and the shearers, but Will protested—"Good God, Hiram, you built the place yourself, worked it, raised your family in this house, and we can't have you crawling off out there like a hired hand"—and Mills, as if to show how magnanimous he was, just shook his head side to side in denial. "If it's good enough for Jimmie"—and here he shot a look down the length of the table to where the boy still lingered in the hope of a glance from Edith, though the pudding was long gone and Adolph and the shearers vanished into the night—"then it's good enough for me, isn't that right, Jimmie? And it's your house now, Will, and I wouldn't want to upset you or your family."

"That's very generous of you, but still it wouldn't be an inconvenience to us, not at all, wouldn't you say so, Minnie?"

She and Edith had stayed on, glad for the company. They each had a cup of coffee before them, but the coffee had grown cold. In the interim, Nichols had produced three Cuban cigars and Will had brought out a bottle of brandy he'd been saving for a special occasion—unlike the whiskey.

They were all watching her. What had Will said? No matter. She shook her head and flashed her eyes as if nothing could please her more than having her house invaded, then raised the handkerchief to her mouth and coughed, just once, choking back the residue. She was tired. Exhausted. She hadn't realized until that moment just how much the evening had cost her. "We thought," she said, struggling to clear her voice, "that Mr. Nichols might want to take the spare room on this floor, across from Ida's—Ida can always share with Edith—and that would leave Ida's room for you, Mr. Mills, *Hiram . . .*" She attempted to cover herself with a laugh, but that was risky the way she was feeling, because a laugh, the slightest tickle in her throat, could bring on a coughing fit. "That is"—she snatched a breath—"if you really don't mind giving up all those bedbugs out there in the bunkhouse."

The detail she didn't mention was that her husband would in that case be sleeping in the master bedroom, if you could call it that, at least until the business had been transacted and the guests were safely out of sight.

"I wouldn't want to put you out," Mills said, softening. He knew what the bunkhouse was like, knew better than anyone, except maybe Jimmie.

"Or me either." Nichols had set down his glass and was giving her that faint smile, the gold outline of his tooth glinting in the light of the candles, which were guttering now in pools of wax.

"Oh, no," she said, her voice so husky she might have been growling, "it's no trouble at all."

But of course it was, as her husband was to discover when he came plodding up the stairs after the others had gone off to bed. She was lying there waiting for him, propped up on the pillows, and she wasn't reading or knitting or doing anything at all except watching for him to come through the door. The handle clicked, rose, fell, and there he was, unsteady on his feet, tipsy with wine, with brandy, looking needy, looking hopeful. "I hope you won't mind," she said, her eyes leading him to the pallet she'd made up in the corner, on the floor beneath the window: sheet, blanket and pillow, the thinnest of horsehair mattresses salvaged from the bunkhouse.

He stood there a long moment, rocking ever so slightly over the twin fulcrums of his hips, and then he began to unbutton his shirt, his hands clumsy, his fingers thick as blocks of wood. She almost went to him, almost slipped from bed to help him out of his clothes as if he were a child, almost relented, but it was all too much, all her resentments rushing back at her on a howling icy internal wind that chilled her to the marrow, to her soul, to the bottom of everything.

"I'm sorry, Will. It's just that I can't bear the weight of you beside me. Not the way I am now. I'm sorry. I truly am."

Nichols

Whether it was because of the excitement of having company in the house she couldn't say, but during the week that Mills, Nichols and the shearers were there, she began to feel stronger, day by day. The coughing tapered off. The phlegm she brought up, especially in the mornings, seemed looser and there was no tinge of blood. She began helping Ida and Edith with the meals and even found time to work in the flower garden she'd planted up against the fence in the front yard. And once, out of curiosity, she'd gone out to the corral to watch the shearers at their work.

It must have been the second or third day of the shearing. The weather was clear for a change, the wind soft, almost balmy. When Will saw her making her way across the yard after breakfast with her parasol and knitting basket, he swung open the gate and came to her, his face lit with a smile of the purest pleasure. He'd wanted her to take an active interest, and here she was, out of the house, in the sunshine, interested. "Minnie," he called, holding a hand out to her, "come and watch. You'll like this, I think."

He was in his work clothes, his trousers spattered with mud, chaff in his hair and all down his sleeves and the front of his shirt as if he'd been out haying. But he hadn't been haying—that was months off yet. He'd been wrestling with the sheep, that was what it was, as she was soon to see, helping the shearers pin them down while they clipped the fleece from their bodies in continuous sheets so neatly proportioned it was as if the animals had been wearing jackets that only needed to be unbuttoned and slipped off. "I hope so," she said. "The whole business seems so mysterious to me." She let out a laugh. "I never imagined wool came from anyplace other than a shop."

His smile died and then fluttered back into place. "Listen," he said, "let me get you a chair and you can sit over there, just outside the corner of the corral, and see what we're about. This is all new to me too, you know."

And so he found her a chair and she sat there, out of range of the mud the animals kicked up when they were flipped over on their backs and their legs pinioned so that the shearers, one man to a sheep, could transform them from squat comfortable-looking things to puny bleating sacks of skin that careened off to huddle in the next pen as if they were embarrassed by their own nakedness. Will waded right in, and it lifted her to see his enthusiasm, the way he snatched up an animal the minute Jimmie or Adolph, whose job it was to go on horseback and round them all up, released one through the gate. And Mills, Mills too. Mills and her husband were working in concert, making sure the shearers were fed a new animal the moment they finished with the previous one, then taking the fleeces and stuffing them into the huge canvas sacks that bloated out like sausages as the morning went on.

The sun was pleasant—heat, for a change, real heat—and she stayed there perched on the chair long after she'd grown bored with the process unfolding before her, the sheep bleating out their terror and broadcasting their hard black pellets of excrement even as the men fought to hold them until they went lax and submitted, then the fleece lying there in the dirt and the naked animal scurrying away to hide itself amongst the naked others. Across the yard, in their pen, the pigs were silent, as if contemplating what lay in store for them. Even the chickens and turkeys, usually so active around the barnyard, were keeping out of sight. She was thinking about that, about how the animals seemed to know what was going on though they weren't conscious in any rational way, or at least that's what she'd always believed, when Nichols emerged from the house and came strolling across the yard to her.

He held himself stiffly, as if he were uncomfortable in his clothes, but his voice was pleasant enough as he called out a greeting to her. "Good morning, Mrs. Waters," he intoned, coming up to stand beside her so that his shadow momentarily took away the sun. "Are you enjoying the shearing? The process, I mean?"

She studied him a moment, a tall man, nearly as tall as Will, and dressed impeccably, as if he were on his way to a gentlemen's club instead of coming out to peer into a muddy pen full of terrified sheep on an island stuck fast in its own solitary sphere. "Yes," she said, smiling up at him, and she was glad she'd powdered her face and put on a bit of rouge, though most mornings she didn't bother, not anymore, not out here. "Or no, truthfully. For the first couple, it's interesting, I suppose, to see how it's done, but I feel sympathy for the poor animals. They seem so terrified."

He made as if to prop one elbow on the rail of the pen—or corral, as it was called here—but then seemed to think better of it. "But they're not actually hurt in any way, are they?"

"No," she had to admit. "Aside from the odd nick and scratch, I suppose. I'm told that the shears get dull quickly here because there's so much sand caught in the wool. Sand," she said, letting her eyes drift beyond the rail and the commotion of bodies there to the distant rising slopes. "It's the curse of the place. It's in everything—your clothes, the bedding. Set the table half an hour before dinner and you've got to wipe the plates clean again before you can sit down to eat."

There was a shout from one of the men, something in Spanish, a curse, and she saw that one of the sheep had managed to kick the shears from the man's hand and break free. It came toward them, trembling, wild-eyed, until her husband, his face reddened with the exertion, managed to seize it from behind and drag it back to the dark little man who was still cursing in his own hermetic language. *Puta,* he spat. *Puta. La reputa que lo parió.*

"You see?" she said. "And the lambs must have their tails docked, of course. I couldn't watch that. It seems so cruel."

"So why do it at all?"

"Something to do with the meat." She glanced up at him then. It came to her that he didn't know the first thing about this, knew even less than she did. Either that or he was testing her. And if he was, she was destined to fail. "It would grow into the tail instead of on the body itself, where—"

"Where you want your lamb chops to be." He gave her his thin smile. "You seem quite well versed."

"Oh, no, not really. I've only been listening to what Will tells me, that's all." She let out a laugh. "I'm hardly a farmwife, or not yet, anyway. In fact, until now, I've never really been outside a city in my life."

"I'd never have guessed," he said, and it took a moment to realize he was making a joke. But was it a joke? Or a criticism?

More shouting from the pen, another animal breaking free to rush pell-mell from one side to the other, giving up its terror in a ragged choking cry of despair.

"All right," he said, turning back to her, and again he made as if to prop an elbow on the rail and again thought better of it, "I concede your point. But each of these animals will live on for years, whereas with cattle or hogs the whole animal has to be sacrificed in order to get any value out of it. And there's very little loss out here, or so I'm told. No wolves or dogs or bears or anything like that. No catamounts. And the only fences you need are to guide the animals in for shearing and keep them out of the pasture until the hay is mowed, isn't that right?"

"Yes, I suppose so." And then it came to her that she should be praising the place, trying to sell him on it so that he would come in as partner and she could go back to town and her things and live like a human being and either get well or not. She wouldn't want to die out here, that much she knew. It was already like being a soul in limbo. She was bored. She was afraid. She wanted release, only that. "It's a remarkable place," she said. "Truly remarkable." And she almost added, *A once-in-a-lifetime opportunity,* but caught herself.

He was studying her out of eyes that were too close-set, too small, as if his face had been pinched in the womb. His heavy mustache masked the expression of his mouth, but he might have been smiling, or at least she thought he was. "Seems like you're trying to sell me on the place," he said.

She wanted to deny it, but she gave him a smile instead, if only to cover herself. "I suppose I am. But it's worth it, worth everything we've invested— the opportunity. I couldn't be happier. I couldn't."

And now he *was* grinning, the mustache levitating above a set of stained lower teeth. "I'm flattered," he said, "but there's really no need. Hiram, Will and I signed the transfer papers last night."

"Yes," she said, "yes," and she didn't know what she was assenting to, her heart pounding, the blood rushing to her face. He shifted again and the full glare of the sun struck her so that she had to raise a hand to her eyes. There was a long expiring gasp from the pen as one of the sheep was released to clatter away on unsteady legs. "When—?" she asked, but couldn't finish the question.

"Your husband hasn't told you?"

"Well, I—he was up especially early this morning, because of the shearing, that is, and I must have overslept . . ."

"Everything's fine," he said, and he held out a hand to her as if to conclude a bargain, but she merely stared at it in bewilderment. "I'm pleased to be your new partner, yours and your husband's. I'm sure we'll all prosper together."

"I don't know what to say. I'm delighted. Truly delighted." She was soaring suddenly, so elated she hardly noticed his embarrassment as he dropped the hand to his side, rebuffed, but then wives didn't conclude bargains, husbands did. "It's just—when will you be coming out to take over?"

"Oh, I won't be coming out. I don't think your husband would stand for it, do you? No, no, you misunderstand me: I'm to be a silent partner only."

"Silent?" she echoed, and she couldn't hide her disappointment.

"Yes," he said, "in name only." And here was that look again: was he mocking her, was that it? Was he intentionally trying to drive a stake through her, torture her, bring her crashing to earth like one of Ord's wing-shot eagles? "Don't worry," he said, "you can plan on staying as long as you like."

The Fog

And then they were all gone and the household went back to normal. The wool—a bumper crop of it, or so Will claimed—was stored in the barn, safe in the overstuffed canvas sacks, awaiting the completion of the final section of the road and the return of Charlie Curner's schooner, promised vaguely for two or three weeks on. Ida put away the big stewpot and went back to setting the table for six, baking every third day instead of every morning. They saw the last of the tortillas, as if anyone had wanted them in the first place—tasteless scorched things as dull as the unleavened corn mush they were shaped from. Evenings were tranquil. No more watching Will, Nichols and Mills sit around jawboning at one another, no more pretense or show. They went back to the Ouija board, to whist, muggins, euchre, to the long silences and the quiet ticking of the stove.

The only thing that was off was the weather. It had held for the shearing, and she thanked God for that, but as soon as the schooner pulled out of the harbor it turned dismal, days of continuous rain giving way to a fog so opaque you couldn't see ten feet ahead of you. When she went out to scatter feed for the chickens, one of the few tasks she actually enjoyed, she had to wait till they emerged from nothingness like the ghosts of chickens, which, she supposed, was what each of them would become in time, their eggs stripped from them, then their feathers and the sweet meat that clung to the bone—pecking ghosts, squawking dismally in the ether of another world. Ida got lost on the way to the spring, which couldn't have been more than three hundred yards away, just above the spot where the road began to dip down into the canyon. The men went off to work the road and as soon as they stepped from the front porch they vanished like coins dropped into a well. Just finding the W.C. was a trial, and she trained herself to keep her eyes on the ground so as to pick out the thin muddy ribbon of a path leading away from the back steps and across the yard, through the gate and into the field where eventually the blistered vertical plane of the latrine's door would loom into view. If your luck held. Two or three times, in the urgency of her need, she'd found herself lost in a damp dripping void, nothing visible but her skirts and shoes and a pulp of slick dark vegetation crushed beneath her feet.

On this particular morning—it was the first of March, two months into her exile—she felt well enough to help Ida clean up after breakfast, standing at the counter and drying the plates as Ida fished them from the dishwater. She put them back in the cupboard as neatly as she could, though what she really wanted was to smash them on the floor, but that wouldn't have been practical, not unless they were going to set up a potter's wheel and start from scratch. The fact was that she'd all but given up on her own crockery coming now. It was lost somewhere, lost in transit—or in Charlie Curner's hold. She didn't want to think of him leaving it behind on the pier or pitching it overboard in a heavy sea. She could picture the box, the newspaper with which she'd wrapped each plate, each cup and saucer and the gravy boat and all the rest, in order to protect them from rough handling, but in the end, she supposed, it hadn't really mattered. What mattered was this: Ida handed her a dish, one of these dishes, chipped and cracked and ugly, and she wiped it dry and set it atop the others. It was something to do. A sop to the boredom. As they worked, Ida did most of the talking, chattering away about anything that came into her head, but it was pleasant enough, calming, the whole house hushed and peaceful in the grip of the fog. Afterward, she sat at the kitchen table with a cup of tea, basking in the warmth of the stove, then took a thumbed-over copy of *Harper's Bazaar,* which she'd already read twice through, and went out the back door to the W.C.

She wasn't really paying attention, thinking about Edith, how she was falling behind in the lessons they'd set out for her—reading mostly, in literature and history both, but some maths and sciences too and the exercises in the French text the teacher at the school in Santa Barbara had thrust on her the week before they'd left—because she lacked discipline and her mother hadn't been able to summon the energy to bear down on her, for which her mother was feeling guilty. Before she knew it, she'd lost the path, one clump of crushed weed looking much like the next and a gray impenetrable cocoon of fog spun all around her. There were no landmarks. The house was gone. The fences. The field. Green Mountain. She kept on, watching her feet, her steps shuffling and cautious. She could step in a hole, turn an ankle, break a leg, and where was the blessed thing? It was in this direction, wasn't it? But no, it couldn't have been because she would have caught the odor of it by now, the latrine, the stink-hole, and why couldn't she have a flush toilet like everybody else in the world? A bathroom, a door that locked behind you, tile on the floor and a sink to wash up after? She paused to sniff the air, but the fog was like a wet rag pressed to her face and all she could smell was the familiar odor of rot drifting up from the shoreline. Then she stopped altogether. Stood still. Listened. There was nothing, no sound at all, not even the droning of the seals.

She didn't know how long she'd been wandering, the magazine clutched in a tight roll in one hand, her insides churning, when she gave up. It was like that night in the bedroom, the night of the lamb, when finally she'd found the chamber pot, but there was no pot here, no toilet, nothing but dirt and weed and the fog that was strangling her till she found herself beginning to cough before she was even conscious of it. Miserable, shamed, she lifted her skirts, squatted there in the void like some barnyard animal and released her bowels.

Nothing but grass to clean herself with. Everything wet, cold, filthy. She tore a page from the magazine, but that was filthy too, the touch of it on her skin, on her privates, like an electric shock. She stood, gathered herself. How had she come to this, this humiliation, this barbarity? Was this what was visited on the dying, this tearing away from the life lived and worth living? This deracination? And here was her epitaph: *Marantha Scott Waters, 1850– 18——? Deracinated.*

She was cold. She coughed, kept on coughing, a spasm sweeping over her so immediately, so desperately, she didn't have time to brace herself, and then the phlegm was coming up inside her and where was she to spit it? On the ground. In the dirt. And why not? She'd paid ten thousand dollars for the privilege, hadn't she?

She spat, wiped her lips on the back of her hand. She couldn't catch her breath. The coughing wouldn't stop, each cough crashing down atop the next like bricks falling from a cliff. Then she was down on her knees in the wet, pounding at her breastbone, and what had Dr. Erringer told her? That phthisics like her (he wouldn't call his patients consumptives, never, because the term gave too much agency to the disease) could more often than not expect a complete cure simply from living quietly, exercising moderately and above all taking in the untainted air of the countryside. Yes, and where was he now? Sitting by the fire in his offices, his feet propped up on an embroidered footstool, the wainscoting glowing behind him, anything he could possibly want just a tap of the bell away, a sandwich, a steak, hot cider, a nurse to come in and ease the tension in his shoulders after a long day of dismissing one patient after another with smiles and promises and the medicines that did nothing but make you feel as if you were dead already. Morphia. Morpheus. Sleep and Poetry.

By the time Ida found her—"Mrs. Waters? Ma'am? Are you out there?"— she was sprawled in the grass like a broken umbrella, chilled through and coughing so violently it felt as if her lungs had been turned inside out. How much time had gone by she couldn't say—she'd been elsewhere, in her mother's arms, racing her sister down the sun-dappled sidewalk to the drugstore, reading aloud from the Book of Revelation ("He will wipe away every tear from their eyes, and death shall be no more") while the pastor and her mother looked on as if she'd just reserved her place in heaven—but it seemed as if she'd heard Ida calling for hours. She tried to respond, tried to cry for help, but her voice wouldn't come. She'd asked Dr. Erringer about that, about the huskiness of her voice, its weakness, the way it failed her at crucial times, and he'd given an abrupt little nod of his head. "Nothing to worry over," he told her. "A symptom of the disease, that's all. The sort of thing all phthisics have to confront to one degree or another."

"Mrs. Waters?" There seemed to be a light in the distance—a lantern, Ida's lantern—and she gathered her legs under her and laid one palm in the cold muck to push herself up, so weak suddenly she sank back down again as if her legs had been cut out from under her. She might have stayed there until the ravens came to pluck out her eyes and the beetles surged up out of the earth to reduce her, to *consume* her, but for the shadow that came hurtling out of the void to fall on her in a rush of churning paws and frantic barking.

"Ma'am?"

"I'm here," she whispered, the dog nosing at her, licking her face, muddying her dress till it was no better than a rag.

Ida's face loomed up out of the void, weirdly illuminated by the lantern she held out before her. "Ma'am? Are you all right? Are you hurt?"

It took her a moment. The coughing came in waves, like breakers hitting the beach. She pushed the dog away. Cleared her throat. And finally, though Ida was right there, seeing her at her weakest and worst, she leaned over to spit in the grass because she couldn't help herself, the sputum grainy and discolored, the taste in her mouth so foul it was as if she'd tried to swallow some dead thing. But then the dead thing was already inside her, wasn't it?

"I'm all right," she said. "I'm fine. I'm just—I seem to have lost my way."

Bao Yu

The days fell away like the skin of a rotten fruit. She was in bed, waiting for the hemorrhage to come on while the household tiptoed round her, Will grave, Edith so white-faced it was as if she were wearing a mask. But then the hemorrhage didn't come—she had a cold, that was all, her eyes itching and her nose running and a bronchial cough compounding the problem, yes, but it was a cold and nothing more, the sort of thing anyone was susceptible to. A cold, that was all.

The fog lifted. It rained. There was a day of sun. And then she was up on her feet again, sniffling perhaps, weakened, humiliated (she'd had to do her business in the chamber pot and it was Ida who had to see it there and dispose of it), but able to work at sewing the lambrequins for the shelves and go out of doors to feed the turkeys and chickens and walk round the yard and even partway down the road for exercise.

She was alone in the house, a Sunday afternoon, the sun high and everyone else taking the day off—or the afternoon, anyway—to go out hunting Indian artifacts, pottery shards, arrowheads. Edith was on horseback, Will on one mule, Adolph on the other, Jimmie and Ida following along on foot. They'd begged her to come in order to make her feel a part of things—at least Will and Ida had, Edith so swept up in the excitement of the horse and the treasure hunt she didn't even try to hide her indifference—and that was thoughtful and she was touched, but she told them she wasn't feeling up to it. Ida made a little moue of sympathy. Or pity. Will had just nodded.

For once, the house was warm. Will had built up the fire before he left, very solicitous—*Can I get you anything? Are you sure you don't want to come? It'll be an adventure*—and with the sun shining and the wind down it was pleasant, even in the corner by the front window where there always seemed to be a draft. She brought her crocheting into the parlor and sat there at the window, where the light was good, thinking to work on the shirt she was making for Edith, but as soon as she got settled she laid it aside. She was bored. Profoundly bored. It was the fault of this place, of course, each day identical to the next, nothing to do but work at sewing, knitting, cooking, cleaning, and the same faces to look into and the same unchanging conversation every night. The same cards even. The four walls. The bowed ceiling. Will would make a comment about the sheep, the barn, his dynamite sticks. Jimmie would say something in return, Adolph staring across the room as if he were working out the metaphysics of sheep dip or the broken haft of a spade. *Edith,* she would say, just to hear herself, *what are you reading?* Edith, looking up from her book: *Nothing. A novel.*

She got up from the chair and drifted across the room to the table where Edith had left her latest book, the one she'd insisted on buying before they'd left the mainland, and idly picked it up. It was by E. R. Roe, a name she vaguely recognized. Light reading, she supposed. Harmless enough. The author had written a preface to this, his fourth novel, and it really wasn't so much a preface as an advertisement. Her eyes fell on the last line: "A glad zest and hopefulness might be inspired even in the most jaded and ennui-cursed, were there in our homes such simple, truthful natures as that of my heroine, and it is in the sphere of quiet homes—not elsewhere—I believe that woman can best rule and save the world."

Rule and save the world. She closed the book and set it back on the table, angry suddenly. If only they'd stayed in San Francisco. If only she'd resisted. Rule? She ruled nothing. And as far as saving the world, she'd give everything she had if she could only just save herself, for Edith's sake if nothing else, because what would Edith do without her?

It was then that something made her look up, some sixth sense, and she caught her breath: there was a face in the window, a man's face, staring back at her. If she'd been home, in the apartment or even the rented house in Santa Barbara, she wouldn't have been so startled—this man, he was a Chinaman, she saw that now, a Chinaman holding something up to the glass as if to offer it to her, would have been a delivery boy from the laundry or a yardman or some such, and Will would have dealt with him. But here, his appearance was so unexpected, so *impossible,* it was as if he were an apparition from another realm, and it jolted her. She didn't move. Didn't breathe. Just stood there staring like an animal in the zoo.

His eyes were fixed on hers. He reached out and tapped at the glass with his index finger, very softly, politely, and gave a discreet shake to the object—objects—he was holding aloft in his other hand. Dun things, flattened, gathered together on a loop of wire. And what were they? Slabs of meat? Fish of some sort? He smiled suddenly, his eyes lost in their creases, his face shining and hopeful. It came to her that he was harmless, a castaway, survivor of a shipwreck, a man in need, perhaps hungry and thirsty, maybe even injured. She went to the door, pulled it open and stepped out onto the porch.

The man widened his grin, gave an abbreviated bow. He was short, shorter than she, wearing an embroidered skullcap and a long silk tunic over a pair of ordinary twilled cotton trousers. His hair was braided in a queue. On his feet, gum boots smeared with the residue of one sort of oceanic creature or another. *"Bao yu,"* he said, holding the dun things out to her.

"Are you thirsty?" she asked. "Hungry? Has your ship gone down, is that it?"

"Bao yu," he repeated. "You take."

He handed her the loop of wire and she had no choice but to take it from him. What she was holding—and it was heavier than it had looked—was dried abalone, that was what it was, and this man was one of the coolies Will had told her about, men brought out to the deserted islands off the Pacific Coast to live in crude huts for months at a time, collecting, boiling, pounding and drying abalone for shipment back to China. And here he was, presenting her with abalone she didn't want, abalone he might very well have taken from these very shores, from her own private stock, stolen abalone. He was watching her closely. This wasn't merely a gift—he wanted something in return.

"You give," he said.

She was no longer feeling generous. "Where did you get these?" she demanded, imagining some hidden encampment infesting the surface of the island like an open sore.

He lifted his chin, still smiling, and shot his eyes in the direction of the harbor. There was a boat there, and how had she missed it? His boat. A sprawling low-slung junk with sails furled and a triangular red-bordered flag gyrating in the breeze atop the middle mast. She'd seen boats like it in the harbor at San Francisco, boats that brought Chinese goods and spices and the coolies to work the railroads and live one atop the other on Grant Avenue as if that was the way they preferred it. She was amazed all over again—had this man actually come all the way across the sea from China to stand here on the porch of her assumed house and bargain with her? The thought was staggering. No, it was comical, absurd. What did she have that he could possibly want?

"*What* do I give?" she asked. "What do you want?"

"You give meat," he said, and it all became clear. He wanted mutton, wanted lamb, of course he did. If you ate nothing but fish, fish three meals a day, you'd want anything else, anything you could get, viands especially—but to offer her abalone, dried abalone, no less, when she lived atop a trove of it, was ridiculous. And he wanted *lamb* in return?

"No, I do not give meat," she said, unconsciously aping his fractured syntax. "And I thank you for this"—and here she tried to return the abalone but he took a step back, thrusting both hands in his pockets and shaking his head in denial—"but I'm afraid we really have no use for it." His eyes were wide, his smile gone. "You see," she began, and she was going to explain that they had all the fresh abalone they wanted, that they owned it and owned the land he was standing on and that he was welcome, as a visitor, to a cup of tea and perhaps some cornbread or the platter of cookies Ida had baked just that morning, but there would be no trading in the offing, especially of meat, which they needed for themselves, for their own benefit and welfare and profit, when she was startled by a movement at the gate across the yard—there was a second Chinaman now, dressed identically to the one on the porch, and he too had a string of dried abalone. The second man—he was older, much older, a thin white beard trailing away from his chin—came across the yard to her, the chickens rushing his ankles in the hope of feed and then scattering just as quickly when they saw their mistake, and he was smiling too.

"No," she was saying, holding up the palm of one hand to discourage him, when both men turned their heads at the rhythmic clatter of hooves thundering up the road. In the next moment, Will came hurtling across the yard in a storm of flying clods, even as the second Chinaman, the old one, froze in place. Will was riding Mike, the horse Edith had left on, and the first thing that went through her head was that Edith was injured, thrown in a ditch somewhere, her leg broken, her arm—or maybe she'd suffered a concussion, maybe she'd been disfigured or worse, much worse.

The horse was lathered. Will's face showed nothing. "You," he said, pointing first to the man in the yard and then swinging round to indicate the one on the porch, "and you. Both of you." He'd raised his voice by degrees and he was shouting now, red-faced and angry. "I want you to clear out of here, go back to your boat."

Neither man moved. They were watching him closely, watching his lips, their expressions blank.

"Now!" Will shouted, wheeling round on the horse. "Don't you understand English? I said, *Get out!*" Mike stamped, blew, his sides heaving. The sun made everything look hard and unreal.

"Will, it's all right," she said, calling to him from the porch, though she could barely project her voice. She felt the relief wash over her: this had nothing to do with Edith. He'd seen the boat. He'd come to protect her, to rescue her. "They're harmless. They don't know what you're saying, they don't understand, they—they want to trade. They want meat, that's all, Will."

But her husband wasn't listening. He was in one of his rages. "Poachers!" he shouted, and he made as if to drive the horse at the old man. There was a scramble of legs, the old man frantically backpedaling until his feet got tangled and he went down hard in the mud. She exchanged a look with the first Chinaman in the instant before he stepped off the porch and took to his legs. What she saw there in his face, the hurt and surprise, the fear, made her feel ashamed.

"Will," she said again.

He jerked the horse round and leaned down to glare at her. "You keep out of this," he said. "They have no right, no right!"

She watched till they were out of sight, Will squared up on the horse and driving the two men before him down the road to the harbor, the water shining in the distance, the embankment looming over them like a dark jagged cloud. At some point she realized she was still holding the string of abalone at her side. She could smell them, fruit of the sea, an astringent smell, a smell of iodine and what's left behind when the life is gone. Across the yard, the chickens had gathered to fight over the second string, the one the old man had dropped in the mud. "Here, chick-chick," she said, coming down the steps. "Here, chick, here."

Bones

She slept late the following morning, slipping in and out of her dreams, vaguely aware of a dull intermittent banging from below, as if Will were rebuilding the house from the inside out. Her dreams were of flight, of escape, eagle dreams, but each time she soared the banging brought her back down again. It was maddening. She'd lain awake through the small hours, unable to sleep, the pain in her chest speaking to her in an intimate whisper of the place beyond, all her fears for Edith and her husband and her own dwindling self concentrated in the shadows the lamp couldn't touch.

She went through the motions of dressing, her limbs heavy as spars—she had a vision of the wrecks spread across the bottom of the ocean, the tide shifting them twice a day, timbers lifting and falling again in silent protest—and then she went down the stairs to the kitchen. Ida was sitting at the table there, leafing through a magazine, a cup at her elbow. "Oh," she said, "you're up." And then: "Can I fix you something—eggs, flapjacks? Toast? Would you like some toast?"

It was gray beyond the windows. The wind was blowing. There was a smell of coffee gone cold in the pot. "Toast," she said. "And make me some coffee. Fresh. I don't want anybody's dregs." She stood there a moment in the doorway, running her eyes over the room, everything dirty, irredeemably dirty, the pans blackened inside and out, the cupboards finger-smeared, breakfast dishes piled up on the counter in a pool of whitening grease. It was disgusting. Life was disgusting. "I'll take it in the parlor," she added, already turning to make her way down the hall, and if there was no please and thank you in the exchange, so much the worse. Ida had begun to irritate her. The way she simpered. The way she made up to Will as if he were some sort of terrestrial god, the sole authority on every matter, president, general and chief justice all wrapped up in one. Even the way she looked with her smooth wide brow and the hair that trailed down her neck no matter how many times she pinned it up, her pursed little doll's mouth and sharp green eyes that never missed a thing. And besides, did prisoners in the jailhouse worry about rules of comportment? Survivors of a shipwreck? Where was the please and thank you in that?

She was in a mood and she couldn't help herself. In the parlor—gloomy, damp, cold as ever—she went straight to the stove and saw that the basket beside it, the wood basket, was empty because Ida was too busy with *The Ladies' Home Journal* to bother with anything so trivial as keeping the house above the temperature of a tomb. She flung back the cast-iron door—barely warm to the touch—snatched up the poker and stirred the coals angrily before settling into her chair. And where was Edith? Why couldn't she help? Because she was out walking or riding or hunting seashells, because she was locked in her room reading *Jane Eyre* or *Northanger Abbey* for the sixth time instead of applying herself to her lessons, because she was thoughtless, that was why. She was about to call out to her, to shout her name up the stairwell no matter the strain on her voice, when she happened to glance across the room and catch herself.

It took her a moment to register what she was seeing. Shelves. Will had built a series of shelves into the far wall while she lay struggling for sleep, which explained the banging, but she couldn't imagine why he hadn't waited till she was up and about. What was the hurry? And why would they need shelves in the first place? They couldn't have had more than two dozen books with them and nothing to display, no curios or drawings or sculpture, not even a mantel clock. But there was something there already, she saw that now, vague shapeless forms splayed across the top two shelves as if they'd washed up in a flood, as if the water had rushed through the room while she lay sleeping, or trying to sleep, and left its detritus behind. Puzzled, she got to her feet and crossed the room for a closer look.

At first she thought she was examining a rock collection, thinking Will had suddenly developed some sort of geological fervor, but then she understood: these were artifacts, Indian things, the fruits of yesterday's expedition, arrowheads, a stone knife blade, shell beads, a mortar and pestle, what looked to be a serving bowl scooped from smooth gray stone and tilting ever so slightly away from its uneven base. She was fingering one of the arrowheads—or no, it must have been a spearhead, as long and tapered as a letter opener,

113

and sharp, still sharp after all this time—when she heard footsteps in the hallway behind her. It was Edith, stepping carefully, cradling something in her arms. She was in her charcoal gray skirt and a light shirtwaist, looking pretty, looking groomed for a change, and she seemed to be wearing some sort of ornament, a pale concave object that dangled from her throat on a thin silver chain.

"How do you like it, Mother?" Edith asked, crossing the room to her.

"What is it?"

"A pendant. An Indian pendant. You see?" Edith set down what she was carrying on the corner of the table—more artifacts, dirty things, things that had lain forgotten in the earth, bits of rock and shell and bone—and lifted the pendant on its chain so she could have a closer look.

It was a worked section of abalone shell with a hole drilled dead-center so that it hung perfectly, mother-of-pearl, catching the light and shining as if it had been shaped yesterday. "Very pretty," she said.

"Jimmie found it."

"Jimmie? And he gave it to you?"

"Mother. He couldn't very well wear it himself, could he?"

She was about to say something, to raise some sort of objection—*Jimmie*—when Edith bent to the table, scooped up a handful of the fragments there and held them out to her, cupped in one palm. "Do you know what these are?"

She did. They were shells, grape-colored, chestnut-colored, the shells of the littoral snails you found when you were wading at low tide. "Snail shells?"

Edith had superior knowledge. She was grinning. Enjoying herself. "Look closer—do you see these holes? Do you see that each one of these has been drilled through so they could be strung on a bit of cord? They're money, Mother—this is what the Indians used for money!"

"Really? Then I suppose we're rich—where on earth will we spend it all?"

Edith laughed and it was good to hear. She'd been moping lately—for weeks, it seemed—and if she wasn't immured in her room she was roaming out of doors like the lost and brooding heroine of one of her romances. She was barely civil at meals, peevish and sour-faced, endlessly complaining about being stifled and bored, as if she were the only one suffering, as if they could just snap their fingers and go back to the apartment they could no longer afford, at least till the wool went to market. If it ever went. If Will ever finished the road and Charlie Curner ever brought his boat back and the

114

world stopped cranking round its axis and the oceans went still as the water in the dishpan.

"How I wish it were true," Edith said. "Even more, I wish the Indians had made things out of gold instead, but Jimmie says they didn't have any gold, only shells. Still, they're pretty, don't you think? I could make a necklace if I could find enough of them."

"Yes, of course," she said, warming to the idea, though the things seemed common enough. "We could use a bit of ribbon to string them, don't you think? Black. Or navy, navy would be nice. Maybe Ida could part with just the smallest length of what you gave her—"

A noise from the direction of the porch made them both look up. In the next moment the front door swung open on Will, in his stocking feet—a flash of light, his thrown shadow—then fell shut behind him. "Minnie," he boomed, "you see what we've done here, Edith and I?" He had a sack slung over one shoulder and she could see that it was weighted, mysterious bulges gathering and shifting as he moved. "And there's more, much more—we really hit the mother lode yesterday, but because of those damned Chinamen I had to leave the better part of it behind. But here," he said, setting down the bag with a click and rustle of the contents within, "see for yourself."

"We went up to Eagle Cave and there were paintings there on the rocks and all sorts of things just lying around," Edith put in. "And then, on one of the bluffs"—turning to Will—"where was it?"

"Harris Point."

"On Harris Point we found a place where there was a whole mountain of shells, thousands and thousands of them, mussel shells, clamshells, abalone, everything the Indians must have been eating since the dawn of time—and there were pits there, depressions in the ground where they'd made their fires, and that got us looking until finally we found where they were buried."

"Under the sand. Probably three or four feet of it just to get to the dirt beneath. But we kept probing, didn't we, Edith? Because we knew we were on to something." Will was reaching into the bag, a magician pulling a rabbit from a hat, and the thing he produced—naked and white and fissured with age—was no artifact. It was a bone. A human bone. He laid it on the shelf beside the rest of the things and then he bent to the sack again, rummaging, its sides swelling and deflating as if the contents had come to life.

She took a step back. She felt flushed suddenly.

Edith said, "I found a bone too. This one, I think"—she held up her right arm and pulled back the sleeve. "Or Jimmie thinks it's this one—the little bone here?"

And now Will: "Here," he said, "here's the prize," and he was holding a skull aloft, a human skull, a skull so small and compact and with teeth so reduced it could only have come from a child.

"But you didn't—those were their graves. Graves, Will. Hallowed ground."

He set the skull carefully down on the top shelf, shifting the stone bowl to one side so that the skull was centered in the middle of the display. "Yes," he said over his shoulder, "they were graves of a sort, I suppose. But certainly not hallowed ground. Not unless one of the Spanish friars took time to consecrate it, but then why would he? In truth, no one really knows much about what went on out here, aside from legends and that sort of thing." And now he turned to her, holding out his palms in extenuation. "They were Indians, that's all. Just Indians."

The rains came back again. The hills got greener, the ocean grayer. The sheep grew into their coats. Coffee ran short, sugar, flour. The wind was a constant. March crept by so slowly she began to score off the days on the calendar, leaning so heavily into her pencil she tore through the paper, and then it was April, April Fools', and she was the fool because Curner hadn't come and the wool hadn't gone and there was no word from Nichols as to whether he'd been able to engage a manager to take over operations and set them free. They'd had plenty of rain, too much rain, a superabundance, and yes, this was an unusual year, Will kept saying, but the dry season was coming because while April might have been the rainiest month back in the east, it wasn't so out here. She felt better, then she felt worse, better again, worse. She spent most of her time sitting by the stove, wrapped in a blanket.

One night, when the thing inside her wouldn't let her sleep, she pushed herself up from the bed, lit a candle and went downstairs to the kitchen, thinking to stoke the fire and put the kettle on. The house was quiet but for the little sounds, the creaking and groaning of the inanimate, the rush of the wind along the outside walls, the patter of mice. When the light of the candle swept over the kitchen in a glancing arc, she saw movement there, a hurried retreat, the creatures vanished in the time it took to recognize them for what they were. Mice. They were nothing to her, one more annoyance, and she'd given up on nagging Will to trap them—what was the use? They were infinite. They belonged here. And she didn't.

She lit the lamp and blew out the candle. Stirred the coals and laid fresh lengths of driftwood in the firebox. The water jug was full, a small blessing, and she tipped it to the kettle, set the kettle atop the stove, then eased herself into a chair at the kitchen table. There was a stack of old magazines and newspapers on the corner of the table, artifacts themselves, long out of date, and though she'd read every page of them twice, twice at least, she picked up a newspaper and settled in to read of events that had transpired in the real world in a time that might as well have been a century ago for all they signified now.

The water came to a boil. She got up and poured out a cupful, flavored it with vanilla extract and a pinch of sugar so as to conserve the last of the tea, and was just about to sit back down at the table when she heard a noise from the hallway. Or no, not the hallway, but Ida's room. It was a cloaked, furtive sound, starting, then stopping, then settling into a rhythmic give and take, slow friction, as if two things, two objects, two *bodies*, were being rubbed together. She froze in place, straining to hear. There it was, there it was again. And then she caught her breath to still the whistling of her lungs and the pain came at her in a sudden triumphant rush, all the air gone out of her, and though she didn't want to give herself away, though she tried to suppress it, she began to cough. It started gently, almost as if she were learning a new kind of respiration, as if she were embracing it, but then it accelerated, harsher and harsher, until her face was aflame and her lungs throbbed and she had to brace herself against the table and spit in the cup and then see it there, her own issue, the only thing she'd ever given birth to, the hard yellow lump of sputum revolving in a wash of tinctured water.

The house had gone silent. Nothing moved. Nothing breathed. Even the wind died. This was a silence of another quality altogether—she could feel it—a deeper silence, a listening silence. Her heart was pounding. Her throat ached. It took her a moment to straighten up, to square her shoulders and catch her breath. Then she started down the hall, very slowly, one step at a time. The floorboards didn't groan—they wouldn't dare—and the ugly whitewashed walls stood mute. When she came to the door of Will's room, the storeroom, the monk's cell, she took an eternity just to lift the handle because she wouldn't make a sound, she refused to, and when the door eased open inch by inch and the uncertain light spilling down the hall from the lamp in the kitchen began to spill here too, she saw the bed pushed up against the wall, Will's bed, and saw that it was empty.

The Weight

After that, things seemed to move forward in a new kind of way, as if the elaborate machinery of the place had been stuck in gear all this time and now it was free to revolve unimpeded. Spring—the drying out—came in the second week of April, just as Will had said it would, fog giving way to a succession of sun-warmed days that seemed to set the island on fire, birds nesting everywhere, the pigs cavorting in their pen, a warm breeze riding up out of the south on a scent of citrus and jasmine. Insects hung over the flowers in the front yard, hummingbirds materialized out of the air and the sheep—mercifully—shifted farther afield, taking their ammoniac reek with them. Will finished the final section of his road and Charlie Curner came at long last to deliver supplies and letters—a whole carton of letters—and stow the sacks of wool in the hold of his schooner, and then the *Evangeline*, her sails gilded with sun and casting a long morning shadow over the waves, made for Santa Barbara, where the market was, where the money was, where Nichols was waiting to get the best possible price and then freight them to the mills all the way across the country. Better yet, Adolph went with him to oversee the transfer, and so they were spared his sourness, at least till the next boat brought him back.

The days lengthened. Sun shone on the porch in the afternoons. She had Edith throw open the windows and doors to let the fresh air scour the mold and carry off the accumulated odors of the place, the reek of ancient grease and cold ash, of dried mud and mouse droppings and people confined through a long wet winter in a house that was no house at all. If she closed her eyes and lifted her face to the sun, she could almost imagine she was in Italy.

Unfortunately, it all came too late, at least for her.

She wouldn't blame Will, though it was the night she'd found his bed empty that the disease came back to claim her all over again, the microbes striking when she was weakest, when she was heartsick, devastated, when sleep was an impossibility and she sat in the chair by the stove and coughed till the house rang with the propulsive ascending notes of it. She wouldn't blame him, not for the disease, but she would never forgive him that night. He'd crept out of Ida's room at first light—she heard the soft click of the latch, the faintest wheeze of the hinges, felt his heavy tread radiating through the floorboards all the way down the hall and across the parlor to where she sat staring out into the ashen dawn. She waited till he opened his own door, shut it behind him and settled into his bed with a single fierce groan of the wooden supports. Then she got up from the chair, light-headed, her breathing harsh and ragged, each indraft roaring in her ears, and made her way across the room and down the hall to his door, but this time she didn't hesitate.

In a single motion she flung back the door, slipped inside and pulled it shut. The room was gray, crepuscular, everything indistinct, and for a moment she thought she was dreaming, that nothing had happened, that she was asleep and well and that her husband loved her and she loved him in turn. But then he lifted his head from the blankets, his torso braced on the twin props of his elbows, his neck craning, his face a pale lump of meat with his features molded in the center of it, and she was living in the moment. "You pig," she said, her voice low and calm, a flesh-cutting voice, cold as a surgeon's knife. "Adulterer. Cheat. You thought I was Ida, didn't you? Ida slinking across the hall for one last embrace?"

He didn't deny it. He didn't say anything, not a word.

"A servant, Will. A serving girl. How could you demean yourself? And with Edith in the house, Edith in the room above you while you—" She couldn't say it, couldn't name what they were doing, what they'd *done*, though she could feel it stirring inside her, deep in her own body, in the place where she'd opened her legs for him in the time when he wanted her and she wanted him.

The bed shifted beneath him. He let out a soft moaning curse and dropped his head back on the pillow. It came to her that he wasn't going to defend himself, wasn't going to plead or extenuate or attempt to comfort her—or lie, he wasn't even going to bother to lie. The thought enraged her. What was he, anyway? A blustering hateful overgrown adventurer who didn't care a fig about her or Edith either, the island king, William G. Waters, Rex et Imperator.

"Poor Irish," she said. "Shanty Irish." Oh, and now her voice rose up till it was like the rattling of husks, like dead cane beating on a dead shore. "A girl half your age, a girl we took in as if she were our own daughter. And you, you—"

"Shh!" he hissed, sitting up with a jolt. "She'll hear."

"Who?" she demanded. "Who'll hear?"

A whisper: "Ida."

"Ida? Ida's already corrupted. You corrupted her, Will, you did. And you dirtied me in the doing of it."

"Edith, then. For Edith's sake."

And that was where reason left her—that he should dare to put this on Edith, to mention her in the same breath with that, that *slut!* She found Edith's name on her own lips then, found it as if it were a blessing, a salve, but by the time he threw himself out of the bed and took hold of her, shaking her in the grip of his two calloused clumsy hands that were like talons, exactly like, she was screaming it.

This time the blood wouldn't stop. It erupted from her as she fought free of his grip and staggered out into the hallway. She tried to contain it, swallowing mechanically, swallowing till she thought she would drown on her own blood, but the cough shook her harder than Will could ever have and the cough was awash in it. She spattered the grubby white wall, spattered the floor, the front of her dressing gown. So bright, her living blood. And the cough. The cough. Will was right behind her, muttering, pleading, but she fought him away and then Edith was there and she clamped a hand to her mouth and her hand came away red. Everything went dark, the whole world folded up and sucked away from her, and then it wavered and came back again. She was on her feet still and how could that be?

Somehow, with Edith's help, with Edith's arms wrapped around her and her feet finding the stairs one at a time and all the breath squeezed out of her as if she were climbing the highest mountain anyone had ever known, she managed to make it up to her room. The door flung open, clapping against the wall. Ten steps to the bed, and then she was down, but she couldn't lie flat. The thing wouldn't let her. Pillows, she needed pillows to prop her up, and here they were, stony and cold, bunched at the small of her back. Edith, her face drawn down to nothing, ran for a towel and when that was soaked through she ran for another.

She thought of Poe and his story of the Red Death, death that comes in a fountain of blood, and she was ready to let go, so weak, so disappointed, infected after all, *fatally* infected, and what did it matter how she'd lived her life? Will, Ida. Iron pills, *plein air,* doctors. James. Edith. Her own mother a continent away. Beyond the window the day was closed up like a fist. Edith sat beside her. She fell out of consciousness, then fell back in. "My medicine," she pleaded, bleeding, still bleeding, tasting it, swallowing it down, soaking the towel till the towel hung at her throat like a skinned carcass. She took the bottle from Edith's hand, put it to her mouth and drank it down as if it were water, and then she dropped away again and didn't wake till it was dark and saw that Edith was still there at her side and that the blood had stopped flowing.

That was when the weight settled on her, the stone as big as the biggest boulder Will had shattered with his dynamite—or no, bigger, bigger still, as big as the island. It *was* the island, the island was crushing her, she'd known it all along and she might have said it aloud, cried it out, might have said anything, cursing and raving in her throes, thinking *This is what death is like, this weight, this crush,* and then she fell one more time down the long shaft of her dreams.

The Cruelest Thing

But this was the thing, the cruelest thing: she didn't die. She was going to die, she'd nearly died, and when she came back to herself on a day as colorless and changeless as the day she'd taken to bed, she wished she had—there was only so much blood in the human body, only so much weight that anyone, even the saints and martyrs, could be expected to bear. The bed was cold. She couldn't feel her toes. The tips of her fingers, though she rubbed them together, rubbed them furiously, felt numb. She called out for Edith because she wouldn't have Ida in the room with her, never again, never, and the first thing she heard was the sigh of Edith's mattress from the room down the hall and then footsteps and then the door was opening and Edith was there, laboring under a frightened smile and asking her how she felt.

And so it was Edith who nursed her, Edith who helped her comb out her hair and brought her her medicine and the bowls of broth Ida sent up from the kitchen, and when Will came in from his work to stand there in the doorway gazing down at her like a mourner at a funeral, she looked back at him as if he were a stranger. There was no need for speech—speech only complicated things. He came and went. She opened her eyes and he was there or he wasn't. Her breath grated, her lungs rattled. It must have been the third or fourth time he came that she felt strong enough to address the situation, to lift her head and shape words around the emotions stabbing at her. She'd dozed off and woken again to the same pewter light at the window and saw him sitting there in the chair, his hat clenched in one hand and a book open in the other. "I want to go back," she said.

His eyes shot to her. He looked startled, as if the walls had begun to speak. He closed the book, his thumb marking the place, and drew up his legs so that his knees swelled against the thin worn fabric of his trousers. "I know," he said. "And I'm sorry for it. Sorry for everything."

The room seemed to whirl as it had that first day, everything in motion, as if she were looking at him through a kaleidoscope. It took her a long moment to push herself up to a sitting position, her arms sapped, the breath caught in her throat.

"Adolph's back," he said. "I sent him to meet with Nichols, and they think—we think—we may have a man to take over here, a hired man who'll come with his family, a manager, that is . . ." He rose from the chair and whether he was smiling or not she couldn't say, his skin so chapped and burned and his features so reduced she scarcely recognized him—and he looked *old,* old all over again. "And he brought something for you, something to cheer you—"

"Who?"

"Adolph."

"Adolph brought something for me?" She saw the man then in quick relief, the clod, heavy-faced, humorless, lewd, *The softest thing in this world but for one other thing I can think of.*

"Shall I go get it? Would you like to see it now?"

What Adolph had brought her—and she froze when Will led him into the room in his filthy work clothes and out-at-toe stockings until she saw it there in his arms—was a cat. Not a Siamese like Sampan, but a silver and black tabby with great all-seeing eyes and a swirl of markings on either side that made her think of marble cake. Adolph came across the room to her, nimble enough for a man almost Will's age, his eyes downcast—he wouldn't look at her though she'd caught him stealing glances at the dinner table, and she could only imagine what she must have looked like now, skeletal, bone-white, her eyes huge and luminous and snatching at the light as desperately as the cat's. He didn't say a word. Just held the animal out to her—an old tom, docile, loving, she saw that in a flash—and then she had it pressed to her so she could feel the engine of its purring through her robe and her nightgown and down into the thin drawn tegument of the skin stretched across her ribs. A cat. Purring. It was a small miracle. "Thank you," she whispered, and smiled at him for perhaps the first time since the day they'd met—and that had been a smile of civility, not of gratitude.

And Adolph? She didn't like him, she would never like him, but here he had his moment of grace, lifting his eyes to hers for just the briefest instant before nodding in acknowledgment, turning on his heels and slipping out the door.

So there was the cat. The cat that had come from shore, where Adolph had been just days ago, mere days, and now there was the promise—or the hope, the hope at least—that they would all be going there, going home, as soon as Will was able to fix things with Nichols and the manager in waiting. In the meanwhile, there was a new cycle beginning, the strength coming back to her in increments and everything revolving around that soaring promise— she forced herself from bed after a full week of inactivity, forced herself to pull open her steamer trunk and hatboxes and begin packing her clothes and hats for the trip back, overseeing things, and when she couldn't put it off any longer, even going downstairs, to the kitchen, where Ida was.

She came down the stairs that first day on silent feet, in her carpet slippers, the cat padding noiselessly behind her. She was walking, moving, but she couldn't feel her legs. They seemed fiberless and weak, as if they'd become detached from her body, as if she were walking on someone else's legs, someone feeble, impossibly old, etherealized already. Ethereal, that was what she was. A spirit. A thing of the air. And if she had reason to doubt it, she saw that the walls of the corridor had been washed free of the taint of her blood, as if she'd never passed this way at all.

She found Ida in the kitchen, bent to the washing, the windows steamed over, heat radiating from the stove, the usual smells at war. For a long moment she stood there in the doorway, hesitating. What would she say to her? How could she look her in the face? How could she live under the same roof without exploding from within like one of Will's shattered boulders? Before she could think, the cat gave her away. He paraded into the room, tail held high, and Ida, her hair in a long frizzled braid that dangled over one shoulder, glanced up at the motion and in that instant they were staring into each other's eyes. "Ma'am," Ida blurted, "oh, ma'am, I don't know what to say—"

Steel, she was made of steel, unbendable, unbreakable, and now she could feel her legs, the muscles tightening there, everything in her gone rigid suddenly. "Then don't say anything at all."

"But I—" Ida's face crumpled. She was in tears before she could draw her hands from the soapy water and rub them spasmodically on her apron.

The table was Marantha's destination. She wanted only to cross the room, sit at that table with a cup of tea and a slice of buttered bread and gaze round her at something other than the four walls of her bedroom, no matter how shabby or disordered, but she never got there because Ida backed away from the washbasin and came gliding to her as if she'd been drawn on a string. Marantha almost held out her arms to her, almost took hold of her and drew her to herself like the child she was, but that wasn't natural, that wasn't right. "No," she said, shaking her head side to side while the girl slumped her shoulders and dropped her chin to her chest in mortification. And though she saw then that what had happened wasn't the fault of Ida, but of Will—of Will and herself too, for allowing him to bring them all out here to this desolate place where there was no society and no affection or manners or common human decency and where the disease could have its way with her—she turned away, went to the table and pulled out the chair there. "Bring me a cup of tea," she said over her shoulder. "And a sandwich. Make me a sandwich."

One-Arm

April faded into May. Her steamer trunk, packed and ready to go, stood just inside the front door, positioned there so Will could see it every time he came in or out, and no, she wasn't going to decorate it with a cloth or a vase of flowers or attempt to disguise it in any way. It was her trunk. And it stood by the door. He could make of that what he would.

She was on the porch with Edith one afternoon, the balls of her feet rising and falling with the motion of the rocker, her breathing shallow but steady, the sheet she was mending spread across her lap in a series of gentle undulating folds and the cat asleep in a golden puddle of sunlight beside her, when the one-armed man made his appearance, entirely unannounced. Edith was the first to spot him. She'd been rocking too, absorbed for once in her studies, Will and the hands nowhere to be seen—mending fence, collecting driftwood, who knew where they were?—when suddenly she let out a low exclamation and jumped to her feet so abruptly the rocker pitched back against the clapboards behind her. "It's, it's Captain Curner, Mother, look! And who's that with him?"

She had to blink twice to be sure she wasn't seeing things. Two figures had just crested the hill, rising up out of the haze that hung in the distance though it was past two in the afternoon and should have burned off by now. There was Curner, sure enough, his face the color and texture of smoked ham under his grimy seaman's cap and with a wooden crate propped up on one shoulder, and how had they missed his sail in the harbor? The fog, that was what it was. It still hovered over the water, as if the sea had pulled the sky down like a shade and left nothing in between. But who was the other man?

It all came clear in the next moment, Curner lumbering across the yard to set down the crate on the edge of the porch while the stranger, following along in his wake, pulled up short at the base of the steps to peer up at her and Edith with a narrowing look of appraisal. He was a slight man, no bigger than Jimmie, in patched and faded work clothes, and his left sleeve hung empty so that he looked as if he were leaning to one side when in fact he was standing straight on, as erect as a soldier. "Good afternoon, missus," he said, his face drawn down to its underpinnings of bone and the straight slash of an oversized nose, an English nose, as it turned out. "And good afternoon to you, miss. Am I correct in assuming that I have the pleasure of addressing Miss and Missus Waters?"

"Yes," she heard herself murmur, even as Curner mumbled a greeting of his own, and Edith, for once at a loss for words, echoed her.

The new man—and suddenly she knew who he was, the apprehension striking her so suddenly she almost cried out in rapture—gave her a horse's smile, all teeth and no lips. "I'm Horace Reed, missus," he said, eliding the *h*, "at your service."

"He's come out for the day—and the night, that is, because we'll be leaving first thing in the morning," Curner said.

"Just to get acquainted," Reed put in. "To see if I'm acceptable to your husband. And you—you, of course."

Another attempt at a grin. And then he was fumbling in the breast pocket of his coat for something, a sealed envelope, which he extracted and handed across to her. It was from Nichols and addressed to her husband, but she was so excited in that moment, so carried away, she couldn't help tearing it open and snatching a look at the letter within.

This is to introduce Mr. Reed, a man who has had large experience in the field of ranching in general and sheep in particular, mostly in his native country but on a ranch in the Santa Ynez Valley as well. I took the trouble of communicating with the owner there, who holds him in high regard. He is eager for the job here, as he has six children and a wife to feed and is currently out of work, his previous employer having sold the ranch to new interests. He assures me that in spite of his small stature and his obvious disfigurement, he is fully capable of managing our operations on the terms you and I fixed upon—that is, he will supply his own needs and receive one-third the value of the flock's increase per annum. If he meets with your approval, he means to take over from you on the twenty-ninth of this month.

She folded the letter carefully and returned it to the envelope, and it was all she could do to keep herself from running off into the fields shouting for Will, because he had to see this, had to read the letter and take a look at the man and sign him on without delay. Her hand trembled as she clutched the letter to her. The new man, Reed, was studying her face, his eyes taking everything in. She'd opened a letter addressed to her husband right in front of him, and if it was a serious breach of etiquette—what would her mother have said?—she dismissed it, because husband and wife were one before the law and she and Will were equal partners in this enterprise, no matter what anyone might think or expect.

"I'm sure you'll be just what we're looking for," she said, "and I'm sure too that you'll find this place everything you could want. It's—" Here she faltered, struggling to present things in a positive light. "It's very peaceful out here. Isn't it, Edith? Quiet. Tranquil."

"Oh, yes," Edith said, shooting her a glance, "very quiet."

"If that's what you want, that is."

He took a step forward, snatched the cap from his head—the same sort of cap Jimmie favored, though this one was clean, or appeared to be. "A farm's a farm, missus, and if you've seen one—" He finished the phrase with his hand. "Peace and solitude, that's what a man wants, doubtless. And please don't think that this"—pointing to the empty sleeve—"will slow me in any way or keep me from my duties because I can do the work of two men all on my own and what I can't manage I've got my boys, Cuthbert and Thomas, of sixteen and fourteen years, to pull along with me."

She wanted to reassure him—he was a treasure, her savior, the one man to lift her out of this, and she didn't care how scrawny and hungry and crippled he was just so long as he was standing on two feet and drawing air—but she didn't have the chance because Curner spoke up then. "Ma'am," he said, indicating the crate he'd set down on the porch, "where do you want I should put this?"

If she didn't recognize it in the exhilaration of the moment, who could have blamed her? "What is it?" she asked, Curner nodding and shuffling, Reed sober-faced, Edith burning up with her own barely contained joy—they were free, free at long last, already on their way!

A shrug. A grimace. "The plates," he said. "You know, that you been asking after?"

She wasn't privy to the conference Will had with the man—she'd gone up to bed early, too overwrought to hide her feelings or preside over the dinner table—but every time she'd looked up for the remainder of the afternoon she'd seen them crossing the yard together or tramping the fields or examining the railway ties that supported the barn as if they were rare works of art. She had a plate sent up, though she was too excited to eat, and when Edith brought it to her they were close as thieves. "Three more weeks," she said, and Edith, giggling, repeated it to her: *Three more weeks.* Then she'd settled in with the back copies of the Santa Barbara newspaper Curner had brought her, the cat—they'd named him Marbles, for his coloring—curled up in her lap, where she could stroke the silk of his ears in a steady, easy, unconscious way. It was past nine and dark beyond the windows when she heard Will's tread on the stairs, his steps uncertain, as if he'd been drinking—and he had, she knew he had, with Curner and the new man, her one-armed savior. She didn't begrudge them. Let them celebrate. She would have celebrated herself but she was afraid of hexing things.

Will was on the landing. He was at the door. And then, oddly, he was knocking, the soft rap of his knuckles whispering through the wooden panels so politely, so reticently, you would have thought they were strangers to each other. "Come in," she said, the door pushed open, and there he was, her husband, looking sorrowful and shaking his head back and forth in negation, and at first she thought he'd lost at cards and then that he'd offered up the bed in the storeroom to the one-armed man instead of installing him in the bunkhouse where he belonged and that now he'd come to her, to be close with her, to sleep in the same bed with her despite all that had come between them.

"I'm sorry," he said, shuffling unsteadily across the room, the hateful room, her prison cell, and he had been drinking, of course he had. She watched him go to the corner by the window for the straight-backed chair there and laboriously lift it and bring it round to her side of the bed, where he set it down on the dried-out floorboards and sat heavily facing her.

"Sorry for what?"

He was still shaking his head. "The new man," he said. "Reed. One-Arm. Whatever you want to call him."

"What about him?" She pictured the man, so reduced he couldn't have weighed much more than Edith, and what was the weight of a human arm? A fifth your body weight? A sixth?

"He's not"—his voice heavy and slow—"going to work out."

She'd been lying flat and now she sat up so precipitously she startled the cat, which came up out of its sleep with a sudden lurch before it could see that it was only her, its mistress, stirring to action. "What do you mean?"

"Just look at him. He's weak, deformed. He looks half-starved."

"He's no worse off than the men you march down Market Street with come Decoration Day—"

"That's different. They're veterans. And we're not hiring any of them to keep us from bankruptcy."

"But I thought, I assumed—" But how stupid of her. It was the Revolutionary War the British fought, and on the wrong side, at that, not Will's war. And if any of them did fight in the Civil War it would have been for the South.

"He lost it in a threshing machine, a farm accident, and who's to say who was to blame. He drinks, though, that's for sure—"

"So do you."

"But that isn't the point. Or maybe it is: I don't trust him to do the work. I don't think he's capable."

"He is, Will, I know he is." She was pleading now and she hated herself for it. "He has two sons, nearly grown, and they—"

"I'm sorry," he said.

"Sorry? Are you actually going to sit there and tell me you don't intend to hire that man?"

"We can't take the risk. What if the ranch were to go bust, where would our investment be then?"

"Investment?" She threw it back at him. "Is this your idea of an investment?"

"We can't simply—"

"We can. And we will."

"I want to stay on, that's the long and short of it. If even for a month or two more. It's summer, Minnie, summer coming on—the air, think of the air."

She let out a laugh then, incredulous, tainted, more a dog's bark than any human sound, and then, though her throat was closing up on her, she dropped her voice to the pitch of absolute certainty, of threat and irrevocability: "If you do, it will be on your own. I'm finished here. Finished. Do you understand me? And you *will* hire that man and I don't care if we have to beg in the streets and every last ram and ewe falls over dead and rots in its hide. Just get me out of here. Get me *out!*"

Departure

Will wanted to leave the cat behind, but she was adamant on that score too—in the short time she'd had it, the animal had become her chief source of comfort, along with Edith, that is—and now, as General Meade jerked at his harness and Jimmie fought the reins and the rocker pitched and yawed with each violent shudder of the sled, Marbles concentrated his weight in the basket in her lap till he was as heavy and inert as a stone. There was wind, of course, a gale of it blowing full in her face so that she had to squint her eyes to keep the grit out of them. Everything had dried up, just as Will had said it would, but that was small consolation to her now. In fact, it was nothing but an annoyance, her dress sheathed in a pale yellow patina of dust before they'd gone a hundred yards and the handkerchief she pressed to her face filthy all the way through. And her gloves—her gloves looked as if she'd been using them to dig up potatoes by hand. She focused on her breathing. Held on as best she could. And entertained herself with the notion that in a few hours—*mere* hours—she'd be at sea.

The road was much improved, she had to admit it, though it still wasn't wide enough for a wagon to go up and down without risk, but that was Mr. Reed's concern now, Mr. Reed with his pinned-up sleeve, listless children and skeletal wife, though who was she to criticize? Still, the woman—she claimed to be thirty, though she looked ten years older, her shoes worn down at the heels, her dress washed so many times it was as colorless as the spring water in the kitchen basin and her eyes a crazed flaring assault of cobalt blue—seemed to her a fellow sufferer. She didn't cough, or not that Marantha had heard or noticed, but then she'd barely spent a moment with her, consumed as she was with the final details of packing up and leaving. The woman—Mrs. Reed, and Marantha never did catch her Christian name—had stood watching from the porch of the bunkhouse, where the family had been temporarily installed, as Jimmie hitched up the mule, lashed the rocker to it and half a dozen crates of things, the unopened dishes amongst them, that were to go back on Charlie Curner's schooner. Mrs. Reed was eager to get herself settled in the house, and who could blame her for that? *Good use of it,* Marantha thought, *welcome to it,* and if she ever laid eyes on the place again it would be from above, high up, out of reach even of the eagles.

Slowly, step by tentative step, the mule worked its way through the turnings and switchbacks and down the final stretch to the beach, braking with its hooves and its big sweating flanks against the downward impetus of the sled with its rocking chair and piled-up cartons and the all but negligible weight she and her cat brought to bear. Jimmie didn't say a word the whole way down, bent on focusing on the task at hand, which was to keep the mule from running out of control and pitching over the side of the canyon. She had nothing to say to him in any case. She'd washed her hands of him and she was glad he'd be staying behind. Where he belonged. He wasn't fit for society, not after what he'd done to Edith—*with* Edith—and Edith was hardly innocent herself.

It had been just after Reed had gone back with Charlie Curner, hired on and prepared to return at the end of the month, as contracted. The day was typically gloomy, the fog lingering well into the afternoon before giving way to a pale high sun that crept by stages through the windows while she sat mending by the stove, determined to repair every last tear in the sheets, bedding and underclothes before they were packed away for the trip back home. It might have been the influence of the sun or just the desire to get out of doors and away from the house, but at some point she set aside her work, put on her hat, took up her parasol and strolled out the door, thinking she'd walk as far as the cliffs and see if she could make out the shore from there. She moved awkwardly, the muscles of her legs gone lax from disuse, yet the day was pleasant and she needed the exercise and before long she began to feel better, stronger, and though it might have been no more than a childish indulgence she was looking forward to a glimpse of the coastline, if only to reassure herself that it was still there.

When she came up the path to where the headland narrowed and the cliffs gave way to the churn of the sea below, she was disappointed. Though the sun was shining above her, the coastline was wrapped in fog, nothing visible but a motionless band of gray thrown up across the horizon. She was standing there, looking out on nothing, when the wind shifted and the sound of voices came to her. Edith's voice—she heard it plainly—and another voice, a man's. Or no, a boy's. Jimmie's. But where were they?

She edged toward the drop-off and peered over. A second ledge jutted out below her, not thirty feet down, a patch of rock and scrub suspended over the ocean like the crow's nest of a ship, and Edith was there, with Jimmie, playing at one of their games. Edith was perched on a rock, hatless, in an old green shirtwaist she'd long since outgrown, and she was so close Marantha could make out the parting of her hair. "I'll bet you're afraid," Edith said.

"I'm not afraid." From this angle, all she could see of the boy was his cap, the thin spike of his nose, two ears, his shoulders.

"Then go ahead, Caliban. Go ahead and kiss me."

And he would have, or he was going to, but as soon as he leaned into her Edith pushed him away, even as the sea below them slashed at the rocks and sucked away again. "No," Edith said, "not there," and she was lifting her skirts so that the sun glanced off the perfect unblemished flesh of her calf, her knee, the hem of her undergarments, Jimmie kneeling, down on his hands and knees, groveling like an animal, and Edith bunching the material till she was exposed all the way up the long white slant of her legs. "Here," she said. "Kiss me here."

And now there was the mule and the boy's narrow shoulders and the canyon that was opening up before her for the very last time. She felt no nostalgia, only regret. And if she'd confined Edith to her room for an entire day and banned Jimmie from the table at dinner—banned him permanently—it was small punishment for the shock she'd received. What had she been thinking when she'd consented to bring Edith out here? No matter how much it would have cost or how much the separation would have hurt, she should have sent Edith to boarding school—and if she had it to do over again, she would have. And Jimmie. She wished she'd never laid eyes on him.

As they emerged from the canyon and started across the beach, the sled gliding over the sand with a soft continuous hiss and the mule going easier now, she saw that the sea was alive with birds, an enormous squalling convocation of them—gulls, shearwaters, pelicans, all of them bobbing and wheeling and plunging into the careening froth of the waves so that the boat, the schooner, was almost lost in the storm of them. This was one of their banquets, the sardines and anchovies driven to the surface by larger fish and the birds there to collect their due, the scene as elemental as it must have been all those eons ago when the mammoths stalked across the countryside and the glaciers stood rigid and taller than the mountains they crushed beneath them. She might have appreciated it in another context, might have enjoyed it—wild nature, a scene Winslow Homer might have depicted—but she'd had her fill of nature. She dropped her eyes to the basket in her lap and the moment the mule came to a halt she got down from the chair and made her way to the skiff even as Curner came up the strand to help Jimmie with the crates. And no, she didn't want to wait on shore for the others—she wanted only for someone to take up the oars and row her out to the boat, where she meant to sit on the bench in the saloon and stare at the walls till she heard the rattle of the anchor chain paying out in the harbor at Santa Barbara.

This time Ida didn't come down to comfort her or see to her needs or even to show her face at all, not for the entire trip, and Edith, having had her fill of the sea, was no company either—she was asleep in one of the berths before they'd left the island. Since Will and Adolph were occupied on deck, tugging at one line or another and sharing valedictory swigs from a bottle Charlie Curner had provided, Marantha had the saloon to herself. She and the cat, that is. She'd kept him confined in the basket till she was aboard and then she let him roam free, though he didn't go far—one circuit around the cabin, a quick stiffening over the scent of the rodents cowering in their holes, and then he was back in her lap, purring himself to sleep. He'd proven a superior mouser in his short time with them, roaming the house at night and present-ing her with the headless corpses of one mouse after another, though it was too little too late. By that point she didn't care if the mice overran the place, piled their droppings up to the ceiling and whittled the walls to splinters. The mice were behind her now. Everything was. The boat rocked gently under her, the sea as smooth as the sheets she'd mended and folded and packed neatly away for the journey home. There was the susurrus of the spray against the bow. It was very quiet. Before long, she found herself dozing.

And then—she had no notion of how much time had passed—Will was there, nudging her awake. "Minnie," he said, his voice soft and apologetic, "Minnie, wake up, we're almost there."

Through the fog of her sleep and the dullness of the thing inside her that was just starting to rise and yawn and unsheathe its claws, she had to take a moment to stare up at him, blinking, and ask him, *"Where?"*

"Where?" he echoed. "Santa Barbara. Don't you want to come out on deck and see the shoreline?"

And now she was awake, fully awake, for the first time in months. "Yes," she said, not coughing, not yet, and she lifted the cat from her lap and stood firmly, planting her feet against the motion of the ship. She touched her hands to her hat, smoothed down her dress—and then, spontaneously, as though she couldn't help herself—she gave him a smile that was as pure and uncomplicated as the evening coming to life around her. "I'd like that," she said, and she could already picture the view from the deck, the boats bobbing in the harbor, the carriages ashore, palm trees, streets and lanes and avenues, and in the houses that ran back from the sea in neat orderly rows, people already lighting lamps against the coming of the dark.

PART II

Edith

Homecoming

Though she slept through the entire voyage back, slept like an Egyptian mummy in the narrow berth that smelled of bilge and hair oil and the private sloughings and parings of the man whose bed it was—Curner, Mr. Curner, *Captain* Curner—she rose the moment her mother came to her and whispered, "We're here." After that, she couldn't sleep at all, not for the next two nights running, for sheer excitement. It was as if she'd never in her life seen or heard or felt or tasted, as if she'd been color-blind, as if her ears had been stuffed with wax and her tongue coated in magnesia. She'd been deprived, that was what it was, locked away on an island like some fairy princess, everything drab and changeless and the only sound the keening of the wind and the weak disjointed cries of the sheep, the seals, the birds. The world had been stilled, and now—in a sudden explosion of color and noise, glorious noise—it had come careering back to life.

On the very morning after they'd returned to the rented house and pulled the covers from the furniture and dusted and swept and sat down to a meal that wasn't mutton or turkey or fish coated in its own slime—steak, Ida made steak and French-fried potatoes with a fresh garden salad, the greens even better than the meat itself, lettuce a revelation, tomatoes sweet as candy and candy available round the corner and ice cream too—her mother made her go back to school, though she was months behind in her lessons and there were only three weeks remaining in the term. The teacher—Mrs. Sanders—looked different somehow, older, thicker, with a perpetual drop of moisture depending from the tip of her nose and hair thinner and grayer than she remembered. The room seemed smaller, the desks shrunken, the map of the United States that decorated the wall beside the chalkboard more worn and faded. She barely recognized her classmates. Still they *were* her classmates, young people, people her own age, and what they thought of her clothes or her attitudes or how they might have snubbed her or not didn't really make a difference, not that first day—it was enough just to be looking at them, hearing them, sitting at a desk in school and listening to Mrs. Sanders drone on as if she were singing in the wrong key.

Though all the girls wanted to know where she'd been and what it had been like, she felt shy of them, overwhelmed by the wheeling gallery of their faces and the way they seemed to talk without pausing for breath, by their clothes and their boldness and the sheer press of them. One girl, Becky Thorpe, the one she remembered best from last December, asked if she wanted to walk home with her after school but Edith just shook her head, coloring, and murmured, "Maybe tomorrow."

Still, she took her time making her way home, peering in the shop windows, lingering outside the drugstore just long enough to avoid attracting notice, going up and down the steps of the Arlington Hotel for the sheer novelty of it. The hotel was her special favorite, a towering glamorous three-story palace dedicated to the society people who came for the air and the sea and the sun, a place that had its own orchestra and, so she'd heard, the best dining room in town. She saw the women arrayed like jewels on the porches that ran the entire length and breadth of the ground floor, the grandes dames from San Francisco and Los Angeles and even farther, from the East Coast maybe, with their silks and furs and their little pug dogs, and she watched them too, studied them as if they were her true curriculum—and they were, or they would be, once school let out and her mother took her back to San Francisco. But she had to laugh at herself, even as a woman came up the steps in a blue velvet polonaise with a borzoi on a leash and the doormen practically fell over themselves to pull back the doors for her, because she'd just gone through her first day at school since before the Christmas holidays and here she was already looking ahead to the end of the term.

No matter. It wasn't math or history or geography that interested her. It was the theater, the Burbank, the Tivoli, the Baldwin. Lillian Russell. *Danseuses.* Stage lights. The orchestra she could feel thrumming in her chest like the wash of her own blood when they were only just tuning up. That was life, not some provincial school, and when she was growing up in San Francisco, for as long back as she could remember, her mother had taken her to the theater and the concert hall, to variety shows and dramas alike. She never tired of the thrill of it, the anticipatory rustling of the audience as the houselights went down, the way the actors emerged from the wings in shirtsleeves and housedresses as if they were in their own parlors with the curtains drawn and no one to see or hear them, or the way the musical performers came right out at you like they were going to rise up and float off the stage.

For a long while she sat on a bench on the hotel grounds, feeling as if she were doing something illicit, and if anyone questioned her she was going to say she was a guest in the hotel, come down from San Francisco with her parents and staying in Room 200, a number she pulled out of the air. But were there that many rooms? She scanned the windows, doing a quick count, fourteen rooms per side, times three floors, and then multiply that by the four sides, which made a hundred sixty-eight. All right, fine. She was in Room 168, and maybe it was a suite, with a marble bath and gold faucets, and who to say different? She was almost disappointed when no one asked.

It was past five by the time she started for home—she had no idea it was that late till she glanced up at the clock outside the bank across the street—and she found herself hurrying, feeling guilty, afraid of what her parents would say. Her mother would start scolding in her rasping worn-out voice that was like the buzzing of insects, of hornets, angry hornets, then her stepfather would take over. *Had she been wasting her time in nonsense? Had she been with boys, was that it?*

She ran the length of the last block, breathing hard as she swung open the gate and started up the walk. Nothing seemed out of the ordinary—there was the porch swing, the varnished rail and the white palings, the windows glazed in sunlight and the curtains hanging motionless behind them—but she had the oddest feeling that someone was watching her. She had to turn round twice and look back out to the street before she realized with a start that her mother was there, sitting perfectly still in a chair set in the front corner of the yard. At first she thought her mother was waiting for her, ready to pounce, but then she saw that her eyes were closed and her head thrown back so that her face caught the full glare of the sun. Which was odd, not at all like her. Her mother would never sit out of doors and risk her complexion, not without her parasol, but her parasol was nowhere to be seen. And more, and worse: her arms hung limp at her sides, her fingers curled and wrists dangling as if they were barely attached to her.

"Mother?" she called, coming back down the steps, her heart slamming at her ribs, and then she was bolting across the lawn, the sunlight bleaching everything so that the shadows flattened and the house stood out as if it were made of pasteboard and she were onstage, shaking her now, "Mother! Mother!"

The moment swelled, huge and hovering, and then, abruptly, it burst. Her mother's eyes eased open. "What?" she gasped. "What is it?"

"I thought—" Edith trailed off. Under the glare of the sun her mother's face looked depleted, the bones standing out in relief, lines tugging at the bloodless flesh around her eyes as if to cinch it tight, tighter, till there was no trace of softness left. "What I mean is . . . I'm home. From school."

"I was just sitting here a moment, trying to catch my breath."

There was noise, all that clamor she'd missed—voices from the house next door, the creak and clatter of a passing carriage, the dull intonation of bells sounding the quarter hour—and it distracted her. For a moment she was gone, back at the hotel, ascending the steps with a little dog in her arms, the doors flung open wide and all the facets of the chandelier glittering like stars in the ballroom at the end of the hall. She didn't want to be here. Didn't want to see her mother like this. Didn't want to be afraid. "Do you need anything?" she heard herself say. "A glass of water? Your parasol—don't you want your parasol?"

Her mother was looking at her strangely, almost as if she didn't recognize her, and then her eyes contracted and she began to cough. The cough was high and hollow, echoing in her diaphragm as if it were the chamber of an instrument, and then there was the wheeze for breath and the next cough and the next until the cough and the wheeze seesawed back and forth and her mother was doubled over in the chair. Edith felt helpless. Once the cycle started it would play itself out whether anyone was there to help or sympathize or not. She began patting her mother's back automatically, though her mother wasn't choking—she was drowning on her own fluids, on her blood and mucus and the dead cells of the disease that was in her and would never leave, not till she lay still for the final time. The truth was there before her, but it was hard, too hard to hold on to. She let it go and felt the darkness sweep through her like the chill through an open door.

Her mother coughed. She patted. Kept on patting. From the palm tree in the next yard over, a flight of dark miniature birds hurtled themselves into the sky.

"Let me go get your medicine," she said.

144

"No. I'm"—the cough tore at her—"I'm fine."

"Water, then. Here, let me help you up."

Her mother pushed her away, arms in furious motion, wrists jangling like bracelets, coughing till something came up and she spat it in the tin cup she kept secreted between her legs. Then she drew in a great wet wheezing breath, the next cough waiting in the wings, hanging there like a bat ready to swoop down and twist through the air, her eyes wet with the effort of turning herself inside out. "I don't"—and here came the cough, racking and harsh—"I just want to, to . . ."

"You need a doctor. I'm going for the doctor."

And suddenly her mother's voice hardened, narrowed, came at her like the filed point of a blade: "I just want to be left alone."

They were three at dinner that night—Edith, her stepfather and Adolph. Ida served—a roast of beef, with baked potatoes and sautéed vegetables and lemon pie for dessert—and when the serving bowls had been set out and the glasses filled, Ida took a portion for herself and went out to the kitchen with it. Edith's stepfather never said a word about school or whether she'd been late in coming home or not. He was in high spirits, the glass before him stained dark with whiskey poured from the bottle he kept right out in plain sight on the table, and Adolph's glass was dark too. The main theme of the evening was business—business couldn't be better, or so she gathered. Wool prices were up and the profit was in, more than anyone could have expected, and her stepfather kept pouring whiskey from the bottle and reaching out to pour for Adolph too. From upstairs, from behind the closed door of her mother's room, came the sawing rasp of a cough that wouldn't let up.

She kept her head down through the meal, surreptitiously reading from the book spread open in her lap and hidden from view by the corner of her napkin, though she found she couldn't concentrate. She was more upset than she wanted to admit, the image of her mother pushing her away driving everything before it, the school, her homecoming, the pleasure she'd taken in the hotel grounds and the fashions of the ladies. She spoke only when her stepfather addressed her—"You like that cut of meat? Beef for a change, huh? I don't know about you, missy, but after all that mutton I think I could eat a whole steer by myself"—and as soon as the meal was done and Ida cleared the table she went out to the kitchen. Ida was at the sink, her back to the door, arms and shoulders working over the dishes. Steam rose around her. Outside, beyond the window, the sun picked its careful way through the red-gold trumpet flowers climbing the espalier against the fence.

"Would you like some help?" she asked.

Ida looked over one shoulder, the sunlight catching her eyes so that they seemed all at once to leap out of her face. "It'd be a mercy, I'm so worn with all this moving from one place to another. Truly, I'm dead on my feet."

Edith took up the dish towel and Ida plucked the plates from the rinse water—her mother's best china, in a pretty rose pattern that made you feel good just to look at it—and handed them to her one by one.

"And what of you? How was your first day back to school?"

"Fine."

"Fine? No more to say than that? Don't tell me it's not a glory to be laying your eyes on somebody your own age besides Jimmie, who might mean well, who might—" She lifted her hands from the dishwater to sketch a picture in the air and they both laughed.

"Oh, no, I don't mean that. It's just strange, that's all, to be back after all this time. Everything seems so busy."

Ida gave her a look. "I'd say busy is just what you want—myself, I felt half-dead out there on the island, dead of boredom for one thing. Do you know I went down to the market this morning, just that, just there and back, and it was like being transported to heaven—and on the wings of angels, no less." She was going to say more but just then there was a fierce breathless burst of coughing from above and they both paused to lift their eyes to the ceiling. "Your mother seems worse today," Ida observed after a moment. "It's the moving, is what it is." She shook her head. "The dampness of that boat . . ."

"She pushed me away." Edith tried to control her voice, tried to focus on drying the plate in her hand and finding a place for it in the stack on the counter, but she couldn't help herself. "She was having a spasm—outside, in the chair, when I'd just got home—and all I wanted to do was, was—" She could feel it all coming up in her, all the tension and fear and loneliness—her mother was dying and she'd been dying a long time and once you started dying it was like being dragged down the side of a hill and all the dirt coming with you. To the bottom. To bury you. "I just wanted to help."

"Hush, it's all right, she doesn't mean it." Ida laid a hand on her shoulder and they stood there a moment without moving. "When people fall ill they're not themselves anymore. It's like dogs, same thing. I can recall when I was ten or eleven maybe and living with my Aunt Maeve—remember I told you about her, my father's sister, the one that took in the three of us? We had a dog, just a mutt, really—Lucky, his name was—and he liked me most of all, maybe because I fed him scraps when no one else would bother with him, but then a wagon ran him over and broke his leg so the bone was showing through and my aunt warned me not to go near him because in his pain he wouldn't know me—"

"But she's so angry all the time. Angry at everybody. You especially. Why is that? It's just not right, the way she won't have you in the room anymore, won't even come to the table if you're there." She looked away, out across the yard to where the woman next door was cutting flowers and arranging them in a vase the little girl beside her held out patiently, the moment crystallizing, butterflies, birds, the sun like syrup poured over everything and all the trees reaching in unison for the sky. "What happened?" she asked, turning back to her. "What did you ever do to her?"

Ida's eyes. Her moon face. The pursing of her lips, dry lips, lips that clung together with a thin film of soft pink flesh. "I don't know," she said, shaking her head. "I just don't know."

The Empty Shell

Then everything changed. They went back to San Francisco, as promised, though it was to rented rooms and not the apartment she'd grown up in because strangers lived there now, and if she walked past it she told herself it was only to get where she was going by the shortest possible route and she never allowed herself to look up at the second-floor windows where her mother had kept her geraniums and Sampan would bunch himself against the glass to bask in the sun so that you could see him there from all the way down the block. There were doctors for her mother, new medicines. The cook—Ida had stayed behind in Santa Barbara and there was no arguing with her mother about it—was an irascible old woman named Mrs. Offenbacher, who could have played one of the weird sisters in *Macbeth*, and without a wig or a touch of greasepaint either. The rooms were dreary, furnished by somebody else, withered plumes of pampas grass sprouting from a vase at the door, the furniture nicked and worn, a smell of dust and disuse in the air. It might have been depressing under other circumstances, but not to her, not after the island. She was in San Francisco, and nothing else mattered. Her friends were here, her true friends, girls she'd known all her life, not just acquaintances like Becky Thorpe and the other girls in Santa Barbara, and they hadn't forgotten her—within days of her arrival she began to receive invitations to parties and dances, carriage rides in the park, picnics, outings at the beach. Better yet, there was money again and that meant she could go back to her ballet and voice lessons.

At the end of August, when it came time to return to Santa Barbara—*For the air,* her stepfather said, *and school, school of course*—she began to feel dejected all over again. She wanted her mother to recover, of course she did, with all her heart, but as far as she could see the air was no better down there than it was here—it was all California, wasn't it? Why couldn't they stay?

Why couldn't they wait till the lease was up on their old apartment and move back in and have a normal life instead of packing up and moving from one place to another like gypsies? She didn't want to whine, didn't want to be a complainer, but she did and she was.

She came up the stairs one afternoon after ballet class, trudging, dragging her feet, angry at the world, the hallway reeking of Mrs. Offenbacher's sauerbraten and the odious woman in the flat next door crowding the staircase with her two brats in tow so that she had to put on a false smile for them though all she wanted to do was tear out her hair and scream like one of the damned in Dante's river of fire, and was surprised to see her mother and stepfather sitting in the parlor at that hour. It was odd to see them together like that, especially in the afternoon. More and more, her mother was confined to bed, where she read or knitted or dozed off sporadically throughout the day and then let her lamp burn into the small hours of the night, and Edith's stepfather was always out somewhere doing whatever he did when he wasn't wrestling sheep on a muddy ranch in the middle of nowhere. Business, that's what he called it—he had business—and left it at that.

Before she could even remove her coat, she could feel the tension in the room. Her stepfather sat rigid in the armchair by the window, his jaws clamped and his gaze fixed on the street below, and her mother—in a pretty plum-colored dress instead of her chintz wrapper—sat just as stiffly across from him. They'd been quarreling, that much was evident. "I'm back," she said, slipping out of her coat and hanging it in the hall closet—it had been brisk out on the street, the fog creeping in over the rooftops to dissolve the sun and a chill breeze running in ahead of it, though she'd never admit it. San Francisco? Cold? Never.

Her mother coughed gently into one fist. "We've been talking, your father and I," she said—and here she shot a look at Edith's stepfather, who wouldn't acknowledge her, wouldn't even turn his head—"and we've agreed that you'll be staying on here, in boarding school, for the academic year."

It took a moment to register the words, and then suddenly it was as if the sun had broken through the fog and struck the room with light, meteoric, blinding. She was there on the edge of the carpet, feeling as if she were at the very beginning of a recital, every head turned to her and the conductor holding his baton at the ready. She didn't know what to say.

"Miss Everton's Young Ladies' Seminary," her mother went on, "where

149

Rebecca Thompson's daughters attend classes. Carrie Abbott speaks highly of it. And the curriculum should suit you perfectly: French, German, Music and Art." Her mother was smiling her beautiful smile, full-lipped, her teeth shining and perfectly proportioned, and for just that moment she looked as she had before the disease claimed her, vibrant, young, sure of herself. "I've already spoken with Miss Everton. You're to begin September fourteenth."

Her stepfather had nothing to say to this. In the next moment he stood abruptly, strode to the closet for his hat and stalked out the door, slamming it behind him. It was the cost he objected to, she was sure of it, as if nothing mattered but dollars and dollars alone. She didn't care. She was soaring—"Oh, Mother," she said, "Mother." And then, just for a moment, she came crashing down again—this would mean separation, a two-days' journey between them, and she'd never before been separated from her mother in her life.

"Of course, we'll wait till you're settled before we leave for Santa Barbara, and we'll see you for Christmas. And write. We'll write every day."

It was a kind of miracle. After all she'd been put through on the island and in Mrs. Sanders' class, where she'd never really belonged—they were hayseeds, rubes, and Santa Barbara wasn't a city at all—now, finally, she felt she'd come home. And felt she'd earned it too. If she'd never been on San Miguel, never seen a sheep or a pig or suffered the grinding boredom of those anemic days and bloodless nights with no one to talk to and nowhere to go, she couldn't have appreciated Miss Everton's school the way she did. To the other girls it might have been usual, more of the same, a ritual society had contrived to prepare them for the next stage of life, which was to marry and marry money, but Edith saw things differently—this was her opportunity, her escape from the ordinary, from ranches and dust and a dying mother and a stepfather who could think of nothing but himself. And though she was an outsider at first—most of the girls had matriculated together through the elementary grades and formed their coteries and alliances—she quickly found her place. By the end of the first term she was earning A's and B's across the board and she was easily the best ballerina—and singer too—in the freshman class. Her French—the language of dance—was still limited (*Chère Maman, J'espère que vous allez bien*) and her German was weaker yet, but she was improving through sheer repetition and Miss Everton herself singled out her performance as Portia in the school's co-production of *The Merchant of Venice* with St. Basil's Academy as the best of the year.

So it went through that fall and the following spring, home for the summer and on into the next term, and if she worried about her mother—and she did—it was at a remove. Each night, just after lights out, her mother's face would float free of her consciousness to hover there in the dark over the bed, and she would say a prayer and close her eyes and the next thing she knew it was morning, girls rustling in the hallway, her roommate softly snoring in the bed beside hers and the smell of bacon and toast and scrambled eggs infusing the air. Then there was the onward rush of school, another day, another night, and no thought but for the moment. When she was home, when she could see her mother struggling to stand upright, her limbs wasted and the lines of suffering lashing her face, she could think of nothing else.

Then, on a rainy afternoon just before Christmas break, everything changed all over again. She was in the middle of her piano lesson with Mr. Sokolowski, who had a habit of beating out the time with the flat of his hand on the bench beside you in a slow steady drop that went counter to everything you were feeling (it was Chopin's Nocturne no. 2 in E-flat Major, the tempo so dragged down and reduced she might have been sleepwalking), when Miss Everton herself appeared in the doorway. Mr. Sokolowski looked up, his lips parted in irritation. She stopped playing, though his hand went on beating through the next two measures. Miss Everton—she was her mother's age, or no, older, dressed all in tutorial gray and with her hair pinned up so severely her scalp was blanched at the hairline—was simply standing there, looking lost. Was there something in her hand—a slip of folded-over paper? There was. And before she could say a word Edith knew what it meant. "Is she—?" she said.

"Your mother's ill, that's all the telegram says. You're to return at once."

She was two days on the boat, the seas savage in the face of the storm that chased them down the coast, and everyone around her was sick at stomach. The smell was awful—like being trapped in a zoo—and she couldn't go out on deck because it was raining the whole time. She'd never been seasick—she had her sea legs, that was what Captain Curner had told her, praising her— but as the hours went on and the smell concentrated itself till she felt she couldn't breathe, she began to feel worse and worse. In the head—filthy, sour, a discolored mop reeking in the corner and somebody pounding desperately at the door—she went down on her knees and hung over the toilet till there was nothing left inside her. The boat rocked and groaned as if it would come apart. Her legs felt weak. When finally she made her way back to her berth she lay there volitionless, unable to change into her nightdress, unable to read or sleep or think of anything but what lay ahead.

Her mother was ill, that was all she knew. But her mother had been ill a long while—she'd lost weight and color and she'd hemorrhaged more times than anyone could count—and yet she'd always recovered because she was strong, the strongest woman alive. Maybe that was what this was: a false alarm. Maybe it was just another hemorrhage, bad enough, yes, but the sort of attack her mother had survived before. That was what she wanted to believe and she fought down the voice inside her that told her she was fooling herself because why else would they have pulled her out of school and wired the money for her passage if the moment of crisis hadn't come? And then the grimmer thought: What if she was too late? What if her mother was already dead—or dying, dying right at that moment?

By the morning of the second day her throat was raw. She was thirstier than she'd ever been in her life, but every time she took a swallow of water it came right back up. The woman in the berth across from her took pity on her and gave her a handful of soda crackers to soothe her stomach. She broke them into fragments and tried chewing them one at a time, but they turned to paste in her mouth and she couldn't seem to get them down. At one point someone said they were passing San Miguel. She never even lifted her head.

There was no one at the pier to meet her—she would have thought Ida would come, Ida at least, and the fact that she wasn't there or her stepfather either filled her with dread. She stood alone on the pier in the rain, feeling light-headed, the other passengers streaming past her, the smell of the sea so overpowering it made her stomach clench all over again. There were people everywhere, faces looming up out of the mob, their eyes seizing on her as if to take possession of her and know her in her grief and fear and need before staring right through her, and she didn't recognize any of them. Adolph— where was Adolph? Anybody? Finally, the umbrella clutched in one hand and the suitcase in the other, she set out to walk the eight blocks home.

It was a struggle, the streets a mess, the gutters alive with refuse, cigar stubs, paper bags, leaves, branches, horse droppings. Carriages lurched by, but no one thought to offer her a ride. The rain plunged straight down. She pushed through it, hurrying, breathless, going as fast as she could, her shoes soaked, her feet cold, the hem of her dress—the one she'd been wearing when Miss Everton escorted her to the boat and unchanged now through two days and a night—sodden with filth. Her hair was coming loose, her hat poking awkwardly at the ribs of the umbrella. All she could think was what her mother would say, how angry she'd be. *You change that dress right this minute, young lady, and here, give me the brush, your hair's a disgrace.*

Up the walk to the house, a single lamp burning in the front window, water cascading over the eaves, then the door, the umbrella, the suitcase dropping from her hand. "Hello!" she called. "Is anyone home? Mother? Ida?" The cat— Marbles—was perched on the footstool before the fire and he shot her a glance, startled, before springing to the floor and vanishing in the shadows beneath the chair. She saw that the fire had burned down. There was a half-filled teacup on the low table beside the chair and a book lying open there, facedown, the sort of thing her mother would never tolerate, *You're ruining that book, Edith. Think of the spine. Think of the cost.* "Hello?" she called again, moving across the floor to the stairway.

There was the sound of footsteps, of a door flung open, and then Ida was there at the head of the stairs. "Edith, is that you?"

They tried to spare her, Ida clinging to her in the stairwell, her stepfather emerging from the upper bedroom with his arms folded and his eyes gone distant, and the man beside him too, the doctor, the doctor with his black bag and his spectacles shining and the dead dumb unflinching look on his face warning her not to go in there, not yet, not until they had a chance to prepare things, but she wouldn't have it, wouldn't listen, and she broke away from Ida and rushed up the stairs knowing only this: that her mother was already dead, dead and gone and extinguished, and that she'd never hear her voice again, never hear the coughing in the night or the soft calming lilt of her words as she read aloud before the fire or recited a poem she'd learned as a girl. Her stepfather tried to block her way, but she fought free of him, careening down the hall to fling herself through the open door and into the room that was lit by the lamp at the bedside and yet was dark all the same with its layers of contending shadow and the blood that wasn't red, not red, not red anymore, but as black as the place where what was left of her mother— the shell, the empty shell—would go to rest.

Double Eagle

Alone in her room in the dark, she listened to the shuffling and whispering from the room next door, the room where her mother lay dead. The smallest sounds: a patter of feet, the sudden startled whine of the wardrobe's hinges, the sigh of a drawer pulled open and the soft discreet thump of its closing. Ida was in there, taking charge. She could hear her stepfather—a heavier tread, but soft, soft, the muted beat of a mallet wrapped in gauze—pacing the hallway, creaking up and down the stairs, his voice cast low. Then nothing. Stasis. Silence. Rain. And here it came again: the buzz of whispered griefs, concerns, question and response, a door opening and closing, the solitary rhythm of Ida's feet on the bedroom carpet. She tried not to think about what those sounds intimated, but she couldn't help herself: Ida was cleaning up, putting things to rights. And what did that mean? That meant preparing the body for the undertaker. For the ground.

But wasn't that a daughter's task? Shouldn't she be there beside Ida, shoulder to shoulder, elbow to elbow, hip to hip, stripping the bloody sheets, stripping the corpse, washing the crusted black blood from her own mother's lips? Ida had said no. Ida wouldn't hear of it. Ida had wrapped her in her arms and led her away from the disordered bed and the effigy of her mother—and the blood, the blood that was everywhere, even on the bedstead, the floor, the wall—and gently pulled the door shut behind her.

Her mother was dead. That was the fact. And the worst thing, worse even than the loss of her, was that she hadn't got to see her before the Lord took her away, and though she tried to imagine her mother in repose, in a better place where there was no coughing, no blood, where there were no sleepless nights spent sweating in a thin gown and spitting mucus into a cup, tried to picture the field of lilies, the wisps of cloud, Jesus radiant on His throne, she could find no relief. If the Lord was so merciful why had He let her die without her own daughter there at her side? Why had He let her die when that daughter was so close, when she was standing confused on the pier in the rain or struggling up the street with the gutters clogged and her heart pounding and no one to offer her a ride?

It had been so close, a matter of minutes, mere minutes. If the boat had only been swifter, if there hadn't been a storm, if the telegram had come a day earlier, just a day, she would have been there to take her mother in her arms, no matter the blood or her coughing or frailty, to bless her and hold her and receive her blessing in return. Instead, she came home to a corpse. And worse: she didn't shed a tear or beat herself like Heathcliff in his grief over Catherine, but just stood there frozen because she couldn't accept that this was her mother, this dead inert thing in its frieze of blood. *It's the shock of it,* Ida had said. *Now come away from there, come,* and Ida led her out the door and down the hall to bed, this bed, her own bed, where when the whisperings finally stopped and the house settled into silence, she fell away into a black and fathomless sleep.

The funeral service was held in the parlor the following afternoon. Her mother lay rigid in the coffin, her eyelids drawn down as if she were asleep and the faintest smile painted on her lips by the mortician. The mortician stood at the back of the room, two small boys in black at his side. They held black silk top hats in their hands and studied the floor. The minister was a stranger—her mother wasn't a churchgoer and she supposed her stepfather must have contracted with the mortician to bring the man along. There were no mourners but for her, her stepfather, Adolph and Ida. Tapered white candles and vases of cut flowers—Ida's doing—gave the room the feeling of a chapel, and the minister, with his sweep of silver hair and crisp clerical collar, stood grave and erect before the coffin. The service was brief—the usual comfortless words, the words she'd heard twice before in her life when friends of her mother had died in San Francisco and they'd gone to services in a great lofty cathedral with a hundred mourners and a choir singing and incense streaming from polished censers—and then they were out on the street, in a light rain, following the mortician's hearse to the cemetery on the hill overlooking the ocean.

There were more words, *earth to earth, ashes to ashes, dust to dust,* black umbrellas, black horses, the seabirds rotating overhead and crying out their indifference. Her stepfather took the shovel from the grave digger and threw the first symbolic spattering of dirt on the coffin. Ida, in a dress that had once belonged to Edith's mother, hung her head and sobbed, and Edith watched her stepfather put an arm around her shoulder to steady her. Edith herself, though she was stricken to the core and would recollect every detail of that day for the rest of her life as if they'd been seared into her brain with a hot iron, didn't break down and cry. Anyone could cry. Anyone could rage to the heavens and tear out her hair. But she was an actress—or she became one that day—and she held herself apart so that she could see and feel and hear and take all the credit away from the kind of God who would do this to her, her face ironed sober and her shoulders slumped under the weight of her unassailable grief. There was a funeral supper, but she didn't taste it. And, finally, there was bed, but she didn't sleep.

The next day sheared away like the face of a cliff crashing into the ocean and then there was another day and another. Her stepfather put a wreath on the door, but it wasn't a Christmas wreath and when Christmas Day came there was no celebration, no exchange of gifts or singing of carols or even a special dinner. Ida put something on the table and sat with them and they ate in silence. In the days that followed, Edith locked herself up in her room though the weather was soft and inviting, clear days giving way to star-filled nights, the trees in perpetual leaf and the flowers along the front walk waving bright orange banners as if to deny the toll every living thing has to pay, and then it was New Year's, a bitter time, the bitterest, the two-year anniversary of their move to the island. It was that move that had killed her mother, she was sure of it. If only they'd stayed in San Francisco—or here, even here—everything would have been different. Did she blame her stepfather? Did she watch him chewing his meat, chewing with his mouth open and one hand clenching his knife and the other his whiskey (he was drowning his sorrow, that was what he claimed) and accuse him in her heart? She did. Yes. Resoundingly.

She didn't like to talk to him, didn't like to talk to anyone, not even Ida, not the way she was grieving, but when New Year's had passed and the new term at Miss Everton's was about to commence, she came to him where he was sitting by the fire, a book open in his lap and the glass on the table at his side, and handed him the printed schedule for the *Santa Rosa*. "I thought tomorrow morning's boat would be best," she said. "Classes start Monday and this way I'd have Sunday to settle in at the dormitory. We could wire ahead to Miss Everton to have someone meet me at the pier—and I don't have much with me, so I can walk to the boat if you like and save the expense of a carriage . . ."

Patches of peeling skin traced the margin of his side whiskers, yellow-edged flakes that dusted his shoulders and clung minutely to his mustache. He'd worn a beard on the island for at least part of the time—too much trouble to shave, he'd said, though her mother had hated it—and the beard had hidden the flaws of his skin. She looked at him now in the lamplight and saw the pits and eruptions run rampant there, his whole face aflame as if all his sorrow had bled out of him and settled in the pores of his face, and she felt a wave of affection for him: he *was* grieving, grieving every bit as much as she was herself. He looked up from the book. His eyes shifted to her, gray eyes, eyes the color of smoke drifting over open water. "I've been meaning to talk to you about that," he said.

She said nothing. She stood there in the pool of light cast by the lamp, looking down at his blistered face, the stippled beak of his nose, the pink revelation of his scalp where the white hair was thinning, giving him her attention.

"Well," he said, closing the book on one finger to mark the place, "the long and short of it is that I've decided—and your mother, before she died, agreed with me on this—that you'll not be going back."

"Not going back? What do you mean? It's school, my school, I must go back."

For a long moment he just looked at her steadily. "I don't know about that," he said finally, and he gave her a smile—or a simulacrum of a smile—that chilled her. "If you ask me, a girl's place is in the home—especially a home like this one where there's been a tragedy so fresh I don't think any of us has had a chance to put it in perspective."

"But"—she was stunned, pleading now—"Miss Everton will be expecting me. Mr. Sokolowski, all of them. My things are there. My studies. My books—"

"That's all been arranged."

"Arranged? What do you mean?"

He took his time, shifting in the chair so that he was facing her, his eyes locked on hers. "Do you know something," he said, and it wasn't a question,

"I don't like your tone." And then he added, "Young lady," as if he were her mother, as if he were speaking in her voice, in her place, and the address rang hollow on his lips.

He was still staring at her, his eyes hardening, and she should have known better, should have backed off and waited till he was more reasonable, but she couldn't help herself. "My mother would never have said such a thing, I don't believe you. She wanted me to have an education, you know she did. You're a liar!"

He rose from the chair so suddenly she didn't have time to react, the book spilling to the floor, his mouth twisted in a sneer, his breath in her face, whiskey breath, hateful and stinking. "No," he said, "I'm no liar. Every word out of my mouth is the truth and nothing but the truth—the truth of your life from now on. You'll not be up there in that city with no one to watch out for you and your, your *boys*—"

"But Miss Everton never—"

"Enough! You listen to me and listen well because as long as you live under my roof not only will you do exactly as I say in every phase of your conduct, but you can put Miss Everton out of your mind for good and all." He swung angrily away from her, stalking across the room to set his glass on the mantel. She saw that his hand was shaking. She kept thinking of Ida— where was Ida? Ida would stand up for her, Ida knew her mother's wishes. But Ida was in the kitchen or out in the yard, and even if she weren't, Ida was only a servant and servants had no say in anything.

The house was still, every mote of dust hanging suspended in the air. The fireplace framed him, the great squared-off ridge of the back of his head rising up out of his collar like hammered stone, his shoulders barely contained by the crudely tailored cloth of his jacket. In the next moment he swiveled round, moving so swiftly she didn't have time to react, and he was right there, thrusting his face into hers and snatching her by the wrist. "Miss Everton," he spat. "Miss Everton's an irrelevance. And so's Mrs. Sanders and the music teacher and all the rest of them. Because the fact is I'm taking you back to the island where I can keep an eye on you. Do you hear me? Do you?"

He was shouting now, but she wouldn't stand for it, wouldn't listen. She jerked her arm away, struggling for balance, and then she was running for the door, the front door, with one thought only: to get out, to get away, to put a stop to whatever it was that was happening to her.

159

"And we leave as soon as I can break off the lease and put this furniture in storage, if you want to know!" Then the parting shot, his words hurtling at her as she pushed through the door and fought her way out into the sunshine that seared the walk and set the trees afire: "Go ahead, cry your eyes out. But you pack your bags. And don't you ever dare call me a liar again."

She kept on running, through the gate and out into the public street, hatless, sobbing, in her plainest dress and the shoes she wore around the house, not caring what anybody thought. People gave her startled looks, stepped aside for her. The boy three houses down, a boy her own age she barely knew, called out in a jeering voice but the words made no sense to her. She ran past him, ran past them all, and she didn't stop till she'd reached the grounds of the Arlington, and even then she veered off the flagstone path and across the lawn till she found an isolated bench—the farthest one in the farthest corner of the property where no one was likely to see her—and threw herself down on it. For the longest time she couldn't seem to catch her breath, couldn't seem to stop crying, and she understood that she wasn't crying for her mother anymore but for her own stricken self, because she'd rather die on the spot, rather kill herself, than go back out there to that island. And she would. She'd take poison. Cut her wrists. Find a serpent like Cleopatra, and if it wasn't an asp then she'd dig up a rattlesnake, with its dripping fangs and furious buzzing tail, and press it to her breast and feel its bite like the kiss of a lover. He couldn't do this to her. He didn't have the right. She was almost seventeen years old and he wasn't her real father, anyway.

Her nose was stuffed with mucus, her face was a mess. She patted her pockets for a handkerchief, but she didn't have one. She didn't have anything, not even a comb. The realization—she was helpless, absolutely helpless, *not even a comb*—started her sobbing again and she couldn't stop, her face buried in her hands and her shoulders heaving, all her misery boiling out of her and no one to see or care. Her mother was dead, dead, dead, and her stepfather was a tyrant and her life was finished before it had begun, and so what was the use of anything?

And then something—a whisper in the grass, a murmur of voices?—made her glance up. Standing there before her was a young couple—very young, no more than four or five years older than she—looking alarmed.

They were dressed beautifully, *à la mode*, the woman—girl—in a gauze veil and a high wide-brimmed hat crowned with aigrettes, and their faces were numb. She saw it all in an instant—they'd come here, to this bench sheltered in its bower of jasmine, to make love, and here she was, unkempt and unfashionable, in her homeliest shirtwaist and scuffed shoes, creating a scene. She was pitiable. Beneath contempt.

The man was saying something, asking if she needed help—*assistance,* that was the term he used, *Do you need assistance?*—but she was so mortified all she could do was shake her head. She watched them exchange a look, and why couldn't they leave her alone, why couldn't they find some other bench, some other hotel, why couldn't they take a stroll along the beach or watch the boats from the pier like all the other tourists? Or vanish. Why couldn't they just vanish?

The man tried again, leaning forward so that his shadow fell over her. "Are you certain? Isn't there anything we can do?"

And now the woman spoke: "Anyone we might call? Your mother? Do you want us to fetch your mother?"

And the man: "Are you at the hotel?"

She was sobbing still—she couldn't seem to stop—but she pushed herself up, turned her back on them without a word and made her way across the grounds and past the front entrance and out into the street, where she found herself running again, but this time she wasn't running blindly. This time she had a purpose, a plan. She wasn't helpless. She had money. A lot of money. Enough to get her far away from here if she had the courage to use it.

The streets were shabby, muddy. The sun mocked her. After a block or so she slowed to a brisk walk, her skirts fanning out behind her, her eyes locked straight ahead. In the drawer of the night table beside her bed was a letter from her mother, her mother's last letter, written in a wavering hand the night before she died. It was all too short, just a paragraph telling her that she loved her and would be looking down on her from above and that her father would provide for her until she reached her maturity and then there would be an inheritance coming to her according to the terms of the will, though she—her mother—wished it were more. In the meanwhile, she enclosed a bracelet of precious stones her own mother had once worn and a twenty-dollar gold piece—a double eagle—for her to spend as she pleased. There was a single dried drop of blood on the envelope, and the valediction—*With All*

My Love, Mother—trailed away till it was barely legible, and the thought of it made her want to break down all over again, but she didn't, because she was calculating now. She would sit down to dinner as if nothing had happened and if her stepfather wanted to make small talk she would oblige him and she would smile when he wanted her to smile. And when he went to bed, when the house was still and Ida was asleep in her room and Adolph in his, she would pack the suitcase she'd brought with her, slip down the stairs and out the door and into the night, never to look back.

The Ticket

The man behind the ticket window at the steamship office said he couldn't make change for a double eagle and so she had to wait for the bank to open and then the man at the bank wanted to know who she was and how she'd come by the coin. She didn't see what business it was of his what she did with her own money or where she'd got it from, but she gave him her name and informed him that her mother had just died and she was taking the one o'clock steamer for San Francisco, where her school was, which would explain the suitcase at her feet. The man—he was wearing a green celluloid visor that took the luster out of his eyes—stared down at the coin where it lay on the counter between them. Then he glanced up at her again, considering, but he made no move to slide it across the counter and into the money drawer or to begin counting out bills. Or silver. Or asking which she preferred. "I'm a second-year student at Miss Everton's Young Ladies' Seminary," she said, offering further evidence of her legitimacy—she was a schoolgirl, that was all, on her sad way back up the coast after burying her mother.

She tried to hold the man's eyes, but she felt her confidence slipping, felt guilty, and she stole a glance at the window next to her, where an over-dressed woman tottering under a hat the size of a birdbath stood chatting with the teller there. The woman gave a sidelong glance and Edith froze—she knew her, didn't she? Wasn't she one of the teachers at the high school? But now the woman had turned and was staring directly at her, and what was her name? It came to her in the moment she spoke it aloud: "Mrs. Parsons, how are you? Don't you remember me—I was in Mrs. Sanders' class the year before last? Edith Waters?"

Clearly the woman didn't remember, but that didn't stop her from chiming, "Yes, yes, of course. And how are you?"

The teller was watching her closely and so she just nodded her head, as if to say she was very well, thank you, then added, "I'm at Miss Everton's Seminary now—up in San Francisco?"

"Oh, well . . . that must be quite a change from our humble little school."

"It is," she said, "yes," and she was going to say how much she'd enjoyed the Santa Barbara school and how advanced it really was, but the teller was already counting out her change, so she merely smiled. She put the money carefully in her purse, taking up her suitcase and stepping aside for the man waiting behind her. "Remember me to Mrs. Sanders," she said in her sweetest voice and made her way to the door.

She'd sat through dinner the night before and then breakfast in the morning, though she'd lain awake half the night, fighting with herself. As much as it appealed to her sense of drama to melt off into the night, an empty bed would have given her away and she couldn't afford that, so she dressed and came down to breakfast. The parlor was quiet, the cat nowhere in sight. There was a vase of flowers on the dining room table, but they were wilted and they only reminded her of her mother. Her stepfather was already there, seated at the head of the table, a greasy plate with a half-gnawed bone on it set before him. He seemed bored and remote, hardly glancing up from the newspaper, his blunt battered fingers clumsy with the thin china handle of the teacup. He only brightened when Adolph came in, pushing back his chair to light a cigar and call out to the kitchen for more coffee.

All the while her suitcase was packed and hidden away in the back of her closet, the image of it glowing in her mind till it wasn't a suitcase at all but a pair of wings, angel's wings, to lift her up and out of this house and this life forever. Too wrought up to eat, she took only a bite or two of toast and a mouthful of scrambled eggs with catsup, sugaring her tea so heavily it was like a parfait and no one to notice or tell her different. She forced herself to bid good morning to Adolph, and even ventured a comment about the weather, but he just grunted and took his place beside her stepfather. Ida drifted in with the coffee pot and back out again and as soon as the door swung shut behind her, the two of them started in on the only subject that seemed to hold any interest for them: sheep. Sheep and the island, that is, and all the minutiae of their preparations for the move back. Adolph said it was a shame the way the Englishman was letting the place go to ruin and her stepfather just nodded his head and reiterated for the tenth time how now that poor Marantha was gone there was no sense in maintaining two separate establishments, no sense in the world. They barely noticed when she took up her plate and went out to the kitchen with it.

After that, it was easy—she didn't let on to anyone about what she was planning, not even Ida, and she made sure no one saw her leaving the house. All she could think was that if she could somehow get back to her room at school her stepfather would relent—he'd have to. Either that or make the trip himself to reclaim her. There would be the question of board and tuition, she wasn't fooling herself on that account, but once Miss Everton saw her there at her lessons with the other girls, in the dining hall, at the piano—saw how she *belonged*—she'd intervene for her, Edith was sure she would. And her stepfather would have to pay. He'd be too ashamed not to.

This was what she was thinking as she walked briskly back down the street to the wharf, one hand occupied with her parasol, the other with the suitcase, and she didn't want to think beyond that. Her feet, buttoned tightly into her best shoes, had begun to chafe, but she ignored them. She was fixated on getting her ticket before the smokestack of the *Santa Rosa* appeared on the southern horizon on its way up from Los Angeles, and then losing herself in the crowd until the boat left the pier and she could breathe again, because there was no telling when her stepfather would discover her missing. Hurrying on, she scanned the glistening apron of the sea as it opened up at the base of the street and fanned out across the channel to the islands. Santa Cruz, the largest of them, was clearly visible on the horizon and not a cloud in the sky. Which meant that the seas would be calm—or calmer than on the way down. Or at least she hoped so.

And then she was in the waiting room, the benches full, baggage scattered about and everybody staring at her as if they'd never in their lives seen a young girl traveling back to school on her own. She took her place in line at the ticket window and concentrated on her posture—chin high, shoulders back, *No slouching, Edith, take pride in yourself*, her mother would nag if she were here, but her mother wasn't here and never would be again. When she got to the ticket counter and presented the precise amount for a steerage ticket as it was listed in the schedule of fares, the clerk just stared at her. "I've gone to the bank for the proper change," she said.

He was an effete little man, no bigger than Jimmie, and Jimmie was only a boy. She could see that he was trying to grow out his whiskers, his face

165

splotched with reddish patches of hair that looked like open wounds at a distance and animal's fur close up. "I beg your pardon?" he said.

"For the double eagle," she said, pushing the money forward. "I'd like a ticket, please. One way to San Francisco, third class."

"I'm sorry, miss, but it's against company policy to issue tickets to unaccompanied"—here he hesitated, snatching a quick look at her face before dropping his eyes to the counter—"children."

"But you said . . . you said you didn't have change."

He stiffened. "I didn't," he said, and the lie lay there between them.

"I'm no child. I'm"—she could lie too—"twenty-one years old."

"Company policy," he said. "You'll have to bring a parent, your father or mother—"

She didn't want to draw attention to herself, that was the last thing she wanted, but she couldn't help it. "My mother's dead," she said.

"Then your father." He spoke softly, sadly. He was already looking past her to the next person in line.

"My father's dead too."

"I'm sorry," he said.

When she saw he wasn't going to give her what she wanted—he was immovable, a mule, an idiot—she swung round abruptly, glaring at the man waiting in line behind her, stalked the length of the room with her heels clattering and the suitcase flaring at her side and flung herself out the door and into the full blaze of the sun. She tried to calm herself, to think things through, but already her anger was shading into despair. She felt exposed. Helpless. Anyone could have seen her there, some friend of her stepfather's she didn't even know, some sheep magnate or deckhand or dry-goods merchant come down to meet the ship. She felt a small flutter of panic. Just then the blast of the ship's horn racketed across the water and she looked up to see the boat riding just offshore, as big as a block of houses, its smokestack fuming. The planks of the pier shifted subtly beneath her. "Here she comes!" somebody cried.

For one mad moment her only thought was of stowing away, of following a family up the gangplank, pressing close to them until they were aboard—if she was going to be taken for a child, she'd act like one—and then hiding somewhere overnight, in one of the lifeboats, in a closet or the head or under a table in the saloon. She had money. She could buy herself dinner, tea, sit

166

there as long as she liked, tell the waiter her parents were indisposed, seasick, green around the gills—anything, anything to get away from here—but she knew she was fooling herself. Very slowly, squaring her shoulders and taking up the suitcase and parasol, she turned away from the ticket office and began making her way back down the pier as if she'd just arrived, ignoring the men in carriages and the fishermen and all the rest of them with their pat stupid expressions and leached-out eyes.

By the time she reached the end of the pier, she knew what she was going to do, though it was risky, riskier even than the boat. She didn't dare try to take a coach—that would be the first thing her stepfather would expect and there was no guarantee that the agent there would take her money any more than the idiot at the steamship office would—but the railway was another thing altogether. Anyone could take the train. Of course, rail service was new to Santa Barbara and she'd never been on the train herself, yet Becky Thorpe had and that was good enough for her. The problem was that the train didn't go to San Francisco, it went south, south only. To Los Angeles. If she boarded the train, she'd be on her own, without a room or roommate or meals in the dining hall or piano lessons with Mr. Sokolowski or Miss Everton's guiding hand, not that Miss Everton had ever guided her personally, but she was there, like a monument, in loco parentis, a buffer between the girls and the harsh hard world they all knew from Zola and Dickens. She'd have to find her way all alone in a city she'd seen only once, with her mother, years ago—she'd have to take rooms, but who would rent to her? And once her money was exhausted, how would she pay?

No matter. She strode into the station, went up to the window and booked passage on the next train for Los Angeles and the only question the agent asked was *Will that be round trip or one way?* and without hesitation she answered: *One way.* She took a seat on a bench in the far corner and settled in to wait. The train was at five-thirty and it would be past dark then. Her step-father would be sure to come looking for her if she wasn't home by dark, no question about it, but then he'd never imagine she'd try to get away to Los Angeles—to school, yes, to San Francisco, where she belonged, but not Los Angeles. Los Angeles was a place he scarcely knew. Still, it was just past one-thirty in the afternoon and who knew but that Ida would have sent up the alarm by now? She could imagine her stepfather sitting down to luncheon after a morning of laying in supplies against returning to the island—the big

167

sacks of rice and beans and flour she'd come to loathe the sight of, farm equipment, tools—and saying *Where the devil's Edith got herself to?* and Ida saying *I haven't seen her all day and I know she's not in her room or the yard either.*

She tried to read to pass the time, but her eyes kept jumping to the door, people going in and out, a garble of voices, inquiries about the timetable and fares and did the five-thirty stop at San Buenaventura? At some point she dozed off, the book spread open in her lap, and then the door slammed and she was awake again. She smelled boot blacking, coal dust, leather. The ticket agent was eating a corned beef sandwich and she smelled that too, hungry suddenly and wishing she'd taken more at breakfast. She started thinking of food, of the places along State Street where she could get cheese and bread or a hamburger sandwich, but she was afraid to leave her seat though it was only just four and the train wasn't due for another hour and a half. Even so, she couldn't risk being seen on the street in any case. They must have known she was gone by now. What would her stepfather think—that she was with Becky Thorpe, though she hardly knew her anymore? Out for a walk? Haunting the shops? But no, that wasn't what he'd think at all. He'd know in an instant—he'd always been suspicious of her, of her relations with boys, though they were practically nonexistent, never satisfied, always maligning her—and it was only a matter of time before he came after her.

The thought frightened her and she shrank into herself. She tried to focus on the future, on the good things that surely awaited her. When she got back to San Francisco—and she would, she knew she would no matter what it cost her—she wouldn't return to Miss Everton or Mr. Sokolowski or to lessons of any kind. She was grown now. She'd had enough lessons. No, she would go directly to the stage door and audition for every part in every play there was and though she'd have to start as an understudy or with one of the subsidiary roles—a walk-on—she would shine and people would take notice and soon, with hard work and luck, she'd be offered the leading roles, the ingénue, the princess, the young love of the count or senator. And when people called out to her, shouted acclaim from the balcony and in the lobby afterward, she wouldn't answer to Edith. Edith was the name of no one she knew. She had a new name to go with her new identity, a name that had come to her in a waking dream after she'd rejected a dozen others, a name that was simple and direct and yet exotic too in the way that Edith Waters or even Lillian Russell could never be. Inez. They would call her Inez, Inez Deane.

At quarter of five the waiting room began to fill up. A woman with a wicker basket brimming with oranges sat beside her, along with her little boy, who kept saying "We're going on a train" over and over and turning periodically to his mother for confirmation, "aren't we?"

"Yes," the woman said, "yes, we're going to Pasadena. To see your nana." She smiled at Edith. "Don't mind him," she said. "It's his first rail trip."

"Oh, he's no bother at all." Edith leaned forward, bringing her face level with his. "And what's your name?"

He looked away, rocking on the balls of his feet, his shoulders swaying back and forth. "Go ahead," his mother said. "Tell her your name."

Still swaying, a look for his mother, then the quick proud glance at Edith: "Jimmie."

"Jimmie?" she repeated, taken by surprise, and for an instant she was back out on the island, the day wrapped round her like an unwashed sheet and Jimmie crouching there before her with his warm wet mouth sucking at the flesh of her inner thigh as if he were trying to extract juice from an orange . . .

"Would you like one?" the woman was saying. "I've got a whole basket here. I'm taking them down to my mother. Go ahead, have one."

It was then, just as she took the orange from the woman's hand, that the door swung open for the hundredth time that afternoon. Almost casually, as if she'd known all along how events would unfold, she glanced up into the faces of her stepfather and the stranger in the high-crowned hat beside him, who, as it turned out, wore the six-pointed star just above his shirt pocket for a very good reason. She didn't start, didn't protest, just handed the orange back to the woman, took up her suitcase and walked quietly to the door.

The Stove

And so she was on a boat again, but it wasn't a steamer and it wasn't the *Santa Rosa* and it wasn't bound for San Francisco. If there was a cruel irony in all this, she couldn't begin to fathom it. She sat stiffly, staring straight ahead, her back pressed to the wall and her feet planted firmly on the floor of the cabin that stank of tobacco, bacon grease, fish leavings and sweat, men's sweat, in the very seat her mother had occupied, and she might have been her mother's ghost, dead and disembodied, caught between one world and the next. The men were above, in the wheelhouse, drinking whiskey, their eyes tense with excitement. "We're going home," her stepfather had crowed, slapping Adolph on the back as they hauled their provisions aboard, and Adolph, a sack of pinto beans suspended between him and Charlie Curner on the deck below, had given him his tight immutable smile in return. Charlie Curner grinned. It was a good day, with a fair breeze, and he was getting paid.

For her part, she refused to look anyone in the eye, refused even to lift her head, and she didn't bother with a parasol or her stays or anything else, staring first at the planks of the pier, then the deck and the steps going down to the cabin, and she wouldn't speak to anyone even if she was addressed directly—if they were going to make her a prisoner, she would act like one. She was mute and she might as well have been deaf too. The boat lurched. There were the waves, the gulls, the mainland that sank behind her like a stone.

It was mid-January, somewhere thereabout, anyway. She wasn't even sure of the date, but what did it matter? The only thing she was sure of was that her will meant nothing, that she was captive, body and soul, no better than an animal in a cage. The man with the badge had searched her and handed over her money—and the ticket, the useless ticket—to her stepfather, who forbade her to leave the house till they were safely aboard the *Evangeline*, and

170

he'd gone with the sheriff to the offices of the stagecoach, the steamship line and the railway to make sure of his prohibition.

"It isn't fair," she said. "You have no right."

"Your place is with your father."

"You're not my father."

"I am. And you're a willful, ungrateful child, and if you don't come to your senses I swear I'll take off this belt and strap you till you do."

"Never! I won't do it. I won't go."

And suddenly the belt was in his hand, jerked through the loops with a snapping ominous hiss, and she turned and bolted across the room and up the stairs and into her bedroom before he could grab hold of her. She heard his heavy tread on the stairs and locked the door, but he put his shoulder to it and the door flew open and he stalked into the room, his eyes as cold as any murderer's, the belt snaking from one clenched fist. "Will you listen? Will you listen now?"

She was on the bed, clutching at her pillow. Her mother was dead and there was to be no quarter between them, she saw that now. "Yes," she said.

"What was that?"

"Yes," she said. "Yes."

She didn't venture out of her room for the next two days and she didn't care whether she starved or not. She heard them below, going about their business. The sun striped the wall behind her, faded, came back in the morning and faded again. At dinner on the second day, there was a knock at her door and Ida was there, a tray in her hand and the aroma of tomato and barley soup running on ahead of her. Her face was unreadable, as if she'd paused to slip on a mask in the hallway, and whose side was she on in this? What had he told her? Had he sent her? "Here," Ida said, setting the tray down on the night table, "you just take a taste of this now."

But she wouldn't, though she hadn't eaten in nearly three days, not since the morning of her aborted flight. Her stomach rumbled. She swallowed involuntarily.

"Sure you're going to have to eat something if you intend to remain amongst the living."

"I don't. I just want to die. I want to be with my mother."

"You can't mean that."

"I hate him," she said. "I hate him with all my heart."

Ida was standing there in the middle of the room, the light from the hallway spilling her shadow across the floor till it reached the foot of the bed and climbed up the wall beside it. She didn't say anything in response, but after a moment she went to the lamp on the table by the window and lighted it.

"He killed my mother. And now he wants to kill me too."

If she expected Ida to contradict her, she was mistaken. Instead, Ida came round the bed and eased herself down beside her. "Edith," she murmured, the lamplight feathering her hair and settling in her features so that she took on its glow. "Here," she said, "put your hand here," and she took hold of Edith's hand and laid it palm down on her stomach. The room was very still. Edith could feel the warmth there beneath the fabric of her dress and her stays and underthings, Ida's flesh, the beat of her heart: it was the most intimate thing that had ever happened between them. "Do you feel that?"

She was confused. Ida's face was right there, inches from her own. She could smell the powder she wore, count the minute divisions of her lashes. "What do you mean? Feel what?"

"I'm going to have a baby."

"A baby?" She was joking, she had to be—she wasn't even married. "But how, how can that be?"

Ida only shook her head, very slowly, side to side. She began to say something, then caught herself. "I'll be going back north, to my mother," she said finally, and she dropped her eyes.

And why was she thinking in that moment of herself, only herself? Because she was going down in a darkening swirl of wind-beaten waves and clutching at anything to pull herself back up and out, because she was a girl still whose only experience of the world was a stolen kiss with a boy from St. Basil's by the name of Thomas R. Landon and the feel of Jimmie's lips on her thigh and the way it made her blood rush, but Jimmie was nothing and she was nothing too. Ida was going to have a baby. There was a male organ, that was how it started—she knew that, everyone did, the girls whispering in the dark after lights out, one lewd thing paraded after another—but nothing could happen without the sacrament of marriage, no babies, that is . . . but then she herself had been an orphan and how had that come about? Had her parents died? Or had her mother, her true mother, been someone like Ida, who just somehow happened to have a baby in a time like this when everything was confusion and all the world had a dark shade thrown over it?

"You'll be coming back," she said, and she was breathing hard now, as if she'd been running uphill, "after, that is, once the baby . . . and the father, the baby's father . . ."

But Ida kept on shaking her head. In a whisper so soft she had to strain to hear: "The baby's father doesn't want me. He doesn't want the baby."

Then the bed rocked beneath her and Ida was on her feet, her shoulders hunched and her hair looping free of the bun at the back of her head. Then she was framed in the doorway and then the door pulled shut and Edith refused to think of the nights on the island or in this very house—this house, this one—when there were noises in the dark, the faintest watery sigh and suck of movement in the rippling depths, as if the dolphins were at play beneath the moonlit waves. She thought of herself, of herself only. And when the door had closed, she picked up the spoon and began to eat.

She came up on deck when the anchor dropped in the harbor, feeling as if she'd been singled out and sentenced for some crime as yet unnamed. The sky was overcast, the island a dun fortress hammered out of the waves. Wind drove at her on a stinging whiplash of spray, and even then, even in the first moments of her sentence that could stretch on for months or years even, it carried the stink of sheep to her and the distant racketing of the seals and sea elephants. Nothing had changed. Miss Everton's Seminary had never existed, nor her mother, nor San Francisco, nor the rented rooms or the house in Santa Barbara. This was all there was, world eternal, *the quality of mercy is not strained,* but it is, it is.

Jimmie there on the beach with his leering eyes and the mule perched like a statue behind him. Harsh words from her stepfather, commands, and no, she wouldn't be riding the sled up the hill, she would be walking—and carrying her own load too. Then there was the house, the paint all but gone, the smell of it, cold grease, colder ash, five p.m. and almost dark and her stepfather taking her by the arm and thrusting her into the kitchen. "There's the food," he said. "There's the stove."

Jimmie

She stood just inside the door, slumped against the wall. The cold was in her feet, in her bones. She could hear her stepfather pounding through the house in a rage, cursing the one-armed man and his wife for the state of the place, everything in disarray, every step he took and corner he turned a fresh outrage and an affront and a keen winnowing disappointment that set him off all over again. He shouted at Jimmie and Adolph. Gutter language. God-damn and Jesus Christ. Fuck this, fuck that. They ran the mule up and down the road that had washed out so many times it was just a glorified gulley now and they crashed through the door at regular intervals to dump the food-stuffs on the kitchen floor in a heap of crates, sacks, cans and bottles. The house boomed and echoed. The gutters rattled in the wind.

For a long while she merely stood there, sunk in despair. The place reeked like a garbage dump—it *was* a garbage dump, trash heaped to the windows and every stained and cracked cup, plate, saucer and bowl crammed into the washbasin in a cold puddle of swimming grease and putrid water, in the center of which the corpses of two drowned mice floated with their naked feet clenched on nothing. It was disgusting. Degrading. She wanted to sit, wanted to use the toilet, but her body was paralyzed and her mind had shut down, the past colliding with the present till she hardly knew where she was. Still, when the light faded out of the windows she found herself crossing the room to light the lantern and clear a space for it on the table. And then she went down on her knees and tried to light the stove too, if only to take the chill off, but the flue must have been stuck or the pipe stopped up because every time she touched a match to the crumpled paper and sticks of kindling, it wouldn't draw.

Her arm—her left arm, just above the elbow—gave a sudden sharp stab of pain where her stepfather had taken hold of her to shove her through the door in his impatience, this hulking bellicose red-faced man who was the only father she'd ever known and who'd been wounded in the war and never let anyone forget about it. Captain. That was what people called him. Not Mister, but Captain. And he expected her to call him father, yet he wasn't acting like a father but a coward and a bully and all she could think was that if she had a gun she would press it to her temple and shoot herself right there on the spot—or no, shoot him, shoot Jimmie and Adolph too, and then all the sheep, every last stupid staring one of them. "Cook," he'd demanded. "But I don't know how," she'd protested, talking now, talking finally, if only to get the words out no matter how deaf the world around her might be. "Then learn by doing," he said.

He'd been poised there in the doorway, urgent and impatient, and his face told her what should have been evident from the moment they boarded the ship or before that even, when Ida had come to her to say she was leaving because she was going to have a baby nobody wanted. There were three men in the household and one girl. Or woman. She was a woman now, by default. And he didn't care if she never saw the inside of a schoolroom again. He needed a cook. And she was elected.

But the stove wouldn't light and the food hadn't been sorted or the dishes washed or the floor swept. She looked round her grimly. There was no water. No apron. Every pot and pan was blackened and crusted over and what was she to scrub them with? Where was the soap? The washcloth?

And cook? Cook what? She'd never cooked a thing in her life, not even an egg. For as long as she could remember, they'd had a cook in the house. Before Ida it had been Mrs. Hedges, who'd served as nanny as well, and on the cook's day off her mother would boil a handful of potatoes to go with the cold roast Mrs. Hedges had set aside the night before. If she was hungry, there was always food, and sometimes, when she was little, Mrs. Hedges would indulge her by allowing her to climb up on a stool and use the spatula to turn her own cheese sandwich in the pan so that it browned evenly on both sides. She'd baked cookies with her mother, of course, like any other girl, and after her mother fell ill she liked to sit in the kitchen feeling blessed and warm and protected while Mrs. Hedges fussed about and the smell of baking bread or corn muffins filled the room, and then later, when Ida took over, she'd drift into the kitchen to gossip as Ida stood at the counter rolling out dough or peeling potatoes or measuring out rice in a cup, but that hardly

175

qualified her as a cook or even a cook's helper. And Ida was gone. And so was her mother.

She got to her feet and wiped her hands on her coat. The kindling just wouldn't seem to catch, each match igniting a ball of paper in a quick crackling bloom that sent up pale snaking tendrils of flame and then died as it reached the wood above, and now it had become a challenge, a contest between her and the powers of the universe. She was angry, frustrated, cold, lonely, hateful, but she set her brain to it. She tried the handle on the flue—it should be straight up and down, shouldn't it? Another ball of paper, another match. Nothing. She crumpled more paper, opened the vents and separated the individual sticks of kindling to widen the gaps and admit more air, blew on the wavering tentative flame till she ran out of breath, and still nothing. Maybe the kindling wasn't dry enough, maybe it had somehow absorbed the dampness of the house. She removed it all, stick by stick, set it beside her on the floor and reached into the box beside the stove for more—and this was dry, certainly it was, dry as the paper itself. Painstakingly, she set one stick across the other, beginning with the smaller ones and working her way up.

She was bent over the open door of the stove, her lips pursed, fanning the ghost of a flame and blowing softly till it quivered and rose and died again, when the back door swung open and Jimmie came in out of the dark. Crouched there on her knees in the dirt, her hair in her eyes and her skirts and petticoat filthy already, she could only scowl at him. "It won't light," she said.

"Won't light?" He gave her a smile that was like a tic, formed and fled before it registered. His arms hung loose, his jaw went slack. This was the first good look she'd had of him since they landed, and if she was miserable, if she hated the sight of this place and of him too because he was part and parcel of it, the presiding spirit, *Caliban,* she was curious at the same time. He'd changed in the year and a half since she'd seen him last. There seemed to be more to him. More breadth to his shoulders, a firmness to the legs she remembered as being so scrawny and shapeless she wondered how they'd managed to keep him upright. He wore the spotty beginnings of a mustache over his lip, twists of dark hair like plants stuck randomly in the soil of a frost-killed garden. His hair crawled down his neck. His clothes were worn to threads. Jimmie. He was Jimmie all the same.

"I've been trying for the past ten minutes." She stood, brushing her hands on her skirt. "I twisted the flue back and forth and I'm sure it's open—"

"Let me have a look," he said, going to his knees so fast it was as if he were diving for cover. Balancing on one hand, he thrust his head through the open gap of the stove, peering upward. "I don't see nothing," he said, his voice echoing in the pipe. In the next moment he was on his feet again, standing beside her, and she felt a pulse of satisfaction: he was still shorter than she was.

"Could it be the pipe? Is the pipe stopped up?"

"Could be," he said, bending to pluck a length of stovewood from the box. "I couldn't say, really, because I've been doing my cooking out in the bunkhouse since Mr. Reed that was here come out to the island. Here, let me try this"—and before she could think to slam shut the door he hammered the pipe with the length of wood, the pipe gave back a corresponding thump and rattle, and there was soot everywhere. "There," he said, and he sneezed three times in rapid succession, "that ought to do it. Go ahead and light it now."

She waited a moment till the air cleared, then bent again to the stove and the kindling there and put the match to it. This time it took and the next thing she knew she was feeding the fire with progressively thicker sticks and it was already rising and snapping and throwing off heat. "Thank you," she said. "I should have thought to do that myself."

There was a silence. She warmed her hands at the fire and he moved in beside her, holding out his palms to the blaze. "Hello," he said.

"Hello? What do you mean, 'hello'?"

"Well, we didn't have a chance—I saw you at the beach, of course, when you came in, but I didn't, not till now . . . What I mean is, we haven't seen each other in such a long while and I thought I'd just say hello. Again. After all this time. How are you? Are you well?"

"I was well," she said, "till I came out here."

"You look beautiful."

She heard him as if from a great distance, as if she were in the dining hall at school and his voice was carrying across the waves all the way up the coast and over the rooftops, and she despised him, she did, but she was already thinking of what he might be worth to her and what he might do for her and how she could use him as an ally in the war she was already engaged in, whether she was ready for it or not. She brought her eyes up. Her voice went soft. "Hello," she said. And then: "It's nice to see you again."

Graveyard of the Pacific

So she became a cook. Not a dancer, not a singer, not a student, but a cook. On an island that was known, if it was known at all, for its wrecks, for the fogs that sucked it into invisibility, the winds that sheared round Point Conception to snap masts and tatter sails and drive ships up on its rocks, for the shriek of rending wood. People called it the Graveyard of the Pacific. She called it Nowhere. At night, when she lay in her damp bed—everything damp, always damp, mold creeping over the mattress like a wet licking tongue and the walls beaded with condensation—she listened to the wind, to the distant tolling of ship's bells and the fading ghostly cries of the foxes that were no bigger than a cat, and her mind spun away into fantasies of escape. She wished she had a boat. Wished she could swim like a fish. Or just walk across the water like Jesus, but then Jesus never faced such surf in the Sea of Galilee. Or wind. Or sharks. Or the ghost of the Chinaman you could hear wailing on nights when the moon was dark because he'd had to sever his own hand with a rusty knife and leave it there wedged between two rocks or drown with the tide.

Her first efforts in the kitchen were clumsy and inadequate, everything tasteless, burned, the beans hard as gravel and the soup so salty it was like spooning up seawater. She was at a loss. The stove was too hot, then it wasn't hot enough. Pots boiled over, meat blackened in the oven. She served the three men at table through breakfast (overcooked eggs and chalky gruel), luncheon (lamb or salt pork fried in lard, with hot sauce, Mexican beans, fried potatoes and bread that was like hardtack because it wouldn't rise) and dinner (more of the same), and sat at the far end of the table with her own plate and watched their faces as they lifted one forkful after another to their lips. They grimaced, sluicing the meat into the beans and the potatoes into the meat, mashing the whole business together and drowning it in grease,

178

hot sauce and pepper, but no one complained, or at least not to her face. In fact, during those first weeks everyone seemed to tiptoe around her, Adolph vague and elusive, Jimmie solicitous, her stepfather going out of his way to conciliate her now that he'd seen she was going to be compliant, if not exactly reconciled to her lot—but then what choice did she have?

He did the slaughtering and showed her how to sharpen the knives and cut chops and sear them in the pan or rub a leg of lamb with thyme and rosemary and bake it so that the juices flowed and it didn't taste like wood pulp. When they had turkey—or more rarely, chicken—Jimmie cornered the bird, took off its head with a stroke of the hatchet and hung it by its feet to bleed out, but it was up to her to scald and pluck and gut it, the wet eviscera steeping her hands and getting up under her nails so that she was forever picking at them and running her orange stick over her cuticles. The first time, she tried to spare herself, poking gingerly at the pale stippled skin with the tip of her knife until Jimmie took it from her and ripped the bird open from the slot at its rear all the way to the breastbone, and when she tried to dislodge the organs with a knife and spoon rather than her fingers, Jimmie just reached in and tore them out. "There's nothing to be squeamish of," he said. "It's just animals. Meat, that's all it is."

The days tumbled past. Her hands toughened. She cut herself or burned her palm on the stove or the handle of the frying pan two or three times a day and learned to ignore it. Out of boredom—and a sense of standards, that too—she cleaned up the kitchen till it was as orderly as when Ida and her mother had been in charge, and very gradually, as a matter of self-preservation as much as anything else, she began to find that she did have a way with cooking after all. Not that there was much range for variation—the meals were standardized to the point of ritual and the household was forever running short of one thing or another so that she had to improvise more often than not—but at least things seemed to taste better, or at least she thought they did. She never did get the knack of baking—her loaves were like wheaten bricks, her bread pudding dense and unpliable. And when she fried abalone steaks, no matter how often she shifted the pan around the stovetop, they were invariably sodden, tasteless and tough. After a while, even though abalone were her stepfather's favorite dish (at least in the abstract, since they cost nothing), he stopped bringing them to her.

She'd heard it said that people could get used to anything, like the Arctic explorers who had to butcher their dogs just to keep from starving and then wear their coats around as if the animals who'd inhabited them had never been their companions and confidants, or the prisoners in solitary confinement who made do with a rat or roach for company—or even Robinson Crusoe, who got so inured to his island he didn't want to leave it—but to her way of thinking adaptability was a curse. She sank into the usual and the usual had nothing to do with her life. The evenings were hardest. During the day she was so busy with the chores she hardly had time to think and when she wasn't cleaning up after one meal and preparing the next she made time to get out and away from the house, tramping the dunes and ridges of the island till she became as strong and fit as an Alpinist and her mind ran free. (If she saw a lamb that had been abandoned she left it where it lay bleating and if Jimmie or her stepfather came across it, they butchered it and ate spring lamb and she didn't think twice about it. She wasn't a sentimentalist, not anymore.) But in the evenings, after the meal had been served and the dishes washed, the emptiness overwhelmed her.

She made a fourth for whist most nights, glad for the distraction, and more often than not chose Jimmie as her partner ("Excellent choice," her stepfather would say, always in his best humor at the card table, "pitting the young folks against the old once again, isn't that right, Adolph? And who do you think'll win this time?"). Jimmie wasn't much use as a player, though— he was too busy gaping at her or gazing off across the room as if he'd been hypnotized and he never gave a thought to protecting his cards so that her stepfather always seemed to know what suit Jimmie was going to bid before he did himself. Still, once in a while they did win a hand, and on rare occasions a game or two, and when they did she couldn't help taking satisfaction in the way her stepfather's face froze up with disappointment. There was the Ouija board too, but without her mother there to guide them, the messages seemed bland and obvious (*Spirits abide; Sheep money; Treasure comes horizon*) and though they were all eager to hear from the beyond, her mother's spirit never entered the room. The men didn't much care for the game in any case and after two or three attempts, she put the board away and never retrieved it again.

But God in heaven was she bored! She took up with Jimmie where they'd left off—she the mistress, he the slave—but it wasn't the same. She'd seen what life was now, Ida exiled, her mother dead, her stepfather set in place to rule over her and all her prospects rubbed off the board as if her own life were a game she'd already lost, and their play-acting seemed to take on an intensity she hadn't felt before. Jimmie had changed. He wasn't content to be her foil, not the way he once was. He was stronger, more sure of himself, and he understood perfectly well that her pool of companions had drawn down to one. "I'm the ram," he said, giving her a look. "And what does that make me," she said in return, "the ewe?" His eyes jumped away and then came back to her again. "Yes," he said, drawing out the single syllable as if this were a philosophical proposition he was mulling over at length, "that's right. That's it exactly." She was bored. He was bored too. And when her stepfather tried to discourage them from spending time together, from hiking, beachcombing, swimming—anything out of his sight and control—they came together all the more determinedly.

It began almost at once, in the very first week. Jimmie was in the kitchen, helping her put things in order—she had him up on the stepladder driving nails into the high beam so that she could hang things there and get them out of the way—and she'd just handed him the cast-iron stewpot when he sprang down off the top step, laughing aloud in a sudden excess of spirits, took her in his arms and danced her across the room to a madcap rhythm all his own. The first few steps were awkward, almost as if they were grappling, but she let herself go and followed him and they went round the room two times, three, both of them laughing now. Everything had been grim—everything *was* grim—and here was this burst of exhilaration to take her by surprise. She was alive after all, giddy suddenly. And when she pushed him away—pushed hard, as if they were children roughhousing on the playground—and then pulled him to her so that they were breast to breast and their faces inches apart, it seemed like the most natural thing in the world to kiss him. On the lips. And this was a different sort of kiss altogether, qualitatively different, nothing at all like when he kissed her hand like a courtier or she'd made him press his lips to her feet, her ankles, her calves and thighs—this was mutual, a partnership, ram and ewe, and she could feel the heat of him burning and burning as if she'd gone right inside of him to live there like Jonah in the belly of the whale.

After that, they began meeting whenever they could, when her stepfather was out riding with Adolph or when he'd sent Jimmie into the fields on one pretext or another and she sneaked away to meet him there. At first, they explored each other through their clothes, fumbling and inexact, stroking and squeezing and feeling what each had to offer, and then she wanted to see him—see what it was, the male organ—and she made him strip naked before her. It was in February, three weeks after she'd arrived, and conditions were hardly ideal. The ground was wet, the day steely and brisk, with a low cloud cover and a wind that sang through the chaparral. They'd found a protected place, deep in one of the ravines, where the rocks hemmed them in and the bushes that had escaped the sheep had begun to flower and sweeten the air. "I want you to remove your clothes," she said, "*all* your clothes."

He dropped his jacket on the ground, making a sort of bed of it, and he pulled his shirt up over his head, eager, grinning at her, his eyes focused and daring. Off came his boots, then his trousers, so that he was standing there in his union suit and stocking feet. "Everything? Even my socks?"

"Go on," she said, and her eyes were fixed on his. "No malingering. What are you waiting for?"

He reached behind him for the buttons, his arms elbowing out, then pulled the garment down to his waist so that she saw the black tangled hair at his nipples and his navel—a sort of Christ's cross of it there—and then he was bent over, stripping the fabric from his groin and legs as if it were a second skin. When he rose back up to stand before her in a confusion of limbs and a torso bleached white as flour where the sun had never touched it, there it was, the male organ, standing out rigidly from the dark nest of his groin as if it were an arrow that had been shot into him and stuck there, wooden and hard. But it wasn't hard. Or it was, but it was soft too. She took it in her hands, chafed it, squeezed, rubbed, slid her fingers beneath it, at the root, thinking of Ida. This was what Ida had taken inside her, this quivering veiny blood-engorged thing that was like an animal itself—that had been how the baby came to grow there, and even then, even with Jimmie standing before her and moving to her touch with his mouth hanging slack and his eyes pressed shut, she refused to admit or even consider who had been the second party involved, though she knew, *she knew.*

But Jimmie, Jimmie was *her* plaything. He was no ram, he was only Jimmie—Jimmie with a whole new set of needs and weaknesses—and she'd been fooling herself to think their relationship had changed. He did whatever she said. Did it gladly, beseechingly, abjectly, no humiliation he wouldn't endure for her sake. As the weeks fell away she became expert in manipulating

him till the white fluid came spurting out of him and very gradually she allowed him favors too, though she would expose only one part of herself at a
time and never removed her dress or underthings no matter how furiously
he stroked or how deeply he kissed her or how much he begged. She was curious. Of course she was. And he satisfied her curiosity—and more: the touch
of him made her blood race, though she wouldn't admit it, not even to herself—
but this wasn't a pact and it wasn't reciprocal and she was the mistress, always, and he was the slave.

Mrs. Caliban

At the end of July, on a fine high clear day that brought the mainland so close it was as if the channel were a tranquil little pond you could swim across in fifteen minutes, she found herself on Charlie Curner's schooner once again. Her stepfather was taking her to Santa Barbara for three days. On business. She was to stay at a boardinghouse for women presided over by someone called Mrs. Amelia Cawthorne and she was not to leave the house for any reason except under her stepfather's or Mrs. Cawthorne's supervision. That was the promise she'd made, and what choice did she have?—it was either promise and go or refuse and be left behind. *I want your solemn oath,* he'd said, and she'd given it, gladly, humbly, with shining eyes and a smile of fawning gratitude. She'd all but curtsied—and would have, would have done anything—except that it might have aroused his suspicions, and she didn't want that. The fact was that in the past three months her stepfather had been twice to the mainland without her—he'd taken Jimmie the second time, as if to rub salt in her wounds, and she'd been left alone with Adolph and the sheep and a misery so deep and all-abiding she couldn't get out of bed the whole time and if Adolph complained to her stepfather because he'd missed his three square meals a day she never knew of it. Or cared. So she made a promise, swore it to his face, *On my soul, on the Bible, as God is my witness,* a promise she had every intention of breaking the moment she was clear.

Mrs. Cawthorne was a large woman, a matron sunk in fat whose husband, a boatwright, had been lost at sea in one of his own creations twenty years past. She had pinched narrow eyes—squinting, always squinting—and a way of claiming all the space in any room she happened to be occupying. The other boarders—there were three—were spinsters in various stages of decrepitude. Her stepfather paid in advance and informed the landlady that he'd be back in the morning to fetch his daughter and take her with him on the rounds of his errands. In the meanwhile—and here he'd given her a significant look before turning back to Mrs. Cawthorne, who stood there in the center of the parlor working one swollen hand in the grip of the other—she was exhausted from the journey and would no doubt want to go up to her room directly after dinner. The landlady had squinted at her, giving her a long look of appraisal. One of the spinsters, ancient, with claws for hands, who'd been napping in an overstuffed armchair by the fire, came awake with a snort and glanced up sharply. Her stepfather said, "Isn't that right, Edith?" Stupefied—he wasn't even going to let her look in the shop windows or take her to dinner or his hotel or anyplace at all?—she just nodded dumbly.

In the night she awoke in the dark to a whole symphony of strange noises, of water shifting through the pipes and the house creaking and groaning as the hours chipped away at it, the barking of the neighbor's dog, a soft hiss from beyond the windows as if a giant were sweeping the streets with a broom made from an upended tree. Her stepfather had given her a single dollar in spending money, as if to say, *Let's see how far you can get on that,* but what he didn't know about, what no one knew about, not even Ida, who'd handed her the envelope, was the bracelet her mother had left her. She had it with her now, wrapped in tissue paper and secreted in her purse. For a long moment she lay listening to the sounds of the house, then she rose from the bed and dressed in the dark.

The suitcase she would leave behind. She needed to be unencumbered, needed to get out, into the streets, and hide herself somewhere until the pawnshop opened, and then she would go there to give over her mother's bracelet and take money in return. And then what? Then she would start walking—on the road out of town that ran up through San Marcos Pass to Cold Spring Tavern, where she would catch the stage north after it left Santa Barbara, and if anyone should come along the road in a wagon or buggy or on horseback, she would hide herself in the bushes till they passed. It would be a long walk—ten miles, fifteen?—and most of it uphill. But it was nothing to her—all she'd done on the island was walk.

The house was as dark as the inside of a closet, the windows shut tight and the shades drawn. She felt her way along the corridor and down the stairs, spots floating before her eyes in random patterns, straining to see and seeing nothing. There was a rustling, a moan, the faint whisper of one of the old women snoring in her bed behind an invisible door. Shuffling her feet, one step at a time, afraid of stumbling into a chair or table and giving herself away, she read the wainscoting with her fingertips like one of the blind. She bumped into something—wood, cloth there, the coat tree?—and then finally she was at the door. She felt for the doorknob, gripped it, twisted it, but the door wouldn't open. The latch, where was the latch? She ran her fingers over the smooth wooden plane, feeling for the latch, but there was no latch, only a keyhole, and the keyhole was empty. She was trying to come to grips with that—had the landlady actually locked them all in? What if there was a fire? An earthquake? But there must have been a back door and that couldn't be locked too, could it?—when there was a noise behind her and the room came to sudden life.

Mrs. Cawthorne, in her nightgown, her feet bare and her expression blank, was standing there at the edge of the carpet, a candle held aloft in a pewter dish. "What's going on here? Who is it now?" she demanded.

She was a very fat woman, fat and lazy and old, and Edith felt a surge of contempt for her. She said nothing.

The light wavered as the landlady took a step closer, her eyes lost in the dark tumid contours of her face. "Is that the new boarder? Edith, is it?"

"Yes. I was looking for a glass of water. I was thirsty."

For a long moment the landlady merely squinted at her, breathing heavily, a gasp and wheeze that scratched away at the silence of the sleeping house. Then she said, "There's a glass and pitcher on the table in your room." Another silence. "Right next to the lamp."

During the course of the next three days, Edith's stepfather took her out for a meal exactly once, at a cheap restaurant where men with snarled whiskers and bad teeth sat sucking at one thing or another and everything stank of sour milk and chili beans, and he took her to the shops exactly twice, to buy toilette things, cloth for a new dress to replace the ones that were so worn and stained they'd become an embarrassment, and, of course, to lay in supplies at the grocer's—more sacks of beans, more rice, more flour. Each sack, as the clerk checked it off in his ledger and she stood there at the counter trying to keep from screaming, was a weight drawing her down, another link in the chain she had to drag behind her like Marley's ghost, dead in life, dead on her feet, dead to the world.

She was up in her room, plotting frantically, when her stepfather came to take her back to the ship. She'd seen no one, seen nothing, and now she was to go back. It wasn't fair. It was criminal. An insult. Hadn't Lincoln freed the slaves? Wasn't this America? For three days she'd watched for her opportunity, even measuring the distance from the second-story window to the nearest tree, but Mrs. Cawthorne was like a watchdog and her stepfather was worse—he was Argus of the hundred eyes, keen to her every movement. Mechanically, she paced from the dresser to the bed, packing her suitcase and listening to the voices rising from below.

"I want to thank you," her father was saying, and then he paused and she imagined them nodding at each other in satisfaction, the prisoner in her hole and a job well done. "I appreciate your keeping an eye on her."

And then Mrs. Cawthorne, her voice level and hard: "Yes, but I'm afraid I won't be available to her next time round."

"And why is that—you're not thinking of closing down, are you?"

"No, it's not that, not that at all. It's just—well, a young girl needs a mother, and I'm sorry to say it. She doesn't look after herself, that's what I mean to say. Her clothes, her hair, her shoes, her corsets. She's ragged. Not at all what I expect from a young lady."

Her stepfather made some sort of meliorating comment—the island, the weather, rough conditions—but the landlady wouldn't be swayed. "It's to do with standards," she said. "My boarders, I've got to think of my boarders. And my own reputation too."

And that was it. She was condemned. Her stepfather called up the stairs to her—"Edith, will you put a hurry on, for God's sake? We can't keep Charlie waiting all day"—even as she stepped to the mirror, pushed her hair back and gave herself a good hard look. It was true. Her hair was dirty, her dress no better than a patchwork quilt. Her face had taken the sun till it looked as if it had been stained in a barrel. Her eyes stared out like a madwoman's. She was like a savage, like Jimmie, like Caliban—or no, even worse, because she'd let him touch her as if he and she were the same, as if she were his wife, not Miranda, not even Sycorax, but worse, far worse, Mrs. Caliban herself.

The Shearers

The shearers came back in August and this time there was a new face amongst them. At first she didn't notice—she glanced up one afternoon and there they were, outside the window, milling around in the yard with their bedrolls flung over their shoulders and that greedy craving look in their eyes, and all she could think of was the extra work they would cost her. Five of them—or no, six—and each one going through three pounds of meat, a stack of tortillas and half a gallon of wine every day, though the wine was to be watered and doled out a glass at a time till they sat down to dinner so as to prevent a general riot, and her stepfather was absolutely strict on that score. They wore straw hats—sombreros, they called them—that were as stiff as tin and finger-greased till they'd taken on a dull gray sheen, Mexican boots that cocked them up off their heels and stained bandannas knotted jauntily round their throats to lend them the only bit of color they seemed able to support. She recognized most of them at a glance, lean reticent stripped-back men in their thirties and forties who spoke a garble of Spanish, Italian, English and Portuguese and maybe Indian too, she couldn't say—all she knew was that it wasn't French and it wasn't German and the thought made her ache all the more for the life that had been taken away from her.

Of course she recognized them—she ought to, since they'd worked her nearly to death when they'd come out at the end of February. There was Luis, in a pair of leather chaps, and next to him Rogelio, quietly spitting in the dirt, and who was that, the one with a concave face like the blade of a shovel? The Italian. They just called him El Italiano. And—but here she caught her breath—there was a new man amongst them, young, with a smooth unseamed face and a guitar strapped over his shoulder atop the bedroll. He was standing there with the others, taking everything in, the chickens, the barn, the bunkhouse and the pigpen and the hills dotted with sheep that must have been replicas of the sheep-dotted hills on all the other islands, nothing new under the sun, and what was he doing here with these old men? Was he somebody's son? Rogelio's maybe? Luis'? That was when he suddenly glanced up at the house, at the window behind which she was standing, and they locked eyes till she was the one to turn away.

That night, when she served at table, he sat up rigidly the minute she came into the room, as if her mere presence had turned some switch in him. The other shearers broke off their conversation and stared down at their plates out of respect, but he fixed on her every movement. Her stepfather was addressing Adolph and Jimmie as usual and he was saying the usual things about the flock and the weather and the turpentine they would dip the sheep's noses in and the whale he'd seen off Prince Island just that afternoon, raising his voice to let the sense of it drift down the table to include the shearers in the conversation. He was feeling convivial, the prospect of another crop of wool before him, and while the shearers—and Jimmie—raised glasses of watered wine to their lips, his own tin cup was filled with whiskey. As was Adolph's, judging from the dazed look on his face.

She set out the two big pewter platters of roast lamb, one at each end of the table, then went out to the kitchen for the pot of beans, the tortillas and the hot sauce Jimmie had helped her concoct from chopped tomatoes, rendered grease and the dried habanero peppers the shearers had brought with them. She was flipping tortillas on the stovetop when the door to the kitchen pushed open and the new man stepped into the room as if he'd lived there all his life. His name was Rafael, he was twenty-six years old and he was a Spaniard (not a Mexican, he'd insisted during the brief introduction she'd had to him out on the porch before dinner), with glass-green eyes and long black hair he slicked back with a scented pomade she could smell all the way across the room.

"I am thinking if I am able to assist," he said, and he was the first man—with the exception of Jimmie and Jimmie didn't count—ever to offer to help. On a ranch, men worked in the dirt and women in the kitchen, their paths never to cross. On a ranch, there were no gentlemen or ladies—there was just life lived at the level of dressed-up apes tumbled down from the trees. If you wanted to talk of poetry or drama or music or have a man open a door for you or get up when you entered a room, then you'd better die and come back in a new life.

She was stunned. She didn't know what to say, but he'd found a pair of dish towels to cushion the handles of the cast-iron pot of beans and was already lifting it from the stove, and then he was gone, backing out the door and down the hall to a chorus of jeers from the others. *Mujer,* someone shouted. *Pícaro!* cried another. A moment later she flipped the last of the tortillas onto a platter, took up the tureen of hot sauce and followed him down the hall, but instead of putting the platter in front of her stepfather or even in the center of the table, she set it down beside Rafael, as a sign of favor. "Oh-ho," Luis crowed, "you see?" and everyone laughed, but for Jimmie, who set his mouth and lashed his eyes at her.

Did she care? No, not in the least. Jimmie had had his chance.

For months now she'd pleaded with him to help her engineer an escape from the island and he'd made vague promises about contacting this fisherman or the other when they anchored in the harbor, but nothing had come of it. The first time she'd mentioned it to him—while they were alone, in their secret spot, after she'd let him kiss her lips and suck endlessly at one bared nipple like the oversized infant he was—he gave her a long look she couldn't quite dissect, at least not at first. "Please?" she'd whispered, and she'd moved her hand to his groin, to stroke him there through the fly of his trousers. "Pretty please?"

"The Captain wouldn't like it," he said after a moment.

"No," she said. "I know he wouldn't. But do it for my sake. Please?"

He looked away, though he'd begun to move his hips to the rhythm of her hand. "I could maybe . . . but then, what about me? I'd be here all alone without you. I'd miss you something terrible, because, well, I've only said it a thousand times, I love you. You know that."

There was nothing to say to this. She wasn't about to exchange vows with him, not if she had to stay there on the island for the next three centuries. She stopped her friction until he laid his hand atop hers and began to guide her. "Will you talk to the fishermen?" she said after a moment.

"What fishermen?"

"Any fishermen."

"The Captain won't like it."

"No," she said, staring into his eyes and working her hand deeper, "no, he won't."

Since then she'd seen any number of sails in the harbor or farther out at sea, ships riding north, fishing boats, sealers, the private yachts of people from San Buenaventura and Santa Barbara who sailed from island to island for the pleasure of it because they had the means and the occasion to go wherever they wanted whenever the whim took them. But not her. No. And every time she mentioned it to Jimmie he gave her that look she had no trouble reading now, a look of greed and fear and self-serving obstinacy—he didn't want her to go any more than her stepfather did. What did she do? She cut him. Cut him dead. She wouldn't look at him, wouldn't touch him—wouldn't let him touch her—and if he spoke to her she ignored him, and yet still he never gave in. Oh, he pleaded with her and made up all sorts of stories about how he'd hailed a boat but it was full of Chinamen or maybe they were Japanese and she wouldn't want to go with them, would she? or how he'd just about talked Bob Ord into it, but then Bob's boat had run aground on a shoal off Anacapa and he'd had to have it towed into Oxnard for repairs and never did come back, but it was just more of the same and all worth nothing. He'd had his chance and he'd failed the test. Now she looked where she could and when Rafael had strolled through the kitchen door nice as you please, she saw the way.

She washed the dishes and cleaned up the kitchen while the shearers filed out to the bunkhouse, Jimmie tagging along behind, then waited till her stepfather and Adolph had settled in at the card table before taking a chair out into the yard to sit there with a book in the declining light of the evening. The book was *Wuthering Heights,* which she'd read so many times the pages had worked loose from the binding. She'd come to hate it, actually, all that rural misery and star-crossed romance she'd once found so exotic and appealing but was now just a burden to her because it was one thing to picture the scene from a sofa in a San Francisco apartment and another to see it out the window, but that didn't matter. The book was a prop. As was the chair. She'd combed out her hair and tied it back with a new red sateen ribbon she'd bought on the visit to Santa Barbara and though her dress was out of fashion it was the best one she had and it was clean and ironed and she'd dabbed perfume under the arms and in the pleats of her collar.

The breeze was light for once, blowing across the yard and carrying the stench of the pigs away with it. Overhead, long ghosting trails of vapor went from gray to pink with the setting sun. She turned the pages of the book, staring down at the words but making no sense of them, working at the trick of shifting her eyes to the porch of the bunkhouse and the clot of dark figures gathered there without giving herself away. For the longest while, nothing happened. She held herself rigid, the light softened, fell away. It was almost dark now and she wouldn't be able to keep up the imposture much longer. She was about to give it up and go back into the house when there was movement on the porch, a figure separating itself from the others, and suddenly it was as if she'd been transported to another world altogether because she was hearing music, music out here in the barrens—a guitar, the elided figures, the strummed chords—and she couldn't help but turn her head.

It was Rafael. He was standing at the base of the bunkhouse steps, one leg lifted to the bottom riser and the guitar resting on his thigh, the fingers of one hand tensing and releasing over the neck of the instrument while he strummed slow emphatic chords with the other. The rest of the shearers were lined up like statues on the benches along the wall, Jimmie amongst them. Rafael was looking down at his hands, deep in concentration. The others—to a man—were looking at her.

The rhythm quickened, beating steadily toward some sort of release, and then Rafael lifted his head, looked across the yard to her and began to sing:

Si tu boquita morena
Fuera de azúcar, fuera de azúcar,
Yo me lo pasaría,
Cielito lindo, chupa que chupa.

She didn't know the song or what the words meant, but when the chorus rang out in soaring full-throated abandon—*Ay, ay, ay, ay*—she knew he was singing not for his compatriots lined up along the wall or for her stepfather immured in the house or the sheep in their coats or the rolling broken dusty chaparral, but for her, for her only.

The shearers were to be there for two weeks and then the boat would collect them and they'd go back to wherever they'd come from till the sheep's coats grew out and they made their rounds once more. It was her intention to be on that boat with them. She didn't know how she was going to manage it, but she looked to Rafael, encouraging him in any way she could, making sure to brush by him in the doorway when he came in for meals, letting her eyes jump to his and then away again, lingering outside each evening to hear him raise his voice in song till her stepfather went out on the porch to spit and light a cigar and call her in. She had to tread carefully—her stepfather was more vigilant than ever with men on the property and Jimmie shadowed her like a spy. *Jimmie.* Jimmie was the enemy now and no doubting it.

Rafael didn't offer to help after that first night, and yet it wasn't that he didn't want to—he was polite and well bred, she could see that—but because the others wouldn't allow it. They'd heckled him at the table and what they must have said to him in private she could only imagine. Let them have their fun. They were crude men, ignorant, unlettered, and what they'd seen of the world was limited to bunkhouses and sheep pens. He was different. And she knew he liked her. There was a sympathy between them—or no, a current as powerful and jolting as anything a magneto and a copper wire could generate. He was handsome, what the Mexicans call *guapo,* with his unexpected eyes and the way he stood out from the others like a prince amongst peasants, taller, straighter, his forearms corded with muscle beneath the fringe of his rolled-up sleeves and his secretive smile that was reserved for her alone.

Near the end of the second week, on the final day of the shearing—and she was counting the days off, tense and impatient, sick to her stomach with the thought of the opportunity passing her by—he slipped her a note as he came in for dinner with the others. She'd rung the bell on the porch as usual and stayed there to greet the men as they came up the steps, and he'd been last, holding back purposely. His hand flitted toward hers as he shifted past her and there was the quick hot touch of him and then the note was in her hand, a twice-folded scrap of paper that fit her palm like a holy wafer. She went straight through the room, down the hall and into the kitchen with it. *Come to me,* it read. *Midnight. Behind the privy.*

It was nothing to slip out of the house. Her stepfather, exhausted from the exertions of the roundup and shearing—nearly two weeks into it now and he an old man no matter his protestations to the contrary—had forgone his cards and whiskey and retired early. By nine, when she damped the lights and went up to bed, she could hear him snoring thunderously from down the hall and he was still at it at quarter to twelve when she crept back down the stairs and out into the night. She eased the door shut behind her and stood there a moment on the back porch, listening. Nothing moved. All was silence.

It was chilly, and the minute she stepped off the porch she wanted to go back for a wrap, but didn't dare risk it. She was wearing the dress she'd put on that morning, though she'd been prepared to change into her nightdress if her stepfather had been up and about—he was in the habit of easing open her door to wish her a good night, especially if he saw the light on, and she wouldn't want him to suspect there was anything out of the ordinary. A fog had set in, but it was thin and diaphanous, the three-quarters moon shining through it to light the way. Not that it would have mattered: she knew the yard as intimately as a convict knows his cell and could have found her way even in the pitch dark.

There were stirrings in the brush. The fog sifted down and it was as if the darkness itself had come to life, pulsing and fluctuating in a tincture of moonlight. Before she'd gone a hundred feet she was out of breath, and it wasn't because she was weak or tired—it was nerves, that was all. She tried to keep her composure, telling herself to proceed with caution, to go slowly with him, to let him see and value her for what she was before she let him kiss her, touch her, but all night she'd felt herself racing as if he were pulling her to him on that thin hammered thread of wire. The W.C. was a black mono-lith, a shadow amongst shadows. The smell of it stabbed at her. She circled round back of it, thinking how clever he was—if anyone should see her, she had her excuse, just going to the privy, that was all. The call of nature. She smiled to herself.

But where was he? All she could make out were the dark hummocks of rock giving back a faint glow under the moonlight and the scraps of ragged vegetation bunched up round her like discarded clothing. Had he forgotten about her? Led her on? Played a joke on her? And if he had—and here she pictured him lying in the darkened bunkhouse with a smirk on his face— she'd spit on his eggs in the morning, slap him right there at the table in front of everyone, tell her stepfather he'd . . . but then one of the dark hummocks before her unfolded suddenly and there he was.

"*Cariña,*" he whispered, taking her by the hand and swinging round to lead her through the brush without so much as a kiss or caress, moving swiftly. His grip was tight, too tight, as if he was afraid she'd break away from him, but she didn't hold back, didn't protest, just followed him, stumbling, her breath coming quick and hard. They moved swiftly, no time for thought or hesitation, and when they came to the fence he stopped to shift his hands to her waist and lift her over into the dried-up field where the hay had long since been cut and the sheep let in to browse the stubble to bare dirt. And then, like Jimmie, he shrugged out of his jacket—or no, it wasn't a jacket but a kind of blanket, what they called a serape—and spread it out on the ground.

She watched the shadow of him bend to the blanket and then he was pulling her down beside him, twisting her round so that her feet went out from under her and she came down hard and all she could think of was a lamb flipped over for shearing. Without a word he began to dig at her, at her skirts, her legs, his hands rooting there, and he pressed his face to hers, not for a kiss but to strain against her. His cheek was a wire brush. His hands were stone. She wanted him to stop, wanted to talk, wanted a promise, and now that it was too late she saw how naive she'd been to think he'd be satisfied with kisses and the kind of manipulation she'd practiced on Jimmie. He dug at her, tore her undergarments, and still he didn't kiss her. His cheek chafed against hers, he rocked and tensed and shoved himself into her and now she was the one made of stone, and not just her hands but the whole of her, as if the weight of him had petrified her.

Afterward, when he was done and he pulled out of her and sat there in the dark whispering *Cariña, cariña,* she lay rigid watching the stars poke holes in the torn fabric of the night, and then he wanted her again and if he did what he liked what did it matter? When it was over, finally and absolutely, and she felt everything begin to dry and tighten and tug at her skin like so many tiny crepitating hooks, she pushed herself up. He was sitting there beside her, burning something—a cigarette, he was smoking a cigarette, the smoke harsh and stinging. She couldn't see his eyes. She could barely make out his face, a dark oval hung there on a hook of nothing. "Rafael," she said, and it was the first word she'd spoken since he'd pulled her down, "I want you to take me away."

He said nothing.

"Please." Her voice seemed foreign to her own ears, a thin tensile rope of sound drawn out of some deep place inside her. She thought she might begin to cry.

"Away to where?" he said finally.

"Anywhere. Just away."

He was silent a long moment. He inhaled and the cigarette flared and still she couldn't see his face.

"On the boat," she said. "When you go tomorrow with the others."

"Captain Waters," he said, his voice low and disconnected, "he will oppose it."

"He won't know," she said, and though she was made of stone and could barely work her muscles or lift her arm from her lap, she took hold of his hand in the dark and stroked it, her thumb moving against the callus of his palm, the gentlest friction, over and over. "Take me," she said. "Just take me."

By the time the first tremulous sliver of light appeared on the horizon she was already up and stirring about the kitchen. Her movements were slow and mechanical, her feet tracing the floorboards by rote as she bent to the stove, put on water for coffee, mixed the batter for flapjacks and set the pot of beans, eternal beans, on the stovetop. Everything was ordinary, everything in its place. If she paused a moment and held her breath she could hear the distant ratcheting of her stepfather's snoring as if some metallic creature were patiently boring through the walls, but there was no other sound. She ground coffee beans and told herself she didn't feel appreciably different, though she was truly a woman now—and here a voice in her head that might have been her mother's took the thought a step further: a fallen woman, ruined, like the heroine of one of the Hardy novels her parents wouldn't let her read. She didn't care. She was numb to it. Something had happened and now it was over. She'd washed herself in the basin after she'd crept into the house at one in the morning and then sat in front of the mirror for the longest time, staring into her own eyes, and there was nothing different there, not a trace—she was Edith Waters, still and always, a very pretty girl, consummately pretty, who was going to go onstage and acknowledge the applause of hundreds and hundreds of elegantly dressed ladies and gentlemen with a deep bow and a flush of modesty.

The water came to a boil. The first bird began to call. And then there was a thump at the back door, the dog nosing there to be let in and fed, and the day, which for all appearances was like any other day, started in. She didn't so much as glance in Rafael's direction at breakfast for fear of giving herself away—or of breaking down, or no, choking, actually choking over the emotion wadded in her throat that was so dense and heartbreaking she could barely swallow—and she took her own breakfast out in the kitchen to avoid his eyes, their eyes, the eyes of the men. He'd made her his solemn promise and the plan had been set in motion. She'd packed her suitcase and laid out her best clothes and gloves and hat. When the men were at work—only a half day today, clearing up the odds and ends, hauling the sacks of wool to the barn, packing up their shears and knives and bedrolls—she would conceal the suitcase in a clump of rocks just off the road that led to the harbor and then, after luncheon, instead of washing and stacking the dishes and scrubbing the counter and sweeping the floor, she would go upstairs and dress and then steal away to wait for Rafael.

Yes. And then, when the others had gone out to the schooner (it was Lawrence Chiles' boat, not Charlie Curner's, thank God, because there was no telling what Charlie Curner would have done when he discovered her aboard), Rafael would claim he'd forgotten something—his guitar, which he'd have purposely left behind one of the rocks at the beach, nothing to it, just ten minutes at the oars, and they'd wait, they'd have to. She'd crouch in the bow, hidden beneath his serape, and when they got out to the ship she'd do her best to slip aboard unnoticed but if they knew and saw it would be nothing to them because this was between her and Rafael and nobody else. She was almost eighteen. She was a woman. She could do what she wanted in this world.

Luncheon. There was extra wine, unwatered, because it was a kind of celebration, the work concluded and the men on their way home, and maybe they had families to go to, wives, mothers, sisters, daughters, sons. She served at table, then kept herself apart, and though she felt Rafael there like a fire burning in the center of her being, she didn't look at him, no more than she had at breakfast. There were handclasps and farewells that traveled from the parlor and across the yard, the dog excitedly barking and the chickens scattering, and then they were gone. Jimmie and Adolph went off into the fields and she waited at the kitchen door to see what her stepfather would do, praying he wouldn't take it in his head to walk down to the harbor to see them off. He'd lingered with the Italiano, who was the last of the shearers to start down the road, but finally he'd turned and come back into the house. She heard him go up the stairs, then there was the sound of his door easing shut and finally the groan of the bedsprings. He'd drunk wine, a quantity of it—she'd made sure to keep his glass full—and now he was having his siesta.

By the time she got to the place where she'd stowed her suitcase, she looked out to sea and saw that the shearers had reached the schooner, which sat the waves as if it had been propped there on wooden pillars, scarcely shifting with the action of the water. The sun was abroad. The sea shone. The men were like stick figures in the distance. She snatched up the suitcase and hurried down the road even as the dinghy swung back round with a single figure at the oars.

As she followed the switchbacks down the road the dinghy floated in and out of view, now present, now obscured by the sharply raked hillside. The suitcase dragged at her—she'd packed it with everything she could, even her books, and she'd had to kneel atop it to force the latch shut—but she kept on as best she could, her blood high, shifting the load from hand to hand till it swung like a pendulum and hurried her on. And then she was there, coming round the final turning, and she saw Rafael in the boat, working hard at the oars, but it took her a moment even to begin to comprehend what she was seeing. He wasn't heading in to shore. He was on his way out. Back out. And from the stern of the boat she could see, quite clearly, the sun-burnished neck of his guitar poking out from the nest of the serape.

She dropped the suitcase and began to run, unencumbered, her arms churning. The dinghy was a hundred yards from shore and he was facing her, leaning into the oars, but he had the sombrero pulled down low so that his features were lost to her. She called out his name. Jerked her skirts high and bolted into the surf—she would swim, swim or drown—but he kept pulling at the oars, pulling harder and harder. The sea swept in. She was wet through, her skirts wound round her legs like the twisted chain of an anchor. She called out again. Twice, three times, bleating his name till the syllables ran up against one another and made no more sense than the inarticulate cry of an animal. The surf slammed at her, drove her down and jerked her back again till she was flung shivering on the beach in a white surge of foam and Rafael slid smoothly over the rail and melted away in the depths of Lawrence Chiles' boat.

Then the sails unfurled and caught the wind and the boat was gone.

Inez Deane

Does life go on? It does. Though she sank low enough to consider the alternative, even going so far as to take her stepfather's rifle down from its hook and caress the trigger where it shone silver from use, and she spent one dismal fog-haunted afternoon suspended over the ocean on a fragment of rock no wider around than the seat of a chair, daring herself to jump. She could hear the crash of the waves, taste the salt-sting of the spray. The damp penetrated her hair, slicked the rock till it might have been greased. There was a cold drip from above. She pressed her back to the wall, closed her eyes and let her mind wheel away from the voice that whispered, *Let go, let go, let go.* She saw herself dancing then, saw herself at the piano, and presently she imagined her fingers moving over the keys, working her way through the melody bar by bar as if it were an exercise and Mr. Sokolowski seated beside her on a platform of cloud beating out the time, and it was the music that held her there. And when finally she removed her shoes so that her naked feet could anchor her and she climbed back up the rock face above her, up to the plateau beyond and the sheep scattered there in all their blank-eyed placidity, she tested each handhold as if it were her last.

She was in the kitchen one interminable afternoon two months later, taking a cleaver to the unyielding carcass of the wether Adolph had shot the day before, her brain gone as dull as the blade she had to keep sharpening over and over, when there came a tap at the door. She looked up from the chopping block, the cleaver poised above the twisted red mass of muscle, skin and tallow. The stove creaked. The faintest distant rumor of the seals barking for the sheer pleasure of it inserted itself into the silence. She thought she must have been hearing things, but then came the second tap and she set down her cleaver. Caught her breath. Wiped her hands, very slowly, on the apron, her eyes fixed on the window set in the door.

There was a figure on the back porch, a hovering shadow, indistinct behind the drizzled panes of scoured glass. It took a moment to understand that this wasn't her stepfather. That it wasn't Jimmie or Adolph. That it was someone else altogether, someone new, a new face and form to align with the only three she knew because in all these hills and gullies and sea-battered coves, there were just the four of them, no one else, but for the shearers who weren't due back till winter or the odd fisherman who came ashore to feel something beneath his feet besides swaying planks and the elastic give-and-take of cold salt water. And now a voice was attached to the form, a voice calling her name softly, a man's voice—"Edith? Edith, is that you in there?"— and she knew that voice, didn't she? Of course she did. It was, it was—

She was already moving toward the door, wiping her hands furiously now, the stink of the dead animal in her nostrils, the apron filthy, her hair a mess—and she couldn't pat it in place, wouldn't dare, not till she washed the offal from her hands—when it came to her: Robert. It was Robert Ord. The sealer. The jack-of-all-trades. The man—the young man—who possessed a boat, his own boat, a craft with a rudder, a sail and a hull that could slice the waves like its own kind of cleaver and carry anything or anybody all the way to the pale indented shore that hovered there on the horizon like a mirage. One more wipe of the hands and she pulled open the door, his name on her lips: "Robert, Robert, what a surprise. How are you?"

He was tall, levitating right up out of his sealskin boots, taller than she remembered, and he was grinning down at her with such burning intensity she wondered if he hadn't been drinking. "Me?" A pause. "I'm just, well, I got a bad sore on my foot, the right one?" He held out his leg and shook it for her, his heavy cotton twill trousers spattered with white blotches that might have been paint, but then what would he have been painting out here—the cabin of his boat? "It don't smell too good, but it's nothing to worry over, nothing I ain't seen before, though I told myself I should of took that splinter out of there the minute it went in, just pus, that's all, and I guess that'll teach me to go walking around in my bare feet . . . but what I mean to say is, how are you?"

She wanted to give him the conventional response, wanted to say she was fine, but instead she pulled the door wide for him and ushered him in, saying, "Crushed with boredom, because nothing ever changes here, you ought to know that. But come, sit at the table and I'll fix you something. Are you hungry? Would you like tea? I can make you toast—and we've got some

200

strawberry jam left from the last time the boat came in." If there was a flutter in her voice, it had nothing to do with calculation, not yet, anyway. She was excited, that was all—transported—because here was something new, a break in the routine, the vast towering wall of the day suddenly crumbling to dust around her.

"Don't go to any trouble," he murmured, hovering, awkward, a bedroll under one arm and his coat patched at the elbows. In the next moment he was trying to ease himself into the chair at the stained table by the window, the space cramped, his legs too long, the slant roof of the kitchen angling down to confine him, and then he was seated. "I fried up some abalone on the boat this morning, so I . . ." He trailed off, then patted his pockets till he came up with what he was looking for—a bottle—and set it on the table. "Want a drink?"

"A drink?" Her stepfather didn't allow her to take spirits. He didn't allow her to associate with the opposite sex or go to school or pursue her musical studies or experience anything anyone would call living because he wanted her under his wing, wanted her to cook and clean and make his bed for him while he went horseback over the hills and sat playing cards at night and drinking from his own bottle. "What is it," she asked, "whiskey?"

"Rum," he said, pulling the cork with his teeth. "Fetch a glass. Two glasses."

He watched her, grinning, as she eased down in the chair across from him and lifted the glass to her lips. *So this is rum,* she was thinking, the rising vaporous odor tearing her eyes, caustic, poisonous, like nothing so much as a solvent, and then the liquid itself burning her lips, her tongue, the back of her throat. She clamped her jaws tight. Let out a gasp of surprise. Next thing she knew she was blotting her eyes with the corner of her apron.

He laughed aloud. "No, no," he said, "you don't sip it, you just toss it down like this, watch." He sat up straight in the chair and jerked his head back, draining the glass in a single gulp. "Go ahead, try it again."

She laughed too because it was funny, tossing rum in the kitchen at four in the afternoon—he was a tosspot, that's what he was. She'd always wondered where that expression came from and now she knew. It was funny. Hilarious. And then she followed suit, a tosspot herself, and the shock of it very nearly seized her up—it was as if a rake had gone down her throat, or one of those enameled back-scratchers they sell in Chinatown, and the heat was inside of her now. Again she felt her jaws clamp. She tried to speak but the words wouldn't come.

"Good stuff, huh?"

"It's horrible. I don't understand how anyone could drink it."

He shrugged, his eyes gone vague. "It's a taste," he said, acknowledging the point. "You get used to it."

"Used to it?" She could feel the effects already, at least she thought she could, a lightening of her limbs, the flutter of some organ deep inside her she never knew she had, a sense that the air had grown dense around her so she could get up and walk on it if she wanted. "I thought you were supposed to like it."

"Here," he said, and he was pushing himself up from the table in a scramble of limbs and holding out a hand to her, "let's try flavoring it for you." She followed his lead as he pulled her across the room to where she kept the basket of oranges, grapefruit and lemons Charlie Curner periodically brought out from shore and stood beside him, watching, while he shoved the carcass of the lamb aside with the palm of one hand and sliced two oranges and a lemon in half. The carcass didn't seem to trouble him, nor the blood on the board either. He gathered up the fruit in one hand and spun round as if he were on a holy mission—and this was funny too, everything comical suddenly—before darting back to the table for her glass and making a show of squeezing the juice into it. "Now," he said, tipping the bottle over the glass to fill it to the brim, "try it this way. And maybe, if it's still too strong, mix a spoon of sugar in."

If the light changed when the sun pulled back from the house and the barn threw its shadow across the yard, she hardly noticed. There was nothing in the world but Robert Ord and the glass before her, though she knew in a vague way that she would have to get up and see to the stove and dinner and set an extra place at some point. All in good time. In the meanwhile, there was Robert Ord and Robert Ord was a gentleman, or the best succedaneum the island could provide, and he let her sit there at her own table as if she were the guest—he insisted on it—while he got up to squeeze the bright orange and yellow rinds over her glass and tint the mixture with the dark burnt sugarcane rum, lovely rum, beautiful rum, rum that no longer smelled of chemicals but of tropical isles and the faraway. The rum was a breeze. It fanned her. Lifted her. She felt as if she were floating.

Then, somehow, her stepfather was there, Adolph peering over his shoulder and Jimmie there too, goggling at her from the open doorway. "Bob!" her stepfather bawled, striding across the room to slap him on the back even as Robert struggled unsteadily to his feet. In the next moment they were crowding into the room, handshakes all the way around, and if Robert was slow with his speech, no one noticed, at least not at first. They were all too enraptured by the novelty of seeing him there where they'd expected no one, firing one question after another at him: *What news? How long had he been out? Had he seen Nichols last time he was ashore? He hadn't brought any newspapers with him by any chance? A bottle? Did he have a bottle?*

It was this last inquiry that caused him to reach down to the table, take up the bottle of rum by its neck and hold it to the light. Dark stuff, dark as molasses, and only an inch of it left to swish round the heel of the bottle. "I've got," he began slowly, so very slowly, "this one . . . and then"—he swayed over his feet and spread a palm on the wall to steady himself—"there's a couple more on the boat."

That was when they all four looked down at her where she sat entrenched in the chair that was pushed up so tightly to the table she could scarcely move, not that she wanted to move. Her elbows were propped on the tabletop and her hands formed a brace for her chin, which suddenly seemed impossibly heavy. The silence pounded in her ears. Her stepfather looked to Robert, then to the bottle, and then, finally, to her. "What's in that glass?" he said.

"Juice."

"Juice, my eye."

She clarified: "Orange juice. And lemon."

He was drawing himself up. His hands were dirty, his forearms, dirt up under his nails and worked into his hair, his trousers stained with dried-up mud and his shirt feathered with trail dust. They'd been out riding to the far end of the island, checking the stock there, seeing to things in the season when there wasn't much to see to. His eyes narrowed. A look of fury came over his face. And when he lunged forward to snatch the glass from her hand and lift it to his nostrils, sniffing, it was no more than she'd expected. "You're drunk," he said.

"I'm not."

"Don't you lie to me. You, you—you're disgusting."

"She—" Robert began, and it was as if his mouth were full of cornbread and he couldn't risk forming his words properly, "I mean to say she was, or I did, I offered her a little drink—"

Her stepfather swung round on him. "You stay out of this." And then he leaned over the table so that his face was so close to hers she could smell the rankness of his breath that was no different from the smell of the meat on the chopping block where the flies had begun to dance and settle. "You're drunk," he said again.

Something flashed in her then, a single whipcord of rebellion. "So what if I am. You're drunk half the nights of the week. You were drunk when my mother—"

"You shut your mouth. Shut it." He bit off the words. "Right now. And you get yourself up from that table and go straight up to your room, or I'm warning you—" He didn't finish the thought. His finger. He was wagging his finger in her face. "You're a disgrace," he spat, and she was already pushing back from the table, already gathering her feet to flee—how she hated him, the hypocrite, the tyrant, and who was he to boss her like a slave?—when the finger curled back into his fist and the fist slammed down on the table. "Now get! Do you hear me? Out of my sight!"

She was sick in her stomach all night, once the liquor wore off, that is, because it was the liquor—she understood this now—that killed the pain. That was its use. That was why the men drank it and women too, even her mother, who used to take a glass of her stepfather's whiskey from time to time and sit sipping it in the corner, her eyes bright and her face gone slack, cradling the glass in her entwined hands as if to extract the last emollient heat of it. Twice in the night she had to get up and vomit in the chamber pot while everything seemed to swirl round her in the dark as if the earth had slipped off its track since she'd laid her head on the pillow. What they ate that night, she didn't know. Or care. At some point the odor of frying onions and seared meat had seeped up through the floorboards, which only made her feel sicker, and she'd heard them carousing below till it was full dark and well beyond.

She was sick. She was weak. Her head ached. But Robert Ord was leaving first thing in the morning because he had three living barking seals tied up in his nets on the deck and he didn't want to risk losing them to death or sickness or starvation before he got them back to Santa Barbara and the man from the circus who'd put in the order for them, and she meant to intercept him when he left the bunkhouse at first light. He'd told her he wouldn't be staying to breakfast—there were the seals, in addition to the fact that his hold was full of the guano he'd shoveled all the morning and afternoon before and there were the friable white streaks on his trousers to prove it, not paint, not paint at all—and at first she'd begged him to stay on. "I'm starved for the company," she said, moving in closer to him at the table under the spell of the rum and the way the light sat in the windows and the whole world that had been so dreary and dull seemed suddenly magical, but then, though her brain was fuddled and the connections came slowly, she began to see the situation in a whole new light. She wrapped her hand around the muscle of his upper arm and leaned in close to him so that their faces were inches apart. "No need to stay on my account," she said.

"Oh, I don't mean nothing like that," he said. "I wouldn't—I like being here with you. Hell, I'd stay a week if I could, if I was welcome . . ."

She would have let him kiss her, guano or no, and it didn't smell, or not hardly, but he didn't seem to take the hint. Maybe he was shy, maybe that was it. She held her face there, as close to his as she dared, and when he flushed and looked away, she dropped her voice to a whisper and said, "You can't know how long it's been since I was off the island."

He lifted the glass to his mouth and jerked his chin—tossing—and then turned back to her. His eyes seemed to swell and recede and swell again. The lines bunched in his face. It was as if he were seeing her for the first time. Very slowly, very tenderly, he brought his lips to hers and they did kiss, almost chastely, as if he were afraid to go too far, and it was the sort of kiss she'd practiced on Jimmie, who had the annoying habit of trying to worm his tongue into her mouth, a dry kiss. He pulled back and stared at her a moment and then she kissed him and she was the one who worked her tongue and when they broke apart this time she didn't ask a question of him or beg a favor—she merely said, "I'm going with you."

"I don't know," he said, and her heart sank—he was just like the others, gutless and weak, afraid of her stepfather, afraid of the law. But then he looked her in the eye, just holding her gaze, and she could feel him working through the tangle, objection by objection, before he let out a sigh and said, "She's riding pretty low in the water, what with all that weight. And those animals aren't exactly the pleasantest things to be around."

"I don't mind." She gestured at the carcass of the lamb, the crude kitchen, the door that gave onto the barnyard.

"And the guano. That's shit, you know, gull shit."

"I know."

"It can smell something awful when it's all packed in like that."

"I don't doubt it," she said.

"Makes your eyes water. And it's bound to be rough, what with her riding low, and I don't know if you can . . . or you'll want to—"

"Hush," she said, and then she leaned in and kissed him again.

This time, though she felt cored out and her head throbbed and she'd hardly slept, she was there to make sure of him when the door to the bunkhouse swung open beneath the pale fading screen of stars. If he was surprised to see her there, he hid it well. She'd been sitting atop her suitcase and when the door opened she rose and came to him and he took both her hands in his and accepted the kiss she brushed against his cheek. He had his bedroll thrown up over one shoulder and a leather satchel over the other. He looked blunted and pale, his eyes heavy in his head, and she wondered about the aftereffects of the rum on him—if she felt this bad how must he have felt? Was he capable of piloting his ship? Rowing out to it? Even walking down to the beach?

It was then that the door of the bunkhouse swung open again and her heart froze till she saw the shadow of the dog there. She watched it lift a leg to the steps of the porch, then shake itself and go off round the back of the barn, and still she stood there, waiting for what she couldn't say.

"Well," he said finally, "I guess that's your suitcase, is it?"

"Yes," she whispered, and they were both turning toward it now, walking in stride. And the thing was, he never hesitated, but just bent to it, took it up by the handle and continued on across the yard and down the road, moving so swiftly on his long legs she had to hurry to keep up. The day brightened around them, just perceptibly, and then, in the distance, the cock began to crow and she could picture it perched atop the shed where she'd seen it spring in a single claw-pedaling leap every morning for as long as she could remember and her only thought was that she would never have to hear it again in all her life.

Then there was the dinghy, drawn up on shore, and he secured her suitcase in the bow and helped her into it like a gentleman so that she didn't even have to get her feet wet. The surf rocked them. The shore pulled back. Ahead of them lay the boat drifting at anchor on a sea so calm it was like the land itself and she could see the pale sun-bleached mesh of the net and the three dark shapes nestled beneath it. The seals. The captives. Wrapped up in their animality and the forlorn fishy stink of them. They were leaving the island, never to come back, and so was she. The oars squealed in the locks and Robert, facing her, gave a quick look over his shoulder, then turned back and smiled at her. It was a simple smile, pure, charged with the excitement of what they were doing together, what *she* was doing, a smile of appreciation, of admiration, of awe even.

It was only appropriate. Because everything had changed. She wasn't Edith Scott Waters anymore, wasn't a girl on a sheep ranch on an island, wasn't ordinary in any way. She was Inez Deane, belle of the stage, and she was going home.

PART III

Elise

Arrival

She was thirty-eight years on this earth and until three weeks ago she'd never been west of the Hudson River—she'd been to the Berkshires, Boston and Newport as a girl, and Montreux and Paris too, but west? Never. The West was a place she knew only from books, from Francis Parkman and Mark Twain and Willa Cather, a huge dun expanse of the map striated with mountains and flecked with plains and deserts, home to cactus, rattlesnakes, red Indians, cowboys, bucking broncos, buckaroos—and what else? Prospectors. Oilmen. Motion-picture stars. She thought of Chaplin eating his own shoe, of Laurel and Hardy selling Christmas trees on a street lined with palms. The West. Terra incognita. Terra insolita. And now here she was, all the way out on the west coast of the U.S.A. and waiting for the cattle boat that would take her beyond the coast altogether, to the last scrap of land the continent had to offer, an island tossed out in the ocean like an afterthought. Thirty-eight years. And wasn't life the strangest thing?

It was early morning, the end of March, 1930. She watched the sun rise out of the mountains down the shoreline to her left, and that was strange too, because all her life she'd known it to emerge from the waters of Long Island Sound, a quivering yellow disk like the separated yolk of an egg, the waves running away to the horizon and shifting from black to gray and finally to the clean undiluted blue of the sky above—if the sun was shining, that is. And half the time it wasn't. Half the time it was overcast, drizzling, raining— or sleeting. There was no sleet here, though, and never would be, not until the next Ice Age came along, anyway. Just the sun, which in that moment swelled to a perfect blazing circle and slipped free of the clutch of the mountains to draw long tapering shadows out of every vertical thing, boats at anchor, the pilings of the pier, the trees along the bluff—some of which, and she just noticed this now, were palms, imagine that, *palms*.

The boat—Herbie had told her to watch for it downshore to the east while he ran off in his excitable trot to see to a dozen last-minute things—was called the *Vaquero,* and it was used by the family on one of the other islands to ferry cattle across the channel to market. She looked off to sea, sniffed at the breeze. The sun rose higher. People moved around her on the shifting planks of the pier, going about their business, maritime business, and no one gave her a second glance. Herbie had left her there to keep an eye on their baggage—a glancing kiss, a bolt from his eyes, *I'll be right back*—but she didn't feel at all threatened or even anxious. If there were any thieves on the pier that morning, she didn't see them.

When finally the boat did appear, it was a distant black pinpoint emerging from the shadow of the mountains to glint sporadically as it rocked into the rising flood of sunlight. She put a hand up to shield her eyes and held it there the whole while as the boat grew bigger and the smell—urine, feces, the close festering odor of glands and secretions and hide, cowhide—came rushing to her on the breeze. Then the boat was there, tethered and gently knocking against the pilings, and a raw-faced man in blue jeans and a wide-brimmed hat came scrambling up the ladder and onto the pier. He was short, shorter than she was, anyway, and so slim and agile it took her a minute to realize he wasn't as young as he'd first appeared, wasn't young at all. There were creases round his eyes, hackles of stiff white hair tracing the underside of his jaw where he'd been indifferently shaved, and she wondered about that, shaving at sea, with the deck pitching under you and the razor—even a safety razor—a hazard all its own.

He stood there a moment as if to get his bearings, then shot her a glance, his eyes dropping from her face to the tumble of suitcases, shoulder bags, trunks, boxes and sacks of provisions scattered round her, before lifting again to settle on hers. Then he was coming forward, drumming across the planks with a brisk chop of his legs—boots, he was wearing cowboy boots— and giving her a smile so wide she could make out the cracked gray remnants of his molars. "So you must be the new bride," he said, tipping his hat, and then he gave his name, which she forgot in the instant: *new bride.*

Yes, she was a new bride, twenty years after she'd made her debut at Delmonico's with a full orchestra to provide entertainment and a young tenor by the name of Enrico Caruso serenading the glowing cluster of debutantes and their families, all the world laid out before her, and fifteen years—fifteen at least—since she'd given up all hope. New bride. She almost blushed.

"Yes," she said, bending forward to nod in assent. "I'm Herbie's wife, Elizabeth. Or Elise. Call me Elise."

There was a moment of silence, the stink of the absent cattle—they'd been off-loaded the day before in Oxnard, she would learn—rising to them from the boat lurching in the swell below. There were gulls, of course. Pelicans. People up and down the pier bending to one task or another.

He ducked his head, pulled at the brim of his hat, looked to her things and then to the ladder bolted to the side of the pier. "Well, lucky for you and Herbie the boat's here today, because if it wasn't for the storm that come in day before last they'd of been here and gone already. And then you'd of had to take the Coast Guard boat."

She must have given him a puzzled look, because he immediately qualified that: "Which is fine, and I don't mean anything by it—it's just that the Coast Guard boys tend sometimes to go off on other business, depending on what comes up on the radio, orders, you know, and sometimes you'll be four or five days aboard before you can get to where you're going."

She smiled. "And what about you?"

He smiled back, made as if to tip his hat again and thought better of it. "Oh, me? Don't worry about me—I'll be going out to Santa Rosa with the boat. And we'll be shoving off here just as soon as they can take on supplies and get you and your—Herbie, that is—aboard."

"Santa Rosa? Which one is that?"

He did a quick shuffle of his feet, maneuvering round the baggage to point off down the length of the pier and across the channel to where the sun striped the flank of the big island lying out there on the horizon. "That one there, straight out? That's Santa Cruz. Now look to the right of that, you see it tucked in there behind that point, almost looks like it's joined to it, but it's not, believe me—that's Santa Rosa, that's home for the Vail and Vickers boys. And me too, at least for the first week or so, till you get settled in—I mean, for your honeymoon and like that."

"But I thought—weren't we supposed to go to San Miguel?"

Laughing now: "Oh, yes, nobody's going to strand you on your honeymoon—San Miguel's the first stop." He'd shifted again and was pointing far off to the right. "You see that? Way out? That little strip of brown there?"

She narrowed her eyes, squinting at the hovering vaporous line of the horizon, due west, all the way out, so far out she couldn't be sure she was actually seeing anything at all. "Is that it?" she asked, looking to him.

"It is, ma'am," he said. "And you can't always see it from here, but you're lucky, as I say. Doubly lucky."

They were silent a moment, both of them staring out over the waves to where the island suddenly came clear, stretched across the horizon like the smallest fragment of a very old rug. "I'm sorry," she said after a moment, turning back to him, "but what did you say your name was?"

"Jimmie, ma'am. I'm Jimmie. Didn't Herbie—I mean, Mr. Lester—tell you about me?"

She was about to say *No, he didn't*, but then she saw the look in his eyes and caught herself. "Yes," she said, "he did, as a matter of fact."

This seemed to satisfy him. His features settled. He pushed back the hat to scratch briefly at his scalp. "Well," he sang out all of a sudden, "no sense in standing here gawking—which of these bags you want aboard first?"

The *Vaquero* was like no boat she'd ever been on, the open high-railed deck more accommodating to animals than people, but the wheelhouse was snug enough and the men gathered there—ranch hands on their way back to Santa Rosa, the ship's captain, her new friend Jimmie—were in a festive mood, their eyes shining, grins playing across their faces like heat lightning. There was a woman aboard, and a new bride at that, and they crowded round her, each one vying to outdo the other, their voices blending and breaking as they offered up an unyielding torrent of stories, advice, jokes and admonitions. She'd never much liked being the center of attention, shy of it, actually, the ugly duckling of her family, thick-limbed and awkward all her life, but this was different—she'd been selected for this—and she found herself enjoying the attention. Or mostly. And when it got too much for her, when the bug-eyed man in the plaid shirt and patched blue jeans leaned across the bench to shout in her left ear even as the one named Isidro contradicted him with a Spanish-inflected tirade on the other side, she just called out to Herbie in French—*Chéri, sauve-moi*—and he was there, distracting them with the jeroboam of champagne he'd somehow managed to get hold of from sources unnamed and had begun pouring before the boat even left the dock.

"*À ta commande, madame,*" he crooned, pouring first for her, then for the bug-eyed man and finally Isidro, who stopped what he was saying—about cattle, his defining subject—long enough to tip back the tin cup he'd produced from his jacket pocket when Herbie had first uncorked the bottle. And then Herbie—*her husband,* and how she loved the sound of those three syllables on her lips—was holding out a hand to her as if he were inviting her to dance, pulling her up off the bench and handing the big heavy dense-green bottle to Isidro all in a single fluid motion, and here she was following his lead, not to an imaginary dance floor but out the door to the deck where the sun poured down and the breeze fanned her hair and the spume broke away from the bow and flew up in sunstruck beads to vanish on the air. The sea was gentle, the air mild—or if not mild exactly, then not cold, at least not yet. To her right was the mainland with its white-fringed beaches and the greening mountains that rose up and away from them, to her left the big island clothed in a patchwork of color, and straight out over the bow, larger now, but still not much more than a blemish on the horizon, the mysterious place where she was going to make her home. Herbie pulled her to him, whispering, "*Ah, enfin, je t'ai seule.*"

The French. It was part of what had attracted her to him in the first place—she'd learned to love the language as a girl and he'd picked it up during the war—and now it had become their secret language, the language they alone shared amongst all these cowboys and sailors and sheepmen. She closed her eyes and he kissed her, right out there in full public view, and she didn't care because she was half-mad with the champagne and the sun and the sheer wonder of the adventure she was on, picturing him the day they'd met, Herbert Steever Lester, dressed in suit and bow tie and with his laughing blue eyes screwed right into hers as she answered the door and he took her hand in his and murmured "*Enchanté,*" even though all he was doing was inquiring about subletting her apartment on East Seventy-second Street. Herbie. Her husband. Her first and only love.

And then, his arm round her waist, they were strolling the deck—promenading—and if she saw the stains worked into the planks or caught scent of the animals that had so recently been passengers here and were now on their way to meet their fate, she wouldn't admit it. Why spoil the day? Why dwell on the imperfections when there was so much beauty to glory in?

She threw back her head and let her gaze roam free, the shore receding, the islands drifting closer, the sun ladled over everything and everything glowing as if the world were slick with a new coat of paint.

For his part, Herbie chattered away, in English now, going on about the island and its multitudinous charms, telling her about the house and their bedroom and how she wouldn't even need to crack her trousseau, except maybe for one of those sheer peignoirs from Paris. Gowns? Ball them up and throw them away! And where did she think his tux was? Back at Bob Brooks' place in Beverly Hills. Where it was going to stay. Forever. Because this was the real life they were going into, the natural life, the life of Thoreau and Daniel Boone, simple and vigorous and pure. He talked on, talked and talked, pacing up and down the deck, as full of enthusiasm as she'd ever seen him.

When finally the breeze got to be too much for her they went back inside and there was another round of champagne and then another and then the shadows began to lean the other way and before she could think San Miguel rose up out of the sea ahead of them like an image on a photographic plate and they were in the harbor there, the anchor chain paying out and Herbie helping her down into the boat that would ferry her across to the place where her life was about to begin, and if through all these years she hadn't believed in reinvention or second chances or just plain dumb luck, she had to believe now.

The House

There was a team of horses—Buck and Nellie—but they were in the barn at the top of the hill where Jimmie had left them when he boarded the *Vaquero* the previous morning, and so she and Herbie hauled all their things up past the tide line themselves, then shouldered their packs and started up the crude dirt road to the plateau above. By this time, the sun was low in the sky and the *Vaquero* had rounded the point behind them and tipped away on the streaming red waves. She watched it over one shoulder, alive in all her senses, everything steeped in the soft declining light. The whole world seemed to be holding its breath. Something darted across the road ahead of them and what was it? A lizard of some sort. Or a snake. But then snakes didn't have legs, did they?

The canyon that gave rise to the road smelled wet and raw, like the inside of a cave, and it funneled the wind so that it was blowing in their faces, blowing cold, and she had to stop to button her cardigan. And once they were up off the beach, everything was mud, so that her shoes were thick with it, each step heavier than the last. She hadn't gone a hundred yards before they were like twin boats—or no, like those great flapping wooden things they wore in Holland, and what were they called? *Sabots?* No, that was French. Clogs. Wooden clogs.

But here was Herbie, dancing on ahead of her in his short pants and Army boots, his shirt flapping and the hair beating round his head, impervious to the wind and the mud and everything else. His mood was soaring, lifting him so high it was as if his feet hardly touched ground. And it wasn't the champagne, which had worn off by now and had only left her feeling sleepy, but his natural exuberance that had him so worked up he was actually trembling like one of those coffee addicts you saw barking at each other like trained seals every time you stepped into a diner. Every thirty seconds he had to catch himself, looping back to her to shove at the weight of her pack as if to push her on up the slope, blowing a kiss in her ear, dropping a hand to her buttocks to pat her there, stimulate her, urge her on. And talking, of course. Talking all the while.

"You see the yellow flowers on the cliffs there? That's deerweed, but the funny thing is there're no deer to eat it."

"Just sheep."

"Right, just sheep. Our sheep. And you'll catch sight of them soon enough. But the other patches of yellow—see them?—with the flowers all bunched? That's coreopsis. Giant coreopsis. Bob says it's only found on the islands, the giant kind, anyway. But you're lucky. This is the season when it's all in bloom, because come summer, when the rains are over, everything goes dormant and it's just this brown thatch—"

She was fighting for breath. She'd tied her hair up in a kerchief and she could feel the sweat at her temples. Good sweat, productive sweat, and how amazing to be here, in a wild place, with her husband beside her, a canvas pack slung over her shoulder and her legs digging at a hill that seemed to go on rising forever—just the two of them and not another soul for miles. Everything in the past three weeks had been a mad whirl, the berth on the train, unfamiliar beds, the hurried marriage that was really more of an elopement because of the murder out on San Nicolas Island. Her sister Anna had exhausted herself planning a formal wedding for them down the coast in La Jolla, but they'd had to throw all that out the window—there just wasn't time to arrange for the license and blood tests, not in California. But Arizona was another story. In Arizona, things got done. And so, because Bob Brooks was subpoenaed to go and testify at the trial of one of his hirelings who'd fired on a poachers' boat and hit the man at the oars—killed him, that is—she had to climb back on another train and rattle across the desert to St. Paul's Episcopal Church in Yuma and then rattle back again, because Herbie was needed here, needed urgently, wedding or no. She wasn't complaining, even under her breath—it had been the most intensely romantic thing she could ever have dreamed of—but she was tired and the hill was steeper than a ski slope and her feet were like lead weights.

"Tell me about the house again," she said. "And our bed. What's our bed like?"

"Oh, it's first-rate, splendid, grandest bed in the world. A big old sleigh bed, made of mahogany, with a mattress as soft as, I don't know, butterscotch pudding with whipped cream on top—"

"And just as cold?"

"Not with you in it, not anymore. And it's got the very highest quality Army blankets tucked in tight and my grandmother's quilt spread over top of them. And pillows. Pillows like your mother's breasts—"

"*Herbie—*"

"Or my mother's, anyway. And there's a stove there, right in the bedroom, to keep you warm through the night—as soon as I can get the stovepipe hooked back up, that is. Plus, the room's big, biggest room in the house, and the house is practically new too, built by Captain Waters and his caretaker not twenty-five years ago with choice planks from the wreck of a ship carrying, of all things, lumber, can you imagine? I guess they just abandoned the old one at that point—whether it was too small or falling apart, I don't know. But I'll show you the ruins of it, amazing, really, the way a place can go to wrack and ruin in no time, everything buried in sand like in that poem, what's it called? You know, the one from your *Oxford Book*. Lord Byron—"

"Shelley."

"Shelley, yeah, Shelley. But the place, our place, has views you could only pray for if you were back there on the mainland"—he was whirling round to point now, walking backward without even breaking stride, feet pumping, the mud nothing to him—"all balled up in that shithouse life that never stops, automobiles and trains and *lunch counters,* everybody running around like they're in a race, some marathon to nowhere . . . and you'll see, it's head-on to the wind, like a big inverted *V* laid out on the ground, with a courtyard in the middle and fences to keep the blow out. And the sand, of course. Because the sand's like snow out here, you've got to understand that, sandstorms coming up out of nowhere and piling up drifts against anything they can't carry off. And—but come on there, girl, we've got to get up top so I can show you over the place and then hitch up the horses and bring everything back up the hill before it's black dark. You wouldn't want your books to get all wet and moldy, would you, your library, I mean, and how many did you say you packed up back there in New York, a thousand?"

She tried to shrug, all in good fun, banter, banter with her husband, but she was struggling too hard to waste the extra motion. "Half that."

"But still," he said.

The place was cold and dark, a long rambling succession of rooms and doors upon doors that could have been the set for a Mack Sennett picture with clowns piling out everywhere except that there was practically nothing in them but for the odd chair or cot, the table in the kitchen, the sleigh bed in the master bedroom. Herbie set their things on the kitchen table and bent to the stove to get it lit, then took her by the hand and skipped her through the rooms—and here was where the shearers stayed and there, across the courtyard, was the smithy and the storage shed he was going to convert into a taproom just as soon as he got the chance, their own private taproom, and how did she like that? Prohibition? What Prohibition? On their own island? And out there, beyond the fence? Those were the shearing sheds. And the barn. Where the horses were.

"Do you need help?"

"No, I'll bring it all up in two trips with the sled. It's nothing. Really."

"In the dark?"

"Yes, in the dark."

She wanted to know if she should see to making something for supper, their first supper in their new home, and he could barely contain himself, his feet jumping in place as if to some jazz band playing in his head, and yes, yes, that would be *splendid,* grand, and maybe she could put the kettle on for some tea?

So she made use of the hand pump at the sink and filled the pot and set it on the stovetop while the firebox coughed and roared and chewed up the wood she fed into it stick by stick. The place was clean enough, spare, almost Essene, the floors scrupulously swept, the counters dusted, dishes washed and stacked, not at all what she would have expected from a bachelor's residence, and she wondered if it had been spruced up specially for her. But no, her husband was like that, orderly, precise, finicky almost to a fault. Though the place could use a woman's touch, she could see that. Curtains wouldn't hurt. A few pictures on the walls. A carpet.

Herbie had been alone here since the first of the year, but for Jimmie (who'd been out on the island as long as the rocks on Green Mountain, or so she gathered). Bob Brooks had relieved him so he could whisk his bride off to Yuma before coming back as full-time caretaker with an option to buy in, but Bob Brooks had a whole host of other concerns to look after, not to mention a murder trial to attend. And Jimmie, apparently, was incapable of doing the job himself, though she couldn't fathom why. Maybe he was untrustworthy. Maybe he was a drunk. Or a dope fiend. Or lazy. Or just one of those men who never seem to grow up no matter how old they are.

She began sorting the groceries they'd hauled up in their packs, vegetables and dairy mostly, because there was no garden out here and no cow either and after the first few days milk was going to have to come out of the can. And cheese. They'd have to husband their cheese—or wife it, if that was a verb, and why shouldn't it be? Eggs too. Herbie had carried the eggs in his pack, six cartons of them, because she was afraid of the responsibility, and as she folded back the canvas flap and lifted them off the top of his pack, she saw—or felt, rather—that a few hadn't made it intact. Which in that instant gave her the inspiration for the first night's menu: *omelettes aux fines herbes avec fromage naturel et pain de l'épicerie.*

Six of the eggs in the top carton were broken, but she was able to spoon them out of their shells and set them aside in a blue ceramic mixing bowl she found on a shelf above the sink. Then she set about putting the rest of the groceries away in the pantry and the cold-storage room beyond it: the eggs, milk, cheese and vegetables went here, alongside a hanging slab of bacon and a whittled sheep carcass that looked—and smelled—none too fresh. The canned goods, sacks and sacks of them, were down at the beach still, but the basics were here on the shelf, tomatoes, pork and beans, sauerkraut and a line of big brown crocks set against the wall that contained, as she was to discover, sugar, flour, spaghetti, noodles and the like. After she'd put everything away she went to the bedroom to unpack her clothes.

The walls were dark—natural wood—and damp to the touch and the room smelled of cold ash and boards bleached and pounded by the sea. The kerosene lamp gave off its own astringent odor, the wick blackened but the globe wiped as clean as if it had just come off the shelf at the hardware store. There was a dresser in the corner—the top two drawers empty and with clean oilcloth laid down for her, Herbie's clothes neatly folded in the bottom drawer—and it took her no more than a minute or two to arrange her own things and tuck them away, since the majority of what she'd brought along was still down below. In the dark. She lingered over the bed, hesitating over which side was his, before deciding to lay her sheerest—her only—peignoir over the pillow on the left. It was a gift from Anna for her wedding night, the sort of thing she wasn't really comfortable with, or hadn't been, but Herbie—as if he needed encouragement—had really come alive when he'd seen her in it that first night. And then she'd switched off the light and he'd come to her and after that it wouldn't have mattered what she was wearing.

She was thinking about that, about Herbie and their first night together and the nights since, studying herself in the mirror, wondering if she should put on a dab of lipstick, rouge, perfume, and trying to do something with her hair—it was a mess, flattened across the crown by the kerchief and teased out on the ends by the wind—when she heard the sound of the horses in the courtyard. She wasn't much for makeup in any case—she was plain and she knew it and makeup just made her look like a circus clown, or that was how she felt, anyway—and it was almost a relief to duck away from the mirror and slip out to help him haul the things up off the sled and onto the covered porch that ran the entire length of the building.

"It looks like I'm going to have to make two more trips," he said, sliding a cardboard carton of books across the dried-out planks and bending immediately for another. "I guess"—the cardboard giving up a sharp frictive whine as it rushed across the planks—"we brought more than I'd bargained for"— bending again, lifting, sliding—"but it's all to the good because you never know when the next boat's going to come by and it's nice to think you've got what you need when you're on your own. We won't be starving. Not anytime soon."

She was working right beside him, unloading books, canned goods, bedding, a pair of matching suitcases her mother had given her as a wedding gift, the exhaustion she'd felt earlier gone now in the excitement of the moment, his things and hers—theirs, conjoined. "Couldn't you leave some of it for the morning?"

He stood up, stretching, and gave her a look. "The fog comes in, it can leave things pretty wet."

"What about a tarp? You must have a tarp of some sort. And if we bring up the perishables, the food, all the food, then the rest can wait. Can't it?"

He was still standing there, the night opening up to infinity behind him. "I didn't even carry you over the threshold," he said. "Shame on me. Shame on us." And then, before she could protest—there was so much to do and what about the horses, what about his back, with all this lifting?—he was tipping her backward into the embrace of his arms and kicking through the door and he didn't set her down till they were in the bedroom and he was pressing her to him for a long lingering kiss. "You're right," he said finally. "Absolutely. Our first night in our new house and here I am worrying about, what—baggage! What am I thinking? Have I gone nuts?"

So he went on out to the barn to unhitch the horses and drag a dusty and somewhat perforated canvas tarp—Army issue—out of the rafters and haul it down to the beach and when he came back the table was set in the kitchen, a candle burning there in a saucer and the aroma of her omelets riding the air. They sat a long while over supper, Herbie chattering on, his internal motor spinning and spinning again and no neutral on the shift lever, praising the house, the island, her cooking, *her*—her most of all—and so what if the omelets were scorched on the bottom and the *fines herbes* had been reduced to salt and pepper and ketchup out of the bottle? He didn't care and she didn't care either. It was enough to be there together with no place to go and no one to please but themselves, and when she rose to clear up he wouldn't hear of it. "Not tonight," he said, his voice sunk to a whisper. "We've got other things to do tonight. Better things."

And then he took her by the hand and led her out of the kitchen and through the house to the bedroom, where the foot of the sleigh bed rose up like an undulating wave and the black silk peignoir lay limp across the pillow. The house was utterly still. There was no sound, nothing, not even the wind. He held up the peignoir to her and kissed her, kissed her deeply. He wouldn't let her go into the other room to change and when she'd changed he wouldn't let her turn the lamp off either. Not yet, anyway.

The Mice

That first week was an idyll, the two of them alone in an untamed place and nothing in the world to intrude on the slow unfolding of a peace and happiness so vast she couldn't put a name to it. She woke each morning exhilarated, everything new, the hills enfolded in fog and the fire going in the big cast-iron stove in the kitchen, Herbie there already with the pot of coffee, and she, in her robe, bending to kiss him before seeing to the flapjacks and bacon or French toast layered with butter and awash in maple syrup, breakfast, breakfast for two. Then there were the walks. Each morning, after breakfast, he took her out over the island, showing it off, the cliffs falling away to the churn of the sea, Prince Island rising out of the waves like the humped back of a whale—and whales too, actual whales, spouting right out there in the harbor. There were the caves up on Eagle Cliff with their Indian pictographs worked into the rock, the elephant seals stretched out on the beach like enormous stuffed sausages, the caliche forest with the haunting twisted shapes of its petrified trees. Wildflowers. Open space. And the sheep, the *raison d'être* of the place, running off wild in every direction.

In the afternoons, he would see to his chores and she turned her attention to putting the house in order, no hurry, no compulsion, just a long slow descent into the drifting rootless pleasure of arranging things, moving what little furniture there was, seeing what chair or table looked best beside the window or set against the wall in the far corner. She took a long while arraying her books according to category on the shelves in the living room, hung her pictures, washed every jar she could find and filled them with the stalks of dried flowers for the simple beauty of them. Nights, there were the dinners she prepared for him—mutton and rice, a fish he'd caught, mussels *marinière*—and then the quiet time when they sat before the stove reading aloud to each other, and finally, bed, and the dark and the feel of him there beside her. She called him Adam, he called her Eve.

When Jimmie came back it was as if a marching band had clattered across the courtyard and into the house, cymbals crashing and horns blaring—she was that used to the quiet and the sound of their own two voices. The first night he talked their ears off about people she'd barely heard of, the Vails and Vickers and their families and hired hands and all the fine points of the little feuds and grievances of this one or that. Herbie had shot and dressed a sheep, the old spoiled carcass, or what was left of it, tossed out on the compost heap for the ravens and the dwarf foxes that trotted around the island like dogs, and she'd made a credible leg of lamb with mint jelly, roasted potatoes and peas out of the can fancied up with pearl onions.

"Bobby Burgos, that works the horses out there?" Jimmie was sunk into his chair at the table, waving his fork like a baton, as if he were about to get up and lead the band off in another direction. "Got thrown and broke his shinbone, clean snap you could of heard all the way over here—you notice the Coast Guard boat? They come for him three days later but he just waved them off, tough old bird—"

Herbie, her Herbie, fingertips drumming and feet tapping under the table, let out a sigh of resignation and sympathy both. He was handsome as an actor, his face smooth and unlined and his hair going to silver at the temples, and she could have sat there all night just watching him, though there were the dishes to clear up and coffee to brew and the dough for tomorrow's bread to knead and cover and set aside to rise. He cut a slice of meat, chewed and bolted it, and now he was waving his own fork. "I suppose so," he said, "but I don't really know the man, since I haven't had the chance to get out to Santa Rosa yet, or did you forget? Tough's what you want out here, though, isn't it?" He looked to her now, grinning his wide lit-up grin and giving her a wink of complicity. "But while you've been out there having your vacation—"

"Vacation? They worked me like a dog."

"I potted that old tom you couldn't seem to hit, though you must've gone through half a box of cartridges."

"You got him? Where?"

"Out behind the barn. He was just sitting there licking himself and I slipped into the house, grabbed the .22 and let fly."

"Tom?" she said. "What tom? You're not talking about a cat, are you?"

"Feral cats." Herbie had uncorked his last precious bottle of bourbon—or what somebody claimed was bourbon in this eleventh year of Prohibition—and he took a moment now to pour out a measure for each of them. "The last people out here before Bob, the people after the Russells? They let their cats go wild, and the cats went on breeding, of course. And then you've got your boaters coming out here with a litter maybe they don't want, figuring they'll set them free on the island instead of putting them in a sack and drowning them. Like any decent person would." Another wink. The light of the lantern shone through the glass and the bourbon gave up its color. "Here's to the memory of Old Tom!"

"Here, here!" Jimmie crowed.

The liquor went down all around, a burn in her throat and then in the pit of her stomach. "I don't understand. Don't you want cats here? To keep the mice down? You yourself said they were all over the place."

"Ah"—he held up a finger—"that's where you're wrong. The mice *belong* here, they evolved here, this is their home. Who was that mouse man from the college, Jimmie?"

"Walter."

"Right, Walter. Walter Franks. He came out here, I guess it was mid-January, studying them, you know? Well, guess what? They're a distinct sub-species of the deer mouse, unique, found nowhere else. We can't have cats killing them. Plus, have you seen how cute they are?"

"Cute? Mice, cute? They're pests, they're vermin. Whoever heard of a cute mouse?"

Herbie was watching her, grinning still, but his eyes seemed to harden ever so slightly—were they having a disagreement, their first disagreement, and over mice no less? "You wait," he said, and he brought his hands together on the table, intertwining his fingers and leaning back to crack his knuckles, "you'll see."

A week slipped by. The wind came on, a two-day gale that picked up every grain of sand on the island and deposited it somewhere else, mostly in their clothes and the bed and the dishes on the shelf, so that she itched all night and whenever she chewed anything it had a fine grit to it, then the fog settled in and it was as cold and gray and damp as the night Scrooge saw Marley's ghost, but it was all bliss to her. The days took on a rhythm all their own, a rhythm dictated not by the subway and the work schedule she'd kept at the New York Public Library these past ten years—nine to five, five and a half days a week—but by the sun struggling up out of the water in the morning and settling back into it at night.

One morning (the honeymoon over now and Herbie out in the yard with Jimmie working at one thing and another the minute breakfast was cleared away) she was in the kitchen, rolling out the dough for an experimental cobbler to be made from canned peaches in heavy syrup, when Herbie burst through the door. "You mun see this," he said, his voice spiraling up and away in his excitement.

"Mun? Have you been reading Burns again?"

"Aye. 'To a Mouse.'" And he began reciting: "'Wee, sleekit, cow'rin tim'rous beastie,/O what a panic's in thy breastie!' But I forget the rest. How do you say mouse in French, anyway?"

"La souris."

"Right, of course." And he repeated it: "La souris. Well, anyway, I've got les souris to show you, les enfants d'une mère qui est morte."

It was then that she noticed the bulge in his shirt, his hand cupped there, the buttons undone. In the next moment the hand emerged and there they were displayed against the hardened callus of his palm: three hairless pink things no bigger than bugs. They had tails, whiskers, pale curled feet. Mice. Les souris.

"Tell me they're not cute," he said.

"They're not cute."

The corners of his mouth twitched, but he held his smile. "Unbeliever," he shot back. "You might not think so, but I find them beautiful, perfectly made, everything wrought in miniature—just look at them. They're babies, Elise, babies."

She shrugged as if to say there were more perfect objects of beauty in the world, then turned back to the board, the rolling pin and the dough. She wasn't squeamish, wasn't indifferent, but they were mice, only mice. "What do you plan to do with them?" she asked after a moment, but she already knew the answer.

"Raise them, of course. I can't just let them die. I was in the shed, where the taproom's going to be, you know, moving things around, clearing some space, and I guess I didn't see the mother till it was too late. So I'm the responsible party here."

"And then?" she asked. "When they're grown? Are you going to train them to sit up and bark and wag their tails?"

She was watching his face—more banter—but he didn't laugh or even smile. He seemed to be considering. "I haven't thought that far ahead yet," he said. "But for now, where's the eyedropper? And would you bring me one of those cans of evaporated milk—you don't think it'll be too rich for them, do you?"

He put the mice in an old sock and left them beside the stove, for warmth, then ducked back out the door and into the fog that showed no sign of burning off. She went about her business, careful where she stepped as she moved around the kitchen, the cobbler taking shape and the soup she'd prepared for lunch boiling furiously on the stovetop. Three times that morning he came in to check on the mice, patiently holding the eyedropper to their snouts, though whether they took any of the milk or not, she couldn't say. After lunch he and Jimmie went out across the yard to work on repairing the fences they would use to funnel the sheep into the pens for shearing, or so he explained, and by the time it began to get dark it seemed he'd forgotten all about the sock in the corner and what it contained. But he hadn't. Even before he washed up or put on the kettle for tea, he was kneeling there beside the stove, eyedropper in hand. "They're eating!" he cried. "Or this one is, anyway. They're going to make it. I really think they're going to make it."

But, of course, they didn't make it. He was in bed, snoring, while she brushed her teeth over the sink in the kitchen, the lantern burning low and the dark pressing at the windows. She thought to check on them before she turned in, if only for Herbie's sake, and they were alive still, warm to the touch. The cobbler had been a success, even if it had dried out in the oven she was still trying to get the hang of, and she took a moment to cover what was left of it with a plate before going to bed. In the morning, the mice were cold, already stiffened, miniature satchels of shriveled leather bound up in a dirty sock. And the cobbler, the plate tipped back ever so slightly, bore the tracks of their cousins outlined in flour. As did the counter and the floor and the wall over the sink too.

228

Blue

That he took it hard was a testament to him, to his kindheartedness, his compassion and gentleness and his ability to see value in the smallest things, that was what she told herself. And yet the way he'd reacted, the way his face had fallen and his voice caught in his throat when he discovered them there at breakfast, was so bewildering she didn't know what to think. She watched him come through the door, light on his feet, whistling and singing out a good morning to her, then watched him bend down beside the stove, fussing there a moment before he lifted his head to give her a numb stare. "They're dead," he said.

She was at the sink, pumping water for the kettle. She looked out the window into the yard, where the fog closed everything in. "I know," she said. "I discovered them first thing this morning."

"And you didn't tell me?"

"The way you've been working, I thought I'd let you sleep." The kettle hissed as she set it on the stovetop. "I thought you'd want to find them yourself."

He rose heavily to his feet, the sock pressed to him. His eyes were flat, without sheen, his face bleached of color.

She said his name then, moved, puzzled, making a question of it—"Herbie?"—and she wasn't frightened, not yet, because he must have been joking, must have been pulling her leg. He was putting on an act, that was what it was, clowning for her. But he didn't say a word. Just shuffled across the kitchen, shouldered his way through the door and out into the yard, the sock cradled in his hands.

She went after him, waiting for him to swing round on her with his electric smile and deliver the punch line to the joke, this joke, this routine, and hadn't April Fools' Day passed already? Because he couldn't be serious.

Couldn't. He'd had no qualms about killing the cat—and, apparently, all the cats before it—and he kept talking about shooting one of the elephant seals, one of the big bulls, so he could preserve the skeleton intact and sell it to the natural history museum in Santa Barbara. Once he'd redeemed his gun collection, that is. And he was going to do that any day now, as soon as he could raise the cash . . .

"Herbie!" she called, but he wouldn't turn round. When she caught up to him he was emerging from the shed with a shovel in one hand, the sock in the other.

"You're burying them?" she asked, because she had to say something.

"I'll do it," he said, pushing past her. "You go on back in the house."

For a long while she watched him out the window. He stood there motionless at the far corner of the kitchen garden, or what passed for a kitchen garden. It was just weeds now. When she'd asked Jimmie about it he told her the wind and the birds would ravage anything they put in the ground, except maybe potatoes—potatoes they couldn't get to. She thought about that and about the seed packets—peas, tomatoes, cucumbers, pumpkins, bell peppers—she'd carefully picked out at the store back in Santa Barbara, which she was going to plant first chance she got no matter what Jimmie had to say, because weren't they going to have to make their own way out here? Or at least try? Fresh vegetables. Where were they going to get fresh vegetables?

Finally, Herbie laid the sock aside—gently, gently—and slipped the blade of the shovel into the ground. Two scoops of dirt, three: it was nothing. The sock disappeared in the hole, the dirt closed over it. But then he stayed there for the longest time, his lips moving as if he were talking to himself—or praying, maybe he was praying.

The whole business was odd, surpassingly odd, the first rift between them, the first thin trembling hairline fracture in the solid armature of them, husband and wife, joined forever, but she didn't know that yet. She merely watched him till she grew calm, grew bored, and turned back to her chores. It wasn't till later, till she was making dinner and happened to go out into the yard to throw the slops on the pile there that she noticed the wooden marker. He'd fashioned it in the shape of a cross and carved an inscription into it with his penknife. She had to bend close to make it out. *Wee Ones,* the crosspiece read, and on the vertical, *R.I.P.*

She tried to be breezy about it when they sat down to dinner, but it was as if he couldn't hear her. Normally he'd be spilling over with stories and jokes and reminiscences, so carried away she sometimes had to remind him his food was getting cold. Not tonight. Tonight he just sat there over his plate, chewing and staring off into the distance. "I probably made too much," she said, sitting across from him. "Thinking of Jimmie, I mean. But I suppose I can just add the meat to tomorrow night's pot, what do you think?"

Jimmie was off on the other end of the island on some urgent mission or other and so they were alone, a state of tranquility she'd been looking forward to ever since he'd come back. Not that she had anything against him. He was a companion for Herbie, inoffensive, even likable, a fount of information about everything from the peculiarities of the stove to the ailments of the horses and what the breeze portended vis-à-vis the next week's weather, and he did seem to pitch in without complaint—it was just that she hadn't had her fill of her husband yet. That first week. She wanted to relive it all over again. And again.

"Yeah," he said. "I guess."

"I'm sorry about the mice. These things happen, though, don't they?"

"Yeah."

"You did all you could. And that was nice, the way you put up a marker for them."

He shot her a glance. "Yeah," he said.

It went on like that through the next day and the day after that, even after Jimmie came back to provide the conversation round the dinner table, and at night, when they undressed for bed, she could feel him slipping away from her. On the third night, after he'd barely spoken a word to her all day, let alone touched her or shown the least sign of affection or even recognition for that matter, she couldn't hold back any longer. "What is it?" she murmured, easing into bed beside him. "It's not the mice still, is it?"

The room was cold, the stovepipe yet awaiting repair. She was dressed in a flannel nightgown, the peignoir folded away in the drawer now, and he didn't seem to notice the difference. She breathed out and saw her breath hanging there in a cloud.

"No," he said, "it's not the mice. The mice just—I don't know what it is. I feel all closed in."

She took his hand, afraid suddenly, trying to think in French, because he was speaking another language now. Closed in? How could that be? She'd never felt freer in her life. *"Chéri,"* she whispered, *"je t'aime. Je t'aime beaucoup."*

His eyes swept over her, then came back into focus. "I don't know what it is. I get like this. It'll pass. It always does."

"You're blue," she said. "You're just blue, that's all."

"Yeah," he said, nodding now, lifting his chin and dropping it as if it weren't a part of him at all, "I'm blue."

Bob Brooks

The shearers came at the end of April and they were a force of nature all their own, a human storm of wants and confusion and noise out of all proportion to their numbers. There was a dog that barked all the time. The sheep paraded through the yard. There was dust everywhere. They were four and they stayed a week, only a week, because the flock was so reduced now (twelve hundred, Herbie said, a quarter what it once was), but the week seemed like a month. She stood over the stove, which never went cold, even for a minute. She pumped water till her right arm was made of iron. Chopped stovewood. Washed dishes.

Herbie was outdoors all day long, sweating and swearing along with them, and she barely saw him till he collapsed in bed at night, but it was all right, she kept telling herself, it was only for a week, and this was the way Bob Brooks paid his bills—if it weren't for the shearing she and Herbie wouldn't be here at all. The wool piled up while she soaked beans and boiled rice and made lamb in every conceivable way she could think of. The shearers slept in the back bedrooms, at the far end of the house, and they ate like twenty men. At night they played cards, drank red wine from gallon jugs, sang in high hoarse voices to tunes that thumped along to a rattling singsong beat. One of them played guitar.

And then, as suddenly as the storm arose, it died away and they were gone. The sheep were let back into the pasture but for the ones going to market, the wool was stuffed into sacks and the shearers turned in their tokens (twenty-five cents for each ram shorn, fifteen cents for each ewe), received their pay from the bankroll Bob Brooks had handed Herbie the day after the wedding and took the boat back to shore. And Jimmie went with them, for a holiday, his own pay thrust deep in one pocket and a grocery list as long as his arm in the other. Peace descended. And Herbie, riding high on the hard physical labor and the satisfaction of seeing it to a successful conclusion—his first time as overseer and all had gone well—was her old Herbie, the Herbie who saw the joy in every form and example of God's creation and took her by the hand out over the hills to point it all out to her.

The sex came back. Came roaring back. He was insatiable. And it wasn't just in bed, but anywhere he found her, whether it was the living room or the kitchen or once even out on the porch. *We're not going to become nudists, are we?* she protested, toying with him, and he grinned his grin and pointed out that they were all alone with the sun and the sand and the sheep and if the sheep had anything to say about it, besides *baa,* that is, he'd let her know. One afternoon, a week after Jimmie and the shearers had left, he announced he'd be out till dark and not to wait dinner for him, and she just nodded, telling herself they couldn't expect to be together every minute of every day and that she had plenty to do, all sorts of things, letters to write, books to read, knitting, sewing, crocheting. She watched him go out the door, then she finished up in the kitchen and sat at the table there, writing a letter to her mother. Half an hour later she was in the living room, lost in one of her books, when she glanced up and there he was, framed in the doorway, his chest bare and his shorts barely containing him. Before she could say a word he pulled her up out of the chair and pinned her to the wall, his mouth hot on hers and his hands at her breasts. The surprise of it, the erotic jolt, shot through her. She touched her tongue to his, felt him, moved against him, her hips in slow rotation. They were like that, in an embrace, intimate, an intimate moment, when suddenly the outer gate flung open with a sharp raking clatter.

"Someone's here," she said.

"It's the wind."

She could feel his heart pounding against hers, both of them flushed, listening now. An instant later the gate crashed back again and he said, "See, I told you. I've got to fix that latch, damn thing's always blowing open," and that was fine, that was all right, until they heard the first footfall on the porch.

A moment later—and she'd instinctively pushed herself away from him, without thinking, really, because it wasn't as if they'd been caught in flagrante delicto and what if they had, they were husband and wife, weren't they, and in the sanctum of their own home out in the middle of nowhere?—Bob Brooks' face appeared in the window.

"Bob!" Herbie shouted, breaking away from her and rushing pell-mell for the door so that she was left there to smooth down her dress and watch the shift in Bob Brooks' expression as he began to register just what he'd interrupted. An instant, that was all it was, and then he was grinning and holding two fifths of Canadian Club whiskey up to the window for her inspection, the real thing, in real bottles with the actual label and the seal still intact. What could she do but smile back at him and fold over the fingers of her right hand in a complicit little wave?

The day was nice, the sun high still and the breeze down, so they sat outside and had their highballs, whiskey and rainwater out of the cisterns at either end of the house, the rainwater preferable to what came out of the ground because it didn't carry the heavy mineral aftertaste. "It's swell whiskey, Bob," Herbie said, clinking glasses with him, then with her. "Aces. The best. Where'd you get it?"

He was sprawled out on the ground, his elbows propped on the step behind him, his feet splayed in the dirt. His Army boots were worn smooth and his legs, tanned by the sun, showed the pale flecked topography of his scars, shrapnel there and shrapnel in his side and scattered up into the muscle of his rib cage too. She and Bob Brooks were on either side of him, sitting in the only two good chairs they possessed, glossy teak deck chairs salvaged from the wreck of the SS *Harvard*. That was one of the benefits of living on an island that projected out into the shipping lanes, she supposed: the furniture came to you. They had the safe from the SS *Cuba* too, which had gone aground here in 1923, and it was a permanent feature of the living room, as familiar to her now as her books and pictures and the sofa Herbie had fashioned from what appeared to be a coffin (empty, he assured her) that had washed up on shore one morning, though how anybody had ever got the safe up that hill, sled or no, was a mystery to her. It must have weighed five hundred pounds.

Bob Brooks just shrugged—and he was every bit as good-looking as Herbie, with the same boyish face and a full head of hair, none of which had turned gray, even though he was the same age as Herbie—forty-two, that is, a time when the average man has begun to show his age. "I have my secrets," he said.

"You're not turning to rum running now, are you?"

"No, but whiskey running, now there's an idea. I'll take this any day"—and he held the glass up to the sun to inspect it—"over rum. All the rum in the world, for that matter."

They were quiet a moment, sipping. A meadowlark folded its wings to drop into the yard and investigate something at the base of the fence. A shimmer rose from the earth where the sun beat at it.

"And how about the court case?" Herbie said, squinting against the light and arching his neck to glance up over his shoulder at them. His hair stood up from his head, shining in a nimbus of sunlit fire. His eyes had never been deeper or bluer. "How did that turn out? They're not going to send you to jail, are they?"

"Whoa, now—I was just a witness. A character witness at that."

"Just ribbing."

"Actually, it could have been worse. The attorney got the charge reduced to manslaughter, and then, of course, the men in that skiff *were* poachers—two Japs and a Portugee, off a whaling boat—and the jury took that into account."

She was feeling blessed, the sun on her face, the men's voices murmuring round her, the clouds stalled in the sky—there were no murders here, no courts, no forms and regulations to observe. She felt sorry for Bob Brooks, even though he was a millionaire—or the son of a millionaire, though who could know what anybody or anything was worth since the crash? He owned the leases from the government on both San Miguel and San Nicolas and he had property in Carpinteria and a home and an office in Los Angeles, and that meant his life was complicated in a way hers wasn't—he had to go to court and attend business meetings and run from one place to another while she got to stay put, out here, where everything held steady.

"I hate the Japs," Herbie said. "They stole from me and I don't forgive that. Was it a Jap that got killed?"

"No, the Portugee."

"So much the worse. But if your man had shot all three of them it would have been no more than they had coming—and I tell you, if any of them tries anything out here, I've still got the Remington. And the .22, if I want to just put a scare into them. Or blow their hats off." Herbie tipped back his glass, then got up to pour refills, and she had to put a hand over hers and tell him she was going to wait till later because she still had to fix dinner, or had he forgotten?

"That's okay," pouring first for Brooks, then for himself, "just hunky-dory—that just leaves all the more for us, right, Bob? But you just wait till I get my guns back because I don't care if they bring a whole army out here, I can hold them off—"

Brooks leaned back in the chair, the fitted joints letting out a sharp squall of protest, and held the glass to his nose, inhaling. "Good stuff, isn't it, Herb? But I didn't just bring you whiskey. Un-uh. I've got a surprise for you down there at the landing—and judging from the weight of the box, you're going to need some *horsepower* to haul it up here."

"You didn't."

"I did. Bought the note back from Hugh Rockwell, so you're square with him. My gift to you—really, it's the least I can do." A widening grin, a glance for her. "And you did just get married, didn't you, or am I missing something here?"

Herbie spun round, balanced on one leg, before going down on his knees and bowing his forehead to the ground, both palms pressed flat to the dirt before him. "Salaam," he said, "o wise one, o great and wise. I'm salaaming you, Bob. Salaam, salaam. That's the best news I've had in a month." And then he spun again, snatching his glass off the porch and plunking himself back down in the dirt with his legs crossed and the glass raised high. "A toast! Another toast! Here, Elise, give me your glass—no, no, you've got to. To Bob! To the greatest boss on God's green earth—or brown earth or umber or whatever damned color it is!"

That night, long after Brooks had gone to bed—woozy from the whiskey, though he'd had two portions of her lamb stew and half a loaf of fresh-baked bread to sop it up—Herbie sat over his guns in the living room. He cleaned and oiled them and then hung them one at a time on an ascending grid of nails he drove into the wall beside the stove where the fireplace was going to go—once they found the time for it, because what was a home without a hearth? She sat beside him, knitting, listening to the wind on the roof and the distant murmur of the surf. From time to time he'd hold up one of the guns—rifles, that is—and tell her about its features and provenance, the

Mannlicher and Lebel carbines he'd got in France, the Hotchkiss, the Mauser, his Jacob's elephant gun.

"Elephant gun? What on earth do you need an elephant gun for?"

"You never know, might be a whole herd of them grazing up on Green Mountain day after tomorrow."

"No, really."

He shrugged. "I just like the way it looks and feels. And I might go to Africa someday, on a big-game hunt, who knows? You have your books, I have my guns. It's a collection, that's all. And it's worth a pretty penny, believe you me. Worth more than anything else in this house."

"Big game? Aren't you the one who wouldn't kill a mouse?"

"That's different."

"Well, if it is, you'll have to explain it to me."

"The mice are—well, they're here. Africa's not."

"But the elephant seal, what about that?"

"That's different."

And so it went, the clock marching them past ten and then eleven until finally she pushed herself up, stretching, and asked if he wasn't coming to bed.

There was the smell of the gun oil, sharp and alien, the white rag smoothing over the gleaming barrel, his hand in motion, back and forth, back and forth, hypnotic. "In a minute," he said.

"You won't stay up too late, will you?"

"No," he said.

She set her knitting aside, moved to the door of the bedroom. "I'll be waiting," she said. But he didn't answer. He didn't even look up.

She closed the door behind her very softly and went on into the cold room to bed.

238

The Matchlock

It was growing light beyond the windows by the time he eased into bed beside her and he was up an hour later, no change visible in him except that he was accelerating through every motion he spun out with his hands and every syllable streaming from his lips. "Where's Bob?" he kept asking. "Is Bob up? Because Bob has a boat to catch and lucky for him the *Vaquero*'s making the round trip or he'd be stuck out here, though there're worse fates, aren't there? Stuck out here? Imagine that!" he sang out, running an arm round her waist and pecking a kiss to her ear where she stood at the cutting board, slicing potatoes and onions for home fries. He sailed round the kitchen, fussing over the coffee pot, hauling in stovewood, cutting out thick strips of bacon to lay in the pan just to hear them sizzle, and he twice went out to the barn to see to the horses and three times trotted into the living room to admire the arrangement of his guns, all the while bawling down the length of the porch for Bob Brooks: "Come on, Bob—haul your lazy carcass out of bed!"

When Brooks did emerge from the back bedroom it was past eight and he came up the length of the porch and into the kitchen in his bare feet, walking gingerly. His hair was mussed. He hadn't shaved. He was dressed in the same clothes as the day before, denim trousers and a flannel shirt with the collar open and the sleeves rolled up, and the minute he pulled back the kitchen door Herbie was there, dancing round him with a cup of coffee held out in offering. "Drink up," Herbie crowed. "This'll put the life in you, strongest coffee in the history of the world because I made it myself and I knew you'd be in sore need of it after last night—"

Brooks accepted the cup, blowing gently into it and shaking his head ruefully. "I never could keep up with you, but then who could?"

She was standing at the stove, manipulating the cast-iron frying pan with one hand, the spatula with the other. "Good morning, Bob," she said, looking back over her shoulder. "Sleep well?"

"Like a rock."

"Rocks don't sleep," Herbie put in. He was at the table now, pulling back a chair, three places set, napkins, knife, fork, spoon and cups all around. "They're inanimate. Never been awake. And if you've never been awake, how can you be asleep?"

"Like a dead man."

"Dead man's not asleep, he's dead."

"All right, Herb, have it your way—you're too rhetorical for me this morning, too rhetorical by half. Suffice it to say I slept well, Elise, and I ought to after that meal you served up—"

Herbie, seated now, his heel tapping and the cup to his lips: "And that sleeping potion."

"Sleeping potion?"

"Canadian Club, wasn't it? And by the way, if there's any chance of getting any more of that, let's say a couple cases, you just let me know."

It went on like that throughout breakfast, Herbie and Bob Brooks trading quips, and Brooks, to give him credit, was a good sport all the way, never impatient or condescending or anything like that. They were friends, old friends, from their days at Walter Reed Hospital after the war, when they were in the business of recuperating, though she never did find out what Brooks' complaint had been. Herbie, she knew, had been wounded when a mortar round hit one of the trenches and she knew that he'd suffered shell shock, but she had no real sense of what that meant. A shell landed. There was a concussion. Fragments went up. And then you recovered or didn't. Maybe at first you flinched when you heard a sudden noise, a car backfiring, fireworks on the Fourth of July, but you got on with life. Herbie certainly had. He was smart and capable, afraid of nothing and as full of life as any man she'd ever known—and that included her father and her brothers too—not at all like that sad pathetic man in the Virginia Woolf novel she never could remember the title of.

At one point, Herbie, in the midst of an encomium to one of his guns—the Japanese matchlock, the *tanegashima* with Japanese lettering, kanji, carved into the stock—sprang up from the table to dart into the other room and fetch it for them so they could see for themselves, and Bob Brooks, seated

240

across from her, looked up from his plate and said, "He seems in good spirits. You're doing wonders for him, you are."

"Him too," she said. "He's doing wonders for me."

"Glad to hear it. More than glad: overjoyed. He's had it rough these past few years, traveling for that machine company, going one place and another with no fixed address half the time—he needed to get away from all that. Needed a fresh start."

She didn't know what to say to this: Brooks was the one in charge here, the one pulling the strings, the boss, and as natural as he was, she sensed she had to be wary, or at least circumspect, around him. "We're grateful for it," she said.

"Oh, no, no, no," he protested, holding up his hands, "I don't mean it that way at all. You're doing me a favor, both of you—it's just that, well, I've had some losses, like everybody else, and I don't know how much longer I can keep up the operation out here. Even if Herb can come up with the amount we agreed on to buy in—" He must have seen the look on her face, because he broke off there and added, quickly, "But all this is premature, and I wanted to let you know, just in case, and what I mean is let's keep this between us, just you and me, because there's no sense in putting any more pressure on him than he's already got." A quick smile. "And you never can tell when things are going to turn around."

And then Herbie was back in the room, showing off the gun, rare treasure, a hundred years old, at least, and did they see these marks here, these slashes and the black ink worked into them? "You know what it says—as far as this Jap that sold it to me claims, anyway?" He was soaring. He gave them a minute, the three of them suspended there in the swelling light of the morning, birdsong running at the windows and the distant muted complaint of the sheep lost somewhere just above the threshold of hearing. She sat very still. Guns. He had guns and she didn't know the first thing about them. Except that hunters used them and there were hunters out here in the Wild West, hunters up and down the coast and all across Arizona, Nevada, Texas, shooting things.

"'Moon in water, blossoms in sky,'" he said. "Can you imagine? Moon and blossoms? What does that have to do with hunting or war or self-defense even? 'Aim true,' that's what it ought to say." And then he clucked his tongue, snatched the gun up and held it to his shoulder, leveling on some imaginary target beyond the window. "Aim true," he said and clicked the trigger on nothing.

"Herbie! Not in the house. What if it went off?"

But he just laughed. "It's not even a flintlock, Elise, it's a *match*lock. You need to light the match first. Isn't that right, Bob?"

Brooks was holding tight to his grin. "That's right," he said. "Nothing to worry about."

Afterward, when Herbie went down to the beach to see their guest off, he took the gun with him, and through the rest of the morning, at regular intervals, she heard the clean sharp snap of its firing as he worked his way down and then back up again. Snap, snap, snap.

Orca

It was August, well into her third month, by the time she realized she was pregnant. Her breasts were tender. She'd begun to bloat in her face and upper arms and around her hips and she couldn't remember how long it had been since she'd got up in the morning without feeling queasy, as if the island were a ship pitching in the sea, and yet still it never occurred to her that she might be pregnant. Young women got pregnant, women in their teens and twenties, not her. She was close to forty—surely the natural mechanism by which these things occur must have shut itself down years ago. *Dried-up.* That was the term that came to her. And though she and Herbie had never discussed having a family, she'd assumed the question was moot in any case. She was too old. Too *dried-up.* A December bride rescued from spinsterhood and assigned the place of helpmeet, companion, cook and laundress, with the sex thrown in as a bonus.

But she was wrong. Gloriously wrong. The realization came to her in an electric flash that practically incinerated her where she stood at the stove over a pot of beans and a skillet of indifferently frying fish. It was late in the afternoon, warm, the doors and windows thrown open despite the flies that sailed in and out at will. Herbie was sitting at the kitchen table, sipping tea from one of the china cups they'd received as a wedding gift and staring into a finger-worn copy of *Field and Stream.* She tried to think back to when she'd last menstruated, to her last sanitary napkin, a supply of which she'd taken pains to remember amongst a thousand other things to pack and bring along because she couldn't just stroll down to the corner pharmacy when she ran out, could she? But how long had it been? She couldn't remember. And because she couldn't remember she felt a thrill run through her: she *was* pregnant. Of course she was. And against all odds.

She looked to Herbie and there he was, his back to her, sipping, absorbed

243

in his magazine. His hair had grown grayer. The backs of his ears were sunburned—red, bright red, redder than the tomatoes she would have had if the birds hadn't pecked the vines right down to the ground, just as Jimmie had said they would. She watched the muscles move in his shoulders as he shifted to turn the page. Her man. Her mate. And what would she say to him: *Herbie, I think I'm going to have a baby?* Or no: *I'm going to have a baby.* Definitely. No doubt about it.

She waited, though, till after dinner, when they were sitting on the porch in the teak deck chairs and she'd had a chance to consult *Thornton's Medical Encyclopedia* and thrill to the lines about the placenta and umbilical cord developing within her to nourish the embryo, the fetus, the child there, and how her breasts were swelling toward their function of providing milk because she was a mammal and that was what mammary glands were for and how her cervix would dilate so that the baby could pass through the birth canal and out into the world to become a daughter or son—her daughter, her son. She'd known all this, of course, as anyone does in passing, but till now— till this moment—it had been strictly theoretical, information about the body and its processes that had nothing to do with her and never would, and she'd known it in the way she knew that the kidneys filtered blood and the two- chambered heart pumped it and the brain thought and the stomach con- tracted when you were hungry. Information. The news as delivered in a biology text.

The wind rattled the gate as if someone were there, but no one was— Jimmie was still back on the mainland because Bob Brooks couldn't afford to have him here and he wouldn't be needed till shearing in any case. So it was just the two of them, just Herbie and her. She smelled the sea, clean and cold. Felt the warmth of the sun on her face, her legs, her blouse and skirt and the blooming breasts and spreading abdomen they clothed and hid from view. She set down her book—a novel she couldn't seem to focus on—and in a voice so soft and tentative she could barely hear herself, she said, "Herbie, I think I'm going to have a baby."

The look on his face. As if she'd said, *They're dropping gold coins from an airplane!*

"You're not!" he said, coming up out of the chair so fast it pitched back and collapsed behind him. "You wouldn't kid me, would you?"

244

She felt her face flush. "I'm—as far as I can tell, that is. From . . . from things. And the medical encyclopedia."

He was standing over her, rocking back on his heels, his arms folded and his stare fixed on her, and then he reached out and laid a trembling hand on each of her shoulders as if he were blessing her. She felt his fingers there, the gentlest touch, and then they were gliding down the length of her arms till he took her hands in his and squeezed them tight. "You haven't been having your period?"

She shook her head no.

"And you've been sick in the mornings—aren't you supposed to be sick in the mornings?"

"Yes," she said. "A little."

And then he had her up out of the chair and he was hugging her to him so fiercely the breath went out of her. "We've got to get a doctor, the best man there is, and we have to get you to the hospital because we can't deliver a baby out here, I mean, I can't—I'm no doctor—and if there's an obstruction, a problem, any problem . . ."

She held to him, rocked with him there on the protesting bleached-out boards of the long straight run of the porch while the wind blew the smell of the sea to her and the soft tremolo of the grazing lambs drifted across the yellowed fringe of the hills. "Hush," she said. "Don't worry. It'll all work out fine. You'll see."

For the next two weeks, Herbie was busy in the toolshed across the courtyard from the house, disappearing after breakfast each morning and not emerging again till lunch, after which he locked the door of the shed and went off on his usual rounds. When she asked what he was doing out there every morning, he gave her a mysterious look and said it was a secret, but when she stepped out on the porch to hang the wash or shake out the tablecloth or sit in the chair with her knitting beneath a fog-shrouded sun or a sky blue all the way to the empyrean, her ears told her the secret had to do with the hammering of nails and the metronomic cleaving of wood with a handsaw. He was building something. And what could it be? A bassinet? A crib? It would be crude, whatever it was—he wasn't a natural carpenter—but she would admire it and exclaim over it all the same. It was the thought that counted. And she couldn't very well order a maple crib from the Sears, Roebuck catalogue—or could she? When one of the boats stopped by—the *Vaquero* or Bob Ord's *Poncador* or the *Hermes,* the Coast Guard cutter—she could send off a letter and then one or the other of them could deliver it when it came in, but what address would she give back ashore? And how could they afford it in these times?

At any rate, there came a day when the banging and sawing and the soft persistent rasp of sandpaper stopped altogether and he brought her out to the shed to show her what he'd wrought. The door stood open. She could smell the shellac before she'd got halfway across the yard. Inside, where the light from the open door fell across it in a savage slant, was a crib patched together from a dozen multihued scraps of wood and glowing under its coat of shellac. It was immense, big enough to hold five babies stretched out end-to-end, and in the depths of it, in lieu of a mattress, were the pillows stripped from the beds in the back end of the house, where Jimmie and the shearers slept. For a moment, she was speechless, and the silence hung between them until Herbie said softly, "I figured shellac instead of paint because I wouldn't want the baby peeling off any flakes of paint and, I don't know, poisoning himself. Because that'll happen."

All she could do was laugh and then take him by the arm, right at the biceps, and pull him to her for a kiss. "It's beautiful," she said. "Perfect." She was going to go on, telling him she loved the way he'd matched up the different woods and how nice it would look in the corner of their bedroom, right next to the stove that was going to have its pipe refitted any day now, but she never had the chance because he beamed his smile at her and said, "How about let's take the day off? A picnic. How does a picnic on the beach sound?"

They went down to the harbor and spread a blanket in the sand. She'd made peanut butter and jelly sandwiches on her own home-baked French bread, or the best simulacrum she could come up with, wrapped some oatmeal cookies in newspaper and poured the better part of a pitcher of iced tea (or cool tea, since they had no ice or means to make or store it) into a thermos, and they sat on the blanket and read their books and ate and gazed out to sea. The day was bright, the sun steady in the sky—early September on through October the best time for weather out here, or so Herbie assured her, and he'd had it from Jimmie—but it was brisk out in the open with no windbreak and she was glad she'd brought a sweater. She was just beginning to think about dinner, a long leisurely walk up the hillside, lamb chops simmering in butter and sage, more French bread, and then an evening spent out on the porch watching the sky change till night came on and they could go in and sit before the stove and talk in quiet voices about the baby and their plans for him—and names, names too—when Herbie suddenly let out a cry, jumping up from the blanket as if he'd been stung. "You see that?" he shouted, pointing out to sea.

She was getting to her feet, struggling up, the extra weight she'd begun to put on making her awkward and uncertain in her movements. "What?" she said, shading her eyes to follow his gaze out across the sun-bleached water. "What is it?"

"There! Don't you see it?"

Something was out there, a rolling undulant thing that shone blackly at the surface, glistening and sparking like an oiled shroud towed through the waves. "What is it, a porpoise?"

"Killer whale. An orca. The one I told you about that's been harassing the seals, eating them, that is—one bite and the water's all blood and the seal's there like a bone crossways in a dog's mouth. But are you okay? I mean, to stay here while I run up to the house for the gun?"

"Gun? What gun?"

"The harpoon gun, what do you think?"

This was a new gun, recently added to the collection thanks to the largesse of Hugh Rockwell, who'd sent it via the *Hermes* as a kind of consolation prize after continually delaying the loan to finance Herbie's bid to buy the lease from Bob Brooks. It was a shining brass thing that might have been a musical instrument but for the barbed spear jammed into the barrel of it and it was Herbie's newest treasure.

"You're not going to try to shoot that thing, are you?" She glanced down the shore to where their only craft—a rowboat—sat beside the crude dock and the shed Brooks had built for storing the wool sacks before they were shipped out.

"Of course I am," he said, already moving away from her.

"But why?"

His shoulders twitched, his feet danced—he was all nerves, all excitement. "We can't have that thing out there killing off our seals."

"Why not? There are thousands of them—and we don't have anything to do with them, anyway, do we? You're not thinking of becoming a seal-skinner, are you?"

Her attempt at humor fell flat: he wasn't even listening.

"It's a killer, that's all," he said. "And I've never—" He broke off then, turned and bolted across the beach to the road, where he never stopped churning his legs, leaning into the grade and running as if he were crossing the tape in the hundred-yard dash—except that this was the mile-and-a-half dash. And all of it uphill. She called out his name, bleated it, but it was no use—he was already gone.

Half an hour later—and she hadn't known whether to stay put or follow him up the hill, finally opting to stay in the hope she could intercept him on his way down and talk him out of it—he was back, racing across the sand at a dead run, the gun slung over one shoulder and his yellow oilskin flapping behind him. She'd been sitting in the lee of a jagged boulder, her eyes fixed on the road, the blanket folded beneath her and the remains of the picnic packed away in the basket. As soon as she saw him she sprang up, waving her arms, but he ran right past her as if she didn't exist. By the time she reached the place where the boat was he'd already dragged it across the beach by its painter and shoved it out into the foam of the surf, wet to the waist and hoisting himself up over the stern to snatch at the oars even as a breaker tossed the boat and the oars grabbed and he pitched forward into the next wave. The wind blew sand in her face and she had to turn her head and shield her eyes. When she looked up again he was a hundred yards out, the whitecaps beating round him and his hair flailing at his scalp.

For the longest while she watched him, mounting higher up the beach and finally partway up the road to keep him in sight, the boat all but lost in the blinding shimmer of the sea. Soon he wasn't much more than a speck on the horizon, out beyond Can Rock, Middle Rock and the huge dun wedge of Prince Island. She was cold. She found a place out of the wind, wrapped herself in the blanket and cleared a spot where she could sit braced against the rocks, wondering whether she should go back up to the house for her coat—and the binoculars. The binoculars would certainly help, because he was so far out now she could barely see him, and the killer whale, if it was there at all and she fervently hoped it wasn't, had faded away to invisibility.

Of course a killer whale wasn't a whale at all, but a dolphin, a toothed

248

dolphin some thirty feet long and twelve thousand pounds in weight, a thing that preyed on the biggest whales in the sea—the blue whale, even, the largest creature in the history of the world. The encyclopedia, which she'd consulted the night Herbie had first told her he'd seen an orca in the harbor, said that they went for the lips and tongue, tore the tongue out—the tongue that alone was bigger than her husband and his rowboat combined. They were savage. Implacable. Killers.

Suddenly she was angry. What was he thinking? Was he crazy? Even if he did manage to shoot the thing, then what—he could hardly expect to tow it back, could he? One man, in a rowboat, in a sea like this? He was impulsive, irresponsible. An hour before they'd been sitting on a blanket celebrating the biggest news of their lives, of her life, anyway, and now he was out there risking his neck without a thought for her or the baby either. The wind keened. She folded her arms across her breasts, pulled the blanket tight round her and stared out to sea at the speck that had become nothing now, that was gone. Outrage beat at her. The cold infuriated her. What would she do without him? What would her life be then, the life that hadn't even begun till she answered the bell and opened the door of her apartment in the crowded churning city to see him standing there grinning up at her in his wing collar and bow tie and with the ends of his mustache freshly waxed? *Bonjour, madame. Or is it mademoiselle? Enchanté.* Hurt yourself out here and you were hurt forever.

It was nothing she wanted to think about, a nightmare, a *cauchemar.* Furious, she turned her back on the sea, on him, and started up the long road to the house.

Marianne

If Marianne had been a boy she would have been named Herbert, after her father, but also after Elise's father and her older brother too: Herbert, the most natural name, the only name, for a male baby. But this baby was female and before Elise had left for the mainland to stay first with Bob Brooks and his wife (who was also expecting) in their big house in Beverly Hills and then with a cousin in the San Fernando Valley, she and Herbie had agreed on Marianne, in the remote eventuality that she gave birth to a girl. Or at least Herbie kept insisting on its remoteness. When she reminded him that the chances were evenly divided, fifty-fifty, he waved her off. "Little Herbie's going to help me dig that new septic field and shoe the horses and work right there beside me when we haul the provisions up from the beach and the wool on down. And he's going to learn to shoot before he can walk."

A girl, a boy, in the long run it wouldn't really matter to him—she knew that—and she was secretly pleased when the doctor, holding out the newest human being in the world to her as she came out of the fog of the ether, announced, *It's a girl*. Herbie wasn't there. Hadn't been there for nearly two months now, so nervous he'd insisted on putting her on a boat to the mainland at the end of her seventh month. If he'd all but ignored her the day of the orca (which still breathed and swam and devoured seals as far as she knew), he'd grown increasingly solicitous as her breasts grew heavy, her abdomen swelled and her clothes shrank till she spent half her time sewing new seams in her dresses, skirts and blouses. He helped with the housework, made her sit in the evenings with her feet up on a stool, pressed his ear to the ball of her stomach—her womb—to hear the baby moving inside her, full of plans, infinite plans, but nervous too. Or not just nervous—terrified that the baby would come prematurely and it'd be left to him to deliver it. "If only Bob had thought to build a hospital out here," he kept saying, his quick grin jumping to life, "we'd have nothing to worry about. Should I write him and complain?"

She missed him terribly during those last two months. At the Brooks' there were servants and she fell into a reverie of the household she'd grown up in, where her father kept a staff of seven, but servants were a thing of the past, of another life in another place, and she felt uncomfortable intruding in any case. With the Whites—her cousins in the Valley—she felt even more ill at ease. She insisted on helping with the cooking and clearing up, doing laundry, making up her own bed and such, but she was moving slowly now and felt tired all the time, and she didn't want to be a burden, especially not to a cousin she hardly knew. And there was noise. Automobiles everywhere, people crowding the markets, the ceaseless chatter of the radio. When Herbie blew through the door of her room at the Good Samaritan Hospital in Los Angeles four days after Marianne had come into the world, all she could say was, "Take me home."

But it wasn't as easy as all that. Herbie had brought Jimmie back to the island and left him temporarily in charge because there was no other option and he needed urgently to get home and put things in order, but the doctor was adamant: the baby was not to leave the mainland until she reached a weight of ten pounds or he wouldn't be held accountable. Ten pounds, that was the limit, the threshold, the inflexible line that kept them chained to shore. Herbie found them an apartment, and what choice did he have? It was a small place, two rooms, a furnished walkup on a busy street ten minutes from the hospital. He burned with energy, impatience, his face gone soft for the baby and hard for her, as if it was her fault they were imprisoned here. He was the one who'd married her, hadn't he? He was the one who'd put his organ in her. He was the one.

They quarreled and made up and quarreled again. Herbie was out all day, from first light to last, looking for work, anything to sustain them and pay off the maternity loan Bob Brooks had advanced them though he was short himself. There was no work, no work of any kind, however menial or ill paying or inconsequential. Hoboes were riding the rails. Men stood on the street corners three-deep selling pencils and apples to finesse the humiliation of begging outright. "What does she weigh?" Herbie kept asking. "Have you weighed her today? This *morning*? What about *now*?"

When finally they were free to go and they drove up to Ventura in Bob

Brooks' car to catch the *Hermes,* her ten-pound four-ounce daughter asleep in her arms and her husband at the wheel beside her, she felt as if she weren't in a car at all but an airplane, soaring high over everything. All she could think of was the sleigh bed with the cradle at the foot of it and the newly functional stove there that threw out heat till the room was as warm as any steam-heated maternity ward or furnished apartment. The sea smelled like paradise, the gulls were winged saints. And if the *Hermes* was on patrol for bootleggers and it took them all day before they finally rounded the point and motored into Cuyler Harbor, what did it matter? They were home.

It was dark by the time the captain lowered the dinghy and had one of the sailors row them ashore. He was a new man, this sailor, someone they hadn't met before, and she couldn't see much of him in the dark beyond the soft pale glow of his cap and the red glare of the cigarette he held clenched between his teeth. He didn't say a word till they reached the verge of the breakers and he eased up on the oars. "We'll have to time this just right," he said as they bobbed there in the darkness, the surf roaring and the long white hem of the wave-tips flaring out on either side of them. "Because we wouldn't want any risk, you understand, to the baby, that is."

They were wearing life jackets, all three of them, Marianne so tiny hers was like a cradle she'd been tied into, cat's cradle, a nest of string Herbie had fussed over for the past half hour. He paused now in the middle of a mono-logue about the wonders of the island to thank the man for his concern, then gave him detailed instructions about where it was best to get in and how to gauge the waves. The sailor said nothing. Herbie scrambled up to the bow to flash a light ahead of them. As soon as he flicked it on, the grand sweeping semicircle of the beach sprang to life as if they were seeing it on a movie screen, faintly brown, faintly yellow, the surf foaming white and the road up to the house a jagged black slash in the distance.

Then they were ashore, the sailor springing out to haul the boat up out of the surf and Herbie there, knee-deep in the water, to take Marianne from her and make sure of her. They were quick and efficient as they unloaded their things, baby clothes, provisions, the accumulation of two months and more ashore, the sailor pitching in without a word. When everything was out of the boat, he asked if they needed help getting it up the hill and Herbie just said, "Thank you again, but we can manage. We do live here, you know."

There was a moment of silence, Marianne asleep in her arms, the surf hissing over the sand and rattling its freight of shells and pebbles and whatever else it had picked up on the incoming tide. The sailor drew once more on the cigarette so that his face flared briefly, almost anonymously—he could have been anyone—then flicked the butt away on a streamer of red sparks. "Yeah," he said finally, "to each his own, I guess. But good luck, huh?"

"Luck to you too," Herbie said.

In the next moment the dinghy was afloat again, riding up the crest of an incoming wave, the oars fanning out like the legs of a water strider and the sailor's white cap the only thing visible until the boat was swallowed up in the shadows. Herbie bent for his rucksack, then flashed the light ahead of them and they started up the road in the narrow tunnel carved out of the night. He was shaking his head, a flickering movement in the darkness, his face ghostly in the quavering beam of the flashlight. "God, it's good to be done with all that, isn't it? All that fuss and bother and everybody running around like it's their last day on earth. I swear I'll never leave this place again," he said, "no matter what, I don't care." He stopped a moment and they both looked back to where the *Hermes,* lights glowing fore and aft, rode the black void of the sea. "Goodbye, world," he sang out, "as far as I'm concerned you can all go to hell."

She stumbled, the baby clutched tight, and he put out an arm to steady her. "You all right?"

"Yes," she murmured and it was a frisson, the faintest delectable tingle of satisfaction, to realize it was true, maybe the truest thing she'd ever uttered.

The Japanese

In the old days it was the Chinese, or so Jimmie told her. They had come out here, to all the islands, really, but to San Miguel in particular, to harvest the abalone, though it didn't belong to them because they were foreigners and they didn't hold the lease on the place, anyway. And they'd poach sheep too and leave behind the charred remains of what they couldn't eat—the fleece meant nothing to them, just a throwaway, putrid, with the skin still on it and all over maggots. Now it was the Japanese. Their trawlers and long-liners came all the way from Japan because the channel was rich in the fish they craved, the tuna and mackerel and halibut they'd overfished in their own waters. Jimmie didn't like them. Herbie didn't like them either. For her part, she was indifferent—she'd never met a Japanese in her life and it was no secret that everybody had good and bad in them no matter where they came from.

So it was a surprise late in that spring, her second spring on the island, Marianne growing and gurgling, with her at all times, even in the kitchen, even then, asleep in a wicker basket and the pot boiling on the stove, when a sleek white fishing boat motored into the harbor flying the flag of the Japanese nation. The flag, it seemed to her, was beautiful, simpler and more austere than the Stars and Stripes: a red circle to represent the rising sun against a bright snapping field of white. She needed the binoculars to see it clearly, and as she hoisted the baby and started down the hill to greet them as she would have greeted any of their rare visitors, whether it be the Coast Guard boys, amateur boaters out of Santa Barbara or whalers from as far away as Norway, she felt no apprehension. They would ask something of her (meat, water) and give her something in return (fish, most likely) and she'd invite them to the house for tea and a meal and if they didn't have any English they'd communicate with facial expressions and gestures. She was glad of the company, always glad.

Herbie had gone out earlier that morning to the southwest side of the island where the elephant seals had their rookery, just to keep an eye on them, he said. He took a gun with him and a safari hat and a pack with a canteen of water and the sandwiches she'd made him. It was three or four miles from the ranch house to the beach where the big bloated males kept their harems, the females two-thirds their size and spread out around them like so many sacks of grain. She'd been out there with Herbie to look at them half a dozen times, and they were appealing enough, she supposed, these things that appeared out of the sea each year as if by magic and had been hunted nearly to extinction for their blubber the same as whales till lamps went to kerosene and coincidentally spared them, but she wasn't as attuned to them as Herbie was, Herbie the hunter. He wasn't going to *donate* the skeleton to the museum, he kept insisting, he was going to sell it, because in these times they needed all the income they could scrape up, what with Bob Brooks cutting his salary to the minimum and precious little money available anywhere, and wasn't that the truth? It was, she supposed, and she knew they were lucky to have any employment at all and to live out here away from the soup kitchens and the hoboes and Okies and everybody else going hungry in a world shrunk down to nothing. They weren't self-sufficient, far from it—the garden a failure, the necessities shipped in from the coast—but they could always eat lamb when others did without. And fish. And the occasional lobster or abalone, which she pounded flat, soaked in evaporated milk, rolled in bread crumbs and deep-fried, with her own tartar sauce to perk it up.

They *were* lucky. Maybe the luckiest people on earth. And Herbie was out stalking his elephant seals and Jimmie ashore or maybe out on Bob Brooks' other island because Bob felt responsible for him and tried to find him work as best he could, and there were strangers in the harbor and the sun shining bright and she was on her way down to greet them with her baby in her arms, just for the novelty of it, and the neighborliness, that too.

There were three of them hauling a rowboat ashore when she got down to the beach and strode across the strand to them, Marianne perched on one shoulder, the sand whispering beneath her shoes. They were dressed like any other fishermen, stained pants, peacoats, watch caps, except that they wore sandals instead of shoes. One of them—the captain, obviously—slipped out of his coat when he saw her coming and handed it to the man beside him. He was wearing a white jacket beneath it, with epaulettes on the shoulders. He said something to her, which she later realized must have been a thick-tongued variant on "Good afternoon," and bowed deeply, as did his two ship-mates.

She didn't know what to do so she bowed back, then rose, smiling, and said, "Welcome, welcome to our island," and she couldn't help adding, thinking of Herbie, "the Kingdom of San Miguel."

In the next moment they'd swarmed round her, their wide dark blunted faces opening up in amazement at the sight of Marianne, this prodigy in her arms, as if a child were the last thing they expected out here, and she wondered how long they'd been at sea and what wives and children they'd left behind. She thought of her own separation from Herbie, first at the Brooks', then the Whites', and how each day had slammed down on her like the door to a vault and how nothing had seemed right, not the sun in the morning or the food on the table or the air moving through the windowscreens, heavy with the scent of orange blossoms. But these men: they were ashore, feet on the ground, and they laughed aloud and held out their forefingers for Marianne to clutch in her tiny fist, made faces for her and talked baby talk in falsetto—their language, in that register, fluting like the wind in the tops of the trees. *"Bebay,"* the captain kept saying, looking from her to Marianne and back again, and she could see the words trying to shape themselves on his lips till he looked as if he were going to implode with the effort, but he got no further.

"Would you like," she said, enunciating very slowly and distinctly, as if that would make a difference, "to come up to the house"—pointing now—"for some refreshment? I can make tea. Sandwiches." She looked doubtfully from one to the other. "Do you like sandwiches?"

An hour later the three men were sitting shoulder to shoulder on the sofa that had once been a coffin, each with a teacup in one hand and a saucer in the other and their spines held perfectly rigid. She sat across from them, Marianne in her lap, and passed a platter of gingerbread cookies to the captain, who was positioned on the end of the sofa nearest her. "Good," he pronounced, after taking a precise experimental bite of his cookie while the other two looked on for a signal as to how to proceed. She wished she could communicate with them, ask them where they were from, if they had families, what their religion was like, their food, what they thought of California, because here was an opportunity she would never have had in New York, where there were all types, but not any Japanese, or not that she could remember. Chinese, yes. But then, looking at them, how could you tell them apart? Maybe she had seen Japanese before without realizing it, but even if she had she'd certainly never sat across from them over a cup of tea and a platter of cookies.

Americans—and she was guilty of this too—tended to treat foreigners like children or idiots, like the deaf and dumb, simply because they had no English or fumbled with it, and yet here were people as articulate and full of passion and hope and experience as she was herself. They were polite. Beautifully mannered. They loved babies. And they had so much to tell her, she was sure of it, if only they could find the words. She set down her cup, shifted Marianne in her lap. And then—and she didn't know why except that it was the language of diplomacy, of the world, and she was speaking before she could think—she tried French. *"Parlez-vous Français?"*

The captain shot her a look of interest, as if all this time he'd been waiting to hear just that phrase. He smiled. *"Un peu. J'ai vécu à Marseilles une fois—il y a plusieurs années."*

And that was it, that was the key in the lock, and though his French was minimal and he spoke it with an accent she could only call bizarre, it enabled them to communicate, if fumblingly. She learned that he and his crew—there were eight more aboard—had sailed out of Yokohama six weeks before and that he knew the islands and the coast of California and its fisheries intimately, having captained *beaucoup* fishing vessels over the years. But it was slow going and frustrating, because suddenly she wanted to know all about him, about his life and his hopes and prejudices, a real live Japanese before her, a visitor from another kingdom. Or empire. It was the Japanese Empire, wasn't it? To *Es-ce que vous êtes marié?* he replied, *Non.* To *Vous aimez la vie de la mer?* it was, *Oui.* And then, after a moment's reflection, *"Beaucoup."*

She was about to ask him if he'd been ashore in America, if he knew any Americans and if so what he thought of them and if the accounts of his country's (how would she say it, belligerence, aggression?) had any basis in fact or if they were just typical newspaper hyperbole, when the door swung open and Herbie was there, the gun slung over his shoulder and the knapsack, crammed with something—driftwood, seashells?—dangling from one hand. Instantly, the three men leapt to their feet. They came up so fast they nearly knocked over the low table that held the teapot and platter, each man clutching his cup as if it were a shield.

She watched Herbie's face work through its emotions, going from surprise to shock to distaste and finally a kind of feigned indifference all in an instant. How it had happened, she couldn't say, but suddenly the room was thick with tension. "Herbie," she called, trying to brighten her voice, "these are our guests, fishermen from Japan—that's their boat in the harbor there. They"—and here she gestured toward them and they all, in unison, bowed, but it was a short bow, a nod of the head only, their eyes fixed on Herbie and his gun—"were just joining me in a cup of tea, paying a visit, that's all. The captain"—another gesture, another bow—"speaks French. *Un peu*." She smiled, first at Herbie, then at the man in the white jacket, but neither smiled back.

Herbie set down the bag beside him, nodded brusquely at the three men, then crossed the room as if he were measuring off each step, shrugged out from under the strap of the gun and with a kind of surgical deliberation placed it back on its mount on the wall. None of the men moved. They remained standing there, the teacups clutched in their hands, until Herbie swung round and leaned back into the wall, arms folded, so that he was framed by the slashing parallel lines of the guns, nine guns in all, from the *tanegashima* to the elephant rifle, and they leaned forward, one by one, to set their teacups back down.

Herbie didn't say hello or welcome or anything of the sort, not in English, French or Japanese, or even in the language of common courtesy. No, he was rude, just plain rude, and it embarrassed her. Fixing his eyes on the captain, he said, *"Ce que vous voulez ici, monsieur?"*

The captain looked to his men, then to her, and finally, Herbie. His face showed nothing. *"Rien,"* he said finally, and he bowed again and moved toward the door, which stood open still on the courtyard and the main gate beyond. In the next moment—and Herbie never flinched, never shifted, just stood there leaning against the wall with his arms folded—the Japanese were bowing their way out the door with murmurs of *"Merci"* and something else, something in their own language that might have meant thank you or good-bye or maybe just *Sorry.*

She didn't want to quarrel, but as soon as they'd left—as soon, that is, as Herbie had got back from following them down to the shore to make good and certain they got in their boat and rowed off to the ship anchored in the harbor—she came right up to him and let loose. "I can't believe how you treated those men," she said.

He was standing in the doorframe, the light a solid wedge behind him, as if it had turned hard, to ice or stone. "What's for dinner?" he said, ignoring her. "I'm half-starved."

"Why were you so rude? They were decent enough, just like anybody else, fishermen, that's all—you should have seen the fuss they made over Marianne."

"They stole from me. I told you that."

"Who stole from you? Those men, were they the ones?"

He shrugged. "I don't know," he said, softening his voice, "maybe. He looked familiar, the one in the white coat. I told you the story, didn't I—about the strychnine that time? The time I was poisoned?"

He tried to take her hand, but she pulled away. "No," she said. "No, you didn't."

"Listen, I'm sorry," he said, and he went to sit on the couch, right where they'd been not an hour before, but she wouldn't let it go, she was furious at him, and she stood over him, hands on her hips, and if the baby was fretting in her basket, so much the worse.

"It was when I first got out here, and Bob was gone and Jimmie too and I was all alone and didn't really know what I was doing—thinking of you all the time, around the clock. Remember all those letters I wrote you? The miss-you ones? The pleading ones? Well, anyway, lambing was coming on and before he left Bob said we needed to do something about the ravens, to keep them off the newborn lambs because they'll kill them, you know that, don't you? I shot a couple, but then, because I was low on cartridges and didn't want to waste ammunition, I put out poisoned baits for them, meat that had gone bad, and I laced it with the strychnine from the bottle out there in the shed. But my mistake—you know what my mistake was? I got done and rolled a cigarette and licked off the paper and smoked it without thinking to wash my hands."

She eased down beside him on the couch. "You poisoned yourself," she said, her voice soft now.

"Yeah."

"You never told me, never said a word in your letters—"

"Why would I? I felt like an idiot. And I didn't want to worry you. But it was bad, and it hit me right away, because I was smoking it, you see? I went into convulsions. Stiffened like a rake. I couldn't breathe. I was out there in the courtyard, in the dirt, thinking I was going to die all alone and nobody'd find me for weeks, and suddenly there was this Jap, come up from a boat in the harbor just like the ones today, looking at me over the gate, and I called out to him for help. 'I'm poisoned,' I said, and then I don't remember, but he must have got me in the house and put me here on the couch and found a blanket for me. I passed out. And when I woke up, the Jap was gone and one of my guns was gone too—and since I only had the three at the time because Hugh had the rest, thank God, I noticed right away. But can you imagine? The son of a bitch leaves me here, dying for all he knew, and all he does is steal my gun? Can you get any lower than that?"

"I didn't know," she said. "I'm sorry. But these men—" she broke off. Suddenly, amazingly, he was grinning at her. "What?" she said. "Why are you grinning?"

"Did you count the silverware?"

And now she was grinning too—it was a joke. He was already joking about it. They had no silverware, no silver of any kind, not even a candlestick or an egg cup. "I'll get up and see in a minute," she said.

"What about the salver?"

"I'll have to check on that too," she said.

The Pain

After that, there was a long stretch of time in which nothing much happened, everything placid, the wind blowing, the sheep grazing, the waves rolling on up the shore and pulling back again. It was just her, Herbie and Marianne, the *Vaquero* coming once a month with supplies, the *Hermes* every week or two with the mail and news of the outside world. Which wasn't especially good as the year wound down and Christmas came on without a tree or store-bought presents, though it was homey and quiet and she and Herbie exchanged little things they'd made—earrings he'd fashioned from mother-of-pearl, socks and a muffler she'd knitted in a shade of red so bright you could have signaled out to sea with them, and for Marianne a stuffed cordu-roy teddy bear with button eyes and three miniature sheep Herbie had carved from a block of balsawood that turned up on the beach one day.

Another spring came and went. The shearers arrived and then they were gone. The days bled into each other, days eternal, each one like the next. Her-bie threw himself into his projects—hooking up a water heater to the stove in the kitchen and running the pipes through the attic to the bathroom so they could have baths without having to lug a sloshing pail from one end of the house to the other; building the fireplace in the living room out of adobe bricks salvaged from the old Waters place; erecting a windmill to pump the water up from the spring and replace the hand pump—and she worked right beside him, hauling brick, mixing mortar, taking the shovel and pick and extending the septic field out and away from the house and water supply. They were too busy to be bored, though there were nights when she would have given anything for a radio or a phonograph even—just to hear music, anything, a polka, a concerto, Eddie Cantor or Al Jolson, it didn't matter. Music. She missed music, but not much else.

The fact was that everything out there beyond the channel began to seem increasingly remote and disconnected. They picked up a newspaper or magazine her mother had sent them and they might as well have been reading about another planet, science fiction in the pages of *Collier's* or *The Saturday Evening Post*. The Depression was worsening and no end in sight, as if joblessness, bankruptcy, starving children and whole families cast out in the street were the normal way of doing things and all that had come before, all the generations of farmers, factory workers and shop owners, all the savings accounts, a quarter a week, build for the future, nothing more than an illusion. Mussolini and his Blackshirts were strutting in Italy and Hitler and his Brownshirts in Germany and when election day came around they discovered that the United States was to have a new president, a socialist by the name of Roosevelt whom both she and Herbie would have voted against if there were a polling place nearby. As if it mattered. And it didn't. All that mattered was the three of them and the way the seasons turned and the ewes dropped their lambs.

Then there came a morning when Herbie couldn't get out of bed. It was just after their second Christmas, a dark late-December morning, the wind chasing round the courtyard and the steady granular tap of the sand grains at the window the only sound in the world. She was up before him, at first light, feeding Marianne and putting on the coffee pot, and at first she didn't think anything of it. Usually he was up first, burning with his uncontainable energy, running from one thing to another, but Marianne had woken her early and she took her out to the kitchen and let him sleep. When he didn't come in, even after she'd fed Marianne her porridge, poured out a cup of coffee for herself, greased the griddle and mixed the pancake batter, she went back to the bedroom and found him lying there supine, his eyes open, staring at the ceiling. "Bring me the aspirin," he said, his voice clenched in his throat. "The whole bottle."

"Are you ill?"

"And whiskey. Is there any whiskey left?"

"Whiskey? At this hour?" She crossed the room to him and laid her palm across his brow. "You don't have a fever, do you? Or your back. Is it your back?"

"It's my side. I don't think I can get up."

She nursed him through the morning, alarmed because he was always so stoic, never sick a day, never idle. His face was drained of color. He wouldn't take anything to eat. She gave him some fruit juice out of a can and found half a bottle of whiskey, one he'd been hoarding, out in the toolshed. For the rest of the day, he alternated sips of whiskey and doses of aspirin, but every time he tried to get up, the pain was too much for him. The problem—and he explained it to her when she brought a plate of supper in to him, supper which wound up going cold—was that the shrapnel in him was migrating, pressing on something there, on his left side, just below the ribs, cutting into him all over again.

She'd pulled up a chair beside the bed and lifted Marianne into her lap. "You need a doctor," she said. "We've got to get you to a doctor, right away."

"No," he said. "I can't do that. I can't leave you here on your own."

"I can manage. It'll only be a day. Or a day there and a day back. That's all. Two days, maybe three. I'll be fine. I will."

"No," he said, "no," and he tried to shake his head for emphasis but the pain grabbed at him and he could only wince.

It went on like that for two days, the whiskey gone, no more than a handful of aspirin left and Herbie taking nothing but tea and broth and no way to contact anyone unless she got in the rowboat and rowed herself out of the harbor, south around Nichols Point and due east to Santa Rosa to try to find someone there to help, but the boat wasn't built for the open ocean and she'd probably just wind up drowning herself—and even if she didn't, even if she managed to make it, what would she do with Marianne in the interval and who'd look after Herbie? No, the only solution was to keep an eye out for a passing boat and pray for the best. But it was the dead of winter, January, and the weather was bad—if it cleared one day out of seven it was cause for celebration—and when the weather was bad the fishermen stayed ashore and the pleasure boaters never left the dock. So where was this miraculous boat going to come from? And how would they know there were people in trouble out here?

By the third day, he was marginally better, sitting up in bed, taking toast and coffee for breakfast and a bit of soup for lunch, but when he got up to use the bathroom he was hunched over and gasping and when he was done there were traces of blood in the toilet. If she'd been alarmed before, now she was frantic. "I can't take it," she told him. "I'm going down to the beach. To signal. There's got to be a boat out there somewhere."

"Signal?" His voice was choked. "With what?"

"I'll wrap a sheet around the broom and wave it like a flag, a white sheet."

He didn't say anything, merely winced and closed his eyes.

The afternoon was cold, the wind stiff, the ocean pounded to a froth. Visibility was poor. She tried to make a game out of it for Marianne, drawing faces in the sand, bending to collect shells, but it was no fun—even with her mittens and scarf and her hood up, Marianne was chilled through, she could see that. Her cheeks were chapped. Her nose was running. She was a baby still, a month short of her second birthday, and taking her down here in weather like this was crazy. It was useless. The whole thing was useless.

She went about her chores that evening as if she were an automaton, making a dinner she alone would eat, feeding the baby and putting her to bed, clearing up, seeing that Herbie was as comfortable as possible. She tried to sit before the fireplace, tried to read, knit, occupy herself, but her mind kept churning. Finally, because she couldn't just do nothing—he was in pain, he could be bleeding internally, *dying*—she went out in the yard with the sudden notion of starting a bonfire, setting the whole island ablaze if need be, anything to get somebody somewhere to see what was happening here.

The wind wouldn't have it. It battered her as soon as she opened the gate, rocking her off her feet and stinging her face and hands with grit as she went about mechanically piling wood in the lee of the house—the precious firewood that had to be dug from the earth or hauled up from the seadrift below, wood there was never enough of. She knelt in front of the pile as if in a pew at church, mouthing silent prayers, but the matches flared out the instant they caught. Eventually, after going through half a box of matches and crumpling ball after ball of newspaper, she managed to work a thin thread of flame through the pile and for a moment she thought it would catch, but a gust snatched it away and the darkness rushed back in. In bed that night, lying sleepless beside her husband, she listened to the wind raking across the island, stretching itself, sucking in air till it was blowing a gale.

And then the miracle. In the morning it was clear, the wind was down and there was a boat in the harbor, a motor yacht that must have come in in the night to take refuge from the storm. She spotted it right away, as soon as she got out of bed to find Herbie bent to one side in the chair by the stove, the empty aspirin bottle clutched in his hand, the baby standing up in her crib and whimpering to be picked up and the binoculars on the hook by the door where she'd left them. "Keep an eye on Marianne," she told him, pulling on her clothes, fighting her feet into her shoes and snatching up the broom with the sheet wrapped round it. "Don't let her near the stove. I'll be right back."

The boat was the *Bon Temps,* out of Ventura, and it had drifted to the end of its anchor line with the incoming tide so that its stern faced straight on when she got down to the beach, breathless, her heart pounding and a shrill tocsin sounding in her head. All the way down she kept expecting to see the boat motor out of the harbor before she could get there and she'd pushed herself hard, risking a turned ankle or a fall or worse, rocks strewn every-where and the sand drifted up to disguise them. For one frantic moment she'd thought of taking Buck, but she couldn't spare the time to saddle him and so she'd just taken off running and hadn't stopped till this moment, when she unfurled the sheet and began waving it wildly over her head. "Help!" she shouted, the urgent squall of her voice carrying out over the water to the mute rocking hull of the *Bon Temps,* which might as well have been a ghost ship for all she could see, but then they'd be asleep in their berths still, wouldn't they?

It couldn't have been much past seven. The water smelled oily and rank. It was calm, flat calm, the stalled sun throwing a hard metallic glint across the surface. "Help!" she shouted, up to her knees in the surf now, the sheet flapping in the breeze she was generating all on her own. "SOS! SOS!" Very gently, almost apologetically, the boat swung round on its tether, then swung back again.

She was thinking of the rowboat, of running for the boat and rowing out to them, when a figure appeared on the deck. It was a man, dark-haired, angular, his face smudged with sleep. She watched him cup his hands and shout, his voice stretched thin as wire: "What's the trouble?"

"It's my husband. He's—he needs a doctor! Help, we need help!"

Now there was a second figure, a woman, her face pale and milky beneath the blond bob of her hair and the flat black slashes of her eyebrows. She watched the two of them put their heads together, conferring, and then the man was dropping the dinghy over the stern, climbing into it and steadying it for the woman. Then they pushed off, the oars dipped, and they were coming.

They made their introductions on their way up the hill—they were the Graffys, Dick and Margot, and they were coming down from visiting her par-ents in Avila Beach when the windstorm drove them into the harbor—and all

Elise could do was apologize for hurrying them up the road till they were out of breath and the small talk fell away to the rasp of indrawn breath and the scrape of pebbles kicking out from beneath the soles of their shoes. The low sun elongated their shadows. The creek below chanted over its stones. She couldn't help thinking what a glorious day it was, or would have been, if only there were no pain and no danger and things could go on as they'd gone on before.

When they got to the house, they found Herbie still propped up in the chair and Marianne—hungry, bored, impatient—perched in his lap with a picture book she'd lost interest in. "These people have come to help," she said, the words all coming in a rush as she bent to lift her daughter and hug her to her. No one was dressed. The room was a mess. She felt ashamed suddenly.

The man—and what was his name again?—stepped forward and bent over Herbie while the wife hung behind in the doorway. "Is it bad?" he asked. He was thin, a man of sticks—she could see his shoulder blades projecting like a wooden hanger from beneath the weave of his turtleneck sweater—and he wore his hair parted just to the left of center and slicked down so it clung to his skull. His clothes were expensive—the sweater, dark woolen slacks, deck shoes with tassels—and he had a stern probing look that for an instant made her imagine he might be a doctor, and wouldn't that be something, a doctor delivered to them out of the storm like an angel of mercy? But he wasn't a doctor. He was a banker, as it turned out, president and chief officer of the Ventura Savings and Loan, one of the few banks that had survived the financial carnage. But he was here. And he had a boat.

Herbie—and this really put a scare into her—wasn't able to respond. He just lifted his eyes, his gaze gone distant, and nodded his head.

"It's his wound," she heard herself say. "From the war. Shrapnel, he says. It's pressing on something—inside. There was blood." She looked away. "In the toilet."

"Can you move?" the man was saying. "Can you get down to the boat?"

"I can't"—the words pinched in his throat—"leave her here."

"We'll take her with us—there's plenty of room. It won't be a problem. And I can help you get down there—and Margot too, we'll both help. Don't worry."

Herbie was shaking his head. "The animals," he said—or no, he was croaking, his voice splintered and reduced. "Somebody has to stay."

266

In the end, it was decided that Margot would stay there with her while Dick ran Herbie to shore, and there were assurances all round that everything would be fine, doctors what they are today, and Dick would take him to his personal physician, best man on the west coast, fix him up in no time, just you see.

There was the first night, Margot a godsend—just her presence, her presence alone—and she couldn't thank her enough. Elise made up the bed in Jimmie's room for her and they sat before the fire and talked about the little things, trivial things, the weather, boats, fashions, life in Ventura and Los Angeles, the motion pictures, never letting a silence fall between them for fear that everything would begin to unravel if they had even a moment to think about what they were doing, strangers thrust together in an emergency, as if their ship had gone down and they were clinging to the wreckage. Margot spent a long time in the bathroom the next morning and when she came out she was wearing makeup, her eyebrows two perfect plucked arches outlined with pencil, her lips a vampish red, her hair blondly gleaming. She sat in the kitchen, looking embarrassed, and she would accept nothing but coffee. They both watched for the boat all through the day but the boat never came. Elise tried to be cheerful, offering to show her guest down to the beach or up to Harris Point for the views, but Margot said she wasn't feeling very well—she hadn't slept, it was the strange bed, it was always like that with her and she just couldn't explain it. "Even on the boat—" she began, and then caught herself.

As the day wore on Elise began to feel a constraint between them, an overpoliteness that became awkward, as if they really didn't know what to say to each other. It was clear that Margot was bored and anxious and was beginning to regret her rashness or altruism or whatever it was that had made her offer to stay on. Which only made Elise feel guilty and inadequate—and foolish too. What were a couple of horses and a flock of sheep that they couldn't be left behind for a day or two? And the house—what must she have made of the house, with its crude furnishings, the guns on the wall, a stove from the last century? And the larger question her guest was too delicate to ask: How could she live like this? How could anyone?

The second night, when darkness sheeted down in increments over the water and it became apparent to them both that the *Bon Temps* wouldn't be returning, Margot looked grim and accusatory. There was no gaiety, no pretense. Elise tried to make conversation: "You know, it really is wonderful to live out here, away from everything. You'd be surprised." Margot just gave a her look. "Though it takes some getting used to, of course. I don't know if I told you, but I grew up in New York, in Rye, with a house full of servants. I never washed a dish in my life." She gave a laugh. "Barely knew how to cook." There was no response to this. Margot fished a silver lighter from her purse, lit a cigarette and blew out a cloud of smoke with a long withering sigh.

At dinner, she consented to take a plate of lamb and potatoes with canned wax beans and a cup of tea, but she excused herself immediately after—and didn't offer to help clean up as she had the night before. Or to mind Marianne while Elise was washing the dishes. She hardly even glanced at her. Just went to her room and closed the door.

It was infuriating. But why should she care? Why should she stand there at the counter and try to make small talk with this woman, explain herself— or worse, apologize? Or be made to feel inferior in her own house while all that mattered was that Herbie was somewhere out there across the waves, at the doctor's, in the hospital, suffering, needing her, and she was stuck here with a stranger whose smile kept tightening and tightening till it was like a screw worked into a plank of smooth knotless wood.

The morning crashed down on them in a sudden burst of rain that hammered at the roof and pocked the courtyard with puddles. She had to force herself from bed: there would be no boat today, no Herbie, no word even. She kept telling herself everything would be fine, it was just a scare, that was all, but she pictured him strapped down on an operating table, his eyes sunk back in his head, the surgeon there with his tools like instruments of torture, and it all became confused with images of the sheep they slaughtered for the table, the heavy bluish sacks of their intestines, the blood that pooled in the bucket till it was like oil, dark and viscous and without sheen. When Marianne, pulling herself up by the slats of her crib, said, "Daddy, Daddy," she almost broke down. And when Margot, hunched by the fire with a cup of coffee and a cigarette, said, "I don't care what the weather is, Dick'll be here, I know it, he wouldn't desert me," she couldn't think of a word in response.

Just after noon, while she sat in her chair reading to Marianne from a book of nursery rhymes, the *Bon Temps,* rocked by a heavy swell, pulled into the harbor. The rain had slackened but the wind had picked up so that it was hard to see anything out there even with the binoculars. It was Margot who spotted it. She'd been out on the porch for the better part of the morning, wrapped in an old coat of Herbie's Elise had loaned her, her hair bound up in a kerchief and the binoculars pressed to her eyes, unfazed by the cold and the rain drooling from the eaves, willing the boat to appear. "They're here," she said, pushing through the door, her voice flat and annunciatory, as if to betray excitement would make it seem that there'd ever been a doubt in her mind.

Margot didn't bother to wait while Elise dressed the baby in her jacket and dug out the umbrella, going on ahead with the scarf cinched tight under her chin and the cloth bag containing the few things she'd managed to bring off the boat with her clenched under one arm. Elise followed her tracks in the mud all the way down the road and across the beach to where the dinghy was cutting through the curtain of rain, already halfway to shore. There was a man at the oars—narrow shoulders, blue cap: Dick—and behind him, in the stern, a figure she couldn't quite make out, though she was sure it was Herbie, Herbie come back to her with pills and emollients, stitched up maybe, but whole. It took her a moment, the oars dipping and rising, the tight slashing bow of the boat coming closer, to realize she was wrong. This wasn't Herbie. This wasn't Herbie at all.

The rain slanted down. The surf crashed. She felt all the will go out of her. She watched the boat as if it were a bullet suspended in slow motion and driving straight for the core of her, where the real pain lived. That was when she recognized the figure in the stern, the little loose-limbed man perched there like a monkey, his hair gone to gray and the slicker drawn up to magnify the fixed black stare of his eyes. It wasn't Herbie. Not Herbie. No—and what this meant she could only guess, and even her best guess chilled her—it was Jimmie.

Jimmie

"He's going to be fine," Jimmie said, flinging boxes ashore as she stood huddled beneath the umbrella with Marianne and the rain drove down till it was hard to distinguish the air from the water. "I guess he called Bob Brooks the minute he got in with Dick here and Bob come up from Los Angeles in his car and took him to his own doctor, not the VA—he don't trust the VA because they'll just put you off—and the doctor said he needs an operation soon as possible." He looked up from beneath the brim of his hat and gave her a ragged smile. "So Bob put me on the boat and I'm to stay and help out till Herbie can . . ." he trailed off, intent suddenly on digging through the inside pocket of his sheepskin jacket. "Here," he said, thrusting a letter at her. "It's all in here."

Dick Graffy was helping unload things, but Margot was already in the dinghy, her face set and shoulders hunched beneath the slicker her husband had wrapped round her. Elise clutched the letter in her hand, struggling with herself. All she wanted was to tear it open, but she had Marianne in her arms and she was trying to work a finger in against the seal and balance the umbrella on her shoulder all at the same time. And Margot was watching her. And Dick. And Jimmie. She wanted a moment's privacy, a moment to herself to absorb the news and defuse the terror that had seized her the instant she saw that it was Jimmie in the dinghy and not her husband. Finally, she turned her back on them, set Marianne down in the wet sand, in the rain, and slit open the envelope.

Dear Elise:

> *My diagnosis was correct, according to Dr. Morrison, Bob's man, and I'm to go into the hospital so they can remove the metal fragments*

that showed up on the X-ray machine. You're not to worry. I'll be home as soon as I'm able. In the meanwhile, know that I love you and Marianne and will miss you every minute until I'm back with you on the island.

Your Loving Husband,
Herbie

P.S. Be sure Jimmie sees to the horses and the sheep if I'm not back by the time the shearers come. And remember to disconnect the blades on the windmill for the water pump if we get a gale so the mechanism doesn't wind up destroyed. Let Bob pay the shearers. And send Jimmie out for wood; I don't want to get back and tear out my stitches swinging an axe.

If I'm not back by the time the shearers come. That was the phrase that leapt out at her: they weren't due for a month yet, six weeks even. How could he possibly be gone that long? What was this operation? What was it exactly? What were they going to *do* to him?

"Elise." It was Dick Graffy. He was right there, right beside her, the rain darkening his blue cap till it might have been black, and he was holding out his hand. At her feet, Marianne scrabbled in the sand, already wet through, and she took Dick's hand and released it and canted the umbrella over her daughter all in the same motion. "We've got to be going," Dick said. "We're way off schedule as it is. The bank, you know. It's my millstone." He laughed. "And Margot's anxious to get back. As you can imagine."

"I understand," she said, so distracted she could barely summon the words. "I'm sorry for all the trouble we've given you—"

"No need to be. I'm only glad God put us here to help. And don't you worry, your husband's going to be fine, better than ever." He glanced at Jimmie, who was piling up the supplies on the dune at the crest of the beach. "And we're leaving you in good hands, I know that."

She thanked him then, the emotion coming up in her so suddenly she had to turn away for a moment. "You're a saint," she said. "And please come back, both of you, when we can have you to dinner and make you comfortable."

"We'll do that," he said, turning to walk back to the boat.

She raised a hand to wave to Margot, then bent to lift the baby and see what she could bring up the hill before the rain carried everything away. She never did see if Margot waved back.

If it was strange to find herself a married woman living under the same roof with a man who wasn't her husband—or unconventional, maybe that was a better word—she tried not to let it affect her. Because it was temporary and necessary and Jimmie was a hired hand—and he was old too, almost like a grandfather. Anybody stopping by—and this wasn't exactly Times Square— wouldn't have thought a thing of it.

They got into a routine, just as she had with Herbie, she managing the household and Jimmie looking after the animals, collecting and cutting fire-wood, wandering the hills with no discernible purpose because he was a man and that's what men did. At the end of the week the *Hermes* brought the mail with another letter from Herbie—the operation had been a success and he'd be home any day now, couldn't wait, and he'd have something for her—a surprise—and a toy for Marianne too. She read the letter over three times— he was all right, he was well, his spirits high—and she read it aloud to Mari-anne and pitched her voice to tell her the news: *Your daddy will be home soon. Daddy!* She didn't care about the weather, didn't care about anything except for Herbie, but it was miserable all the same. Rain and more rain. The week dragged by and then it was gone and still no Herbie. Then there was another letter, delivered by one of the local fishermen.

This letter, the third one, caught her by surprise. There had been complications—an infection they were treating with sulfa—but nothing to worry over. If it was up to him he'd have got up and walked out the door days ago, but he had to listen to the doctors and to Bob Brooks too. Bob was insis-tent and she knew how Bob could be, didn't she? He had to admit he was weak still—and the sulfa made him feel strange, as if he were hardly there at all, as if he were made of paper and liable to tear, and it seemed to be affecting his vision too so that he couldn't even read to pass the time—but still she shouldn't worry and there was no reason in the world for her to make that long trip to see him with the baby, especially in this weather, because he'd be home before she'd even had a chance to really miss him, he promised. She'd see. Don't count old Herbie out yet.

So it went on. The week became two weeks, became three, then a month. She didn't know what to do. Every time she made up her mind to pack up and go to him and damn the consequences, another letter arrived to say she should stay put and that he'd be back on the next boat, the whole business nothing more than a hiccup in their lives. She lingered over the bed in their room, gazed at the pictures on the wall, the deck chairs from the SS *Harvard,* the fireplace they'd built together, and felt that she was the one made of paper.

She was with Jimmie one night in the kitchen—he was good with the baby, dancing her round the room while she did the dishes—and after she put Marianne to bed she sat chatting with him. He was a good talker, though his subjects were limited, and he was unfailingly cheerful, even when he neglected to fill up the woodbox or tracked mud into the house and she had to scold him. He was sitting at the table with a cup of coffee and she sat down across from him with a cup of Postum because she didn't want the caffeine, not at night. "You know," he said, "that daughter of yours is a doll, a real living doll."

"Yes," she said, "but she's Herbie's daughter, you can see that. The energy of that child. She wears me out."

He seemed to consider this, staring past her and sipping reflectively at his coffee. After a moment he said, "You know, there was another girl out here on the island. Years ago, this was. A real natural beauty. And wild. Wild as all get-out. But she wasn't a girl, really, more a young woman." His eyes sank into the memory and then he looked directly at her. "Maybe you heard of her? Captain Waters' daughter—or stepdaughter, that is?"

She shook her head.

"Inez Deane," he said, leaning across the table on the pivots of his forearms. "You never heard of Inez Deane?"

"No," she said softly.

"The actress? She was famous, all manner of famous. And I knew her when I was no more than a boy myself. Edith, her name was then. Edith Waters. You should of seen her."

Inez Deane

Edith—Inez—had escaped with Bob Ord ("Yes," Jimmie drawled, forestalling her, "the same Bob Ord, but he was younger then, a whole lot younger, but then who wasn't?"). She lived with him on his boat two days and a night off Gaviota, where he gave her the money to take the stage north. What she'd given him in return, Jimmie couldn't say, though he'd quizzed Ord on the subject for close to forty years now and Ord would just get a faraway look in his eyes and say that a lady's secrets were her own to keep, and a gentleman— and he was a gentleman whether he scraped shit off a rock and sold it to farmers and munitions makers or not—would never tell. The Captain never gave her any money, not a nickel, though her mother had left him something and the ranch too, but she had a valuable piece of jewelry hidden away in her bag or maybe sewed into her hem and when she got to San Francisco she was able to hock it for enough to get her a room and some new dresses and combs and makeup, enough to hold her while she went the rounds of her auditions at every theater there was in town.

"I seen her once on the stage—in Los Angeles, it was. The Burbank Theater. Captain Waters never knew about it, though by that time—it must have been aught-two or somewhere in there—he knew what she'd become, married and divorced and a mother already. I saved the handbill they give you all these years because it was the most remarkable thing I ever seen—I admit I haven't maybe seen much, but I've been to picture shows since and the vaudeville too, and this was the best, truly. She was playing in *The Tar and Tartar,* the starring part, and it had a whole slew of songs in it. I remember she come out to the front of the stage to sing a duet with Herbert Wilke—'Let Us Pretend'—you know that song? No? It's a beautiful air. If you heard her sing it, just once, you'd never forget it. She had an angel's voice. An *angel's.* And I knew her. Right here on this island."

The night had settled in. The house was quiet, but for the usual sounds, a creak and groan of the timbers, the fugitive gnawing of a mouse under the floorboards, wind—the eternal wind. "How long did she live out here?" she asked. "In the other house, I mean. The old house?"

Jimmie had to think about it. He extracted a cigarette from his shirt pocket, licked it and stuck it between his lips. "Well, she was here in eighty-eight, when her mother was alive still, and that's when I first met her. And then she come back with the Captain for a stretch—he wouldn't let her go ashore for fear she'd run off, which is just what happened, of course—and that must've been ninety or ninety-one. We were close then because there was just the two of us young people out here. You could say we were play-mates, I guess." He struck a match and lit the cigarette, looking satisfied with himself. "If you catch my meaning."

"She was your sweetheart then, is that it?"

He looked away, exhaled. A thin smile settled on his lips. "Yeah," he said, "she was my sweetheart. But once she left here she was on her own and within the year up there in San Francisco she married some actor she was in a play with—or I don't know if she was in a play yet. I think she started out sewing costumes and the like. But she married him and she had a baby, Dorothy, back down in Los Angeles where they moved so she could be in something at the Merced and I don't guess she was more than twenty years old at the time. He was no good, though. Didn't pay his way, is what I heard, one of that type that think a woman's supposed to be the support of a man, which never would have happened if she'd wound up marrying me, that's for sure."

She tried to picture it, the young girl, the actress, who'd once lived out here with all the space in the world, abandoned and living in a bleak walkup apartment like the one they'd had to rent after Marianne came, streetcars clattering past the window, drunks shouting in the streets at all hours. A baby to take care of. And no parents to turn to.

"What happened to the baby?"

He shook his head. "That's a sad story."

"She didn't die, did she?"

"No, no, she didn't die. Or not then, anyway. Edith—I mean, Inez—left her with a woman in Los Angeles and went back up to Frisco. 'See if you can't find someone to adopt her,' is what she told her, "cold, just like that. And that was the strangest thing—like begets like, I guess—because Edith herself was adopted, you know. Nobody knew who her parents were. Mrs. Waters adopted her before she married the Captain when she was just an infant, but then, and I'm sorry to say it, to give up her own daughter like that is what I'd call a hard case.

"Of course, and I followed this in the newspapers when it all come out, Dorothy, who I guess must of resembled her mother—pretty, that is, very pretty—got adopted not by just anybody off the street but a certified millionaire in the oil business. And then he got divorced and when he died—it was just two years after that, when the baby was only three or four years old—all the money went to her, to Dorothy. Millions. Can you believe it?"

Jimmie rose and crossed to the stove to pour himself another cup of coffee, then sat back down at the table and dumped enough sugar in it to make the spoon stand upright. He winked at her. "I like it sweet—never could get enough sweet things all my life, though it's been hell on my teeth. But you only live once, right?"

She nodded. Sipped at her Postum, which tasted like what it was, scorched grain with hot water added, a taste she didn't really like—a taste nobody could like, except maybe C. W. Post himself when he was alive. Awful stuff, really. But if she had a cup of tea—or coffee—she'd be awake all night long, worrying over Herbie.

"Edith was no dummy, though," Jimmie said, blowing the steam off his coffee and rooting around in his shirt pocket for another cigarette. "She got herself a lawyer and sued the old wife, the divorced one, for custody of her daughter—little Dorothy, who she wouldn't of even recognized if she didn't have a picture in front of her. But she was the mother, and I guess, from what the papers said, she put on the performance of her life in that courtroom, and in the end she got her daughter back, no strings attached—but plenty of money. A thousand a month. Which is more than I've seen in my entire life—and a whole lot more waiting for when Dorothy grew up and came into her inheritance.

"No, she was sharp, a real trader. When the Captain died in nineteen-seventeen, she went ahead and sued the estate for the money her mother had left for her and her part of the ranch too and she won that case against the Captain's brother and his son from his first marriage." He lit, drew in, exhaled. "Edith. She married three times, did you know that? And every one of them a divorce. I know all her names by heart, Edith Waters Walker Basford Burritt, and of course the one that made her, Inez Deane."

"Is she still living?"

He had the coffee at his lips, the cigarette clenched in the corner of his mouth. His eyes were drawn down to slits against the smoke. "Last I heard. She's up in B.C. someplace, Victoria, I think it was, sitting on a pile of money. Her daughter's dead, though. Dorothy. Never made it out of her teens."

"She didn't—there wasn't any foul play involved, was there? Anything irregular, I mean?"

"No," he said, looking up sharply. "Edith wasn't like that. Once she had her daughter back she would've raised her up like anybody else, like you with your own daughter. It was the influenza took her."

They sat there a moment in silence, contemplating the escape of one daughter and the death of another, contemplating life and the island and the narrowing path they were all on, everybody alive, then Jimmie pushed himself up with a sigh. "I guess I better be heading off to bed," he said through a yawn, "because there's always work to do—and you know when Herbie comes back he's going to lay into me if anything's amiss."

"Yes," she said, "that's a good idea. I'll put out the lamp here." And then she was on her feet and moving, and if for the past hour she'd been able to forget about Herbie and where he was and the vacuum in her life that was opening inside her till there was hardly anything left of her, it all came rushing back in the instant she switched off the lamp and the house fell into darkness.

Eighty-Six Proof

When he did finally return, a little more than a month after he'd limped down to the boat supported by Dick Graffy on one side and her on the other, Herbie was his old self from the minute he walked in the door, no change detectable in him but for the paleness of his skin and the softness of his hands. She'd been busy with something, deep now into the marooned life and its daily demands, and hadn't noticed the *Hermes* cruise into the harbor. He'd walked undetected up the road with one of the Coast Guard men, both of them carrying rucksacks crammed with supplies—and not just staples, but treats: liverwurst, Neufchâtel, soda crackers, pâté, fresh milk, eggs, a white paper sack of éclairs fresh from the bakery, as well as a doll for Marianne and a marcasite brooch for her—and she hadn't known he was there until the door swung open and he called her name. It was a transformative moment, a moment out of a novel she'd long ago read and couldn't place, she turning to the door, Marianne looking up from her coloring book at the table, Jimmie somewhere out in the yard and Herbie, with his mile-wide grin and his arms spread open, rushing across the floor to her.

They had a celebration that night, the Coast Guard man prevailed upon to stay though he was wanted back on the ship. But why not invite the whole crew up, Herbie kept insisting until it was done and they were a party of nine for a dinner that started with pâté and crackers and drinks all around from the bottle Herbie had brought back with him and ended with fresh-brewed coffee and éclairs. When Marianne had been put to sleep and the men had left and Jimmie gone down to his room, Herbie took her to the bedroom and made love to her with all the quick-breathing urgency of a man starved for it, his hands like a stranger's hands, soft and uncalloused, but his body so familiar it was like an extension of her own. They were lying there under the comforter, thinking their own thoughts, her head propped on his shoulder and a candle guttering in the dish on the night table—awake and dreaming, both of them—when he broke the silence. "You haven't even asked to see my scar," he said.

"All right," she murmured, smiling up at him, "if you think I should."

He threw back the covers then, exposing himself all the way down to his toes, a lean terrain of etiolated flesh punctuated by his two flat nipples and the graying nest of his pubic hair. "You see? See what they've done to me? Neat job, huh?"

She saw a long curving cross-stitched line running up his side like the tracks of the electric trains in the window displays at Christmas, the flesh still red and angry where the needle had gone in and the sepsis had done its work.

He let out a laugh, then took her hand and put it there so she could trace the line of it with her forefinger. "This Morrison could have been a seamstress, don't you think?"

Shadows flickered and gathered in the eaves. She felt very calm, very happy. "Yes," she said, running her finger over the eruptive scar, "he did a beautiful job. But are you sure you're all right now?"

"What do you think?" he said, and pulled her to him.

What came first, the discovery of the whiskey barrel or the intuition—or no, knowledge, definitive knowledge—that she was pregnant again, she couldn't say. It was all bound up in the drift of the days in that spring of 1933, memory as indistinct as the weeks that ran up against each other without the distraction of weekends or holidays or anything beyond dawn and dusk to break the routine. She had Herbie back. They walked the hills, hand in hand, picked mussels from the rocks at low tide, sat before the fire at night and warmed each other in bed. And she had Marianne, who toddled round the house all day, chattering to herself and taking her naps whenever and wherever the mood struck her and each night climbing determinedly into her father's lap for her bedtime story when dinner was done, the dishes washed and the light failing out over the ocean.

All she remembered was that somewhere in there was the day when Herbie came charging through the door in a state of high excitement, calling out, "Bottles, give me bottles, every bottle you can spare!"

It was late morning, the house quiet but for the intermittent rap of Jimmie's hammer from across the courtyard, where the taproom—soon to be christened "The Killer Whale Bar"—was taking shape. Marianne was on the floor in the living room, playing with the alphabet blocks Herbie had made her, and she herself was busy with her latest project, repairing the punctured seat of a wicker chair she'd discovered in a pile of refuse out behind the barn. And now here he was, blowing through the room to the kitchen, calling for bottles. "Come on, girl, get yourself up," he shouted over his shoulder. "No time to spare. What about those vanilla bottles, from the extract? Where are they? Are the corks still intact?"

She found him in the storeroom, digging through things. There was twine here, spare cookware, bottles and containers she'd washed and saved, a shelf of old newspaper and magazines, her broom, mop and bucket. "What is it?" she said, caught up in the pulse of his excitement. "What did you find?"

"Where's the basket? I need a basket. And a length of tubing and my drill, but Jimmie's out there in the shed, isn't he? All right, all right, I'll just have to be sly about it, that's all, otherwise he'll know we're up to something—but come on, come on, bottles, girl, bottles."

"You still haven't answered me," she said.

He paused then, just for an instant, to give her his grin, smug and piratical. "The find of the century, is about all. But don't breathe a word to Jimmie. Quick now, wrap up the baby, grab your jacket and meet me outside the front gate—if Jimmie sees us he'll just think we're going off for a picnic lunch."

What he'd found, on the windward beach between Simonton Cove and Harris Point, was nothing less than buried treasure. A ship carrying a cargo of flour, sugar and Kentucky bourbon whiskey, amongst other things, had gone down on the rocks there at the turn of the century, and for weeks after sacks of flour kept washing up on the beach—flour that the Russells, who were caretakers at the time, managed to retrieve and make use of for years to come, though it must have been uncommonly salty—but the whiskey casks had all been lost, as far as anyone knew. Jimmie had told the story twenty times around the table, tantalizing Herbie with the notion that some of the casks must surely have washed ashore and been buried in the restless sands— and it was true that all sorts of things would appear after a storm or a particularly low tide, including the mast of an old sailing ship Herbie had dug out the week before and erected in the courtyard as a flagpole. He'd been off on one of his beachcombing expeditions that morning and detected just the smallest irregularity in the plane of the beach ahead of him and begun digging with increasing excitement until he'd uncovered enough to see that it was a barrel—more than a barrel, a cask of the sort used for wines and liquors, and too big to dig out. He scraped and poked and smoothed away the sand until he could read the legend branded into the hooped belly of the thing: *Kentucky Bourbon, 86 Proof.*

"Of course, I rapped it with my knuckles," he was saying as they headed off across the plateau, the bottles, tubing and drill secreted in the basket that swung from his arm, "and I have my hopes up, but for all I know that's seawater in there now."

She was out of breath, struggling with the weight of Marianne in her arms and the frenzied pace he was keeping, as if the waves were going to mount up and drag the cask back out to sea after thirty years and more of waiting. "You never know," she said, between breaths, "maybe we'll get lucky."

It was a hard climb down and Herbie kept darting ahead and coming back to help her until finally they got to the beach and she let Marianne down to walk at a child's pace—at which point Herbie lost all patience and shot on ahead of them, jogging into the distance until he was just a hazy linear stroke against the flat pan of the beach and the rolling horizontality of the sea. The mist closed in. The air smelled of dead things. She tried to keep him in sight, tugging at Marianne's hand whenever the child bent for a starfish or seashell, but he kept shifting in and out of focus, Herbie the impetuous, Herbie the mirage.

When eventually she did catch up to him through the simple stratagem of keeping the ocean to her right and the dunes on her left, she found him on his knees in the wet sand, cranking the hand-drill round and round over a scrap of wood fixed there before him. She watched the shavings coil away until a dark hole no bigger than her little finger appeared in the glistening rim of what she realized was the cask—and how he'd ever spotted it she'd never know. It wasn't two inches above the sand, all set to disappear again with the next tide. Wet wood. A faint gleam. It looked no different from the other wrack scattered up and down the beach.

His hands were trembling as he threaded the rubber tubing through the hole and into the depths of the cask. Before he put his lips to it he gave her a look and said, "Well, here goes. We're going to have something very special here—thirty years aged, VSOP, can you imagine it?—or just more of this." He waved a hand at the waves clawing their way up the beach and all that water floating off to the horizon behind it. Then he closed his eyes, put the end of the tube to his mouth and sucked in his cheeks.

She watched him swallow, suck again, swallow, and still he didn't take the tube from his mouth or open his eyes. "Well?" she said. "If it's salt water you must have had enough by now."

And then his eyes flashed open and he gave her the most beatific look. "You try it, girl, and you just tell me what you think."

It might have been that night or the next or maybe a week later that she told him she was pregnant again. It was somewhere in that period, that was all she remembered, and if the memory came intermingled with the faint floral savor of the smoothest, ripest, most ethereal liquor she'd ever known, that was no bad thing either. It was all a gift—manna, manna from heaven. "No doubts this time," she said. "No need for the medical encyclopedia or the doctor either."

He didn't say anything for the longest moment, just focused his eyes on hers as if he could touch her all the way across the room. "We're getting to be old hands at this, aren't we?" he said finally, laughing aloud. "But I'm the luckiest man in the world. And the happiest." Then he got up and came to her where she was sitting on the couch, easing in beside her and wrapping her in his arms. "Herbie Junior," he said, raising his eyes to the ceiling, "where've you been all my life?

"But wait, wait," he said suddenly, jumping to his feet and darting across the room to the bookcase, where he'd hidden one of the scored brown vanilla extract bottles of straight Kentucky bourbon behind a book there. She watched him slide out the volume—*An American Tragedy*—and feel around for the bottle.

"Why Dreiser?" she asked, relishing the moment.

He turned to her, smiling, the bottle in hand. "Because the man knows sorrow and whiskey's the cure for it," he said, ready with an answer as always. "Old Theodore, old Ted, he'd drink bourbon at a time like this, don't you think?" He uncorked the bottle and sniffed. "Even if it smells just the faintest wee little bit like vanilla. But at least this time around"—and here he held the bottle aloft like the trophy it was—"we've got something to toast the baby with."

A pair of glasses. Two fingers for her, three for him. He leaned over the couch to hand her hers and then they clinked glasses. "To Herbie Junior!" he sang out, and drained his glass in a gulp.

She sipped at her portion, savoring it, even as he refilled his own glass, and if she was thinking anything at all it was just this: There's plenty more where that came from.

The Travel Air Biplane

Elizabeth Edith Lester was born in December, a compact pretty baby with her father's eyes and her grandmother Sherman's retroussé nose. This time Elise had convinced Herbie to let her stay on the island till she was well into her eighth month and when she did go ashore it wasn't to the Whites' and only briefly to the Brooks'. She'd been unfailingly gracious to the fishermen and pleasure boaters who stopped by the island—it was reflexive, really, part of her nature, the sort of innate generosity of spirit she displayed for anyone, even the Japanese—and now she found her graciousness rewarded in invitations, half a dozen or more of them. There was no need to rent an apartment or to worry over inflicting herself on distant cousins who had their own lives to lead. This time she went where she was wanted, taking Marianne with her and rotating amongst couples she knew, spending a week or two at a time with each of them—social visits that enlivened her and got her back into the swing of things ashore, the radio programs, the daily newspapers, gossip and idle chat and earnest discussions about Fascism in Italy and the threat of war in Spain, and though she missed Herbie and Christmas on the island and was more than ready to come back home once the baby had put on the requisite ten pounds, the hiatus this time hadn't seemed nearly as stifling as the first time around.

Herbie took to the baby—they called her Betsy for short—just as he had to Marianne. If he was disappointed in being denied a son yet again, he didn't let it show. By the time Betsy was able to take hold of the finger he offered and smile up at him, he was as smitten as he'd been with Marianne, a good father, sound and giving and patient. The days settled in. The sky arched high, crept low, the rain came and went, the wind blew from the north. She mixed infant formula on the stove, hung diapers out to dry. She cooked and cleaned and looked after her daughters and her husband. This was life, this was release and joy—not tedium, not tedium at all. Yes. Absolutely. And now they were four, a twofold increase in the population of San Miguel since the census taker had recorded his data in 1930.

One summer morning she was out in the yard with the girls, tending masochistically to her flower garden that was doomed by poor soil, incessant wind and the birds that seemed to have nothing else green to attack for miles around, when she was startled by a ratcheting mechanical whine that seemed to be coming from every direction at once. She looked up, bewildered, and there it was: an airplane circling the house, one man forward, another aft, and both of them wearing leathern helmets and goggles that glinted in the light of a pale milky sun that was just then poking through the mist. As if this wasn't startling enough, the thing dipped its wings and shot down like a needle toward the sheepcote in back of the house, leveling off just above the ground before circling once more and coming in for a landing. She watched it jolt across the field, the propeller a blur, wheels bouncing over the ruts, the fuselage jerking back and forth as if it were being tugged in two directions at once, and then it lurched to a halt and the two men were climbing down to earth like visitors from another planet.

Herbie was nowhere to be seen—as it turned out, he'd been down on the beach collecting driftwood and was already running at full bore up the road to the house, as startled and amazed as she—and Jimmie was off the island altogether, working for Bob Brooks at his ranch in Carpinteria. She put down the trowel she'd been using to loosen the soil around the withered stems of her geraniums, wiped her hands on her dress, snatched up the baby and took Marianne by the hand, then started across the yard and out the gate to see this marvel up close.

The taller of the men—a good six feet and two hundred pounds, forty years old or thereabout—was smoothing back his hair with one hand and hoisting a satchel to his shoulder with the other. He was dressed in shirt and tie and there were reddened indentations round the orbits of his eyes where the goggles had pinched the flesh there. The other man was Herbie's size and looked to be in his thirties. He was wearing a leather flight jacket and doing his best to look blasé, as if he'd been landing here every day of his life.

"Elise?" the first man said, coming forward and holding out a hand to her. She shifted the baby and took his hand, giving him a wondering look: how did he know her name?

"Yes," she stammered. "I'm Elise, I'm she—"

"I'm George Hammond, from Montecito," he said, pointing vaguely behind her and across the channel. "At Bonnymede? My mother's a friend of Mrs. Felton."

Now she was at an utter loss. Ten minutes ago she'd been secure in the knowledge that she was one of only four people on one of the most isolated and forbidding islands in America, part of a tribe, a family, society reduced to its essence, and now she was standing before an absolute stranger—two strangers—in an old rag of a sweater, with dirt on her hands and two oily patches of the same on the front of her dress where her knees had pressed into the earth while she dug in her garden with a hand tool and the children played beside her and her own private clouds drifted overhead. And the stranger was speaking with her as if they'd casually bumped into each other at a charity ball or cocktail party. She couldn't help herself. "Who?" she said.

"She's a friend of my mother."

Still nothing.

"Who happens to be a cousin of *your* mother—Una, Una Felton?—and who, at the suggestion of your mother, felt that John and I (this is John Jeffries, by the way) might want to stop by and say hello. And to see, well, if everything's going forward and if you might need anything, that is, if there's anything that John and I might be able to help you with."

And now suddenly it came clear. Cousin Una. Her mother. These men with the flattened hair and circular marks impressed round their eyes—they were two missives in the flesh sent here from Rye, New York, that was what they were. Her mother had always been suspicious of Herbie—*that Lothario*, she called him, *that adventurer*—seeing their marriage as the classic case of the spinster swept off her feet by a suave ne'er-do-well whose motives would always be suspect, no matter if they were married for fifty years. Her letters had been increasingly strident of late, calling into question her daughter's judgment, not to mention sanity, in trying to raise babies, her own grandchildren, in a place out beyond the end of nowhere, a dangerous place, isolated and bereft, where anything could happen. And that anything, of course, never incorporated notions of happiness, fulfillment or serenity but exclusively the calamities that befell people living on islands—and she sent on a stream of newspaper clippings in evidence, accounts of people starving in the Hebrides or drowning off Block Island or Martha's Vineyard or dying of strokes, seizures and in one case an apricot pit lodged in the windpipe, before help could arrive. Her mother was looking out for her. And here were George Hammond and John Jeffries, dropped down from the sky. What could she do but thank them and invite them into the house?

They were seated on the sofa in the living room, the door open wide to the sun and the hearth gone cold because it was high summer now and the weather had warmed into the sixties despite the persistent blow, when Herbie came bursting through the doorway, and it wasn't at all like the day the Japanese had come. The two men had been minding the children a moment while she went out to the kitchen for refreshments, Marianne playing with a scatter of homemade toys at their feet and the baby laid out on a blanket between them. She'd just set down a platter of sourdough biscuits and a saucer displaying the last of their butter, with a glass of water for Hammond and a cup of hot tea for his companion, and was bending to take up the baby again, already overflowing with gratitude for these amateur aviators who'd braved the wind and fog to bring her secondhand greetings from her mother and a satchel of letters to back them up (not to mention six dozen eggs, a twelve-pound ham and a live turkey hen in a wicker cage), and here was Herbie, a volcano of excitement rattling over the floorboards in his hobnail boots, eager to pump the hands of their visitors and know everything there was to know about them and their insuperable biplane.

Introductions went round. Herbie slipped Dreiser aside and produced the vanilla-scented whiskey, and while Hammond begged off—"Can't fly cock-eyed, you know"—his partner accepted it gladly. There was a moment of silence, all of them watching Jeffries' face as he first sipped gingerly, then threw back the glass.

"That's thirty years—and more—in the cask," Herbie said, pouring for himself now. "You ever tasted anything smoother?"

Jeffries made a show of smacking his lips. "Goes down like water."

"You don't mind the scent, the vanilla, I mean?"

"Vanilla? No, not at all. I don't smell a thing. But then"—and he held out the glass, grinning—"maybe I'd better take another sample, just to be sure."

And so they drank a second round and Herbie recounted the tale of the ship going down and the miracle of the cask revealed in the sand. "I had Bob Brooks—he's the man I work for here, do you know of him, millionaire from Beverly Hills?—bring me a bunch of five-gallon tins when he came out with the shearers. It took the two of us the better part of three nights to siphon off the whole business and haul it up to the house, and believe me I was careful to keep the thing covered up with kelp and a couple shovelfuls of sand—and to erase our tracks too. All I could think was that somebody else'd get to it before we could drain it. Not only the shearers—they'll drink anything—but the hired man here, because if you don't dole out the booze with him he'll drink till he drops down blind. But you know how hired hands are, I'm sure."

This last was addressed to Hammond, who just gave him a smile and nodded his head. The fact was, as they were later to discover, George Hammond didn't know the first thing about hands, hired or otherwise. Servants, yes. A Japanese gardener. A chauffeur. But he was no rancher—he was independently wealthy, living with his wife and mother at his mother's estate on the ocean just east of Santa Barbara, where he'd constructed his own airstrip. He had one passion only, and that was for aviation.

"So tell me about your aircraft," Herbie said. "It's a real beaut."

"Well, thank you. I like it, I do, but I'm looking for something with a bit more oomph, if you know what I mean. Took us what, John—just over forty minutes to get here? We can do better than that."

"It's a Travel Air, isn't it?" Herbie had pulled up a stool and was sitting kitty-corner to the couch. She sat across from him in the chair, supporting the baby on one shoulder, and if she could foresee the fog coming down and their guests having to spend the night—or even two nights, three—so much the better. Marianne was crabwalking round the floor, clacking her blocks together, as excited by the company as her parents were, and she kept clacking them till Herbie leaned down and told her to hush.

"That's right," Hammond was saying, "two hundred twenty horsepower, and that's fine, don't get me wrong, but I've got my eye on something bigger—a Cabin Waco or maybe even one of the new Beechcrafts. Do you know the Beechcraft?"

Herbie didn't. But he was all ears and she could see what he was thinking: *Forty minutes to shore and that was too slow?* With an airplane, their whole world could open up, no more waiting for the cattle boat or the Coast Guard or a passing fisherman or Bob Brooks to send supplies once a month if they were lucky. They could have some of the things the outside world had to offer, things they'd done without, things to make life easier. A phonograph. A radio. A generator for electricity. *Travel Air Biplane. Cabin Waco. Beechcraft.*

She repeated the exotic names silently to herself, almost as if they were an incantation, though she couldn't have known what she was wishing for.

The fog did come down that afternoon, the sun gone before they knew it, the hills swallowed up and the harbor erased so completely you wouldn't have known they were on an island at all—they could have been anyplace, a field in Nebraska, a mountaintop in Tibet, Fifth Avenue with all the plugs pulled and the traffic swept off to the moon. Everything was soft and gray, the fog so dense you couldn't see the plane from the front door. And with the fog came the quiet, ambient sounds muffled and nothing moving beyond the windows, all the world reduced to the room they were sitting in. Hammond—George—opened up once he saw that they wouldn't be leaving till morning, if then. He sampled Herbie's whiskey, regaled them with stories of what was going on in Santa Barbara society and in Los Angeles and beyond and John Jeffries had his own stories to tell while Herbie leaned forward to interject and magnify and urge them on, flying from one subject to another, never happier. She served lamb stew at the table in the kitchen. Marianne fell asleep in her arms. And afterward, because the chill had come back now and no denying it, Herbie built a fire and they sat around talking, the four of them, till the gray deepened by degrees and finally gave way to a starless night.

Christmas

Christmas that year was a wonder. For the first time ever they had a tree—the girls' first Christmas tree, festooned with strings of popcorn and figurines of colored paper, with a tinfoil angel perched on top—and there were store-bought toys and catalogue things too. The tree might have been scraggly and lopsided and no more than three feet high, not at all the kind of thing she remembered from her girlhood, when the whole family would go out into the stripped and silent woods with the horses and drag back a perfectly propor-tioned spruce eight or ten feet tall, but it was a tree, the only tree on an island that had none. She wouldn't have thought it would make such a difference, the sight of it there on a piece of white felt draped over a stool in the living room—and the smell of it, of pine sap and the stiff fragrant needles—but it did. Just that. Just the tree. It brought back a cascade of memories—and cre-ated them too, the future memories. For her and Herbie and the girls.

They had George Hammond to thank for it. He'd become a fast friend, flying out weekly, sometimes twice a week. He brought them eggs, milk, fresh greens. Delicacies from his mother's garden parties, squab, cold cuts, bakery bread, the cheeses she couldn't get enough of. Once news got around of what they were doing on the island—pioneering, that is, living like the first settlers in a way that must have seemed romantic to people inured to the grid of city streets and trapped in the cycle of getting and wanting and getting all over again—people began to deliver things to Bonnymede expressly so that George could take them out to San Miguel in his new Cabin Waco and lighten the burden for the Lesters. It was amazing in its way—they were gaining notori-ety just for drawing breath in a place that fired the imagination, already undergoing the transmutation into myth the press would later work on them, she the devoted and intrepid wife whipping up gourmet fare on a woodstove, Herbie the wounded war veteran withdrawn from society and seeking peace in nature, the girls growing into their depthless blond beauty in primordial innocence while the rest of the world churned with its hates and factions and the hard knocks of experience.

As Christmas grew nearer, Herbie took to calling Hammond Santa George, the bringer of gifts and good tidings. He'd split the boon of his whiskey with Bob Brooks, fifty-fifty, because Bob *was* the lessee, after all, and he wanted to be fair, but there were gallons of it hidden away in the storeroom—enough to last years, and no more parceling out pennies to have Brooks add a bottle or two of the cheapest rotgut to the grocery list. Oh, no. Herbie was possessor of the finest stock in all the islands and up and down the coast too. So when George flew in two days before Christmas with the tree and an armload of presents—and a Christmas goose to replace the turkey that had fallen victim to the foxes before it had its chance to appear on a platter—Herbie concocted a holiday punch so potent it ensured that George would have to spend the night if he downed so much as a cupful. And he did, of course. And she did too. They sang carols before a snapping fire, took turns reading "'Twas the Night Before Christmas" and Dickens' Christmas stories aloud to the girls, and then went out to hand-feed the goose in its cage in the yard while Herbie clucked over its fate.

"Well, it's fat enough, George," he said. "Fat and prime." He was holding the flashlight, the goose giving back the reflected light in the pans of its eyes as it cocked its head to pick up the sound of their voices. Overhead, the stars leapt out in a mad white display. She felt the punch massaging her veins. It was cold. She thought of the sheep out there in the darkness beyond, huddled, with their legs folded under them. Christmas. It was Christmas on the island.

"You don't think I'd bring you a scrawny one, do you?"

"No, not Santa George. You're the—the best friend I ever had." Herbie's voice had run off the tracks, thick with its freight of whiskey and something else too, something maudlin and overworked. "Except maybe Bob Brooks." A pause, the night pouring down, the goose snatching at the light, trying to get a fix on them. "And Elise. Elise, of course. Finest woman alive. Aces. Aces all the way. Don't you agree, George? Isn't she aces?"

"Yes, sure she is."

"And you—I mean it—you are the most generous, the most—"

"Herbie," she said as gently as she could, "don't you think we'd better go inside?" And she tried to make a joke of it: "For the goose's sake? She's got a big day ahead of her come Tuesday. She'll need her sleep, won't she?"

"Her beauty rest."

"Her beauty rest, yes." She laughed. And George, good sport, joined in.

"But that's not a goose at all," Herbie put in, his voice thick, congealed into a kind of sobbing bray. He'd had too much to drink, maybe they all had, because it was Christmas, almost Christmas, and they were celebrating. "No goose," he said, louder now, an edge of sudden anger slicing through him.

"What do you mean?" George said. They were all three following the beam of the flashlight to the animal's cocked head and the firm golden lockbox of its beak.

"It's a gander," Herbie burst out. "Can't you see that? Look at the size of him. Look at that neck. A gander's no goose. A gander's a—a, a *gander!*"

George couldn't stay for the holiday—he was due back at Bonnymede to celebrate the occasion with his family, which was only understandable. In the morning, though the winds were volatile and threatened to flip the Cabin Waco before it could get off the ground, George hopscotched down the runway, found the air under his wings and was gone. She and Herbie stood there, arm in arm, and watched the plane recede into the sky. They had their tree and their presents—he would surprise her with a phonograph and three records, including a recording of Beethoven's piano pieces as interpreted by a thirty-one-year-old Chilean genius, across the cover of which he'd written *Für Elise* in his neat rounded hand—and the greater gift of their daughters, who would awaken on Christmas morning to see what Santa had brought them. And they had the goose too—the gander—which snaked out his neck and hissed and honked round the courtyard, master of all he surveyed and destined to lead a long and prosperous life as Herbie's special pet, while she poked the coals in the oven and laid on wood to stoke the temperature to three hundred seventy-five degrees, just right for leg of lamb.

Swiss Family Lester

The years scrolled by, 1935, '36, '37, '38, the outside world canting toward the conflagration to come, tension ashore, tension at sea, Tojo's troops in Shanghai and Hitler eyeing the Sudetenland. In the Lester household, there was tranquility. The phonograph brought the strains of civilization to a place where no music had been heard in all eternity but for the erratic strumming of a sheepman's guitar or the rasp of an Indian's rattle over a crude campfire, and she and Herbie and the girls listened over and over to the Beethoven till it was so worn it began to sound as if it had been recorded in the midst of a bombing raid. The next year she added Borodin's Second String Quartet and Mozart's *Requiem* to her thin shelf of recordings, though Herbie claimed he could barely stand to listen to them, the music made him so sad. Still, it was pleasant to sit there during the evenings and hear something other than the wind while they played cards or read aloud before the fire—and besides, wasn't sadness, the ability to feel and feel deeply, what made us human? And joy, joy of course. She had the "Jubilate" for that.

The radio came next. Or rather, the generator to produce the electricity to make the radio something more than just another piece of furniture. Her mother, still worried over them, always worried, had sent the radio, a big glistening Zenith Tombstone model George managed to fly over in his plane, but it was mute until the generator began to turn and the first tentative squeaks and squelches of the forgotten world cohered in the mellifluous tones of an announcer's voice, which came clear so suddenly you would have thought he was there in the room. Marianne nearly jumped out of her skin, staring wide-eyed at the fabric-covered mouth of the speaker, not quite believing there wasn't someone hidden inside, while Herbie maneuvered the aerial and fine-tuned the dial like an impresario. She made popcorn and they all sat round this new marvel, transfixed, while dinner went cold and the sun faded from the sky, unseen and unappreciated.

All in all, it was a mixed blessing. On the one hand, they were glad for the broadcast concerts and the programs they gathered round to listen to each night—*Amos 'n' Andy, Flash Gordon, Major Bowes' Original Amateur Hour*— but on the other hand, the news of the world came at them relentlessly, infecting them like some new kind of plague. Like it or not, they were part of the world now, drawn in almost against their will. Herbie began to fret over things happening halfway around the globe, the news bad, exclusively bad, bad all the time. She tried to tune out the announcer's voice, her fingers busy with her knitting, her mind wandering, but her ears wouldn't let her. And then there was the racketing blat-blat-blat of the generator that annihilated the silence of the yard so that she could barely tolerate going outside when the electricity was in use. Which, fortunately, wasn't very often—the generator devoured coal oil, and coal oil not only cost money they didn't have, but it came in fifty-gallon drums that had to be hauled up from the beach behind the steaming haunches of Buck and Nellie.

Then the first reporter—Richard Blakely, of the *Santa Barbara News-Press*— introduced himself by way of a letter contained in the canvas mail pouch George Hammond had got in the habit of bringing out to them each week. He was a friend of the Hammonds and had heard of the "wonderful things" they were doing out there on the island, things the subscribers to the paper "would certainly be interested in," and he wondered if he might not come to visit them for a few days with the notion of interviewing them for a feature article in the Sunday edition, which, as they no doubt knew, was the most widely read issue of the week. Herbie slit open the embossed envelope with his penknife, careful to preserve it intact, then unfolded the letter and read it aloud while she and George, seated comfortably at the kitchen table, looked on. She could tell from the welling of his voice and the way he tried to give life to the reporter's stale phrases that he was excited by the prospect. "Great news!" he concluded, handing her the letter. "Just what I've been hoping for—a little publicity. What sort of man is he, George?"

"Oh, he's on the up-and-up. Very amenable."

"Nice guy?"

"Yeah, nice guy."

"So what do you think, Elise? Ready to roll out your Sunday best and cook up an island feast for the fourth estate? I'll butcher a lamb. And set out the lobster traps. And George can bring us some more eggs—right, George?—so you can make one of your extra special deluxe chocolate layer cakes for him, show him what island living's all about—"

She was silent a moment, Herbie leaning forward to retrieve the letter and fold it reverently back into the envelope. George sat across from her, hovering over his coffee cup and wearing a benign smile. She felt the first stirrings of something she couldn't name, a kind of superstitious tension, as if she were a girl all over again and going out of her way to step on every crack in the sidewalk to see what the fates had in store for her. "I don't know," she said finally. "But truthfully? If you want to know, I don't think it's such a good idea."

"Not a good idea?" His face took on a look of incredulity. "What do you mean? We're going to be in the papers—we'll be famous."

She shrugged. "That's what I mean." A look for George. "We've got all the society we want right now, what with the friends we've made from the yacht club and people coming out almost every week it seems, in good weather, at least. Do we really want more of them? Strangers trooping up here at all hours, bursting in on us as if we were put here solely for their amusement, and then, of course, we've got to be courteous to them no matter what. Or those boys in the powerboat taking target practice on the seals, when was it, a month ago? You really want more of that sort of thing?"

He looked hurt, astonished. "No," he said, insisting now, "no, you're crazy. Publicity's good, the best thing that can happen to us. It means money, Elise"— and here he turned to George to make the characteristic gesture, thumb and first two fingers rubbed together over an open palm—"and money's been in short supply lately. I made twenty-five dollars for that lecture I gave to the Adventurers' Club, don't forget. And I've got feelers out to the museum and the colleges down in Los Angeles too. People are fascinated by what we're doing out here, Elise, they are. They just wish they could live like us, live free, I mean. Isn't that right, George?"

Richard Blakely appeared a week later, swinging open the door of the Cabin Waco and hurrying across the blistered stubble of the lower pasture, George, laden with the mailbag and half a dozen packages, bringing up the rear. The reporter was young, younger than she would have thought—not much more than thirty—and he wore a double-breasted suit with exaggerated shoulders and he used so much pomade on his hair it shone like neon from all the way across the field. He hadn't even got to the house before the questions started in: *How did they like the isolation? Weren't they ever bored? What about the movies—didn't they want to go to the movies? Or shopping. What about shopping? He heard they had a radio now—how was that?* Amos 'n' Andy? *Oh, yeah? That was his favorite too. But what was that noise? Seals? Was that the seals?*

He was thin and slump-shouldered, he wore a little dandy's mustache and had the habit of winking his right eye—or was it a tic?—when he asked questions, and for the next three days he never stopped asking them. She barely knew what to say—and he was underfoot the whole time, except when Herbie took him out to show him over the island, an expedition he didn't seem particularly enthusiastic about, before or after—but Herbie matched him syllable for syllable, and the two of them chattered on from breakfast until late into the night when she excused herself and went off to bed with Richard Blakely's voice ringing in her ears: *Really? Only twelve hundred in the flock? Is that because the place was overgrazed in the past? Is that the reason for all these sand dunes? What about the sandstorms? Tell me, what are they like?*

The article, which George flew out to them the Sunday it appeared, was titled "The Happy Family That Rules a Kingdom." In it, she was described as "the Queen of the realm, dressed in a gingham skirt and a white pullover she'd spun from the wool of the very sheep her husband kept watch over in the lorn and lonely meadows of the misty isle far from shore." Herbie read it aloud, crowing over one phrase or another, as proud as if he'd written it himself, and he read it to the girls too, though the little one could barely make sense of it and Marianne only perked up when he got to the phrase ". . . and their pretty young daughters, the princesses of the sceptered isle, are as fair and sweetly innocent as the diminutive heroines of their own fairy tale."

George had thought to invest in three copies, two of which Herbie laid carefully in the trunk of keepsakes in the bedroom before taking his scissors to the remaining copy. He cut out the entire article, including the hazy photograph of the four of them posed at the front gate with dazed eyes and fixed smiles, and thumbtacked it to the kitchen wall just below the calendar from the Remington Company that depicted a vigorous-looking man in a flannel shirt cleaning his gun while his faithful retriever looked wistfully on.

That story opened the floodgates, not only on the central coast but throughout the state and across the country too. The Associated Press picked it up and syndicated it nationwide so that her parents and her two brothers and two sisters found it laid out on the table when they came down to breakfast in their households back in New York. Her mother wrote her immediately, on the rebound, all hint of complaint replaced by a glow of reflected pride ("Perhaps you have made the best decision after all, and I was just too blind to see it") and she heard from people who hadn't written in years, distant cousins, forgotten acquaintances, her roommate from her days in the flat on East Seventy-second Street, who wrote to say she'd like to come for a visit. There were more reporters, more stories. The headlines vied with one another for attention—"Eight Years in Solitary"; "Couple Rules Lonely Island as Absolute Monarchs"; "War-Torn Veteran Turns Back on Society to Find Peace in Solitude of Isolated Kingdom"—but the stories were all more or less the same.

Still, people couldn't seem to get enough of them. The way Herbie saw it, they were only getting their due, because they were special, singled out, anointed, above and beyond the run of the common wage slaves out there, but she didn't see it that way at all. To her, the whole uproar was nothing more than a case of escapism, people beaten down by the Depression and fearful of the coming war and only wanting to rest their eyes and let their minds roam free over the idyll the papers presented, all the sweat and toil and scraping and scrimping conveniently left out of the scenario.

Letters began to pour in (care of George Hammond, Esquire, Bonnymede), letters from utter strangers who wanted to advise them, congratulate them, criticize them, move in with them, and with the letters came unasked-for gifts. Steamship lines sent them framed oil paintings of ships at sea, magazines sent free subscriptions. There were Coleman lanterns, a butter churn, a pair of axe handles, a peanut butter jar of assorted screws, hand-knit mittens, sweaters and caps, a braided throw rug, a year's supply of Wrigley's gum. Patiently—at first, anyway—she answered each of the letters, no matter how odd or unctuous they were, and sent thank-you notes in acknowledgment of the gifts, which began to accumulate in the toolshed to the point where you could hardly get in the door there anymore. And every time the flood seemed to subside, another article would appear and it would rise all over again.

Kate Smith featured a tribute to their pioneer spirit on her radio program and the actress Jeanette MacDonald heard it and sent them a cream-colored puppy named Pomo in token of her admiration and solidarity, the first of a whole menagerie of pets people shipped via boat or dropped off personally. The gander—they called him Father Goose—soon had plenty of company, including a trained and very vocal raven Ed Vail personally handed her on stepping off the *Vaquero* one afternoon and a series of cats people misguidedly gave them (or abandoned on the beach), despite Herbie's prohibition against them. But then you couldn't very well give a kitten back once the boat had pulled out of the harbor or wrench it from your children's arms either, and so there were cats on the island again and the mice just had to suffer. ("I'll shoot them all," Herbie muttered, but then she came in one night to see him sprawled on the couch with the white Persian the girls had named Mr. Fluff asleep in his lap, and he never mentioned the mice again. As a subsidiary benefit, things quieted down in the pantry in the dark of night, when Mr. Fluff made his rounds.)

Then—and this was probably the height and culmination of the whole whirling circus that had swept them up whether they liked it or not—*Life* magazine sent a reporter and two photographers out to the island to document their day-to-day life for the edification of the magazine's millions of readers. The photographs were first-rate, she had to admit that—Herbie shone and the girls were angelic, though she couldn't help feeling she looked fat and unkempt in the two that featured her and she couldn't stop thinking about how they'd be displayed for anyone to see in every drugstore and newsstand and dentist's office in the country. The thought made her stomach sink. She pictured strangers—men on streetcars, greasy hoboes in stained trousers, mechanics, sailors, drunks—sneering over the photos, maybe doctoring them with beards and devil's horns or worse. Perverts, even.

The article itself was no different from what had come before, except for some elaboration here and there, but it was the headline, "Swiss Family Lester," that caught the public's attention and brought them more mail than all the other articles combined. Herbie couldn't have been happier. For her part, she laid two pristine copies of the magazine atop the other articles in the trunk of keepsakes and hoped they were the last.

She was in the living room with Herbie one fogbound night, listening to the radio and working through the latest batch of letters addressed variously to the Lesters of San Miguel, to Herbert Lester, Esq., or King Herbert, or simply to San Miguel Island—"fan mail," as Herbie called it—when the deep booming lament of a ship's horn cut through the room and brought her back to herself. "Thick out there tonight," Herbie observed, looking up at her from the puddle of light the lamp threw over his desk.

"Thick in here too," she said, "with all these letters." She was seated in the wicker chair, a writing tablet in her lap and a fountain pen poised over the paper, answering what must have been her tenth letter of the night. "Sometimes I wish we'd never let that reporter come out here."

"Which reporter?"

"The one from the Santa Barbara paper, the first one."

He was wearing a pair of reading glasses, pushed halfway up his nose. The light of the lamp sparked in them as he turned his head to her and the room seemed to jump and settle again. "What," he said, "you don't enjoy writing to Mr. and Mrs. Anonymous every week?"

"No," she said, "frankly, I don't. And I wish we'd never started this business."

He was quiet a moment, the corner flap of the letter he was writing propped up on the arch of one hand. "It's got to pay off," he said. "I know it will."

"In what—all that junk they send us?"

"It's not all junk—the axe handles, I found a use for them. And Pomo"—at the mention of his name, the dog lifted his head from where he lay sprawled before the fire, then dropped it again—"and Fred the raven."

"I know they mean well, it's not that—it's just that they have a picture of us that isn't true, isn't real—"

"We're not hardworking? We're not in love? We don't have the two smartest, sweetest, most beautiful little girls in the world?"

She smiled. "They all make too much of it, that's what I mean. We're not special, we're just like anybody else, only luckier, I guess."

He lowered his head to look at her over the glasses and she saw how his hair was going white across the top now and saw the gouges beneath his eyes and the damage the sun had wrought on his face. Was he old? Was he getting old? And if he was, then she was getting old too, and once you were old you had to start thinking about what came next. "Lucky, yeah," he said, "but we haven't made a nickel off any of this yet. But I've got a couple of schools on the line—I'm trying to set up a lecture tour back east, Saint Andrew's, Saint Paul's, Yale, Harvard, Princeton, the very best—but I need one of the pieces to fall into place before I can even think of going, and they all plead the same thing, no money, hard times, wait till next term—"

The foghorn sounded again, so close they might have been sitting on the foredeck of the ship itself. "Like soup," Herbie said.

"I just hope they don't go aground."

"They won't."

She was going to ask him how he could be so sure, but he distracted her by snatching up a letter from the desk and waving it like a flag. "God," he said, "you've got to see this one," and in the next moment she rose and went to him and he pressed the single sheet flat on the desk beneath the halo of light. The paper was thin, the script minute, as if indited under a magnifying glass, the characters printed discretely, rigid black letters marching across the page in the way Marianne might have arranged them with her blocks.

DEER MR. AND MISSUS LESTER:

I AM AN OLD MAN SEVENTY TWO YEARS ON THIS URTH LIVING IN NORMAN OKLAHOMA AND I HAVE NOONE TO LOOK AFTER ME. I NEVER DID MARRY NOR HAVE ANY SONS NOR DOTTIRS AND I AM ON MY LONESOME ALL THESE YEARS. I AM STRONG YET AND VIGROUS AND I AM AFRAID TO DIE ALONE. WILL YOU TAKE ME IN TO LIVE WITH YOU AND YOUR BOOTIFUL FAMILY. I CAN EARN MY KEEP BETTER THAN MANY A YOUNGER MAN. PLEASE HEER ME AND SEND FAIR FOR THE BUS TO CAL.

VERY TRUELY YOURS,
MORRIS T. SWENSON

They were silent a moment, the house still, the light pooled on the desk. She could hear the dog's breathing decelerate into sleep and then the first quavering whisper of a snore. Herbie turned to her. "You're going to have to answer this one," he said.

"No," she said, "I can't."

"You have to."

"I wouldn't know what to say."

"Tell him he's going to have to die alone."

"Herbie."

"Or no, tell him we're lucky, that's all. Just lucky."

"And he's not?"

"Right. He's not."

The King of San Miguel

There was no telling how Herbie would react to the news that came to them over the radio. Sometimes, he'd flick it off in disgust, right in the middle of a program, and go stomping and swearing through the house in a rage over the idiocy of the world and the way they were being corrupted by it, even out here. Other times, and this was true of the newspapers too, he would extract a few threads of information from one account or another and weave them into a salvatory scheme he talked up day and night till it began to sound plausible, even to her. His biggest bugbear during this period was Mussolini. When they got news that the little potbellied Italian clown prince had invaded Ethiopia, he'd taken it hard. This was Africa, the continent he dreamed of every time he glanced up at the elephant gun on the wall or took it reverently down to show it off to a visitor, and here the Italians were trying to colonize this huge expanse of it, and for what? he kept asking. To rape it and bleed it and force their will on natives in loincloths? "What next," he said bitterly, "nomads eating spaghetti carbonara off the backs of their goats? Campari and soda in Addis Ababa?"

He sat riveted by the radio, agonizing over the reports of a modern army equipped with motor vehicles, tanks and machine guns cutting through Haile Selassie's overmatched forces, whose antiquated weapons belonged in a museum and whose starving horses and blundering mules were shot out from under them and left for the vultures on their black soaring wings. "Spears, they're using spears, Elise," he kept saying. "We've got to do something. We can't just sit around and let these people be slaughtered."

She commiserated, of course, but to her mind the whole business was merely an exercise, a passing phase, another of her husband's obsessions that would occupy him for a week or two and then fade away as the next arose on the horizon, and she was right, to an extent, but this time he really did try to take action. One afternoon, when they were expecting George to fly in, he called her into the living room and asked her to proofread a letter he'd spent the better part of the morning composing. It was addressed to His Highness, Emperor Haile Selassie, the Lion of Judah, care of the Ethiopian Embassy, Washington, D.C. In light of the fact that the Ethiopian army was outgunned, he was offering his entire arsenal on loan for the duration of the war—or as long as it took to achieve victory—and he further offered his own services as an instructor to drill the emperor's men in the use of small arms. No matter that the emperor's men were halfway round the world and she and Herbie could barely afford to get to Los Angeles, let alone New York, the Canary Islands, Gibraltar and points east, Herbie was dead serious and here was the proof of it. She didn't say a word. Just read through the letter, handed it back to him, and told him how good it was of him to think of it and what a noble gesture it was. George came, the letter went off, and that was the end of that, as far as she was concerned.

There was plenty enough to occupy her—occupy them—without having to worry about the fate of a medieval society she'd barely heard of, an empire nonetheless. World events swept on to other things, Herbie fired off letters to FDR, Will Rogers, Lewis B. Hershey and Father Coughlin in support or protest of whatever was on his mind at any given moment, and the life of the ranch went on. They had more visitors now, and the reporters never stopped coming—and, of course, reporters and visitors alike required feeding and a place to sleep and an expanding portion of the time she needed to devote to other things, like her daughters' education, for instance. As Marianne and Betsy grew—and reports of them spread—questions arose in certain quarters over the quality of the education they were receiving, or if they were being educated at all. There were letters from various cranks and retired schoolteachers and professors too, espousing one scheme or another, and then finally an official letter arrived from the superintendent of the Santa Barbara schools, reminding them that the law required that all children on reaching the age of five years must attend school. To this point—Marianne was seven and Betsy not quite five—she'd done her best to instruct them herself, sitting them down at the kitchen table on weekdays and teaching them to copy simple sentences out of the children's books her mother and various friends had sent on, as well as the rudiments of arithmetic, French and geography, but it was far from ideal, considering the distractions.

She showed Herbie the letter from the superintendent's office when he came in from the yard that day. She watched his face as he scanned the letter and then read through it again, slowly this time. "What do you think?" she said finally, and why did she feel light-headed all of a sudden? Why was her heart pounding? Nothing had been decided—it was only a letter, that was all. An inquiry. "I was wondering if we should send them to the mainland—I've been thinking about this for ages, dreading it, really. To boarding school, I mean. I can't imagine how we'll afford it, but the fact is we've been selfish, we have—and don't give me that look. We've been thinking of ourselves, not the girls—they need schooling like any other kids."

"What's wrong with you teaching them? And I can help. With reading, anyway. And math. And French, what about French?"

"It's not the same thing. They need a curriculum."

"I'd rather shoot myself than see those girls leave this island. It'd tear my heart out. Yours too. Admit it."

"But I can't teach them under these conditions and you know it, what with the pot going on the stove and the dog at the door and the cats . . . and every time they look up from their books, even Betsy with her coloring book, there's something going on outside. I can't keep their attention. Nobody could."

"In the old days," he said, trying to make a joke of it, "they used to have itinerant schoolmasters. Ichabod Crane. Maybe we can get him out here. Or no, I guess he's just a fictional character, isn't he? And he'd be dead by now, anyway."

"It's not funny, Herbie. There are laws, regulations. They could take the girls away from us as unfit parents. And don't we want the best for them? Don't we want them to be able to go out and take their place in the world? Someday, I mean?"

The solution—or at least the beginnings of it—came in the form of a gift from Ed Vail. He'd come up to the house one evening for dinner after helping Herbie unload supplies from the *Vaquero,* and somehow—maybe because she couldn't get it out of her mind—the conversation shifted from the weather, conditions at sea and people they knew in common to the letter from the school district and how upset it had made them. "What you need is a schoolhouse," Ed said, pausing over the lamb chops he was always happy to see when he came for dinner on their island, because, as he liked to say, *I'm up to here with beef.* He held the moment, then took up his knife and fork and began cutting. "I've got just the thing for you."

The next time the *Vaquero* came round, there was a brightly painted structure dominating the foredeck. From a distance it looked to be a second wheelhouse, though that was impossible—this was a working boat, as she well knew, and the deck was needed for sheep and cattle. When she got closer, she saw what it was—a wood-frame playhouse, white with sky blue trim and a narrow door that must have been no more than five feet high. The whole thing wasn't much bigger than the toolshed and it had to be partially dismantled to get it off the boat and up the hill, but she was thrilled with it. Ed had built it for his own children, now grown, and it was a regular little house, with windows cut in the exact center of each of the walls, and a sturdy peaked roof. Herbie set it in the middle of the courtyard, beside the flagpole, up which he ceremonially raised the Stars and Stripes once the schoolhouse was anchored in place, and then he went out to the barn and came back with Buck and the sled and the three-hundred-fifty-pound bronze ship's bell he'd dug out of the beach the year before, frame and all.

The girls, who'd been slamming in and out of their new schoolhouse as if they were on holiday (which they were, at least for the time being: she'd have to see to desks, maps, a globe and a chalkboard to make the conversion complete), stopped in their tracks when Herbie led the horse through the gate. "What's that for?" Marianne asked, pointing to the bell, and Herbie, sweating from the effort though the day was windy and overcast, made as if he didn't know what she was talking about.

"What do you mean?"

"That," she said, coming up to touch a tentative finger to the brass shell while her sister held back as if it might erupt with a life all its own.

"Oh, that?" Herbie said, as if he'd just discovered it there on the sled. "That's your school bell. And you know what a school bell is for?"

"No."

"So you never have an excuse to be late. Or your sister either."

After that, they kept regular sessions, eight to twelve and one to four, with an hour off for lunch, following the curriculum—and the texts—the school district sent out to them, and Elise made sure to test her pupils and send in the results as required at the end of each term. Though she didn't have a teacher's credential, the school district waived the requirement, considering the special circumstances of the arrangement, and the San Miguel Island school, with its enrollment of two, was officially sanctioned for business.

The biggest problem? Neither of the girls knew anything of the outside world and so they were forever interrupting their reading with questions about things anyone else would have taken for granted. ("Mother, what's a coin? Mother, what's a car? Mother, what's a pig? Is it a kind of sheep?") There were illustrations in the encyclopedia, of course, and the pictures she cut from magazines and tacked up on the walls, but there was nothing like doing and seeing—they'd never laid eyes on a tree, either one of them, or maybe Marianne had, but she would have been too young to remember—and so, the following summer, at the end of their first school year, she got Herbie to ask Bob Brooks and Jimmie to stay on for a few days after the shearers left so they could take the girls to Santa Barbara. On vacation. Summer vacation. It was high time they expanded their horizons, that was the way she saw it, and if they came across three-story buildings, street crossings and stop signs or the railway with its locomotives and the passenger cars clanking behind, automobiles, bicycles, the market and drugstore and all the rest, so much the better.

Of course, the press got wind of it, and everywhere they went they were trailed by reporters and photographers, the Swiss Family Lester treating their progeny to shoes in an actual shoe store and dinner at a restaurant where you sat down and people came up to take your order and serve you, to a tour of the bank and the courthouse, and best of all, to the drugstore for the first ice-cream cones they'd ever raised to their lips. And so what if every drip and lick was recorded for posterity? The girls were their shy and sweet selves and Herbie beamed and strutted and crowed and kept up a patter with the reporters that could have filled the next dozen editions of the newspaper. She made the girls pay for the ice cream themselves—or hand over the coins, that is, a nickel each—because that was part of the lesson too. Yes, there was a world out there beyond the island. And yes, there was ice cream in that world, and yes, my darlings, my daughters, my loves, people paid for things there with pennies, nickels, dimes and quarters.

And then there was a day, it might have been in 1939 or even 1940, she couldn't remember, a day of overarching light and gusts so strong they threatened to tatter the flag where it snapped at the pole, when a package wrapped in brown paper and trussed up firmly with half a ball of string appeared as if by magic on the front doorstep. She'd been in the schoolhouse with the girls, drilling Marianne on long division and Betsy on alternating columns of addition and subtraction, and Herbie had been out on one of his reconnaissance patrols to check on the far-flung sheep and sniff out signs of poachers, so no one had seen a thing. Nor had she or the girls heard the gate open and close, and that was because they were absorbed in their lessons. And because of the wind. Which tended to rock the schoolhouse on the pallets that kept it just off the ground while it shot under the eaves with a dull roar that more than once had fooled them into thinking George was coming in for a landing in his new Beechcraft Staggerwing airplane. At any rate— and this had happened before—she concluded that one of their yachting friends must have stopped by and delivered the package, and not finding Herbie and not wanting to disturb the lessons, had stolen away without a word. But why then hadn't they at least left a note? It was a mystery. As was the package, which Marianne stumbled over when she and her sister raced each other across the courtyard and darted in the door for lunch.

It was addressed to Herbert Steever Lester, Esquire, San Miguel Island, California, U.S.A., and the return address was stamped *Ethiopian Embassy, Washington, D.C.* She brought it in and set it on the kitchen table, and though she was eaten up with curiosity and the girls kept pestering her to open it, she left it for Herbie—he was the one who'd written the emperor, after all—and made use of the opportunity to give the girls a geography lesson after lunch. Where was Ethiopia? "Right here," she said, revolving the globe halfway round to show the dark continent and the mountainous wedge of the ancient land on its eastern horn, right across from the Arabian Peninsula. "And you know the Arabian Peninsula, right? Where the Arabs are? Remember *The Arabian Nights*?"

Herbie came in looking exhausted. He'd stumbled across the remains of a campfire on the beach at Chinese Point that was so fresh the embers were still glowing, and had searched the entire shoreline, fruitlessly, as it turned out, and he'd gone far out of his way and used up all the water in his canteen so that he had to find a seep just to wet his mouth. He must have fallen too, judging from the fresh wet scab glistening on his left knee. The minute he walked in the door, the girls jumped in his arms, but instead of dancing them round the room as he usually did, he just hugged them to him and dropped them down again, then lifted his head to give her a tired grin. "How about a little splash of whiskey before dinner?" he said. "Will you join me?"

"Yes," she said, "that sounds nice. Oh, and by the way, this came for you."

As soon as he saw the package he came to life—or no, he took off like a rocket, every cell and fiber of him alive with excitement. He turned it over in his hands, reading out the return address in a voice of wonder. "What do you think of that, girls—all the way from Africa. You know where Ethiopia is?"

They both nodded impatiently. "Open it, Daddy," Marianne pleaded, and in the next moment both girls were jumping up and down, chanting, "Open it, open it!"

She brought him a knife and he cut the string and tore the paper away from the box, which was the size and shape of the boxes shoes come in. "What do you know," he said, mugging for the girls, "Haile Selassie sent me a new pair of shoes."

Inside there was a letter from the deposed emperor—or one of his subordinates—thanking Herbie for his generous offer and his support for the regime in exile, which only awaited the day when the Fascisti were defeated and the Lion of Judah could return to his rightful throne. No mention was made of the years that had gone by since Herbie had made his offer or of the fact that it was moot now because the Italians were in Addis Ababa and looked to stay for a good long while, but in the depths of the box, wrapped in tissue paper, were two shining gold-braided epaulets, given, the letter said, to grant the addressee royal status in the emperor's court.

Dinner could wait. Whiskey could wait. There was nothing for it but that Elise had to sit right down, right that minute (well, okay, he would pour the whiskey now, in celebration) and sew the epaulets to the shoulders of his best white shirt. When it was done, he modeled the shirt in the mirror, happy as a schoolboy, and then he drained his glass, filled it again, and took the elephant gun down from its mount, slung it over one shoulder and marched the girls round the courtyard—*hep one, hep two*—until dinner was on the table and they could sit down and give thanks not only for the food before them but for the wise and beneficent Lion of Judah and his steadfast ally, the King of San Miguel.

Bluer

Little money had come in, no matter how wide their fame had spread, but when the National Weather Bureau decided to establish a reporting station on the island—to set them up with a two-way radio and instruments for measuring temperature, wind speed and barometric pressure and pay them a wage for sending in reports twice a day on a regular schedule—Herbie jumped at the chance. Ten years back, when they'd first come out to the island, he might have dreamed of buying out Bob Brooks, but the Depression had put an end to that—and to his bid to have Hugh Rockwell step in as silent partner and rescue him. That had been a blow he never fully recovered from, and it had hurt him too that none of his schemes for lecturing or capturing seals or selling the bones of sea elephants ever came to fruition, but he never stopped scraping for sources of income. Now, though, with the twenty-five dollars a week the weather bureau was giving them, for the first time at least they had something coming in that wasn't dependent on Bob Brooks or Hugh Rockwell or any other millionaire businessman, current or former. Things were beginning to look up. Or at least that was the way she saw it.

Still, they had to get up in the dark every morning, take the measurements and transmit them to a station ashore and then do it all over again at night, seven days a week, without fail, and she wasn't really at her best that early or that late either—and neither was he. The schedule began to wear on them. One anonymous winter morning, the rain and wind relentless, the house freezing, they both struggled out of bed and right away he started carping at her and she snapped back at him and before she could think they were shouting at each other.

"It's you," he accused. "It's all your fault. And why I ever let you talk me into this shitty weather job, I'll never know."

"Me talk you into it? You were the one who couldn't stop going on about how it was like picking money off a tree—"

"I don't care, I want to quit."

"And what about the money?"

"To hell with the money. I say we write Billy Rose—or no, go ashore and wire him, wire him right this minute, today—and tell him we accept his offer."

"We've been through that already." Billy Rose was one of the impresarios of the San Francisco Exhibition and he'd wanted to fly them up there to be his guests onstage for a limited engagement, the Swiss Family Lester arrayed for everyone to see while Billy Rose teased out the jokes about sheep and islands and cooking on a woodstove, then turned to Marianne to mug and wink and lean in close and ask, "You like any of the kids in your school, honey?" while the crowd howled and the dollars poured in. They'd both rejected it, as they had the offer from Movietone News to make a newsreel feature, because they both—*both*—agreed that they wouldn't want to subject the children to that kind of poking and prodding and cheap commercialism.

"I don't care. I want to wire him."

"No. Absolutely not."

"It's a chance to make money, maybe big money—"

"No."

"Who are you to tell me no? I'm the authority here, I'm the King of San Miguel, not you. You're not the one they all want to come see, you're not the one they interview—it's me. *Me.* And I'll do as I damn please, whether you like it or not."

She had a cold, she was irritable, her nose was dripping and her head ached, and Marianne, running a low-grade fever, had kept her up half the night. She wasn't herself and she should have left it there, she knew it, but she couldn't. "Stop fooling yourself," she shot back, "we're the king and queen of nothing, it's a joke," and her voice wasn't even her own—it was somebody else's, somebody strident and heartless. "Are you kidding me? We're as broke as we were when we got here—what do we own besides your guns and my books and the clothes on our backs? And we're at the mercy of Bob Brooks, who could close this operation down tomorrow if he wanted to—and you know it."

He was leaning over the bedside, lacing up his boots, his hair mussed, his shoulders slumped, his every motion jerky with anger. The stove had gone cold. The house smelled of ash, cats, something gone rotten in the walls. She was at the bureau, wondering what to wear (not that there was a lot of choice: she tended to wear the same thing every day, skirt, blouse, sweater, support hose and flat shoes), when all at once he jumped to his feet, snatched his white shirt off the arm of the chair and shook it in her face till the epaulets blazed in the light of the bedside lamp. "I'm king," he shouted, "whether you want to admit it or not. And Bob Brooks would never in his life even think of doing anything to hurt us and if he ever did that's just all the more reason to wire Billy Rose right this minute and get on that airplane."

They never quarreled. Or hardly ever. It set a bad example for the children, for one thing. She could read his moods, play to him, wait him out. And more often than not she gave in to him. But not this time. Not where the children were involved. The rain grew suddenly louder, as if they were hearing it broadcast over the radio and someone had turned up the volume. "No," she said.

"Elise," he said.

"No," she said.

"Jesus Christ," he said.

Gray skies, a month of gloom, no visitors, one day indistinguishable from the next. Three meals to put on the table. Seven hours in the classroom. Twelve midnight at the weather station and right back there again at six a.m. Floors to mop, pets to feed, dishes to wash, laundry to boil up in a pot on the woodstove that choked her lungs and made her eyes smart, her hands as rough as if they'd been carved of oak, her nails chipped and black with their half-moons of dirt no matter how faithfully she tried to keep them up. The girls were restless, the sun was a memory and Herbie was always out somewhere, shoeing the horses, mending fence, wandering far afield, as bored and weighed down as she was—blue and getting bluer. That month—it was March of 1940, Marianne nine and Betsy six and both of them growing out of their clothes—she found herself drifting around the house like an automaton, her legs in motion but her mind a thousand miles away. For the first time she almost wished she'd relented and let Herbie fly them all to San Francisco—at least it would have been a break in the routine.

One Saturday afternoon, when she felt she just had to get out of the house or go mad, she asked Herbie to look after the girls, shrugged into her jacket and went out for a walk. The girls had begged to come, but she was firm with them—"I just need a few minutes' peace, that's all, and I'll be back for dinner, don't you worry," and then she told Herbie to keep an eye on the spaghetti sauce simmering on the stove, and she was off.

The day was mild, the wind light and blowing up out of the south for a change. It was spring, the first breath of spring, and the revelation took her by surprise—she'd come out to the island a new bride in this very month ten years ago, not knowing what to expect, and here she was living an adventure she could never have dreamed of when she was a girl at school. It was as if she were the heroine of a novel, like the stalwart mother of the shipwreck story the press kept identifying them with (who also happened to be named Elizabeth, which, in light of things, had seemed to her an ominous coincidence).

But what was wrong with her? Everything was fine. The girls were growing, everyone was healthy, the ewes dropping lambs and the wool bringing in a regular if niggling profit, while Herbie was doing his best to mask his disappointments and throw himself into the work of the ranch. And here it was spring and she was out walking in this grand majestic place she had all to herself. The sky stretched flat overhead, sheep glanced up at her, startled, and trotted off on stiff legs, still chewing, the ocean smells drifted up the cliffs and the gulls shone white against the bruised gray backdrop that ran out over the water and faded away to infinity. She felt sustained. Felt whole and free. At first she walked aimlessly, letting her feet take her where they would, and then on a whim she decided to go out to Harris Point, Herbie's favorite spot, a place where they'd picnicked and gathered arrowheads and where the views wrapped round you as if you were in the crow's nest of a ship at sea.

It wasn't far, no more than three miles or so, though the terrain was rough, a checkerboard of the usual dips and gullies, loose sand, scree, dirt compacted like concrete. She traced her way along the narrow peninsula and hiked up to the point, where she cleared a spot for herself with a vigorous sweep of one shoe before spreading a blanket so she could sit in comfort and look out to sea. She didn't know how long she stayed there, letting her thoughts wander till she wasn't thinking anything at all, but eventually she pushed herself up and started back, the image of the stove and the steaming pot rising before her. The children would be hungry, Herbie impatient. And she would come in the door to their various murmurings and mutterings and the excited barking of the dog, boil the spaghetti, grate the cheese and serve the meal, as always, and be thankful for it too. As always.

She retraced her way across the broad apron of the plain, moving quickly now, the sun burning suddenly through the clouds to hover over the water in promise of better things to come and the sheep scattered in dense white clots across the hills. The breeze was light still, still warm, and even before the ranch house came into view, nestled like a long low fortress behind the running line of the perimeter fence, she could smell the smoke of the stove and the faint sweet scent of the marinara sauce mixed up with it. Before long she was there, making her way along the outside of the fence, listening to the gander stirring up a fuss in the yard and feeling better, infinitely better—she'd just needed to get out, that was all.

As she came round the corner to the front of the compound, she pulled up short: Herbie was standing there at the gate with two strangers dressed in city clothes. Which was odd enough to begin with, but what was odder still was that Herbie was blocking the gate, rather than stepping aside to invite them in. The first thing she thought of, absurdly, was Fuller Brush men—or Jehovah's Witnesses. And then it came clear to her—reporters, more reporters. As she got closer though she could see that Herbie was agitated, his shoulders squared and his face gone dark, and why would that be? He loved reporters, welcomed them all, the more the better.

"No, no you won't," he was saying, his voice caught high in his throat. "You don't have the right."

The men—they were nearly indistinguishable, but for the fact that the one nearest her was chewing gum, working his jaws furiously as Herbie gestured in his face. "It's nothing to get agitated over," the man said.

"Agitated? You think I'm agitated? If I was agitated I'd go in there and take one of those guns down off the wall. No," he said. "No, it won't happen. Bob Brooks, you talk to Bob Brooks—"

That was when they became aware of her. They all swung their heads to take her in as she passed along the outside of the fence and came up to where they were congregated at the gate. "Hello," she said, looking first to the strangers, then Herbie.

Both the men fumbled with their hats. The gum chewer gave her a strained smile. "Mrs. Lester? Hi. I'm John Ayers, and this is my associate, Leonard Thompson—we're with the Department of the Interior and we'll be out here for the next week, conducting a survey of the vegetation and wild-life, and we just thought we'd stop in to say hello. And introduce ourselves." He tipped his hat a second time, a quick reflexive gesture. The gum snapped. "Just to be neighborly."

"We just got here—on the Coast Guard boat?" the other put in. "We'll be setting up camp on the beach down there in the harbor. Beautiful place, by the way, if only we'd get a little more sunshine, huh?"

Herbie had nothing to say to this, though she could see how upset he was—any encroachment on the island set him off, and though he understood perfectly well that the land was under the aegis of the federal government, which granted the lease for grazing rights to Bob Brooks and could pull the plug on all that any time it wanted, he tended to forget that fact, or brush it aside. Or deny it altogether. The federal government was an abstraction, dis-tant and insubstantial, but he was real and so was she and so were the build-ings and the sheep and the land beneath their feet—the land he worked and possessed and took the value of. Federal government. FDR. He held them in contempt, the same sort of contempt he held for the poachers who came ashore to steal their sheep.

"So you're here to do a survey," she said, just to say something.

"That's right," the first one said—Ayers. "It's nothing to concern yourself over, is it, Leonard?" The other man shook his head. "The survey is only to assess the grazing damage here, with an eye to—"

"Improvement," the other man put in.

It was only then that she began to understand. The island's jurisdiction had passed from the Bureau of Lighthouses to the Department of the Interior and there had been talk of the National Park Service stepping in to oversee management of the land, but that talk, like all rumor, had flitted round them briefly and then gone on over to Santa Cruz and Santa Rosa for the ranchers there to bat around for a while. And yet here it was in the flesh, right on their doorstep. She felt afraid suddenly. Or not afraid, exactly, but off-balance, as if they'd come up and shoved her from behind.

"I don't know how long you've been here—" Ayers began.

"Ten years," Herbie said, cutting him off. "And Bob Brooks has held the lease all the way back to nineteen-seventeen. Is that long enough for you?"

"—but as I'm sure you're aware the range here has been severely over-grazed, leading to substantial degradation of the land—desert, the whole place'll be desert if things continue as they are—and let's call this a feasibility study toward the end of reforesting the island, after making a determination with regard to reducing the grazing population, that is, because that's the first step in any recovery program—"

"I told you, you can't do that. There's a lease in effect."

A laugh now, a wave of the hand. "Oh, we're aware of that, of course we are, and we don't mean to imply that anything's going to go forward at present—"

And now the other one put in: "But we have to inform you, and I have the official notification here, that oversight of San Miguel Island has passed on to the Navy now, for strategic purposes, you understand, as long as there's a threat in the Pacific. And that we're looking to long-range improvement of the resources here."

"Which means getting rid of the sheep, is that what you're saying?" A muscle under Herbie's right eye began to twitch. He balled his hands into fists. "Even though ranching's gone on here for a hundred and sixty years—since the time of the Spaniards, for Christ's sake?"

She said his name aloud—two syllables, emphasis on the first—to draw him back, to warn him: *"Herbie."* And then, in French: *"Ce n'est pas le moment."*

He ignored her. "You better bring your lawyers with you next time, a whole squad of them." And then he caught himself. "Or are you the lawyers, is that what you are?"

Ayers said quietly, "No, we're not lawyers. We're land management men."

Herbie threw it right back at him. "I don't care who you are. You talk to Bob Brooks. He's a millionaire, you know that? He's got resources. He'll fight you every inch of the way."

Both men took a step back. Neither was smiling now. "Let me empha-size," Ayers said, shifting the gum from one side to the other, "that this is all just in the talking stages. It's up to the Navy now. And you know the Navy—"

"No, I don't," Herbie said, fighting to control his voice. "I was an Army man myself. And you go ahead and do your survey because I don't have the authority to stop you. But you'll hear from me—and Bob Brooks too, I prom-ise you that." He turned as if to shut the gate, then spun suddenly round again. "And you stay out of my way, you hear me?"

That night at dinner Herbie hardly said a word. It was as if all the fight had gone out of him the minute the two men had turned and started down the road to the harbor. He didn't touch his food. Throughout the meal, no matter if she tried to keep a conversation going or if the girls addressed him or not, he just stared at the wall as if he could see through it to a place they could only imagine. When the girls were finished and had got up to slide their smeared plates into the dishpan, she took them into the living room to read them their bedtime stories. Neither of them asked about the men who had come to the gate or why their father was still sitting there in the kitchen over a full plate of food, staring at the wall. She read for longer than usual that night—Kipling's *Just So Stories* and "Rikki-Tikki-Tavi," their favorite—as if the magic of talking animals and the strangeness of India could insulate them from what was happening in their own house. Finally, when she put them to bed, Betsy asked if their father wasn't coming in to kiss them good-night and she had to say he wasn't feeling well.

"Is it the flu?" Marianne asked.

"No," she said, "it's not the flu. He's just feeling a little blue, that's all. You know that's how your daddy gets sometimes—me too. We all do."

He came to bed late, stripping down to his underwear wordlessly while she lay there propped up on her pillow, reading. His every motion—pulling the sweater up over his head, bending to his shoes, unbuttoning his shirt—seemed to take forever, as if he were deep undersea and struggling against a heavy current. Earlier, in the kitchen, she'd tried to snap him out of it while she stood over the dishpan, washing up, but it was like talking to a stone. Did he want to listen to a radio program? Or just sit with her by the fire? Did she know that Betsy had added up five columns of three-digit numbers that afternoon—and perfectly too? Was he going to take Pomo for a walk or should she just let him out in the courtyard? He'd shuffled in his seat a bit—there was that much to show that he was alive—but if he answered her at all it was in twitches and grunts.

Now, seeing him there slumped over his discarded clothes as if he couldn't summon the will to pick them up and lay them over the chair, she closed the book and set it on the night table. She knew what was going through his mind, knew the way he let things get him down. Those two men were out there somewhere in the dark—on *his* island—and he couldn't bear the thought of it. "Come to bed," she said, patting the mattress beside her. "You'll feel better in the morning—a good night's sleep, that's all you need."

He gave her an absent look, then eased himself down on the bed and pulled back the covers.

"It's nothing to worry over. Really. I mean it. You heard them—they said it was only a study. And you know how these government studies go. Everything's a study. And nothing ever gets done."

"I know," he said after a moment. "I know. You're right."

"We'll be old folks by the time anything happens. In our rockers, side by side out there on the porch and the girls all grown up and married."

"The Navy," he said, his voice submerged. "What would the Navy want with us out here?"

"They probably don't even know themselves. Bureaucracy, that's all it is. Somebody shuffling papers in Washington." It was only then that she noticed he was trembling. "You're shivering. Are you cold?"

He didn't answer.

She swept back the covers and held them open for him. "Here, move in close and I'll warm you."

"What if they evict us?" he said, sliding stiffly in beside her. "Then what? Where'll we go?"

"They won't evict us."

"But what if they do?"

"No matter what happens," she said, holding tight to him, "you'll always have me and the girls. Always. No matter what."

But he was bitter that night, bitter and blue to the core. "Small comfort," he said, and he rolled away from her and pulled the covers up over his head.

The Gift

As usual with these things, nothing much came of it. The Interior men went around the island taking notes—she saw them only once, in the distance, two crouched figures grubbing in the dirt at the base of a stunted bush, no different from the sheep except that the sheep bore wool—and then they were gone. Herbie came out of his funk once they'd left and he wrote a series of impassioned letters to Bob Brooks, the Secretary of the Navy, the Department of the Interior and their local congressman too, whose name nobody seemed to know till one of the Coast Guard men supplied it, and then he went back to being Herbie, bounding from one thing to another like the bees dancing over the geraniums that had somehow managed to struggle through the soil in the courtyard.

Things held. Time moved on. The Nazis took Paris and drove the British Expeditionary Force into the sea at Dunkirk, 1940 became 1941, the sheep went on grazing and she served lamb five nights a week, week in and week out, while Herbie's moods soared and fell on his own mysterious schedule and the girls grew taller and smarter and saw their test results rank in the highest percentile for their age groups nationwide. The winter was rainy and the spring wet, which made for fat sheep and abundant wool just when demand was growing because of the war in Europe. Summer rose up to loom over them, vast and static, and the girls, let out of school, roamed the island like wild Indians and learned to invent games for themselves. There was the radio, there were letters from her mother, visits from friends and a precipitous falling away of the interest of the press in the Swiss Family Lester in light of the rush of events, which, to her mind at least, came as a blessing.

In the fall of that year, they had a brief spell of sunny weather that rode in on the hot winds off the Santa Ynez Mountains across the channel, mountains they could suddenly see from the yard, revealed to them where no mountains had been for weeks on end. After school each day that week she packed a snack, gathered up towels and a blanket and took the girls down to the beach for a swim, Herbie leading the way and the girls racing the last hundred yards in a pure shriek of elation. Herbie was a great one for swimming and he'd taught both girls to do a creditable breaststroke and Marianne the crawl and butterfly, but mostly they swam in chilly water under a leaden sky, so this was a treat, a real treat, and as long as the weather cooperated they took advantage of it. She'd just come out of the water herself one afternoon, everything slow and lazy, the girls taking turns burying each other in the sand and Herbie propped up on his elbows with a book, when the *Hermes* suddenly emerged from behind the headland to the east to slide across the harbor on a long glimmering train of light. "Look at that—it's the *Hermes*," she said, almost as if she were thinking aloud, and in an instant Herbie was on his feet and the girls up out of the sand and waving their arms over their heads. "But that's odd, isn't it? I didn't think they were due for what, three or four days yet?"

They stood in the fringe of surf and watched as the ship came to anchor and a clutch of familiar faces appeared along the rail. The girls jumped in place, kicking up jets of spray and crying out, "The *Hermes*! The *Hermes*!" in a singsong chant. It was a moment of high excitement, and if she thought with a pang of dinner and what she could possibly serve—or eke out—it was a fleeting thought. She waved and grinned and so did Herbie. They kept on waving as the dinghy was lowered and the oars flashed and the sun leapt up off the sea and fractured and regrouped all over again. She recognized the seaman at the oars, but the man in the bow was a stranger—and it looked as if no one was coming ashore but him, since typically the captain and at least two or three others crowded into the boat to come visit with them.

The mystery was resolved a few minutes later, when the stranger bounded out of the boat, neatly sidestepping the outgoing wave so that his boots didn't even get spattered—boots exactly like Herbie's, and he was wearing short pants like Herbie's too. He had a backpack, a tent and two canvas duffels with him, and they helped him haul it up the beach. And who was he? He was Frank Furlong and he was a surveyor.

Herbie bristled. "You're not one of these land management people, are you? Because I thought I made it clear—"

"No, no, no—I'm a civil engineer. I specialize in remote sites—out of doors, that's where I want to be, not hemmed in in some office someplace. The Navy sent me out here to survey two possible sites for a beacon, but it's your guess as good as mine whether in these economic times they're ever going to get it built." Even as he spoke he was patting down his pockets in search of something—which proved to be individually wrapped pieces of saltwater taffy, which he solemnly handed to the girls, Betsy first, then Marianne, who just stood there gaping up at him as if they didn't know enough to say thank you.

"Girls?" she prompted.

"Thank you," they said in chorus.

"You're very welcome, little ladies. And if your mother allows it—and your father—maybe we'll just find another little piece of taffy for later on."

Before she could think she said, "Won't you join us for dinner? It's nothing fancy, I warn you—"

"Fancy? I wouldn't know fancy if it came up and bit me." He was squinting against the sun, his eyes a pale rinsed-out blue. She saw that he hadn't shaved in a day or two, whitish stubble crowning his chin and climbing up into his sideburns. His hair hadn't gone fully over to gray yet, but to see him there in his hobnailed boots, short pants and soft-collared shirt, he might have been Herbie's twin, minus the epaulettes. "Most nights when I'm out on the job," he said, bending to heft the pack, "it's pork and beans out of the can."

The first night they invited Frank to pitch his tent in the courtyard, out of the wind, but by the second night he was installed in Jimmie's room and frequenting the Killer Whale Bar with Herbie. Herbie took to him right away, once his initial suspicions were allayed, and even went out in the field with him when he could spare the time. She was glad of it. Herbie needed a little male companionship—Jimmie hadn't been around in months and Bob Brooks' visits were sporadic at best—and for the week and a half Frank was with them, his mood just took off like George Hammond's airplane, and when George flew in the three of them sat out in the bar for hours, their voices running up and down the ladder and the sharp bursts of their laughter rolling across the courtyard till the windows rattled in sympathetic vibration.

One night after George had flown back home, she, Herbie and Frank were in the living room listening to the radio, the girls in bed and the wind blowing a gale. At some point the radio went out—the wind, Herbie said— and they sat by the fire, talking in low voices and listening to the wind-borne sand scratch at the windows. "Sounds like a thousand cats out there trying to get in," Frank said, getting up to poke the fire.

"Where *are* the cats?" Herbie asked, turning to her.

"Mr. Fluff's in with the girls," she said. "The others are out prowling, I guess."

"On a night like this?"

"Don't worry, they can take care of themselves. And who knows, they might even catch a mouse or two. Did you know, Frank, that Herbie has a soft spot for mice, if you can believe it?"

"Mice? You're not serious, are you?" Frank shot a look over his shoulder, the poker arrested in his hand. "I hate to say it, but they're dirty animals. Turn your back a minute and they're up on the counter getting at your plate. And believe me they're hell when you set up camp and then you're gone all day in the field. They gnaw, that's the worst of it. Leave anything around, and I don't care what it is—a hammer, your underwear, your toothbrush even— and they'll chew it up."

"Everything's got a right to live," Herbie said.

The fire sent up a burst of sparks. Frank prodded it again—more sparks— then propped the poker against the wall and settled back in his chair. "Yeah, I guess," he said, "but the cat's right seems to interfere with the poor mouse's, doesn't it?"

"The Law of Nature," Herbie said. "People too. Look at the Japs. Or the Krauts. Or the Duce."

"You look at them. It just makes me sick even to think about what's going on in the world today. But you people—at least you're protected from it."

They all sat there a moment and thought about that, about how far out of the sphere of things you'd have to go, geographically and spiritually both, to be safe, truly safe. If it was possible even. After a while Frank said, "You ever get lonely out here—or depressed, I mean? With this weather. A night like this?"

"No," she said too quickly.

"Sure," Herbie admitted. "But it'd be the same thing anywhere, wouldn't it?"

Frank shrugged as if to say, "Point taken," leaned back in the chair and propped an ankle on one knee, exposing the underside of his boot. She saw that the heel was worn down to nothing and the sole rubbed so thin it couldn't have provided much more protection than a sheet of paper and it made her think of all those hundreds of miles he'd tramped in desolate places, up granite mountains and across deserts strewn with cactus, through canyons and riverbeds. Things underfoot. The horizon receding. Can of beans and a fire of twigs.

"You know," he said, "I got so low once—this was two, three years ago, when I was living in San Pedro and couldn't get work and my wife was at me all the time and then I had this accident where I lost sixty percent of the sight in my right eye, just like that, *pow*—I really thought seriously about doing myself in."

"I don't believe it," she said. "You? You're one of the cheerfullest people I've ever met—"

He just shook his head ruefully. "I even bought a gun, a pistol, what they call a .38 Special? And I planned out how I would do it in the dunes some-place so nobody'd have to clean up the mess, let the gulls take care of it, you know? But I didn't do it. And things got better between Marjorie and me, though that's gone sour since, I'm sorry to say—and then I got this job up here . . . but here, let me show you—"

He got up then and left the room. A moment later he came back with something wrapped up in a scrap of stained cloth. He bent forward to set it on the coffee table so they could contemplate it a moment, then unwrapped it to reveal the gun itself, snub-nosed, blue-black and glistening with oil. "I've been carrying it around with me for years, telling myself it's for protection when I'm out on a job someplace, but that's just a lot of gas. I know what I bought it for. And I don't want it in my life anymore." He glanced up at Her-bie, who sat there perfectly motionless, as if to move would be a violation of trust.

"I want you to have it," Frank said. "For your collection. It's not much, I know, but let's call it my way of thanking you—thanking both of you—for all your kindness, for taking me into your home just like I was a member of the family. It's meant a lot to me. It really has."

322

The Japanese

Frank was gone by Halloween, so that it was just the family for dinner, doughnuts and apple cider, after which the girls—who'd both dressed as Snow White, the heroine of the only movie they'd ever seen—got a lesson in trick or treat. They went up and down the porch, rapping at each door, behind which Herbie had stashed a dish of sweets, and just when they began to get the hang of it he sprang out at them draped in a sheet, gyrating and moaning and stamping over the floorboards in full display. "I'm the ghost of Captain Waters," he roared while the dog howled and the girls dissolved in shrieks, "and I've come to reclaim my own!" For her part, she drew exaggerated circles under her eyes with a stick of charcoal and came as the wicked queen, but it was Herbie who stole the show.

There was turkey for Thanksgiving, a dressed bird George flew out to them—"At least the foxes won't get this one," he said, "though I guess I'm depriving the goose of a playmate, isn't that right, Herbie?"—along with all the trimmings. Herbie printed up a menu which began with "Cream of Celery Soup" and ended with "Apple Pie, Home-Brewed Beer, Pipe and Tobacco," and they did their best to make the day festive. As for Christmas, neither of them had really had a chance to give it much thought when news came that the Japanese had attacked Pearl Harbor and all bets were off.

She was sitting in the rocking chair out on the porch, knitting and listening to the Philharmonic broadcast, Sunday afternoon, a weak sun running to milk in the sky and the temperature tolerable because the wind was down. The girls were out in the meadow throwing a ball and playing keep-away with the dog, whose high joyous yips had been punctuating Beethoven's Sixth Symphony—"The Pastoral"—for the past ten minutes, and Herbie was at the far end of the porch, dismantling the clock that had suddenly stopped working that morning. What was wrong with this scenario? Nothing.

Nothing at all. It was a picture of domestic tranquility and the deepest indwelling peace, one more day in a succession of them, husband, family, home, the sky above and the familiar boards of the porch beneath her feet. And then the announcer came over the air and interrupted the broadcast and nothing was ever the same again.

They listened to the president's speech the next day, trying to make sense of what had happened. It had been a sneak attack, premeditated, the Japanese ambassador in Washington as false as a three-dollar bill and the emperor's fleet simultaneously attacking Malaya, Hong Kong, Guam, the Philippines and Wake and Midway Islands, spreading east across the Pacific. She couldn't believe it. It seemed fantastic, like the Mercury Theatre broadcast that had caused such panic three years back, only the invaders were the Japanese this time, not the Martians.

Herbie couldn't sit still. He twisted the dial. Paced the room. Muttered under his breath. All the while, the president's voice came at them, humming, buzzing, fractured with static: *Hostilities exist. There is no blinking at the fact that our people, our territory and our interests are in grave danger.* She tried to focus on the words, but it was as if the president were speaking from the bottom of a very deep jar, every syllable ringing and resonating till all she could hear was the phrase "a state of war," but that was enough. More than enough. She got up out of her chair and went to Herbie, to her support, her pillar, and took his hand. "What does it mean?" she asked.

"What does it mean?" The look he gave her was savage. He'd fought in the war to end all wars, given his blood, his flesh, a full year and a half of his life, and here was the next war sweeping them up whether they liked it or not. "It means they're going to try to evacuate us, that's what—this is just the excuse they've been looking for."

"But why? Certainly we're not in any danger, not way out here, are we?"

"The Pacific Fleet's gone, Elise, don't you understand? There's nothing between the Japs and us. And you can bet they're going to hopscotch island to island till they take Hawaii and then they'll come for us, for the whole west coast, and we're defenseless without warships." He squeezed her hand—too hard, much too hard, almost as if he didn't know what he was doing—then abruptly dropped it. "But I tell you, I'm not going anywhere."

"Can't they force us?"

He gave a wild look round the room, the radio going still, more static, another announcer, more failure, more hate, more fear, then strode over to it and flicked it off. In the next moment he was across the room lifting one of his rifles down from the wall and raising it to his shoulder to sight down the barrel. "I don't know what they can or can't do," he said. "I don't know anything anymore." He leaned the gun against the wall, then lifted another down and hefted it in both hands. "But I tell you, anybody comes here to threaten us, whether it's the U.S. Navy or the Japs themselves, I'm going to be ready for them."

Christmas was dismal that year. All aircraft had been grounded, which meant that George wasn't able to bring out the tree or supplies or the gifts they'd ordered for the girls (one headline, which she wouldn't wind up seeing till well into January, read, "War Grounds Santa: Christmas a Bust on San Miguel Island"). The authorities were putting restrictions on boat traffic as well, imposing a blockade on all ships in the Western Combat Zone, extending out one hundred fifty miles from the coast, Mexico to Canada. No one stopped by, not even the Vails, who were under the same proscription as they. There was no mail, incoming or outgoing—no letters from friends and relatives, no magazines or newspapers, no Christmas cards. Even the Weather Service froze up communications. Herbie managed to fashion a wreath of ice plant, but the shade of green was all wrong and within a day the whole thing had turned yellow and begun to drip a colorless viscous fluid that ran down the front door in riverine streaks to puddle on the doorstep.

She did her best to craft presents for the girls—rag dolls, paper animals, necklaces of seashells—but supplies were limited, and Christmas dinner, while it did feature fresh-caught halibut in a sauce of flour and evaporated milk made piquant with a sprinkle of dried red pepper left over from the shearers' last visit, was short on potatoes and fresh vegetables, and the Christmas pudding wound up being represented by an eggless, butterless and very flat vanilla cake sprinkled with raisins. Even worse, from Herbie's perspective, was that there was no whiskey, the old trove long gone and the two bottles of Grand Sire that George had brought them at Thanksgiving drained to the last drop. About the only thing that made it seem like Christmas was a program of faint scratchy carols they were able to get on the radio, but even the radio signal was sketchy in those days and weeks after Pearl Harbor.

The two Navy boys—and they were boys, eighteen and twenty respectively—showed up on New Year's Day. They came slouching up the road from the harbor carrying knapsacks and with a single rifle between them. A Navy gunboat had apparently dropped them off, but neither she nor Herbie had seen or heard it—the first indication she had that anyone was there came from Marianne. "Mommy, Mommy!" Marianne cried, dancing into the kitchen, "there's somebody coming up the road!"

She and Herbie dropped what they were doing and went out to the gate to meet them, Herbie flicking imaginary dust from his epaulettes and she pushing the hair out of her face. For their part, the Navy boys seemed to be in no hurry, dawdling even, swiveling their heads right and left, looking pained and wary. *City boys,* she said to herself. The thought was automatic: she'd earned her bona fides, she was the pioneer here and they were the mainlanders, the neophytes—she wouldn't be surprised if they'd never been farther than a block from a streetcar in their lives. Just look at them, creeping along as if they expected the sky to fall on them.

When they reached the gate, the taller one—an ectomorph with an Adam's apple as big as a goiter—set down his bag and saluted Herbie. "Seaman First Class Reg Bauer," he said, "at your service. And this here's my shipmate, Seaman Apprentice Frederick Fredrickson."

The other man—boy—had an amiable face and small soft girlish hands. His feet, in their now-dusty standard-issue shoes, couldn't have been much bigger than Marianne's. He doffed his cap and gave a brisk nod of his head. "Call me Freddie," he said.

There was an awkward interval. Herbie was no help—he was bristling again, his hair mussed, the book he'd been reading dangling from the fingers of one hand. The girls, same as with Frank Furlong, just stared as if they'd never seen another human being before in all their lives, and that was something they needed to get over, this island shyness. It wasn't right. They had to learn how to manage in society. Finally she said, "I'm Mrs. Lester—Elise—and this is my husband, Herbert. How can we help you?"

The first one let out a laugh. "Oh, no, ma'am, you don't understand—we're here to help *you*. We're to be billeted here and keep watch for enemy activity. And, of course"—and here he tapped the rifle slung over his shoulder—"to serve as protection in the event hostile combatants do appear. Show up, I mean. The Japanese, that is."

"Yes, we've heard of them," Herbie said in a withering voice. "They're those little yellow bastards with the buckteeth."

"Yes, sir," the other one said, trying out a smile now. She saw that he had acne spots on his face and throat and that his eyes were red, as if he'd been drinking, or—and here she made a leap of intuition—working through the dregs of a New Year's Eve hangover. "The same," he said. And then the smile was gone.

"Let me get this straight," Herbie said, shifting his weight so that he was leaning into the gate now, as if to bar their way as he had with the men from the Interior Department. "You're going to protect us from invasion—with one rifle between you? And an antiquated firearm at that? We used the Springfield in the first war, or didn't anybody tell you that? They couldn't even issue you the M1 Garand?"

"Well, no, sir," the first one said, ducking his head, "that's not possible at present. Captain Hill—he's the one gave us our orders?—says we're short of small arms and we've got to make do with what we have on hand, until we can, or they can—"

"Who can? You talking about rifle manufacturers here in this country gearing up for wartime production? Because if you are, it's going to be a long wait, I'm afraid." He shot her an exasperated look, then lifted his eyes to heaven as if to say, *How can they expect us to suffer such fools?* Out of the corner of her eye she saw the dog come trotting across the yard to investigate, then drop back on his haunches at a safe distance. The breeze came at her, cold and insinuating, and it carried the smell of the sheep. And then Betsy, her hair blowing round her face, sidled over to her father and clung to his leg, shifting back and forth to play peek-a-boo with these fascinating creatures who'd serendipitously appeared on her doorstep. "But you said something about being billeted here?" Herbie said.

"Yes, sir." And here the one with the gun—Reg—saluted again. "Those are my orders, sir."

"And who do you think's going to feed you? Billeted, my ass. You think you can just waltz in here with that Springfield rifle and order us around as if this is some kind of military camp or something?"

The short one, Freddie: "You don't understand, sir, we're here to protect you—to serve you, that is. Your whole family. And to watch out for—"

"Suspicious activity?"

"Suspicious activity, yes, right."

Herbie crossed his arms over his chest and cocked his head back as if he were examining them from a great distance. "Don't make me laugh. You even know how to use that thing?"

The tall one—and now he was bristling: "We've been drilled."

"You betcha," the other one put in.

"I'm sure we'll all sleep better tonight knowing that." Herbie turned to her, his eyebrows lifted in mock surprise. "Did you hear that, Elise? They've been drilled. What a relief, huh?"

They put them up in the shearers' room just off the kitchen. The letter the boys carried with them from their commanding officer gave Herbie and her the choice of evacuation—which meant leaving everything behind that wouldn't fit into one suitcase apiece—or submitting to the Navy presence. Everyone had to sacrifice in this time of need, Captain Hill went on to say, pointing out that the government was pressing all private aircraft into service and any number of seaworthy vessels as well, including passenger liners, tugs, tankers, trawlers and even private yachts, thus it was their duty as Americans and patriots to billet Seaman First Class Bauer and Seaman Apprentice Frederickson, who could be expected to assist with household chores as needed and to patrol the island on a regular basis in order to protect them from enemy infiltration and assault. Further, each man had been provided with ten pounds of rice, ten pounds of beans and a quantity of dried and cured meats, including but not limited to ham, bacon and chipped beef, to contribute to the general stores.

Herbie wasn't happy about it, nor was she. There were strangers in the house and they weren't invited guests or members of the Mexican-Indian crew who came out twice a year for the shearing and whom they'd come to know over time as friends and employees both. Where was their privacy? What did these boys expect of them and what were they to expect in return? From the very first night they felt constrained in their own home, but the country was at war and there was a quid pro quo at work here: billet the sailors and stay or refuse and be forcibly evicted. The government held all the power and now more than ever it would be a simple thing for some official to revoke Bob Brooks' lease, making it an issue of national security, and no one understood that better than Herbie. If that wasn't enough, there was the appeal to his patriotism. There was no one, not in Washington or aboard any ship still afloat in the Pacific, who could question his loyalty, that was how he saw it—and he let her know it, lecturing on late into the night, airing his grievances, pacing up and down the room flinging out his hands like a soap-box orator, as worked up as she'd ever seen him. "I'm a veteran, for Christ's sake. I fought for my country and I'll fight again, if that's what they want from me. Patriotic duty. Don't make me laugh. It's an insult is what it is."

By the next morning, he'd come around. He was unusually quiet at first, hovering over a cup of coffee and sitting there at the table staring out into the gloom while she stirred oatmeal and sliced bread to toast in the oven. He'd mumbled a good morning when he came into the room, but hadn't said another word till finally, out of nowhere, he announced, "The Navy's not the problem. I see that now." He shifted in his seat, set the cup down and began tracing an invisible figure on the tabletop with the bottom edge of it. "Of course I do. It's the Japs, the Japs are the problem. And we've all got to unite against them."

It was seven a.m. and the sailors were asleep still—or that was her presumption, anyway. Maybe she was wrong. Maybe they were already out on patrol, trading the rifle between them.

"Still, it burns me up to think they'd send us a couple of idiots like this—babies, that's what they are, probably cry for their mother the first time a shell goes off. And if they think they're just going to laze around here like it's some kind of rest home, they're nuts. I want you to lay out kitchen duties for them—they'll wash dishes and scrub this place till it glows, by Christ—and I'll let them know what's needed in the yard, wood detail, for one thing. We're two more mouths to feed now, two more adults, and that means double the firewood, double at least—"

When the boys did come in—at quarter of eight—they looked even more subdued than they had the night before. Their uniforms—their blues—were wrinkled, as if they'd slept in them, but they seemed to have washed their faces and hands and their nails looked clean enough as they sat down at the table and she served out their bowls of oatmeal and set a platter of toast and a jar of jam before them. Herbie was already out in the shed, doing whatever he did on cold damp socked-in mornings like this, and that relieved some of the tension. The girls had already eaten and since the holiday was over, she had them in their room getting ready for school, which would commence as soon as she'd fed the sailors and gone out into the yard to ring the bell.

Reg, the taller of the two, the one with the caramel-colored eyes and the pink slashes of scalp showing through his crew cut, ate with the kind of four-square rigidity you'd expect of a military man—or boy—but his compatriot, Freddie, slouched over his plate and bowl as if he'd never had any discipline in his life, not even from his mother. After a good five minutes of silence, during which the only sounds were the metallic clank of the woodstove and the click of their spoons against the rims of their bowls, Reg spoke up. "I'm sorry to bother you, missus, but you wouldn't have a little butter for the toast? Please, I mean?"

And now she was embarrassed in her own kitchen. Butter? She hadn't seen butter in weeks. "I'm afraid you'll have to make do with jam for now because, well, since Pearl Harbor we haven't been able to get any regular supplies—"

"Really? We've got crates of the stuff back at the base, right, Freddie?"

"Yeah, we could've . . . if we'd known, that is—"

"It's all right," she said. She was standing at the counter, tidying things before going out to ring the school bell. "We've learned to make do. Not that it isn't hard sometimes. This past month especially."

There was a silence, then Freddie spoke up. "But what do you do out here normally—I mean, before all this started? For entertainment, I mean?"

She shrugged. "Oh, there's plenty to keep us busy. You get used to the solitude after a while. There're the girls, of course. And we play cards, read, listen to radio programs, I suppose, just like anybody else."

She saw them exchange a look. "That sounds swell," Reg said finally.

And then, because it was five of eight and she made a strict rule of starting school on time, she folded the dish towel across her arm, replaced it on its wooden rack and stepped to the door. "I'm sorry, but it's time for school," she announced. "You'll hear me ringing the bell"—she checked her watch—"in exactly three minutes. You won't mind cleaning up your dishes, will you? You'll find the soap under the counter here."

The Horses

For the most part, the Navy boys kept out of the way. They appeared regularly for meals—they never missed a meal, give them credit there—and the girls came to worship them as if they were celestial idols set down on the earth and given the power of speech and animation, but as the weeks went by she saw less and less of them. If they weren't in their room leafing through comics and back issues of Herbie's sportsmen's magazines, they were wandering the island—aimlessly, she suspected—propped up by the single gun they shared between them. They never said a word about Herbie's collection, which had grown to some thirty-odd firearms now, except to let out a few exclamations of surprise and approbation the first time Herbie led them into the living room to show it off—and if they resented the fact that a private citizen had an entire arsenal at his disposal while they went half-armed, they never let it show.

That they were bored was a given. There was nothing on the island for them but duty as defined in their orders—they wanted life, nightlife, gin mills and dance halls and girls their own age, movies, automobiles, swing bands, Harry James and Benny Goodman—and she couldn't blame them. What she could blame them for was neglecting the chores she and Herbie set out for them—more than once she had to remind them that appearances to the contrary she wasn't their mother, and if they wanted to eat they had better make sure they set and cleared the table, washed the dishes and kept the woodbox full to overbrimming. And if Reg wanted to help Marianne with her arithmetic or Freddie read aloud to Betsy, so much the better, but they did that on their own time.

They were good with the girls, she had to admit it, but the diversions of children's games, hide-and-seek, red light–green light, checkers, Old Maid and Go Fish, only went so far. She registered the tedium in their faces, every day the same, nowhere to go, nothing to do. The one thing they did manage to show interest in—besides eating, that is—was the horses. At lunch one afternoon, the girls giggling and generally being silly vying for their attention and the dog looking up fixedly as the platter went round the table, Reg cleared his throat and turned to Herbie. "So the horses out there in the barn—Buck and Nellie? Do you ever ride them or are they strictly for hauling things up from the harbor?"

Herbie was in an ebullient mood, chasing after the subject of the sheep and how well they were doing because of what was beginning to look like a well-watered and prosperous winter no matter what the Interior Department, the Navy or the Japanese might have to say about it, and he'd just pointed out to her that more of the ewes seemed to be throwing twins this time around, when he paused for a moment to lift the soupspoon to his mouth and Reg slipped in his question. Herbie took a moment, setting down the spoon and delicately patting his lips with the napkin, always fastidious—he had beautiful manners, whether he was knocking on a door on the Upper East Side with his mustaches waxed or sitting here in the dining cum living room of a patchwork house framed by the sea. "Oh, we ride them," he said, "of course we do—the exercise is good for them, Nellie especially. Buck, I'm afraid, is pretty much on his last legs—"

She looked up sharply. This was a sore subject between them. Betsy was eight and Marianne had just turned eleven, and while they were old enough to understand that all things had to die, especially on a working ranch—the sheep Herbie shot for meat, the turkey the foxes had made off with, one of the cats that had crept under the porch to give up the ghost in peace and was discovered only when it began to emit an odor—the horses were in a different category altogether. They were pets as much as anything else. The girls had grown up with both of them, and Buck, a big patient bay roan, had been the one they learned to ride on. He was old and stiff, they knew that—according to Jimmie, Buck had been on the ranch since Bob Brooks took over—but she didn't like Herbie to mention it in front of them. Once, after he'd gone on about Buck staggering on the road up from the harbor ("He damned near pitched over the side into the ravine and me with him"), Betsy had asked, "Is Buck going to die?" and she'd tried to be forthright with her. "Yes," she'd said, "everything dies, even Buck. But not for a long while yet, so don't you worry about it." "Why?" Betsy asked, and whether she was asking why she shouldn't worry or why everything dies, Elise didn't know. And in any case she really didn't have an answer.

"He's got to be twenty-six, twenty-seven years old. But he's been a good old horse." Herbie looked to where the girls sat side by side, staring up at him over their plates. "Right, girls?"

They both nodded solemnly.

"So would you mind then if we took the horses out?" Reg persisted. "It would make it a whole lot easier for us to patrol—get out to the other end of the island, I mean, out to Point Bennett and such."

Herbie was feeling grand and expansive, riding one of his currents. If they'd asked her, she would have said no. The boys were well meaning, she supposed—or well meaning enough—but once they got out of sight of the house there was no telling what they might do. She was afraid for the horses— and for them too. That was all they needed: a boy sailor with a broken neck. But Herbie just waved a hand grandly and said, "We'll see."

On the night of February twenty-third, a Japanese I-17 submarine—a huge thing, longer than a football field—slipped into the Santa Barbara Channel undetected by anyone, not the Coast Guard or the Air Corps or the two boy sailors sent out to San Miguel Island to protect her and her family from attack. It was theorized that the submarine was piloted by a man who knew these waters intimately, either a former fisherman or perhaps captain of one of the Japanese tankers that regularly took on crude oil here before the out- break of war. In any case, just after seven that night, the submarine surfaced and began shelling the Ellwood Oil Field just west of Santa Barbara, intent on destroying the oil storage tanks and setting off a firestorm. It was the first attack on the continental United States by a foreign power since the War of 1812 and while none of the shells hit its target, the sirens went off, a blackout was imposed and people up and down the coast were thrown into a panic, thinking an invasion was under way. On San Miguel Island that night—and she remembered it clearly—they were all sitting around the fire playing cards while the girls did their homework and the wind assaulted the house with its grab bag of shrieks, whistles and growls. Nobody heard a thing.

They only learned of the attack the following morning, when the short- wave radio—given over now strictly to naval pursuits—began to buzz with the news. A pall fell over the house. They all gathered in the living room, even the girls, who couldn't be kept away, the voice of the naval operator hissing and crackling over the bare details, *Enemy submarine, nineteen hundred hours, casualties as yet unknown*. The sailors sat there perched on the edges of their chairs, white-faced and stricken, as Herbie communicated with shore, their feet tapping nervously and their eyes darting to the windows as if they expected to see the Imperial Army out there secreted amongst the sheep. Herbie was outraged. He kept accusing them, as if the whole thing were their fault, as if they could have been expected to identify an enemy submarine forty-two miles away in the dark of night. "Where were you when we needed you?" he demanded. "If you'd been out there on patrol you might have spotted them and radioed their location to shore—we could have called out the planes and bombed them, could have wiped them out, the dirty sneaking Nip bastards."

She watched Herbie fuming over the radio in the impotence of his rage, his arms flapping at his sides and his hair on end, and all she felt was a hopeless sinking fear. Their sanctuary was gone, the invaders at their doorstep—they could be anywhere, already landed at Simonton Cove or right down there in Cuyler Harbor for all she knew. She thought of the Japanese fishermen who'd come to the house all those years ago, saw their faces arrayed before her, such polite men, so mild—and so delighted with the baby. How could men like that threaten them? They were decent at heart, she knew they were—the captain spoke French even. But then—and the thought chilled her—there were the Japs she read of in the newspapers, demonic twisted little men spitting babies on their bayonets, raping women wholesale, murdering, thieving, leaving Nanking in ruins and Shanghai in chains. That was the reality. And this, this cockeyed dream of wide-open spaces, of freedom and self-reliance and goodness, simple goodness, was the delusion.

"Over and out," Herbie pronounced, his voice too loud by half as he switched off the radio and spun round on the sailors. "What are you waiting for? You want to ride the horses? We'll ride the horses. Here"—and he crossed the room to the wall decorated with guns, chose one and handed it to Reg Bauer. "And you, Freddie, make sure you have extra clips of ammunition for that Springfield of yours—they did give you ammunition, didn't they?"

Freddie had half-risen from the chair, looking stunned. "Yes," he said, "yes, I think so," and he straightened up to his full height—which couldn't have been much more than five-foot-four—and tried his best to look martial. And what was she thinking? That this was what stood between her and the Imperial Army? This boy? This and the other one, who looked as if he'd never even raised his voice in all his life?

"All right," Herbie was saying, and he'd taken down a gun for himself, one of the big ones—was it the elephant gun, was that it?—"we're going out that door in two minutes flat and we're going to patrol every square foot of this island. You have your binoculars?"

The boys just gaped at him.

"Well, get them! And be quick about it! Who knows but that"—and here he caught himself in mid-sentence. She knew what he meant to say—*they're already here*—but he didn't want to alarm her, she could see that. Or the girls. Or these two boys either. This was the moment of crisis and she felt herself go out to him: he was equal to it. If she'd ever doubted that, here was proof of it.

"And when we get done with the first circuit of the island," he was saying, "you know what we're going to do?" He didn't wait for an answer. "We're going to go around again, that's what."

The following week the *Hermes* came to anchor in the harbor and when she saw the boat shining there in the distance it was as if the great American eagle itself had come swooping in to the rescue. She'd been living in dread all week, neither the shortwave nor the Zenith bringing them anything concrete by way of news except to say that the shelling had been an isolated event and that the Japanese, far from initiating an invasion, were stuck all the way on the other side of the Pacific and if the U.S. Navy had anything to say about it, that was where they would stay. Later, much later, when the war was over and the great cities of Japan were crushed under the weight of their own shame and the American bombs that had paid them back a thousand times over for Pearl Harbor and Bataan and all the rest, she learned that the Ellwood incident was an aberration, the only attack on the American mainland in the entire course of the war, and that the submarine's captain—who had in fact piloted an oil tanker in these waters before the war—had been on a personal vendetta to avenge an insult he'd suffered at the hands of the refinery's American workers. The submarine's gunners had been inept, missing everything they fired on. And the submarine itself, having delivered its salvo, had turned tail and run halfway across the ocean.

But she didn't know that then. All she knew was that the Japanese had struck and could strike again at any time. She couldn't go out in the yard after dark without feeling as if the night had turned hostile, every sound transmogrified till she heard the roar of cannon in the crash of the surf or the keening of an aircraft engine in the sudden sharp cry of a gull. She was afraid for the girls. For Herbie. For herself. She went on as if nothing had changed, cooking, cleaning, sewing, keeping school, mending Herbie's clothes and feeding the pets, but all the while she felt the tension deep inside her as if it were a physical abnormality, as if her stomach was a knot of twisted wire, barbed wire, the kind they used to repel invasions.

The *Hermes* brought relief from all that. The sight of it alone was enough— here were their true protectors, undaunted, patrolling the waters as they always had and always would, *My country 'tis of thee, sweet land of liberty,* and she never thought, not for a minute, that they'd come to evacuate them. Not these men, not now, not when every American had to stand united. They'd come with supplies, with relief—they'd come because they cared.

The whole household erupted. She couldn't find a hat, Marianne was barefoot, Herbie pulling on the first thing that came to hand. There was no thought of the stove or the livestock or keeping a watch over the house—they were out the door, all of them, hurrying down to meet the boat, the sailor boys, the dog, she and Herbie and the girls, who were positively giddy at being let out of school early. And before they'd even got the supplies unloaded, they had the news and the news was what she wanted to hear: the danger was minimal, nothing really, and in any case it had passed. Did she believe it? Not really. Or not entirely. And Herbie was barely mollified, though he quizzed the captain and crew for hours and when they'd left read through the mail and the newspapers they'd brought along like an exegete bent over the Book of Revelation, weighing each phrase for nuance as if he could see through to a truth the world was hiding from them.

There were six letters from her mother, each more gut-wrenching and strident than the last, as if they'd already been taken prisoner and sent to some resettlement camp in the jungles of Malaya. Wasn't this enough? her mother demanded. Wasn't it proof in the pudding? If there was ever a sign from God, wasn't this it? Her mother wrote in an elegant backslant that tended to crimp and run off the page at the end of each line and she could picture her sitting there at the secretary in the parlor at home all the way across the country, her mouth compressed and the pen clamped firmly in her gliding fingers. Each letter ended with the same imperative, underlined twice: *Come home!*

Though she had no idea of when she'd be able to post it, she wrote a long letter in reply, assuring her mother that everything was fine (though it wasn't and never would be again till the Japanese crawled back into their holes and the Interior men filed their surveys in the wastebasket), and that she couldn't imagine any life but this. Then she went on for pages about Marianne and Betsy and their accomplishments and how the peace and beauty of the island would not only see them through this war as it had seen them through the Depression, but that they'd be stronger, purer and more self-reliant as a result. She sealed the envelope, licked the stamp and almost believed it herself.

The weeks dropped by. Herbie, clacking along on the rails of an idea, indefatigable, unswerving, kept up a watch over the island whether it distracted him from her and the children and took him away from his chores or not—he was out at dawn, the binoculars dangling from his neck, a rifle slung over one shoulder and two cartridge belts marking an X across his chest, and he made the rounds again at dusk. Reg and Freddie, though, soon lost interest once it became apparent that the threat had dissolved and the days were as long as they'd ever been and the shore just as far away. They began to slack off on their chores, disappearing immediately after meals—reconnoitering, as they called it—so that Herbie had to lay down the law every other day it seemed. She saw the collision coming, both boys bridling under the whip, until finally Reg had had enough and spoke up in the middle of one of Herbie's lectures on personal responsibility. "I'm sorry, sir," he said, stroking the lump of his Adam's apple with two tense fingers and shooting Herbie a look, "but you're not our commanding officer—"

"Lucky for you."

"And we do feel"—a glance for Freddie—"that we're doing everything the U.S. Navy expects from us."

"Yeah," Freddie put in. "And more."

They were at the table. Another evening. Another meal. The pans piled up in the kitchen and the grease hardening on the plates. The smell of woodsmoke, of ash, of the dog wet under the table. Herbie pushed back his chair and gave them a withering look. "If the girls weren't sitting here at this table, I'd tell you in no uncertain terms exactly what kind of job you're doing around here. And I swear I don't know what the U.S. Navy might or might not expect, but I'm in charge of this household and you'll work to my standards and like it. That woodpile is a disgrace. And I haven't seen anybody touch a shovel out in the yard for a week—a week at least. No, listen, I'll make it simple for you: you get up off your rear ends and get out there in the kitchen right this minute or tomorrow morning you don't eat."

Neither of them showed up for breakfast the next morning, the first meal they'd missed in the three months and more they'd been billeted on the island. They'd cleared up in the kitchen the night before but they were sullen about it and afterward they went out wandering and didn't come back till late—she was awakened by the scrape of their footsteps on the porch, followed by the faint metallic sigh of the door to their room easing back on its hinges, and checked the clock at her bedside: 1:35 a.m. There was no firewood in the box by the stove when she woke and she had to go out to the woodpile herself to fetch enough to make breakfast. She saw right away that it had been neglected—most of what was left were the big pieces that needed cutting and splitting—and she made a mental note to take the boys aside at lunch and remind them before Herbie found out, but then they didn't come in for lunch.

Herbie had spent the morning patrolling on foot, hiking up Green Mountain to glass the waters to the north and west, and he exploded when he saw they weren't there. "The little crap artists," he spat, and she had to warn him to watch his language even as the girls looked up from their plates and an indecisive April sun sketched a panel of light on the wall and then took it away again. "If they think they can defy me . . . Let them eat dirt, then, I don't care. We'll see how long they hold out."

What she didn't tell him, in the interest of peace, was that a loaf of yesterday's bread had turned up missing, along with several chunks of lamb crudely hacked from the joint in the cool room, as well as the last of the basket of apples the *Hermes* had brought out to them. What she did say was, "Maybe you were too hard on them last night. They have their pride too, you know. Remember yourself at their age, what you must have been like?"

"Hard on them? Jesus! It's amazing they have the energy to wipe their own asses—"

"Herbie," she warned.

"Herbie, what? We've been through all this before. I'm fed up, that's all."

"But they're here and they're not going away, not as long as there's a war on—and the war hasn't been going very well for us, has it?"

"You can say that again." He was mopping his plate with a crust of bread and he paused to glare at her as if she'd personally started the war and armed the Japanese till they were all but invincible.

"We just have to face facts—the Navy's in charge now and they're going to do whatever they want, not only here but up and down the coast. Just be thankful they didn't send us fifty sailors." She got up from the table and began clearing away the unused place settings, then paused to hover over the girls. "Girls, you'd better finish up and take your plates out to the kitchen— I'll be ringing that bell for afternoon session in twenty minutes on the dot." Both girls shoveled up their food—it was baked beans today, with two strips of bacon each and a can of creamed corn—picked up their plates and retreated through the door.

She watched Herbie a moment, his jaws working so that a hard line of muscle flexed on either side of his mouth. She let out a sigh. "I don't like it any better than you do, but I say we all just try to get on as best we can, all right?"

"No, it's not all right." He glared up at her, his jaws still working. "I'm going to report them, that's what I'm going to do—get somebody else out here, men, somebody who knows what work is. Hell, even Jimmie's worth the two of those idiots combined."

It was then that Freddie's face appeared at the window—the uneven crop of his hair (engineered privately, in his room), the too-big forehead and dwindling eyes—and right away she could see that something was wrong. Her first thought, and it clenched her heart, was that the Japanese had come, but that wasn't it at all. He gestured wildly, then pushed open the door, his breath coming hard. "It's the horse," he said. "He—"

Herbie jerked to his feet. "What horse? What are you talking about?"

"Buck. We were—Reg was riding him—and he turned up lame."

"Riding him? I told you, I warned you—you don't ride that horse unless I say so."

"He's having trouble—he's just standing there on three legs, and we can't get him to walk."

The next question was where—up on the bluff at Nichols Point—and then Herbie was muttering curses and angrily thrusting his feet into his boots while she hurried out in the yard to ring the school bell. The girls had been in their room playing, and now they came slouching across the courtyard, looking put upon. "You said twenty minutes," Marianne complained.

"Something's come up. I've got to go with your father for a minute."

She could see the fear seep into their eyes—they knew why Santa hadn't come at Christmas, knew why the sailors were there and that the shells had fallen on Ellwood—and more than ever in that moment she hated the war and the constant tension and what it was doing to them all. "It's nothing to worry over," she said, and heard the falseness in her own voice. "Just one of the sheep. It's nothing. And I expect you both to do your reading assignment just as if I were here—and I warn you, you'll be writing reports the minute I get back. So no dawdling."

Nellie was just outside the gate, where Freddie had left her. She was lathered and her sides were heaving. Herbie took one look at her and swung round on Freddie. "You take this animal up to the barn and rub her down. And then you feed and water her, you hear me?"

"Yes, sir."

"Goddamn you, you better."

In the next moment Freddie had turned to lead the horse to the barn and she was following her husband along a sheep path through the dunes and chewed-over scrub. Nichols Point was less than two miles off and mostly downhill and they moved quickly. "You think it's bad?" she asked, but he never turned round and never bothered to answer. He was worked up, she could see that, and she almost felt sorry for Reg—almost, though whatever he had coming to him he'd brought it on himself.

When they got close she could see the horse framed in the distance against an ocean the color of soapstone and a sky that went just a shade lighter. It was misting and the wind had cut off altogether. Reg was standing off to one side, his hands in his pockets. The horse—Buck—had his head lowered, but he wasn't cropping grass, and he was favoring the left front leg.

"I don't know what happened to him," Reg sang out when they were still a

340

hundred feet away. "I was just riding him along the bluff here, looking for the enemy, you know? And he pulled up lame."

Herbie ignored him. He went up to the horse and patted his shoulder to calm him. With an effort, Buck raised his head, but the motion staggered him so that he had to put weight on the bad leg, just for an instant, and that staggered him again. Herbie knelt beside him to run a hand over the injured foreleg, taking his time, feeling for a break. Then he rose to his feet and still he said nothing.

Reg was cupping his hands to light a cigarette. "Well?" he said. "What do you think?"

"Get out of my sight," Herbie spat.

"But I didn't do nothing. You yourself said he was old—"

"Just go. Go on, get!"

They both watched the sailor adjust his shoulders and start back across the wet field, trailing smoke and sauntering as if he didn't have a care in the world.

"It's broken, isn't it?" she said. He didn't answer. *"Mon amour,"* she said. *"Parlez moi."*

He just shook his head. Buck set his hoof down, then jerked it back again so that it hung limp in the air. "We're going to need to move him twenty feet or so—to the edge of the bluff there," Herbie said finally. "Can you grab hold of his halter while I take the saddle off him?"

It came clear to her then. "You're not going to bury him?"

His voice was hard, as if he weren't talking to her at all but to Reg or Freddie or the Japanese in the white coat who'd had the effrontery to sit there in their living room like an authentic human being: "You want to dig the hole? Christ, it'd take a week."

And then the saddle lay in the dirt and Buck moved under her hand in a series of three-legged jerks, a foot at a time, until he stood poised there on the verge of the cliff that gave onto the bay below. He was a horse, only a horse, and he'd outlived his time, she understood that, told herself that, but when Herbie pulled the black snub-nosed pistol—the gift—from his pocket and pressed it to the animal's head, she felt as if she were dying herself.

All that was left was the report of the pistol—two reports, in quick succession—and Herbie jumping aside as the failing legs kicked out and the big roan body hit the ground and the ground shifted and it was gone.

The Accident

So he was angry, so he was furious, and the whole way back to the house he kept muttering and cursing and he never thought to offer her his hand or put an arm round her shoulders, as if her feelings counted for nothing, as if she hadn't been as attached to the horse as he. Buck had been a good gentle animal and if he'd ever been hard to break or as skittish as his name implied, it was before their time. They didn't even know who'd named him or what he'd been like as a colt—he was just a presence on the ranch, already middle-aged when she came up the hill from the harbor that first time—and though she knew he'd have to be replaced eventually it was a thing she didn't like to think about. Or hadn't liked to think about. And now she'd had to take the shock of seeing him hurtle off the cliff to the rocks below, useless and abandoned, fit only for the ravens and the gulls and the big red crabs that swarmed in on the tide. She followed her husband's rigid back up the long gradual rise to where the barn and house came into view, and she wouldn't cry over a horse, she wouldn't let herself. Just as she hadn't let herself look over that cliff either—for all she knew Buck had sprouted wings like Pegasus and glided off on the breeze or landed in a deep surging pool and swum away to wherever horses go when they die.

Pomo wasn't there to greet them when they came in the gate—he would have been out in the schoolhouse with the girls. She'd already determined not to say a word about what had happened till the girls were done with their lessons, and then, later, perhaps after dinner, she'd tell them Buck had died. Though not how and not where. The last thing she wanted was for them to go looking for the remains and if they asked she'd say they'd buried him on the spot. She could already hear Marianne asking, *Where? Where? Out there,* she'd say, and point in the opposite direction altogether. In a week there'd be nothing left on the rocks at Nichols Point, not with a good high tide—and the moon was full, wasn't it? With any luck the bones themselves would be lifted off the rocks and swept out to sea. And she'd talk up the fact that they'd have to get a new horse now—Bob Brooks would just have to cough up the money or bring one out from his place in Carpinteria—and how nice it would be to have a new animal here, one they could maybe even name themselves and ride as much as they wanted without having to worry.

That was what she was thinking as she slipped up on the schoolhouse so furtively even the dog didn't know she was coming. She eased herself onto the doorstep, held her breath, counted three and whipped open the door like a magician, expecting to catch the girls out. But they weren't chattering or doodling or wasting their time at all: they both had their heads down, absorbed in their lessons. They looked up in unison and Pomo slapped his tail twice and sprang up to greet her. "Good, girls," she said. "Good for you. You just finish up your reading now and I think we'll go ahead and postpone the essays till tomorrow, okay?"

The room was warm still, but she went straight to the stove Herbie had installed in one corner, pulled open the cast-iron door and laid a knot of ironwood on the diminished coals. She had a story all ready for them and when Marianne asked where she'd gone she told her that two of the lambs had fallen into a hole and couldn't get out so their father had asked her to come help him rescue them. Which she'd done. And the lambs were fine, just a little thirsty that was all—and their mothers were right there waiting for them.

"Why couldn't Reg help him? Or Freddie?"

"Oh, you know how it is," she said. "They're busy patrolling. And they're not used to ranching and such—and I am, so your father asked me. It was nothing, really. If I wasn't here, you could have helped him."

"Where would you be if you weren't here?" Betsy asked.

"I was just saying—theoretically. You know what 'theoretically' means?"

"Reg and Freddie took the horses," Marianne said. "Reg was on Buck."

So the whole elaborate lie would unravel, she could see that. But not now. There were still two hours of school to go, which meant history, geography and then, if they were good, a chapter of *Black Beauty* she'd read aloud to them. All she said was, "Yes, I know."

It must have been half an hour later—no more than half an hour, she was sure of it, because they were still on history—when Herbie had his accident.

He'd gone directly to the barn on getting back, ready to chew out the sailors, but they weren't there. He'd found Nellie in her stall, but Reg and Freddie were nowhere to be seen. Then he'd gone into the house to see if they were there—and they weren't, which only made him angrier—and the house was cold and the wood basket empty, so he went out to the woodpile, cursing them, kicking at anything in his path, working himself up. And when he saw the state of it, the larger pieces unsawed and the snarl of roots and driftwood casually dumped in the dirt where any rain could soak it, he flew into a rage. In the next instant he'd snatched up the maul and begun lashing at one piece after another, sweating and cursing, and then he began on the hard twisted roots he'd dug out of the ground, bringing the hatchet to bear now. He might have gotten into the rhythm of it, left hand to balance the wood on the chopping block, right to swing the hatchet and drive it through, the ends falling away and the next root there to replace it, automatic, like clockwork—or he might not have. He might have let the rage carry him into another place altogether, a place where he was blinded, careless, accident-prone. All she knew was that the root slipped. And that he reached out to steady it, brought down the hatchet and missed his mark.

She heard his scream and then the barrage of curses that followed it, and she was out the door of the schoolhouse and running, knowing it was bad— he was howling now, howling like an animal—and when she got there she saw him clutching the mutilated hand to the shirt that was dyed red from his chest to his belt. She saw the chopping block and the way it had gone red too. And she saw the detached fingers, two of them, lying there curled and useless beside the slick blade of the flung-down hatchet.

The Spider

This time he was gone a month, a full month, even longer than when he'd had his operation all those years ago. Infection had set in and they'd had to dose him with sulfa, to which he'd had a bad reaction. Like the last time, the drug had affected his eyes—and, as she learned from the medical encyclopedia, there was the risk of other side effects too, including depression, anemia and various skin disorders—but there really was no choice. Penicillin was then in its infancy and it would be two years yet before streptomycin came into use, so it was either sulfa or risk losing the hand to gangrene or even dying of septicemia. The fingers—the middle and index fingers of his left hand—were lost. By the time he arrived at the hospital, blanched from loss of blood, they were nothing more than an afterthought.

She didn't know any of that in the moment. All she knew was that he was hurt, hurt desperately, and the shock of it flared up and burned through her. She was on him in an instant, fighting for his hand, thinking only to pull it away from him and stop the bleeding, to heal him and put everything back the way it was. He wouldn't have it. He lurched away from her, protecting the hand, stamping and crying out and fending her off with his hips and shoulders. "Stop it! Stop it right this instant!" she commanded, and then she dropped her voice the way she did with Marianne or Betsy when they fell and bumped their heads or took a splinter from the porch in their bare pattering feet: "Let me see, Herbie, let me see. I won't hurt you."

She grabbed hold of him and spun him round, surprised at her own strength, and then she tore at his shirt till she had a strip of cotton cloth to wind round his arm just above the elbow. She cinched it tight, then thought to bend to the chopping block and scoop up the dying fingers before heaving her full weight into him and pushing him toward the house, and if that was strange, his fingers clenched in her hand like meat on the bone, she put it out of her mind because her mind was racing and she could think only of getting him inside so she could stop the bleeding. She kept pushing, thumping at him as if she were kneading bread—he was in shock, that was what it was—and he staggered forward and then they were on the porch and through the door, where she sat him down in a chair and bound up the wound as best she could with a bandage cut from one of the bath towels. "Keep it elevated," she admonished, "over your head. Your head, Herbie, do you hear me?" Then she went to radio for help.

The day was thick, visibility poor, not at all the sort of conditions a pilot would welcome, but the Navy scrambled a plane and the plane was touching down in the sheepcote within the hour. But what an hour it was. If she ever missed ice, it was then. As it was, she wrapped the stiffening fingers in gauze and stuffed them into the pocket of the jacket she helped him work first over his good arm and then up over the bad one, though she knew there was no way to reattach them. The girls, their faces as bloodless as his, insisted on being there with him. She kept trying to reassure them even as she fed him aspirin and whiskey, pouring out one shot after another till his head lolled back and his eyes began to flutter. By the time the pilot arrived, he was groggy, but he was able to walk out to the field and climb into the cockpit unassisted—and then, as the door pulled shut and she and the girls and the dog stood huddled there in a scene Goya might have rendered in ink, he raised his right hand in a thumbs-up, the propeller snatched at the air, the wings shuddered and the plane slammed across the field and vanished into the gray curtain of fog.

He came back a different person. There was no other way to put it. She told herself he'd come around, that it would take time, but he seemed wooden, stripped of emotion, as if he'd never been Herbie at all, as if they'd put somebody else inside of him in some macabre experiment. There had been letters— first from Cottage Hospital in Santa Barbara and then the Veterans' Hospital in Los Angeles, where they'd taken him to recuperate—but the letters were nothing more than notes, really, distracted and disjointed (*I hope you are fine, the children too; The nights are dark here; Jell-O, they feed me Jell-O*). He never said he missed her, never asked how she was getting along without him, never mentioned the ranch at all. Still, it wasn't till he stepped off the plane that she saw what a toll the whole business had taken on him.

346

The children rushed for him, but he didn't swing them in the air the way he normally did, just stood there passively and let them cling to his legs, while the dog, careening toward him in a frenzy of rapturous barking, might have been somebody else's dog for all the response he showed. He spread open his arms for her and she fell into them but it was wrong, all wrong, and she could feel the alien thing in him beating like an irregular pulse. He was thin. They'd cut his hair too short, she saw that right away. And while she'd expected him to be pale, the bleached-white cotton shirt only made him look paler, as if his skin had been bleached and pressed too. The oddest thing—the thing her eyes jumped to—was the black leather glove on his left hand. He didn't mention it, didn't say a word about it, but he wouldn't take it off, not to eat dinner or even to change his clothes for bed. "I'm mutilated," he said finally, sitting slumped in the chair in the corner of the bedroom, one sock in his hand, the other still on his foot. "That's all there is to it." They went to bed that night like strangers.

The next few days were an agony. He claimed he couldn't see what he was eating—"Dark spots, that's all I see, dark floating *spots*"—and kept wandering from room to room in constant search of one thing or another, a nail file, his pipe, the tobacco. "Elise," he kept calling, "where the hell's the tobacco? Elise, where're my slippers? Elise?" He ignored the sailors completely. They would address him at the table or out in the yard and it was as if he didn't hear them. He showed no interest in the radio programs he used to adore and spent hours staring into the fire. If she asked what was wrong, he said, "Nothing." When she commiserated over the problems he was having with his eyes, trying to get at the source of it, find a solution, assuage him, cheer him—"What about glasses? Couldn't you get glasses?"—he cut her off. "It's not correctable. It's degenerative. My eyes are shot, Elise. Shot."

It wasn't until the end of the first week he was back that he went out to the barn to have a look at the new horse—Hans, a black three-year-old gelding Bob Brooks had sent out on the *Vaquero*—and when he did he was out there so long she went looking for him, afraid suddenly, though of what she couldn't say. The barn door stood open. The muted light of late afternoon made inroads into the shadows of the interior so that she could make out the sharp ribs of the rafters and the soft hummocks of the baled hay they had to ship in for the horses. The smell was dull, grassy, as if all the fields she'd ever known had been enclosed and concentrated here beneath the sloping wood-shingled roof. It was very still. She found him in the back stall, brushing Hans and talking quietly to him. She almost backed away to tiptoe out of the barn and leave him to himself, but it was getting late and she'd have to put dinner on the table soon, so she called his name softly, barely breathing it. At first there was no reaction and she was afraid he hadn't heard her, but then he turned to her, his good hand working over the horse's flank as if he were smoothing a blanket, and gave her a trace of his old smile. "Fine animal," he said.

The next morning he saddled up Hans and went out riding. He didn't come back for lunch and that started up the anxiety in her again, but she told herself it was the best thing for him, just to get out and see over the island and let it come home to him. It was nearly dark when he got back. She'd held dinner for him—his favorite, spaghetti with meatballs fashioned of ground lamb and bread crumbs, with beaten egg to bind them and a good splash of Worcestershire and a sprinkle of dried red pepper for bite—and he came into the kitchen with his head thrown back, making a show of sniffing the aroma. "Just what I want," he sang out. "No more Jell-O for me, eh?" And he came to her and hugged her and she felt the burden lift ever so perceptibly.

They danced in place for a long moment, Herbie crooning a snatch of a song from the radio in a low moan, his breath hot on her ear. "'So much at stake, and then I wake up,'" he sang. "'It shouldn't happen to a dream.'" She could feel him pressing into her, down below, where he was hard. She swiveled round in his arms, the relief flooding her in a quick erotic jolt. "You had a good ride?"

"The best, the very best. What a piece of horseflesh that Hans is. He—but we're not missing old Buck now, are we?" And then he pulled her close and kissed her for the first time since he'd stepped off the plane.

The mood carried him through dinner. He joked with the girls, crowed at the sailor boys ("I didn't see a single Nip out there today—you must have scared them all away"), insisted on pouring out half a water glass of whiskey for each of the adults and even proposed a toast. "To San Miguel, fortress of the Pacific!" But then, just when she thought he'd finally shaken off his anomie or the blues or the effects of the drug or whatever it was, he raised his gloved hand and said, "How about a little striptease? You know what a striptease is, girls? No? Well, watch this."

He worked the glove off by measures, playing to his audience, and then at the last moment tore it off with a flourish and laid the damaged hand on the tablecloth. It was a shock, something the girls didn't need to see, or not in that way, not as if he were rubbing their noses in it. The two fingers were gone almost to the knuckle and the skin there—the stump—was burnished and red as if the flesh had been scalded. "Look, girls," he said, splaying his good hand out beside it and then curling the fingers under, "eight of them. And how many legs does a spider have? You know, Marianne?"

Marianne looked as if she were about to cry.

"Come on, you know."

In a very small voice: "Six?"

"No," he said, "not six. Eight. Look"—and he bunched the fingers and moved both hands forward so they crept across the tablecloth—"I'm a spider now. Do you like spiders?"

"That's enough, Herbie," she heard herself say. Both girls had gone pale. The sailors shifted their eyes.

"I'm a spider," he repeated. "But I don't guess I'll be spinning any webs soon, do you?"

The shearers appeared a week later and Bob Brooks and Jimmie with them. The Navy had opened up the channel to commercial boats after the initial scare—they had no choice if the wartime economy was to go on—and the *Vaquero* had been given permission to go about its business. She and Herbie had always looked forward to shearing, despite the tumult and the burden of extra work. It brought society to their little corner of the world twice a year, at least for a week or so, and it not only marked time in the way of the seasons and the great global shifting of the tides and the orbit of the moon round the earth and the earth round the sun, but reaffirmed their purpose—it was necessary, profitable, undeniable. This was what they were here for, to earn a living for themselves and for Bob Brooks and Jimmie and the shearers too. And if she looked forward to it more than ever this time, almost as if it were a holiday, she told herself it was for Herbie's sake, but that wasn't the whole truth of it. The truth was that she needed help, desperately.

At first, Herbie threw himself into the work in his onrushing manic way, shouting and jeering and joking, delighted with himself and with his old friends, flying so high she thought he'd never come down. But as the week wore on, she could feel the enthusiasm leaching out of him, the poles of his temper drifting toward equipoise and then tipping off-balance again, sinking, sinking. He complained of the dust—"I can't see the hand in front of my face out there," he said, and then let out a bitter truncated laugh. "But I guess it's not really a hand, anyway, is it?" And then he found he couldn't grip the lambs properly, not with one hand inoperable. And he was exhausted, worn, out of shape. She watched him sink down beside Bob Brooks at the long plank table she'd set up in the courtyard to accommodate everybody at lunch. "I'm just no good, Bob," he said. "I guess you can't expect to lie up in a hospital for a month and then go out and wrestle sheep, can you?" By the fourth day he was merely looking on. On the fifth, he mounted Hans and went off into the hills, turning his back on them all.

Bob Brooks took her aside that night after dinner. Herbie hadn't been there to preside over the table and everyone had tried to keep up the pretense that everything was all right, but the raucous ongoing fiesta atmosphere of the first few nights had settled into an ordeal of silences and polite requests for the salt or the hot sauce, and as soon as the plates were cleared the four shearers and Jimmie disappeared into their room and the sailors—displaced temporarily—into the tent they'd set up in the far corner of the courtyard.

Brooks came to her in the living room where she was listening to the radio sotto voce after having put the girls to bed. "Mind if I join you?" he asked.

"No, please," she said, indicating the chair nearest the fire, Herbie's chair.

He sat heavily—he was exhausted too—and the dog came up to him and put his head in his lap. "I just wanted to know if everything's all right," he said after a moment.

She looked up. "You mean Herbie?"

"Yes."

"He's still recovering, if that's what you're asking."

"He told me he had to go patrol for Japs," Brooks said.

"Yes, he does a lot of that. He takes it very seriously."

"But isn't that what the sailors are here for? Especially at a time like this, when we need every man we've got—"

"He doesn't trust them. They're just boys, he says."

"Yeah, well, we were just boys too when they sent us marching through France and we came out all right. Can't he let it go?"

"You know Herbie." She waited for an affirmation, but he didn't say anything. He was stroking Pomo's ears, rubbing them between his forefingers as if he were assaying a grade of fine fabric. She wanted to open up to him, to tell him how strange Herbie had become, how worried she was, how she couldn't sleep thinking about it, how every day seemed to close like a fist on any hope she had, but she drew back. He was the boss here and as sympathetic as he was, he still expected a return on his investment, expected everything to be in order—he wasn't running a nursing home, but a ranch, a working ranch. He was the boss and to say anything more would have been a betrayal. "It was the accident," she said. "The drugs they gave him. And this business of the war has him on tenterhooks"—she gave a laugh—"all of us, really. Who wouldn't be? But he's getting better by the day. And Hans, Hans has been a godsend." She drew in a breath and lifted her eyes to his. "It's just a matter of time and he'll be back to his old self, believe me."

"You can't keep old Herbie down."

"No," she said, "no, you can't."

The smile he gave her was odd, barely there, as if he hadn't meant to smile at all. "You know," he said, bent forward still, still stroking the dog's ears, "I was thinking maybe when we come out in June for the wool, you might like to have Jimmie stay on for a bit. What do you think?"

And then, very gradually, things began to settle. If Herbie still wasn't his old self, his moods altering so quickly she never knew whether to expect a joke and a kiss or a long impacted stare, at least he'd come awake. There was a ranch to run, and the necessity of it, of seeing to the accumulation of details the whole enterprise depended on, from tinkering with the generator and the windmill to providing meat for the pot and looking after the horses and the far-flung water sources for the sheep, seemed to speak to him in a way she wasn't able to. He was up before dawn each morning, pounding the floorboards in his hobnailed boots, the stove lit, the coffee brewing and the kitchen swept by the time she joined him for breakfast. Then he went out on morning patrol, careful to be back by noon for lunch, and when he returned, the panniers he'd made for Hans were heavy with the wood he'd collected along the way. In the afternoon, he'd see to the house, moving from one project to another. It was his idea to build a lookout on the highest peak of the roof so the sailor boys could have a vantage over this part of the island and he made sure they were manning it (or boying it, as he said just to needle them) throughout the daylight hours. In the evening, he took Hans out and patrolled again, and when he came back he sat with the girls in the living room while they read aloud to him from their storybooks. Then it was the radio, then bed.

The first week of June brought word of the victory at Midway and he soared on the news, skipping round the living room and pumping his arms in the air till all the color rose to his face. "We've hit a grand slam this time!" he shouted. "Allies four, Nips zero." And here came the whiskey. "A toast to Nimitz! To the brave boys of the *Yorktown*! And to our own sailor boys too. Reg, Freddie! To you! And to the defeat and unconditional surrender of those sneaking yellow bastards. Goodbye, Yamamoto! Goodbye, Hirohito! R.I.P. to the whole shitty lot of you!"

The next morning, she overslept. And when she did wake, at half past six, Herbie was still in bed beside her. She eased herself up, careful not to disturb him, thinking he must have been feeling the aftereffects of the celebration— he rarely drank more than two or three whiskeys at a sitting and she'd never known him to be hungover, but here he was in bed still and what else could it be? She made breakfast for the girls, left plates on the stove for the sailors, who also seemed to be sleeping late, and then sat at the table and ate by herself while the girls got themselves ready for school. At quarter of eight, when Herbie still hadn't made an appearance, she went back to the bedroom to rouse him—he wouldn't want to miss his morning patrol, which had become a kind of obsession with him.

The room was dark still. It smelled of him, of his sweat and the plain brown soap he used and the faint sweetness of witch hazel, which he liked to slap on his cheeks after shaving. But he hadn't shaved. He was in bed still, lying on his back, perfectly composed, his arms at his sides and his feet making a tent of the blankets. She couldn't tell whether his eyes were open or not. "Herbie, it's getting late," she whispered.

His voice came back at her, the dead voice, the one she dreaded: "I know."

"I just thought I'd come in to wake you, for your morning patrol."

"I'm not going."

"Not going? But you've gone every morning since you got back."

There was a noise from the courtyard, the gander squabbling with one of the Rhode Island reds Bob Brooks had given them so they could have eggs in the absence of George's deliveries. They hadn't seen George since the war began—and wouldn't, she supposed, till it was over. There were rumors that the Air Corps had conscripted his plane, one more hardship to rise above. But at least the eggs were fresh, at least there was that. "If you hurry," she said, "I'll fix you some eggs—I've got fifteen minutes before the girls start school."

He still hadn't moved, but she could see that his eyes were open now, a dull sheen in the pale oval of his face, staring at the ceiling. "It's no use pretending," he said. "I can't see a goddamn thing out there, even with the binoculars—especially with the binoculars. If the whole Jap fleet came to anchor in Simonton Cove, I wouldn't know the difference."

"You need glasses, that's all. We'll send you to shore to the eye doctor when Bob comes back."

"And my hand's useless. I can't steady anything with it. The boys had to build practically the whole lookout by themselves. I just stood around."

"And directed them."

"A blind man can't direct anybody."

"You're not blind. We're going to get you glasses."

"Get me a cane."

"Stop it. You're just making yourself crazy. And me too. Now, you can lie there feeling sorry for yourself all day if you want, but I've got the girls to see to." She was at the door now, all the fret and worry of the past weeks souring in her till she could taste it in her throat. "And if you want eggs—or anything else, for that matter—you're going to have to fix it yourself."

The Note

Two weeks later—June eighteenth, the last day of school for the girls—she was as busy as she'd ever been, up before dawn to prepare a feast for Bob Brooks and company, who were due later in the day. He'd be bringing Jimmie with him and two of the shearers to help haul the wool sacks down to the harbor for transshipment to Santa Barbara, and she wanted to make a holiday of it—especially for the girls, who'd worked hard and were looking forward to their summer vacation. In addition to two legs of lamb, mashed potatoes, chili beans and the traditional hot sauce, she was planning a pudding of canned pineapple, odds and ends of bread, cornmeal, sugar and the leftover bananas that had gone black and densely sweet since the last delivery, the whole to be tied up in a muslin sack and steamed in her big pot. To start, there'd be clam fritters wrapped in bacon and half a dozen loaves of sourdough bread—and the wine Bob was sure to bring with him, lest the hands set up a revolt.

By seven, she felt she had things under control, or mostly, anyway, the lamb scored, studded with cloves of garlic and set aside in the cool room, the hot sauce simmering on the stove, the loaves browning in the oven, and breakfast—oatmeal with brown sugar and cinnamon, and coffee, of course—all ready to go. Reg and Freddie came in first, both of them looking pleased with themselves—they were looking forward to a break in the routine as much as she was. "Smells good," Reg said, hovering over the table, cap in hand. "Need any help?"

"No," she said, glancing up, "I think I can manage." If Herbie was still at odds with them, she wasn't. Over the course of these past months, she felt she'd come to understand them—it wasn't their fault they were stuck out here. They were good at heart, both of them, and they'd gradually begun to pitch in more, once they began to realize how lucky they were—as lucky as the lucky Lesters—to be out of the real fighting, where every day men were drowned, crushed, burned to death in a rain of bombs and torpedoes. To be bored was a small price to pay.

"Today's the big day, huh?" Freddie said. He'd removed his cap too and was standing just inside the door, careful to stay out of her way as she flew from the stove to the counter and back again.

"Wait till you see how excited the girls are," she said.

"God, I hated school," Reg said, casting his eyes to the ceiling. "Couldn't wait for the last day. And then summer seemed to go by like nothing and it was back to school again. It was like prison."

"Oh, it's not so bad, not for my girls."

A compliment now, from Reg, who wasn't above currying favor: "But they've got a special teacher. If I had a teacher like you instead of those nuns that didn't seem to care about anything except seeing how hard they could whack you with a ruler, I'd probably be president of a college someplace now."

"Yeah, sure, Reg," Freddie put in. "You're a real scholar. But, Mrs. Lester, should we help ourselves today or are we going to sit down with the girls?"

"Catch as catch can this morning. Coffee's hot. And you can spoon out your oatmeal and take it into the dining room. Herbie's not awake yet and I'm up to my elbows here."

The morning flew by. She had Marianne in the schoolhouse doing her final exams, so she brought Betsy out to the courtyard and sat her down in a chair on the porch to test her on her reading. The day was cool and overcast, typical for June, but she was comfortable enough in a sweater and the temperature had held steady through the night so she didn't really need to start a fire in the schoolhouse. She was down on her knees in the garden, edging the flowerbed with abalone shells she'd been collecting on her walks with the girls, looking up from time to time to correct Betsy's pronunciation and keeping an eye on the harbor—they expected the boat in the afternoon, but there was no telling when it might come. She'd seen it pull in hours before they'd expected it in the past. Betsy's voice flowed on, fluid and musical, though the text was difficult: "'The counterpane was of patchwork, full of odd little parti-coloured squares and triangles; and this arm of his tattooed all over with an interminable'—is that right, Mother?"

"Yes, 'interminable.' Go on."

"'Cretan laby-rinth—'"

"Labyrinth."

"Right, 'Cretan labyrinth of a figure, no two parts of which were of one precise shade—owing I suppose to his'"—and here she broke off and Elise looked up to see Herbie standing there above her on the porch. She'd seen him going back and forth all morning, from the shed to the forge and in and out the gate, but hadn't taken much notice—he was busy with something, that was the important thing.

"Elise—sorry to interrupt, and that was good, Betsy, very good—I was just looking for that pad of notepaper, and I wondered if . . . I can't seem to find it."

She looked at him oddly. It would have been right on the desk in the living room where he did his accounts and she sat down to write letters, but there was something in his voice that caught her out. He was asking her for a reason, asking her to take note. Did he want to say something to her privately, out of Betsy's hearing, was that it? She pushed herself up, rubbing her palms together to brush off the dirt. She looked down at Betsy, who sat poised at the edge of the chair, the book spread open in her lap. "All right, honey," she said, "why don't you take a five-minute break?"

And then Herbie followed her into the house, where she went straight to the desk. She saw the book she'd been reading the night before lying there amidst the usual clutter of papers, unanswered letters, envelopes and stamps, the large manila folder from the school district for the children's exams and the desk calendar, and there, beneath it and only partially obscured, the notepad. "Is this what you're looking for?" she asked, swinging round and holding it out to him.

"Yes," he murmured, his voice subdued, "that's it."

"You need an envelope?"

"Yes."

She pulled open the right-hand drawer, separated an envelope from the stock there and handed it to him. "Just one?"

He nodded.

"All right, well, if you intend to send out a letter be sure to leave it where I can see it or I'm apt to forget all about it—I mean, today of all days."

There was a moment when they both stood there inches apart, husband

and wife, something unspoken hanging between them, something she couldn't quite put her finger on. He looked into her eyes, then down at the notepad, and the moment was gone.

Ten minutes later he was back out in the courtyard, interrupting her again. He'd changed into his white shirt, the one with the epaulettes he wore for special occasions, and put crème oil on his hair, which always tended to curl up across the top, and brushed it tightly to his scalp. He waited till Betsy became aware of him and stopped her reading. "I just wanted to say that I'll be out on foot, gathering wood, and don't know when I'll be back." He paused, fingering the pocket of his shirt, then waved a hand in front of his face as if to scatter the bugs away, but there were no bugs, not that she could see, anyway. "So be sure to send the boys down with the sled when the boat comes in. All right?"

"Yes," she said, "I'll be sure to tell them."

He bent and pecked a kiss to Betsy's cheek, then leaned forward to kiss her. "You think it'd be okay to interrupt Marianne for just a second? I can't go off collecting wood without saying goodbye, can I?"

She wasn't thinking. She wasn't listening. "Sure," she said. "But just a second—and don't distract her."

He walked off across the courtyard and she saw him pull open the door of the schoolhouse, vanish a moment, then reappear and carefully shut the door behind him. He didn't look up as he passed by on his way to the gate, Betsy on to the next passage now—" 'In black distress, I called my God,/ When I could scarce believe Him mine./ He bowed His ear to my complaints—/ No more the whale did me confine' "—and then he pulled back the gate on its creaking hinges and went on out of the yard.

When the boat came in just after four, the boys were there to meet it with the team. She was too busy to go down herself, fussing over the table setting, basting the lamb, rolling the clams in bread crumbs and greasing the frying pan, but she let the girls go down with them, and she contented herself with picturing the scene, Bob Brooks spreading his arms wide, the presents she'd ordered for the girls' matriculation wrapped resplendently in gold foil, Jimmie hauling things ashore like a man half his age, the dog yapping and the waves rushing in. It was a scene she'd been part of a hundred times, her pulse quickening and her face flushed with the joy of company, of relief and

357

resupply, of things made beyond the shore and presented against the backdrop of the dunes in an accelerating fantasy of privilege and abundance. The parcels came ashore. They found their way to the sled. The sled found its way to the house. That was the way it always was and always would be. Never mind that she'd had to make do with onions that were soft down to the core or that the twin roasts had eaten up the last of her garlic and she was nearly out of flour, cornmeal and sugar, the boat had arrived!

By the time the horses came into view, Jimmie leading them on a short halter and the girls running on ahead, the sun had driven through the mist to play off the rocks and ignite the chaparral with color. The sailors, Bob Brooks and the two hands caterpillared along behind them under the weight of full packs, and all she could think of was those African expeditions she'd read about, Speke and Burton and the native bearers weaving their way through the uncharted lands. She watched them out the kitchen window, busy to the last moment, but when they crested the hill, she put down what she was doing, slipped out of her apron and went out to the gate to greet them. She had to shield her eyes against the brightness, the hills and fields that had been so dull all day lit suddenly with sienna and gold and a green so pale it was nearly translucent, while overhead the haze had dissolved and the sky opened up to a solid clear blue, not a cloud in sight. The day had turned out nice, after all—more than nice, beautiful, the kind of day that reaffirmed every choice she'd ever made. She came across the yard, breathing deeply, gratefully, taking it all in.

The girls got there first—racing the last hundred yards, Marianne, with her longer legs, in the lead all the way—and she saw that they were both chewing something, Wrigley's gum, as it turned out. Their knees flashed in the sun, their hair, which she'd cut short for summer, sparked blond, and then their elated faces and quick squealing gasps for air burst suddenly on her: here they were, darting round her, singing out their excitement—"What did you get us? Come on, tell us!"—until she put out a hand to stop them. "Now, don't you run off," she warned. "We're going to need you to help bring the things in—and then we'll see about dinner. And *then*, once everything's been cleared away and put back in order, you can open your presents."

Pomo was next—he'd been guarding the flank like a good sheepdog, and now he broke free to sprint across the field and through the gate, flushing the chickens and terrorizing the gander, which flapped to the roof of the shed and let out a long withering hiss of disdain. And then the sled, and Jimmie, who tipped his finger-greased straw hat and gave her a smile that opened up around a new gap where his front teeth used to be. Bob Brooks and the others were winded, she could see that, and before she did anything more by way of greeting than call out each of their names, she led them into the kitchen so they could set down their packs and she and the girls could get started on filing everything away. She thought of Herbie then—this was his favorite part of the ritual of resupply, sorting through the groceries and putting everything on its proper shelf in his precise way, the cans stacked with their labels turned out, the sacks of rice, beans and pasta upended in the big brown crockery jars set aside for each, greens in the cool room and onions, potatoes and garlic in the root cellar—but she supposed he'd got distracted and let the time slip away from him, which seemed to be happening more and more lately. He'd be making his way back by now, and if he felt bad for missing out on the sorting of the canned goods, he could always come out to the pantry later on and shift things around to his heart's content.

Before long they were all gathered on the porch, their feet up, cigarettes at their lips and the bottles of red wine and whiskey circulating. She served the fritters and bread out of doors to take advantage of the weather. Bob Brooks had brought the latest newspapers—war news and not much else—but she didn't do more than skim the headlines because she didn't have time, for one thing, and for another, this was supposed to be a celebration, Betsy matriculating to fourth grade and Marianne to seventh, and she didn't want to spoil the day. There would be plenty of time for her and Herbie to read through every last line and suffer all over again because the world was fraught and savage and men had to make war to justify their place in it.

Both Manny and Jesus, the shearers Bob had brought along, praised her hot sauce, into which they dipped their fritters delicately before leaning out over the dirt to bite into them so that any excess wouldn't stain the floorboards that had been stained a thousand times before. Jimmie rocked back on his heels, spinning out stories, the sailors joined in and Bob Brooks stirred his whiskey with a twig he'd snapped off the hacked remnant of a sage bush growing just outside the gate, grinning happily. "It's for the flavor, Elise," he said, "you ought to try it."

They all asked about Herbie and she covered for him as best she could. "He's patrolling," she said. "The Japs, you know? They really put a scare into us with that business back in February." Everybody chimed in in agreement and the conversation took off in the direction of the war, though she hadn't meant it to. In any case, she had dinner to serve, and she went on into the house and took the lamb out of the oven to sit while she mashed potatoes and worked in a good dollop of the butter that had just arrived.

Dinner came off beautifully, the conversation free-flowing, the guests uncritical and appreciative of the chef, old friends and new gathered for the feast, and if they missed Herbie—and they did, every one of them, of course they did—they tried to work around it and ignore the vacant chair and unused place setting at the head of the table. "He probably went all the way out to Point Bennett, that's probably what it is—he'll be back anytime now," Jimmie offered when they sat down at the table, and that seemed to put the issue to rest for the time being. Still, at every noise from the kitchen or thump from the porch—Pomo scratching fleas or a raven lighting on the roof— everyone looked up expecting Herbie to come sailing through the door with a bottle held high and a story spilling from his lips.

Then it was coffee—and with the coffee, the pudding and the pineapple upside-down cake she'd baked for the girls and had meant to hold back till Herbie showed up—and afterward the girls' presents. It was half past eight now. The light was nearly gone and the fog beginning to seep in. Dinner was over, the plates strewn with crumbs and the guests easing back in their chairs and lighting pipes and cigars. She couldn't have kept the girls waiting any longer—it just wasn't fair—and if she'd felt a sudden flare of anger for Herbie, so much the worse. What was wrong with him? He knew how much this meant to them. And certainly, no matter how blue he might have been feeling—if that was it—he wouldn't want Bob Brooks to know about it or guess just how deep it went.

It was then—just as she was getting up to clear the dessert plates while Marianne turned over the pieces of her new chess set and Betsy made wide blue streaks on a sheet of construction paper with her new watercolors—that she thought of the note. The thought came hurtling at her, suddenly broken free of the cage in her mind where she'd kept it locked up all through the afternoon and through dinner and into the evening, even till now, when it hit her so hard she nearly dropped the plate in her hand. She saw the look of Herbie's face when he'd leaned over to kiss her, his jowls gone heavy with gravity, the furrows digging at the corners of his eyes, the white bristle of his

360

sideburns. She heard the deadness in his voice. *Nothing to worry over,* he'd said. *It's just a note. I'll leave it in the house.*

No one noticed as she set the plate back down and crossed the room to the desk, the conversation gone on into another mode now, the after-dinner-and-cigars mode, men's talk, moistened with whiskey—sheep and war and boats and money. She couldn't seem to catch her breath. There was a new rhythm inside of her, a drumming premonitory throb she couldn't fight down. She snatched at the scatter of papers, tossed the book aside, slammed through the drawers. Bob Brooks' voice, distant, otherworldly: "Elise, is everything all right? What are you looking for? Elise?"

She couldn't answer because the power of words had left her. She whirled round and waved her hands to silence him and then another thought came to her, a deeper thought wrested from a deeper place, and worse, far worse than the one that had brought her here. Then she was down on her knees, working the dial on the safe that had come from the wreck of the SS *Cuba,* welded steel, adamantine and impregnable even to the pounding of the surf, and if the conversation had died and Bob Brooks was watching from across the room, it didn't matter, because there was the envelope on the top shelf with her name written across the front of it in her husband's hand and the note neatly folded inside:

Dearest Elise:

You'll find me at Harris Point, on the knoll there. I am sorry for this, sorry for it all, but I will not be a burden to you, I will not. There is nothing I can say except that everything is so damned heavy. The air. The air is crushing me. It's like lead, air turned to lead.

Mon âme est sortie de moi. Le roi est mort.

Herbie

Departure

They found him in the morning, as soon as it was light. She'd wanted to go to him in the dark and she'd fought with them, the whole room of them, Bob Brooks crushing her so tightly to him all the air went out of her and she couldn't breathe and then she could and screamed at them till they were nothing more than hollow faces hung round her like pictures in a gallery, but they wouldn't yield. It was impossible to go out there in the dark of a moonless night with the fog closing in, she should know that if anybody should— the terrain was too rough, the cliffs too jagged, the ravines too deep. They'd never find him. It was too risky. Better to wait. *Better?* she threw back at them. *What if he's hurt? What if he's only hurt?* No one had an answer. But Bob Brooks wouldn't let go of her. They rocked in place, just as she had with Herbie that night in the kitchen, but this was no dance and it went on till her legs gave way beneath her.

That the girls had to see it—or see the first cascading moments when she had the note there in her hand and Bob Brooks wouldn't let go of her and the noise that came out of her was like the high choking gargle of a dying animal— made it even worse. Somebody, some one of them with their hollow faces and dumbstaring eyes, swept up the girls and took them out the door and down the porch to their room. Reg, it was Reg, and Freddie right behind him. The sailor boys. Doing their duty. Vigilant boys, vigilant after all. But her legs wouldn't work and she was sitting in the chair, Herbie's chair, by a dying fire, and she had to get hold of herself, had to see to the girls and then prepare herself for the vigil that would take her to first light and Harris Point and what she would find there, because what if he'd missed his aim? What if he'd changed his mind? What if the whole thing was a ruse? A plea for sympathy? A cruel joke?

The girls were both awake, Jimmie stationed outside their door, Reg and

Freddie perched on the edges of their beds, talking to them in low voices. As soon as they saw her there in the doorway, they got up and slipped silently from the room.

Marianne's voice came at her in a soft tremolo, no pause, no respite: "What happened? Reg wouldn't tell us or Freddie either. Is it Dad?"

"Yes." The room was lit only by a candle, a sepia glow straining for the ceiling and falling back futilely, over and over.

Betsy now, the faintest breath: "Is he all right?"

"We hope so."

"Why isn't he back? Where is he?"

"He's"—and here she had to pause to get control of her voice because control was what was needed now, control above all else—"at Harris Point."

"Is he going to stay there all night?"

"Yes."

"Is he camping out?"

"I don't know."

"Is he lost?"

"Yes," she said, "he's lost."

He'd been steady to the last, his aim unflinching, the blue-black revolver still clutched in his hand. He was lying on his side, napping for all anybody knew, but when she was still fifty feet from him, she could see the truth of it. No one had to tell her. She didn't need a doctor or a coroner or a priest or anybody else.

She was mounted on Nellie and Bob Brooks was beside her on Hans, the fog trembling with the first flush of morning light, the surf roaring below and the seals roaring back at it. There was a feathery mist leaching out of the air and a smell like a fire that's just been doused. When she reined in the horse and got down to kneel beside him she saw the crusted spot at his temple and the black dusting around it, such a small thing, this hole no bigger around than her wedding ring. His eyes were closed, shut tight, and his face was locked against the violence the next instant was to bring. She didn't turn him over, though she wanted to—she wanted to lift him from the dirt and press him to her one last time, just hold him, but he wasn't there anymore and never would be again.

They brought him back to the house on the sled and Jimmie took the couch from the living room out into the yard and reconverted it to its original use, fashioning a lid for it out of a sheet of plywood he found in the barn. Manny and Jesus, their mouths set and their eyes drawn down to slits, carried the pick and shovel up to Harris Point and dug the grave there high over the ocean while Bob Brooks searched through the Bible in the living room and Reg and Freddie got the stove going in the kitchen and heated up the leftovers so people could eat. It was up to her to prepare the body and she did the best she could, steeling herself—or maybe she was just numb, maybe that was it. She washed his face with a hot cloth and laid a compress over the left side, where the bullet had gone through, but she left him dressed as he was when she'd found him, in his short pants and boots and the white shirt with the epaulettes shining on his shoulders. The girls knew the truth by then and they were inconsolable. She arranged for Betsy to stay behind with Jimmie, but Marianne insisted on coming out to Harris Point to watch the coffin lowered into the grave—she wouldn't be turned or dissuaded. The wind was up and they all had to keep averting their heads to keep the sand out of their eyes. Bob Brooks said a few words and read a passage from the Bible. She threw the first shovel of dirt in the hole and then they all stepped forward and it was done.

There was a day of high sun and scudding clouds sometime toward the end of the following week, one day out of a succession of them, each as bleak and unfocused as the last. She was in the living room, packing things away for the move back to the mainland, trying not to linger over one object or another— this was a winnowing, a selection, and yet each thing she touched took her out of herself till she lost track of where she was or what she was doing or even why she was here. She didn't feel betrayed or bitter or abandoned, only sad, just that. Sad for Herbie, for her daughters, for herself. She could have stayed in Manhattan, setting herself up in the apartment with the view of the East River she'd had her eye on and gone through life as if she were gliding on a string from home to work and back again, shuffling through the card catalogue, unwrapping a sandwich for lunch at her desk beneath the tall windows, taking dinner at the corner restaurant with the burned-down candles on the tables and the daily specials chalked up on a board over the bar. She could have gone to Paris or back to Montreux or home to her mother in Rye, where every day was a replica of the one that had come before and the only change was the change of seasons. But then Herbert Steever Lester had come knocking at her door and she'd taken the leap and put herself here on this island that was nothing to her now, a widow with two daughters to provide for and educate and see through to their own chance at life.

She had a fire going in the fireplace she and Herbie had built for the comfort of it, hauling the bricks up from the ruins of the Waters' house in a wheelbarrow till their backs ached, mixing the mortar, plying the plumb bob and laying each row as straight as eternity, because you couldn't have a home without a hearth and home was what sustained you. The lamp on the desk was lit, though the sunlight filtering through the windows was bright enough, but she'd lit it anyway, without really thinking. On either side of the chimney, dark rectilinear shapes stained the wall where she'd taken down her pictures and packed them away. The guns were gone too, the entire collection packed up and sent to shore for sale at auction, but for the elephant rifle, which she'd laid in the coffin beside him, and the final one, the fatal one. That one, the snub-nose, the cold steel thing she'd pried from her husband's dead hand though she could barely breathe from the shock of what was happening to her, was at the bottom of the ocean—flung high out over the cliff on a current of rage that burned through her like lightning on a dry plain.

It was too warm for a fire really, what with the sun on the roof, but it was necessary: she was burning things. This was part of the winnowing too, all these *things* and she couldn't begin to take half of them with her. There wasn't room on the sled or on the Coast Guard boat that was coming for her in two days' time. Or in the apartment Bob Brooks had found for her in the heart of downtown Santa Barbara, from the front window of which you could just make out the ocean in the distance.

The girls were ashore, hustled away the day after the funeral to stay with friends there until she could come for them, and the others had gone too—Bob Brooks and the shearers back to their business on the coast and the sailor boys to bivouac in a tent down by the boat shed at Cuyler Harbor. Only Jimmie had stayed behind, to safeguard the place and keep her company.

Which was fine, but she didn't need company, she needed her husband and her daughters and for things to return to the way they were.

The fire snapped and brought her back to herself. She seemed to have something in her hand—a record, the *Requiem*—but she knew enough not to put it on the phonograph. No, there was only one place for it: in the fire. Angry suddenly, enraged, she flung it into the flames and watched the cover blacken and the vinyl inside quicken and die back. She wouldn't part with any of her books—she'd brought them here all the way across the country and the channel too and she'd bring them back again—but there were letters and bills and papers, magazines, recipes, clippings, old art projects, drawings and photos everywhere she looked, and these she fed into the fire without a second glance. She dumped an armload of papers into the flames and felt the heat flare on her face, and then she turned to the chest of keepsakes. It was made of cedar, open-grained, smelling of high forests and perpetual shade. She lifted one end of it experimentally, but it was too heavy. Keepsakes. What were keepsakes, anyway?

She raised the lid and there were the magazines and newspapers with their names splashed all over them, *Life* and *Look* and *The Saturday Evening Post*, Swiss Family Lester, the Pioneers, Wounded Vet, Lonely Isle. She didn't know then that the Japanese would go down to defeat or that Bob Brooks would find an elderly Norwegian couple—the Eklunds—to take their place or that his lease would be summarily terminated by the Navy six years later and that every last ram, ewe and lamb would be herded aboard the *Vaquero* and taken to slaughter. She didn't know that the Navy would use the island as a bombing range or that the house she was standing in would burn mysteriously twenty-seven years later so that only the chimney remained amidst the blowing ash. And she didn't know that the Park Service would finally take charge of all of San Miguel and its waters and that anyone who wanted to come here or dream here or walk the hills and breathe the air would need to have a permit in hand.

What she knew was that the island had turned alien, as strange to her now as when she first walked up the hill as a bride and Herbie lit the lamps up and down the house so that when she went back out to the courtyard to carry in her new leather suitcases the windows glowed against the night that was absolute all the way to the threshold of the stars. She knew that luck gave out. And she knew that there was nothing to keep, nothing to hold on to, that

366

it all came to nothing in the end. She reached into the trunk and lifted out all she could carry. The fire leapt up. The pages crumpled, the images vanished as if they'd never been there at all. If she'd gone outside she would have seen the smoke twist out of the chimney, reaching as high as it could go till the wind flattened it and drove it out to sea.